Will Be Done

A Tale of Family Conflict

by

Laura Arbree

info@barringerpublishing.com
Copyright © Laura Arbree
All rights reserved.

Barringer Publishing, Naples, Florida
www.barringerpublishing.com

Cover, graphics, layout design by Linda Duider

ISBN: 978-0-9989069-2-8

Library of Congress Cataloging-in-Publication Data

Printed in U.S.A.

Will Be Done/Laura Arbree

Dedication

To My Families

Acknowledgements

Special thanks go to the anonymous men and women who contributed to this work even though they may not have known they were doing so. I also wish to thank my publisher and editor, Basil, who helped me with this work.

Any errors of fact regarding the procedures, or professions, represented in this novel are either a result of my misunderstanding of the information given to me, or a result of my decision to take literary license and dramatic liberties. Also, I have altered information given to me in confidence.

Section One

Chapter One

The women entering Daisy's restaurant turned heads and appeared to be a happy family going out to lunch together. Tallest of the three middle-aged women, thin and stately, about a 40 DD, Mary led Ginny, her mother, by the hand toward a sunlit round table in the corner of the dining area, next to a window, with a faded, silk daisy. Savory aromas from the kitchen wafted toward them. A gentleman got up, came over, and pulled out a chair.

"Thank you," they said in unison, as the kindly man helped the elder into her seat and then retreated to his table.

Mary sat next to her mother and motioned with her head, "Cathy, you sit on Mom's other side." She offered no direction to Linda, the remaining sibling and, in fact, appeared to ignore her.

Tall as Mary, with dark, gray-streaked hair and vibrant green eyes, Cathy dutifully obeyed. She took her mother's purse, which she was clutching to her chest as if it held her life's belongings and hung it on the back of the chair.

A shrimp compared to her siblings, Linda took a seat across the table and smiled at her mother.

Handing out menus, their waitress inquired about drinks. Iced teas all around, water, no lemon. The girls pondered the menu, nothing fancy, just the usual fare.

Ginny Cray, mother of these politely subdued women, searched for her purse, forgetting it was behind her, on the back of the chair.

"Right behind you, Mom," said Cathy. "See?" She pointed to it.

The waitress reappeared with drinks, paper and pencil held waist high. "What's your pleasure?"

"I'm going with a roast beef sandwich." Mary asked her mother, "You want a sandwich, soup, or salad?"

Mother, nodding vigorously, grinning and overly excited for a casual lunch, missed the question completely. "It's so good to be here with my girls! All together again!"

Linda exchanged glances with her sisters. *Would they do this after Mother is gone,* she wondered. Cathy had flown in for an overnight, her usual stint, but it had been some time since she'd been around. They usually socialized with each other when a parent was present, mostly to preserve law and order.

"She'll have the same as me," Mary said to the waitress, since her mother couldn't seem to decide.

"Why don't you let *Mom* choose?" Linda asked.

"Because I've already made that decision," Mary snapped with annoyance.

Linda clutched the glass, wishing it held something stronger than tea, and exchanged a glance with Cathy, as she bent over to arrange a napkin on Mother's lap. She waited until Cathy straightened and leaned back against a ruffled, floral pillow tied to the chair posts. "How's the weather up there?" she asked. Her younger sister lived in Maine.

"Nice now. When I get home, I'm going to be busy planting pansies in my garden." She smiled, knowing that was Linda's favorite flower.

Linda returned the smile, remembering how her younger sister had planted purple and yellow pansies by the front door when she'd flown up to visit some time ago. They had been closer then. "I know how much you enjoy being outdoors. It must be stifling being in the clinic all day."

Cathy nodded stiffly.

An awkward silence ensued—heavy with aborted emotional reactions.

The waitress delivered lunch. Mrs. Cray played with her sandwich, taking off the bread, picking at the lettuce with fingers like a child.

Mary placed a finely manicured hand over her mother's. "Don't play with your food." She put the bread back on top of the lettuce. "Go like this." Mary held up her own sandwich and showed her how it was done.

Reluctantly, the elder followed her example, then took a big bite, as if suddenly remembering.

Cathy observed her mother's worsening state of dementia and frowned, then quickly looked away as if nothing unusual had just happened—nothing to be concerned about.

Linda noticed her concern and tried to distract her with a light topic. "How was your shopping trip this morning?"

"Good. Too bad you couldn't make it." Cathy spiked a piece of lettuce on her fork and bent over, mouth open.

"I wanted to, but I had a doctor's appointment."

Mary launched into a detailed explanation of their trip. ". . . and Mother looked tirelessly through the racks but didn't find anything. Cathy bought a pair of blue pants, and I got a red top."

"Red?" said Cathy. "I thought it was orange."

Everybody laughed heartily, too heartily, as if relieved they could still share a laugh.

"Well, it could pass for orange," Cathy added. "It's kind of a bright, orangey-red." She was used to diffusing a quarrel-in-the-making.

Today, they were on their best behavior for Mother, who hadn't stopped smiling since they sat down. No fights, no arguments, and no rivalry—not this time.

As they exited the restaurant and hurried toward the car, Cathy took hold of Linda's arm and drew her aside, letting Mary and her mother walk ahead.

"Mary and I took Mother to Attorney Nestor Brown, for estate planning," Cathy said.

Estate planning? Linda thought. *Mother can't even order lunch.* She felt the betrayal like a sock in the face because they'd excluded her, beaten her to the punch by getting there first. A dirty ambush. *Uh oh. What else are they up to? . . . Am I still in the will?* she wondered.

She remembered Brown. She and he had sat at the same table at an Estate and Financial Planning luncheon years ago—a fancy affair at a prestigious country club, with gleaming silverware on white tablecloths and invitation only. She'd arrived a few minutes late, ducked in the side door, and hurriedly claimed a vacant seat at a table in the back of the room. Brown sat across from her, his basketball-sized stomach pressing against the table.

"I'm the only attorney in this town who specializes in elder care," Brown said, "and I'm the only one with the experience and knowledge to be able to talk about it."

She strained to hear the speaker over Brown's voice.

"I don't know who this jerk is they brought in from out of town, but he doesn't know what he's talking about."

Linda searched the room for another seat but couldn't see any. She considered asking him to shut up. She looked at him. Brown's thick, black-as-coal hair fell over his brow, as he waved his fork in front of his mouth. A little gravy flew from the fork to stain the white tablecloth. His eyes grew wider as he chewed on a piece of chicken smothered in brown gravy, as if dying to swallow so he could pontificate again.

What was the rumor about him—The estate shrinker! She groaned inwardly, came back to the present scene, and faced her sister with a forced smile. "I know about estate planning; I would have appreciated a call."

"I'm surprised to hear that," Cathy said.

"Excuse me?" Linda was shaking.

"Mom's going to buy Mary's house so that we get Medicaid coverage. We'll get the money after she passes." She said it matter-of-factly, as if it were a simple process. She seemed pleased with herself.

A roaring in Linda's ears quickened her heartbeat. Over the years, she had plenty of opportunities to observe how Mary operated. *Calm down,* she told herself. "How'd you find Brown?"

"He's got a great web site on elder care. I've done quite a bit of research," Cathy stated proudly. "You know, I only have so much time because of the demands of my clinic and the animals."

To hell with the website. Just ask around . . . Oh, God, what are we in for?

Desperately craving a drink, Linda ran to her car and called a friend from A. A. "Call your attorney," the friend suggested. The last shred of trust she felt for her older sister disappeared. *Mary will keep the entire estate,* she thought, *and swindle both of us out of our rightful inheritance.* Pauperizing Mother would make her dependent on Mary.

Chapter Two

"Jim Cott, please," Linda announced to the receptionist on the phone. She and Jim had conducted investment seminars in the past under the title of Estate Planning and had become good friends as their mutual success grew. Handsome, Jim kept his physique trim with rigorous workouts, including running. His hazel eyes were friendly but could penetrate to the heart of matters quickly. Linda trusted his expertise explicitly.

He came on the phone and greeted her in a friendly manner.

"Jim, I think I've got a problem with my inheritance."

"What's going on?"

"Well, my sisters met with an attorney behind my back and probably had my mother change her will . . . I'm so mad I want to sue!"

Jim had heard the sad tale before. "Before you do that, tell me who's the attorney and what's he doing?"

"Nestor Brown."

"Brown—Oh . . . Yeah, I know him. Bit of a hothead. I've seen him in court—he gets pretty worked up."

"He wants my mother to buy my sister's house. Knowing my sister, once she has that money, we'll never see it again." She took a deep breath. "I swear, I'll sue!"

"Hold on. I think I know what he's doing. Sounds like he's trying to pauperize your mother for the health benefits, but there's the Three Year Look Back Rule you have to consider, meaning, if she dies within three years, it doesn't count."

"So what do I do?"

"Call your sisters—"

"What if they won't answer?"

"Leave a message. Say—"

"Hold on—let me get my pen." Linda grabbed a pen and wrote.

"Let me see if I've got this right." She read back what he'd said. Most terms familiar to her from their business seminars would be like the 'Navaho Code Talk' to her sisters, but they had their attorney to interpret for them.

"That's it."

"I'm going to call my sisters and read it to them."

"Don't change a word. Just say it like I told you."

"Okay."

She pocketed her cell and reflected. She thought she should have seen this coming. Years after her father passed, her mother had acted strange. Extremely codependent and weak, afraid of her own shadow, she'd become sad and needy, morose and desperate at the slightest provocation, which she met with disturbing and unusual behavior. A doctor diagnosed Alzheimer's.

A slender woman of medium stature, Ginny's hair had turned white long ago, resembling a dandelion turned to seed. A tuft of dark hair snuggled against the base of her neck, with eyes light green, and an undeniable proboscis.

When planes exploded into the Twin Towers in New York City, Ginny was frightened. She'd seen many wars in her lifetime, had prayed for her husband's safe return from missions to Japan, and had spent many a sleepless night worrying about her son-in-law, Brad, who'd served in Vietnam, but now the madness of war was on their front doorstep. The television was on all day, and she listened attentively whenever President Bush spoke. Ginny's reaction might have been normal, considering her past and her current emotionally unstable state, but there was more to it.

For Ginny, Alzheimer's blurred the stark realities of the new age. She knew she was slipping; living alone was no longer an option. Each day she had one less faculty. She'd wake up and ask herself, "What's missing now?" Terrorized by her disease, she contacted her daughters.

Ginny's oldest daughter, Mary, seemed the most available. Linda was recuperating from a near fatal car accident. Between that and burnout from ninety-hour workweeks in the Securities Industry, she shied away when asked for help with investments, even though she'd managed her parents' financial accounts for decades. Her youngest daughter, Cathy, immersed herself in a veterinarian career in a northern state. So, Ginny had sought Mary's assistance, not realizing the hungry tiger that lay within.

A bright, inquisitive first born, Mary had the new parents' attention, when the world was focused on re-making itself, after the war. Her father struggled in business, trying to make ends meet, and she'd missed out on some opportunities, because of the timing of her father's success. She'd married after school and started a family shortly thereafter. There wasn't much chance to go back to school, earn extra, or put something aside for the future. Ginny knew that Mary felt deprived. She tried so many times to make it up to her. This time, she decided, she asked Mary if she could come live with her after she sold her house.

The house had sold quickly after a brief bidding war during the real estate bubble. Mary pocketed the cash, built an elaborate extension to her house, and kept the details to herself. She remembered Linda's persistent questions. "Where's Mom's money? Why won't you talk to me?" and her chagrin when she noticed the new swimming pool, car, and other luxuries.

An opportunist, Mary saw her chance to level the playing field. Her sisters had advanced degrees and made good money—those silly, giggling blondes. Linda was a stuffed-shirt stockbroker and Cathy, a bleeding-heart veterinarian. They'd made names for themselves, traveled around the world. Oh, sure. her parents babysat her children, gave her and her husband, Brad, many things, like a twenty-eight foot cruiser, though she had to lay a ton of guilt on them to get it, but that hardly made up for the difference.

Then there were legal matters. How convenient the law allowed individual family members to seize control. Federal law went right to the core of family sovereignty, upholding the power to exclude. All she needed was Power of Attorney.

SHORTLY BEFORE LUNCH AT DAISY'S

Safely ensconced in Attorney Nestor Brown's office where

various ego-satisfying plaques about his career adorned the walls, Mary carefully adjusted the lapels of her black and white, striped suit jacket. Her eyebrows, like thick black commas, mimicked the black diagonal stripes of her lapels. *The big moment had come*, she thought. *Just get Mother to sign the newly executed document lying on his navy destroyer-sized desk.* If only that facial tic would behave.

Cathy sat calmly beside her mother in a red leather chair, with bronze studs running up and down the length of its arms. She crossed her long legs and modestly lengthened her skirt over her knees. Occasionally, she and Mary exchanged conspiratorial glances like pirates hovering over ransom money. This meeting had been in the works for months, without a word to Linda. They'd gone to great lengths to exclude her.

The old will, executed a year earlier by an Italian attorney, a friend of the family, created the *Ginny Cray Revocable Trust*, naming Mary the trustee. If anything happened to her, then the beneficiaries would designate a successor trustee. Linda and Cathy were designated personal representatives. Ginny had left a sum of money to her only nephew, Tom, and her grandsons; the remaining assets were to be distributed equally to her three daughters, share and share alike. It was a will you would have expected Ginny to write.

The new will told a different story.

Brown addressed his client, Ginny, who was sitting nervously between Cathy and Mary. In his thoughts, he dismissed that she should have been represented by a court-appointed legal guardian. "Let me summarize what we're doing here today. Is that all right, Mrs. Cray?" Although Ginny was his principal client, the two sisters present were also clients. The missing daughter, Linda, was not a client.

Ginny looked from him to Mary and Cathy, both nodding vigorously, and gave him her response—an anemic nod.

Satisfied, Brown continued, "Basically, it reads like your old will, but there are a few changes. Here on page two, it states that you devise all of your right, title, and interest in and to your home place subject to any encumbrances thereon, and its contents, and all rights you may have under any insurance policies to the owner of the house you currently live in."

Clear as mud to the three women.

"In other words, the addition that's part of Mary's home will belong without question to her."

A pause allowed the impact of his words to sink in. Mary smirked. Cathy gazed at a fly on the wall. Ginny stared stoically straight ahead. "If something happens to her, it goes to her husband Brad, then to her issue, meaning her children."

Ginny's lip quivered as she nodded.

"Mary is the trustee, and Cathy is the successor trustee. Is that right?"

Ginny had closed her eyes and appeared to have dozed off. Mary nudged her with an elbow, and she bolted awake, with a newfound attentiveness.

"Yes."

On that note, Mary leaned over the large desk and pulled the papers closer to her mother. Ginny extended her hand, and Mary deftly guided it to the signature line. A strange squiggle trailed north of the designated line and appeared above Ginny's typed name. It was the best she could manage in a tough war against Alzheimer's.

Mary and Cathy let out a collective sigh of relief that could have blown the rest of the papers off Brown's desk.

Attorney Brown produced another document and held it toward her. "This is your appointment of Mary and Cathy as durable attorneys, health care surrogates, and personal representatives under the HIPAA act." Excluding Linda from any position of responsibility was apparent. He waited for any reaction? He waited a moment before sliding the papers toward his client.

Once more, Ginny bellied up to the table. When she had finished signing, once a simple feat, Ginny sat back in the chair, not knowing she'd planted the seeds of her family's destruction.

Mary's smile broadened deeply, having deftly acquired the necessary titles: A successful power grab. There was only one place where Linda's name was mentioned: the distribution of assets. She had tried to have that removed, too, but Brown had strongly advised against it, stating that she would only open herself up to a lengthy and costly lawsuit. She had already confiscated more than half of Ginny's estate, with more coming. Cathy, veterinarian with the big bucks, didn't mind and offered no resistance. The greatest coup, however, was that she had gotten away with it smelling like a rose. Even that pesky, other sister of hers couldn't deter her, and with the rest of the family on her side, she was feeling particularly confident and strong.

The new will was a silver bullet.

With a dazzling grin that things had gone so well, except maybe his main client who wouldn't be around to protest, Attorney Brown escorted Ginny to the door while Mary and Cathy, arms draped across each other's shoulders and heads touching in sisterly affection, brought up the rear, with relaxed, sauntering steps, as they discussed where to have lunch.

Chapter Three

Rehearsing Jim Cott's lines a few times and trying to sound like she knew what she was talking about, Linda left voicemails with her sisters.

"The plan to have Mother buy Mary's house is ill-advised. It ignores the Three Year Look Back Rule," Linda read slowly. "Mother is incompetent. There's no tax, or probate, because we are equal beneficiaries. Please drop it." Just before disconnecting, she added, "Check with your attorney if you like."

Done! She was calm on the outside, except for a racing heart. The Three Year Look Back Rule meant that a person couldn't claim poverty to avoid taxes and die within three years.

Shortly after the call, Cathy, who'd read her caller ID, responded. "What's up?"

"Oh, Cathy! Thanks for calling. I just wanted to say that . . . this is difficult, but I have to be blunt . . . Mary will try to get that money."

"I don't care. She can have it. Look what she's doing for Mom."

Linda couldn't believe her ears. Was veterinary practice that lucrative? As for Mary, she didn't have that income, yet there was plenty of evidence of newfound wealth: A cruising boat parked in the backyard, a shiny red BMW in the garage, and a swimming pool. "It's Mother's money, Cathy. What if she needs it?"

"Let me get back to you. I've got a room full of meowing cats and barking dogs." Cathy pressed the disconnect button.

Cathy was shy and introverted as a child. She took to quieter pleasures in life such as reading and holing up in her room with a good book and one of her cherished pets—anything to avoid the numerous family conflicts and her sisters' arguments. Things changed dramatically during high school when a guidance counselor reported that she had unusually high scholastic aptitude scores. A strong inclination toward science, with a deep compassion for animals, Cathy did exceptionally well in college and pre-med, and then the medical kingdom opened its doors to her, as usually happens upon discovery of unusual talent, or skill. Her internship was in another state, not that she minded. Once she found her strength and independence, she wanted to be far away from the mega center of chaos. After she opened her veterinary practice, work occupied most of her time.

A day passed, and Cathy called Linda. "Mary and I decided to abandon our original plan. I tried to explain to her how you probably felt, having been left out of the estate planning."

"I appreciate your sensitivity to my feelings and your being neutral where Mary and I are concerned," Linda replied. "I know you want to avoid conflict."

"I do."

Linda surmised a good amount of intimidation also. As for Mary, Linda had that she deliberately intended to exclude her from anything to do with her mother's care, so she could operate with a free hand and accomplish her own objectives.

"I asked her how *she* would feel," Cathy explained. "I'm just trying to keep us all together. I feel torn. You two are always feuding about one thing or another."

"I feel like I'm always defending, or protecting myself, but thank you, Cathy." Her baby sister had stirred emotions connected to childhood. Linda remembered a tight bond between her and Cathy when they were roommates. Was it still there? "I'd like to see Mom's financial statements."

Cathy coughed loudly. "I don't really want to get into it any further. I'm willing to let Mary do what she has to do. If you've got a problem with that, why don't you ask her yourself?"

"I have—several times. She's stonewalling."

"Give her time." The attempt to patronize Linda and avoid Mary's rancor fell with a thud in their dialogue.

"It's been weeks. Tell her that she can send them to me, or . . . an agency."

The implication revolted the veterinarian. "You're not serious!"

Linda smirked, recalling her similar reaction when Dr. Peter Hall had first mentioned this course of action. As days rolled into weeks, Linda had grown impatient and then angry by Mary's lack of response. It was not like her to become so angry. Usually, she had a slow simmer. The difference was this time the dispute involved her invalid mother.

"Yes, I am."

"Mary's a saint for what she's doing!" Cathy insisted.

"It's nice she took Mom into her home," she said aloud, thinking, *for a quarter million dollars,* "but let me see the numbers."

"Linda, I trust Mary . . . Don't you?"

She would have loved to tell her younger sister what she thought, but held back and rephrased words. "Let me have a chance to review things..." *How much further can I go with this conversation?* She asked, "Do you know what happened to the cash Mom set aside?" There'd been a hundred thousand for each, held in trust by a local bank.

Cathy rose to the bait. "Well, I know that she let that young financial planner—what was his name? Oh, I remember—Elmer Overton! Anyway, he put some of it in multicurrency." She hesitated nervously, "I think he was a . . . little more, er . . . more aggressive in your account. Mary said it was all right for him to do so."

Linda blanched. A bigger problem than expected. "You've got to be kidding! You could lose your shirt in minutes with that kind of investment!" Her jaw clenched, making her teeth ache. Multicurrency hinged on the value of the dollar, amounted to trillions of dollars in volatile and speculative daily trading. Experts ventured there, not a local broker wet behind the ears.

"I told Mary we needed to be more conservative."

Thank God for that, Linda thought.

Cathy continued, "Elmer took care of that. He was really nice. He used to visit Mom and bring her flowers."

Visits and flowers—big commissions, Linda knew, having played that game herself. Now, on the other side of the table, she wanted to wring Elmer's scrawny neck. Briefly, she considered a visit to his office, but Mary held the cards of authority. *What good would it do?*

"It's all there, Linda." Cathy was talking, but her voice sounded far away. "The three hundred thousand is still there . . . Linda . . . ?"

Linda wrestled with words, suddenly tongue-tied.

Cathy stiffened self-defensively on the other end of the line. "Are you still there?"

So as to calm down and not throw gas on a smoldering fire, Linda considered that as long as the principal was intact she needn't make a call to her lawyer—not yet, anyway. Was Attorney Brown encouraging this fiscal recklessness? "Cathy, have you considered replacing Brown?"

The question annoyed Cathy. "Not yet," she responded icily.

Click.

Round one, going down in a heap at her sister's feet, Linda sat for a while, the cell phone in her limp hand, and reflected on Cathy's impression of the benefits her mother had derived from living with Mary. She was usually left alone in the house with only domestic animals.

Only after Linda insisted on healthcare companionship had Mary hired private nurses. Half a day was better than nothing. Afterward, Mary groused about the cost. Then, the next time Linda had visited her mother, she'd noticed Mary's closed office door. Funny, before she'd asked questions, it had been open. She had meant to threaten Mary into providing financial statements about her mother's assets. The paper trail might explain things, but Mary's refusal to provide information left Linda with few options and much suspicion and distrust.

She remembered her father, a U.S. Air Force captain and war hero. How fortunate they were to have such a father. He'd given them every opportunity for success, including a good education.

Her mother and father believed in family unity. Were the daughters honoring their parents by being at each other's throats? Linda felt sadness—so far, they were failing as a family.

What was she going to do about it? Now, she'd worked herself nto a fine dander, struggling with feelings of persecution, abandonment, and rejection. She was angry. With a sleazy attorney, a wimpy kid sister, and Mary marching with POA boots, the entire operation was so . . . undemocratic!

She thought, *This is not just about money, but about everything I value in life . . . and Mother.*

She had two choices: bleat with frustration and allow it to continue or make the call to the agency.

Taking a drink popped into her head. *Why not? It always feels so good when it hits the stomach. Then, when my heart pumps it into my veins and it goes to my head—ooooh, how nice . . .* She could hide in the bottle, escape reality, and avoid confronting her sister. She shook a firm "no."

Mother cared for me every day of my life and is now totally vulnerable. She thought of Mary and asked herself, *What nice thing did Mary ever do for me . . . ?* She couldn't think of a single one. It was more like Mary had always wanted her out of the way. Like a ping-pong ball, her mind sailed back and forth, over an invisible net.

Days passed . . . then a month.

She tried to reach her younger sister once more.

Sunlight streamed through the window shades and fell on the round table as Linda was finishing her morning coffee. She liked sunshine, liked things to be clear, open, honest and direct. There was little furniture in her house because she craved openness. The sliding curtains had been crunched to let in maximum light. A plastic white cup with a photo of her mother, a token from a visit to the mall from one of the many kiosks littering the walkway, stood by the sink. She never drank from it but used it as a pencil holder. A bowl of half-eaten Wheaties lay next to her coffee.

She thought about her father who'd stood up to his father about a career choice.

On the kitchen table, a pile of history books, mostly about WWII, lay strewn. An avid reader, she'd been drawn to Winston Churchill, identifying with his compassion for the persecuted. Feelings for her father, mother, and country suddenly infused her with courage. She reached for the phone. Little did she foresee the juggernaut coming her way, as she dialed the number for the Department of Families and Children.

Chapter Four

Mary arrived home from work late, which was not unusual, and found a card on the front door. She and Brad owned a home in a remote section of the county, making it difficult for anyone to drop in unexpectedly. Customarily, agents left their calling cards after several unsuccessful attempts. This one was from the Department of Families and Children, Division of Elder Abuse. On the back of the card, "Call me," was scribbled as if in haste. It took a few seconds to register its impact, and then she became apoplectic with rage. Turning to her husband Brad, she fairly hissed the words. "After all we've done! Cooking and cleaning and everything else! We've worked ourselves to the bone!" Her eyes narrowed as she scanned the neighborhood. "Who reported us?" She suddenly remembered Linda's threat if she didn't produce the financial statements. The rage intensified. "That bitch of a sister did this! Look!" A facial tic pulled up the right side of her lip.

"Hon, try not to get so upset." Brad tried to console her, as he glanced at the card. His eyebrows rose, eyes widened. "What are we going to do?"

"I know exactly what I'm going to do. She'll be sorry!"

Attorney Brown reacted hotly. "She did—what?" Instantly, his hand reached for a calculator, and his fingers began rapidly clicking off numbers. "Yes, yes, come in first thing in the morning, and we'll plan a response. No, no. Don't return his call! Don't do anything until you get here. I'll handle this." Negotiating with a state agency entailed careful planning and finesse, requiring more than the usual billable hours. A smile appeared. Plus, it was sort of an emergency considering the state his client was in. The Cray case was getting more lucrative every day.

The extended family sided with the one apparently wronged,

without attempting to remain neutral, or even hear the other side. In this family, first came the patriarch, and then the matriarch, the first born, and the rest took their places in the hierarchy. Differing opinions, or values, were subject to censure. When Ginny went to live with Mary, most everyone understood that Mary was the new matriarch. She ruled. If she were the pope, she could have had Linda excommunicated.

Cathy's voicemail scorched Linda's phone. "Daddy would be so ashamed of you! You are not to see Mom, or talk to Mary, or go anywhere near Mary's property. If you do, you will be arrested." The rest of the message became garbled as Cathy broke down in tears.

A letter from Attorney Brown arrived in Linda's mailbox. "Your sisters do not wish to have any further contact with you. If you have anything to say, it will be through me."

Aunt Dolly, always so gentle and kind, spoke to Linda on the phone. "You didn't do such a nice thing."

"I was protecting my mother."

"There won't be any chit chats, or lunches."

"Chit chats? Lunches . . .with my sisters?" Linda chewed the pencil she'd been holding. "Aunt Dolly, I can't miss something I never had." She picked off a piece of the pencil from her lip. "You want to know something? I had a premonition when I was younger that I'd have a money problem with my sisters."

Her aunt clicked her tongue. "Be at peace. Let it go."

Linda felt no peace in being a Cray. There was no peace in Cathy either, and certainly not in Mary.

Were it not for Recovery, Linda would have given up. She couldn't make a move in her family without tripping over history and bad blood. An idea formed—from the ancient custom, from her grandfather who'd left Italy and immigrated to America in 1895—*vendetta*!

Recovery began years ago, during her divorce, when Linda's mother was the first to notice the change in her daughter. "You drank a lot," she said to her one afternoon. "I'm glad you stopped." This happened before her mother got sick and her father had passed.

Her parents, Mary and her family, and Linda and her husband lived in Florida, on the western coast where things were more laid back and down-to-earth.

Some said Buena Vida was years behind the rest of the country, but the influx of tourists and tourists-turned-residents changed things. When the town was first settled some hundred years ago, it was a sleepy fishing village, accessible only by boat. A service industry, which catered to the rich and famous, had grown so large it soon needed its own service industry. Hospitals, nurseries, and schools sprouted. It became an affluent resort city where families mostly from the Midwest and the Northeast visited, escaping the harsh northern climate. Then the dot-com families bought up all the land along the coast. The town had become its own melting pot of nationalities and lifestyles, but most everyone dressed about the same: in shorts, T shirts, and sandals.

Linda was one of an increasing crowd of year-round residents. In the winter, traffic snarled and you couldn't get a seat in a restaurant. In the summer, it was too hot to leave the house. The weather had been turning warmer each year since their family had arrived, but it was still considered semitropical. Ages ago, this was a densely foliated swamp, with alligators lurking in the shifting shadows, black bears roaming, and panthers slinking low to the damp ground. With a little nudge from nature, it could easily revert to swampland again.

The members who attended the A.A. meeting this night reflected the town's profile. Linda paraded in with them and entered the wide hall of a Presbyterian church. They took their seats around a narrow rectangular table. It was the usual crowd ranging in age from eighteen to eighty. They came from all walks of life and had varying lengths of sobriety. A few came straight from work dressed in suits and ties. The retired members huddled at one end of the table like ducks at the edge of a pond. One fellow adjusted an ankle ID under long pants. They were tall or short, dark or light. Some were "double blessed" or addicted to more than one substance.

When she first moved here, the meetings were small. But the weather drew many more. Their size had gone from half a dozen to forty, or more. She was not good with faces or names, but she knew shoes. She liked to count the loafers, sneakers, and sandals during the meeting.

A sign on the far wall read: "Many meetings, many chances, few meetings, few chances, no meetings, no chances." Linda recognized a few familiar faces. They came regularly because they knew what happened to those who didn't: hospitals, jails, and cemeteries were full of them.

The leader for the night read the introduction from a laminated sheet. After a moment of silence, everyone recited the serenity prayer together. They took turns reading from their prescribed literature and then had a discussion.

"I used to ask myself how bad I really was." Stuart, an Australian, had entered the program in his mid-forties. Each time he got drunk, he bought a new tattoo. His open shirt indicated descending tattoos and black ink scrolled down his ankles to his toes, visible through flip flops. From neck to toe, Stuart had decorated himself. "Here's the answer right on this page—anything! Anything is better than the way I was. I was tore up from the floor up; needed a checkup, from the neck up." There was a round of hearty laughs from the members.

"To me, A.A. is like breakfast," said Wayne. "The chicken is involved, but the pig is committed." Light laughter.

"All are welcome here. That's like a great wind blowing through my mind," said AT, short for Arnold Thomas, a man with an IQ in the stratosphere who, after three divorces, lived in a small studio apartment on the outskirts of town. "I had to get rid of my toilet bowl-thinking and start anew. I found I could do that here. It's not that hard. There are two days I can drink: yesterday and tomorrow. I just can't drink today." He closed with a lopsided grin as he stretched out his legs before him, a habit he had developed whenever he spoke.

Harry had thick brown hair, brushed straight back, and slicked down. "I went straight to God. I asked Him, 'Can you give me a buzz, God?' Drugs and alcohol weren't working anymore." His head bobbed up and down, as he took in their attentive faces. "It wasn't long after that I found joy. I realized that I came in just in the nick of time. I hadn't killed anybody. Hadn't eaten out of a dumpster. Hadn't slept on a sidewalk. A park bench, maybe . . ." There was a big laugh here.

Sam, from Nova Scotia, said, "I heard that *yet* is an acronym that stands for 'you're eligible, too.'" He exchanged a look with Harry. "I just saw something I had never seen before. I watched this guy start his car by blowing into this thing. After we went a few miles, he did it again. He told me he had gotten a second DUI and has to do this for a year. That was enough for me to see."

"You could draw a line in my life when I became sober. There was Claude before and Claude after." Soft spoken, but with a strong message, Claude was ranked one of the top market timers in the nation. "I am a completely different person. I live in a different space. What used to bother me no longer does. I don't regret the past, because it brought me to where I am today."

The room became quiet as they waited for the next member to share.

"I'm Linda. I'm an alcoholic." Her short, blonde hair clung to the sides of her face in soft curls. She wore a light shade of coral lipstick, which blended in with the rest of her tanned complexion. There were those in the room who considered her to be attractive, but she saw herself as a tomboy with average looks.

"Hi, Linda!" the group members responded.

"There are only a few ladies in the room, but I need a temporary sponsor while mine is out of town." No sooner had she said it than Jenna picked up a yellow schedule sheet. She jumped up and brought it around to the other women to write their names and phone numbers. Damien, one elder of the group and a man who looked like he could be an Italian godfather, nodded his approval.

Members from every corner of the world shared their experience, strength, and hope, continuously renewing and enriching the fellowship. No matter the age, they always had energy, ideas, and ways of putting things that gave a fresh perspective to a problem.

At nine o'clock, voices hushed.

The leader looked at the clock on the wall. "We have time for one more," he said. Silence. The leader's eyes scanned their faces. He shrugged as if it mattered little to him. "We have a nice way of closing. Mary Pat—" He nodded to a woman sitting at the end of the table.

Everyone stood and joined hands in a circle.

Mary Pat looked from left to right at the bent heads. "We hold hands to remind us of the truth that we're no longer alone. Our prayer is for the still suffering alcoholics in these rooms and on the streets. Hold on to the hand of the person next to you like your life depends on it . . . Someday it may. Who keeps us sober?"

Our Father. . . Linda was saying the words by rote, until they came to the line "*Thy will be done,*" and her thoughts flew to her mother's will, and she prayed in earnest.

After the meeting, everyone dispersed into the parking lot where some gathered in small circles and talked for a while longer.

"Hey, Linda," said Kent. "How's your mom?" Kent and Linda had been friends for years.

"She's all right. Thanks for asking."

"You don't look too happy—something bothering you?"

"Yeah." She looked at him. "It's my sisters."

"What's going on?"

"My older sister is trying to prevent me from seeing my mother."

He frowned. "That's not good."

They stood talking while the others left the parking lot and headed into the night. Afterward, Linda drove along the freeway, thinking about her family and their origins. Her mother, a beautiful woman from the Midwest who had met, fallen in love with and married a man from New Jersey, during the war. Her father's family took a liking to her and readily adopted her into their culture. She recalled family reunions: grandparents, parents, aunts, uncles, and cousins used to get together almost every week and sit around the dinner table for hours while the adults recounted the past. Holidays and special occasions—she remembered those evenings best because of the banter and laughter. Her mother used to sit at her father's side, approving the scene.

Afterward, there was the usual pile of empty wine jugs. Someone, she couldn't remember who, had given her the first insulting drink at the age of fourteen.

Cousins were like brothers and sisters. She had been close to them, particularly those near her age, until everyone went away to school, started careers, or married and then she didn't hear from them again, which seemed strange and unsettling. Her cousins were still living, and she missed them and the fun they used to have. The thought of her aunt made her smile. Her aunt had been her godmother, responsible for her religious instruction, but she'd given her so much more.

Linda's family roots traced back to the late nineteenth century when her grandparents, along with millions of others, migrated to America from Europe by boat. They passed through Battery Park. The registrar at the orphanage where he lived shortened Grandpa John's last name from Creare, meaning to create, to Cray. The new name stuck.

While immigrants poured in from every country, some racing across the wilderness in search of gold, John Cray settled on the eastern Coast where industrial workers filled the sprawling cities and smokestack plumes spewed white clouds across the skyline. Towering over the harbor, the Statue of Liberty greeted the newly arrived, offering escape from rigid hierarchy and the fresh, sweet opportunity of a government based on democracy.

Foraging on the streets for his livelihood, John met Marsha in Paterson where she worked in one of the silk factory sweatshops that dotted the city, a result of Alexander Hamilton's efforts to transform the city into the famous "Silk City," the country's center for dyeing and weaving silk.

After a brief courtship, John and Marsha married, in a Catholic church. Elaborately decorated with silk trimmings, Marsha took pride in her handmade dress. John raised his four children with a strong patriarchal hand while Marsha took the position of dutiful wife. Although they stayed together their entire lifetimes, as was common in those days, their marriage took a rocky, estranged path. Such was her family history. But now, in the present where her own family was on the same path, *nothing would stop her from caring for or seeing her mother.*

Chapter Five

She knew where to find her mother. It was because of a decision they had made months ago. She remembered how it went.

When Ginny began to exhibit signs of Alzheimer's, Linda had rebelled, thinking her mother was fooling around, playing a game, pretending to be helpless in those things she used to do so well. She didn't get it and became annoyed, a little aggressive, which didn't help either of them. A dementia support group recommended literature to help her understand and deal with the disease. She became more attuned to the dangers that lay in wait for the unsuspecting dementia patient who needed constant care. Particularly disturbing was the increasing possibility of her mother wandering off in a store, on a highway or into a swimming pool. Ginny's accommodations seemed like a disaster waiting to happen. Since Mary and her husband Brad slept on the other side of the house, Ginny could easily slip out the door in the middle of the night and wander off toward the busy interstate down the street, and no one would be the wiser, except perhaps the dogs. For most of the day and early evening, Ginny was alone in the house, with a list of household chores, such as ironing, to keep her busy and she had to fend for herself while Mary and Brad worked.

Linda was losing sleep worrying about the situation.

One day, as if to confirm her worst fears, Linda had arrived at Mary's house and found her mother covered in blood, wearing an idiotic grin, and oblivious to the spectacle she presented. By asking questions and listening intently, Linda gradually pieced together what had happened: her mother had been walking the dogs in the backyard when a turtle stepped out from behind a bush and crossed their path. Startled, the dogs reacted, yelping and barking, and ran around in circles, lashing Ginny with their leashes as they spun about and cutting her delicate skin. Ginny had fallen on some rocks, and the dogs had dragged her around a bit.

Linda had led her mother to the bathroom and washed off the blood. She settled her down, but her mother still had the same silly grin. That night, Linda made several rather urgent phone calls to Mary, her tone of voice a little strained. "Mother should never be left alone! Not even for a minute. It's too dangerous!"

Mary was not about to take orders. "There's an adult day care center down the road. I pass it on the way to work."

Yes, and—? Linda waited for something more, like a promise to stop by and maybe pick up some information. Nothing. After an awkward moment of silence, Linda jumped in.

"I'll get some information."

"Good idea." Her tone was clipped and short.

Mary's house nestled at the end of a street with no outlet and butted up against the interstate highway with eight lanes of raging traffic. It was partially obscured from the quiet neighborhood by dense foliage. Their property of several acres was narrow and long, surrounded by similar bandage-shaped lots.

When Linda arrived at Mary's house a few days later, she stood in the winding driveway, listening to the roaring traffic sounds from the nearby highway, and shuddered, picturing her mother wandering toward it in the voiceless dark of night. She visited her mother, but she and Mary would have a conversation about custodianship. She rang the bell on the large wooden door and, upon hearing "Come in," pushed it open and entered. The dogs recognized her instantly and welcomed her enthusiastically as she bent to greet them. "Yes, yes, I missed you, too. Down, dammit!" From what she could observe by the room's occupants, her arrival was not so welcome.

Ginny sat on a straight-backed chair she had dragged from the nearby dining room table and was facing the front door, anxiously awaiting Linda's arrival, with a not-too-happy look on her face. Mary sat behind her, on an overstuffed sofa, in the deep shadows of the living room, arms defiantly crossed over her chest and legs tucked underneath her angular body.

Having finally freed herself from the dogs that pranced off to lounge by the sofa, Linda glanced tentatively from mother to sister. "What's up?" Her lungs had started to freeze, and she was finding it difficult to breathe.

"Mom saw the envelope from the adult day care center when I brought in the mail," Mary said with a sly smile. "It was on the dining room table." Ginny's glare intensified. Obviously, there had been some sort of exchange between them. Mary looked like she had taken a beating.

"So?" Linda prompted, with a innocent failure to understand. "What's the problem?"

"She doesn't want to go!" Mary blurted, losing patience.

"*I'm your mother!*" Ginny's indignant cry, followed by a forceful foot stomping, startled everyone including the dogs who perked up, ears pointed. "How *could* you?" Her independence, although precariously perched in her daughter's house, was worth fighting for.

Linda looked from her mother to her sister, Mary, whose disingenuous smile taunted, "You asked for it, smarty pants. Go ahead. Let's see you handle this."

Linda picked up the brochure from the coffee table positioned between them and appeared enthused as she read. "Mother, what a cool place! Look, they have all these activities and games." She pointed to the list on the printed page. "There are people your age there!" Their mother sat rigidly, like a stone statue, still against the idea, but willing at least to listen. "It's much better than being *alone* all day." Her emphasis challenged and provoked Mary who raised an arched eyebrow. "I wouldn't mind going there myself. Looks like fun!"

Ginny shifted in her seat and seemed to show some interest. Encouraged, Linda proceeded. "And the food . . . check this out— hamburgers with French fries, soda, ice cream. They have butter pecan, your favorite!" *A lie but, heck, it might work.* Linda turned to Mary, as if to elicit support, and Ginny followed with her eyes.

Mary nodded her head up and down enthusiastically. "C'mon, Mom. It'll be good for you. Try it and see. You can always change your mind."

"Give it a chance, Mom," cajoled Linda. "I'll take you over there so you can check it out—no commitment, just take a peek."

Slowly, hesitantly, her mother softened her posture, nodding with an almost imperceptible move of her little gray head.

"Oh, all right. But if I don't like it, I'm coming home."

"Of course," Linda agreed, feeling the tension evaporate. She could breathe again.

"That's okay." Mary unfolded her arms and stretched her legs on the sofa.

And so it had been decided: Ginny went to adult day care. At first, she went a few days a week and complained about everything, but then she grew to like it and didn't complain nearly as much. After that, she wouldn't miss a day. She even made the front page of the local newspaper when a journalist, writing about the benefits of adult care centers, captured her exuberance, in a dance class.

Linda drove across town to the adult day care center and waited to speak to the manager. A casually-dressed woman met her in the front office, which resembled a dining room. The building was a modified house converted into a care facility.

"What can I do for you?" Arlene asked.

"I'd like to speak with the manager."

"I'm the manager. May I help you?"

"My family's engaged in a dispute. My older sister is legal guardian, but she's trying to prevent me from seeing my mother."

Arlene seemed genuinely sympathetic. "As long as your mother doesn't object, you can do that. What's her name?"

"Ginny Cray."

"Oh, Ginny! She's such a sweet lady. You'll find her in the main room. They're relaxing before snack time." Arlene stood and pointed the way to Linda.

Linda walked uncertainly into a large room—a former living room. Chairs had been set around the periphery, and a couple dozen, elderly people were sitting on them. She passed the kitchen and saw little plates of Jello and cut up pieces of fruit being set out on a table. The staff spoke quietly and congenially as they worked. Linda scanned the room and spotted her mother near the kitchen door. Unsure how she'd react to her being there, Linda approached tentatively and greeted her softly. Ginny raised her head and stared. Her face turned bright red.

"What are *you* doing here?" Ginny lashed out.

"I came to see you, Mother."

Ginny seemed very perplexed and the confusion reduced her to tears.

"Don't you want to see me, Mother?"

Ginny's voice tightened, and fear took hold of her. "Mary said I was not to talk to you," she whimpered.

That was all Linda needed to hear. She stepped forward and put her arms around her mother—a soft touch, so soft and loving. "I'll only stay a moment," Linda said, "I just wanted to make sure that you're all right."

Ginny calmed.

"I love you, Mother."

"I love you, too, Linda." Her mother's smile returned.

Linda took another look at her mother, so weak and vulnerable. A protective strength arose, a new, strong feeling. She had never felt this way toward her mother. To think that Mary threatened her mother like that was—*unbelievable*. By trying to hurt her, she had hurt her mother, and that really bothered Linda. Anger gave her energy. A trip to the gym was definitely in the works and probably a long bicycle ride to work off homicidal urges.

She located Arlene in her office, and they chatted for a few moments. "I might return in a few days," Linda said to Arlene.

Arlene smiled. "Same policy—no matter when you return."

As Linda turned to go, Arlene called out to her. "You have no idea how common your situation is. I see it all the time. You're not alone. It's sad, but true."

"It must be awful," Linda replied. *Common? How many families go through this horror? What is the matter with us that we can't transfer wealth without a family shipwreck?* Why hadn't someone thought of a better way than allowing an aggressive sibling to seize control? Father always said, "Family comes first." Yes, family was important, but so was personal integrity, which had caused him to pursue aviation rather than the livestock commission merchant company his father had developed and wished to pass on to his sons.

Linda knew it took courage for her father to stand up to her grandfather and venture out on his own. Grandpa John was upset at first but later reconciled with his son, who achieved success doing what he loved. Maybe it would be that way with her, too. *Never fear bullies, especially powerful bullies, because victory is sweeter,* she remembered him saying. She would not let her sisters get the best of her. She had heard nothing from her sisters, or their attorney, for a short while, but she sensed something, whatever it was, was up.

A few days later, Linda received Brown's letter: "You are allowed to have your mother visit you for the weekend. You must give Mary advance notice, and if you are late in returning her, Mary will summon the police."

Wonderful. Now I can visit with Mom without having to storm an adult day care center.

A pre-arranged visit was set up through the attorney.

Exhilarated to have her mother to herself for the weekend, Linda brought Ginny to her home and helped her unpack a small suitcase. Mary had left a note inside about Ginny's daily medicine schedule and a pillbox full of multi-colored tablets. Linda kept her mother busy. They looked at cars, stopped at the chapel and looked at the garden where Ginny admired a large, red hibiscus in bloom, and spent time shopping at Ginny's favorite, local department store. Linda bought a DVD with Bugs Bunny singing Christmas carols.

Back at her house, Linda popped the DVD into the player, and the two sat on the couch, shoulders touching, holding hands, while they followed the bouncing words along the bottom of the large TV screen singing with the animated characters. Linda grew hoarse, but Ginny kept on singing.

After breakfast the next morning, Linda helped Ginny shower, then dashed to her room to shower while Ginny dressed for the day.

When Linda returned to the guest room, her mother was wearing two bras, one where her pants should have been.

"You already have on a bra, Mom. You don't need another." Linda helped Ginny to dress appropriately, hiding the shock and dismay she felt.

When it was time to take Ginny home, Linda picked up the small suitcase with reluctance. Neither of them wanted the weekend to end, but they were on a tight schedule and didn't want to keep Mary, or the police, waiting.

On the way to Mary's house, they stopped for brunch, which was more like a contest of wills to see who would be more successful at feeding Ginny. Her mother laid the maple syrup bottle on top of her pile of pancakes then stared at it as if wondering what to do next. Her brain, ravaged by Alzheimer's, was not giving her any answers. Linda reached over, grabbed the bottle, and poured a little syrup over the pancakes, which she cut up into small wedges. Ginny took up her fork and speared a wedge of pancake, only to have it fall in her lap. Linda leaned over, retrieved the piece with a fork, and attempted to feed it to her mother who rebelliously pushed aside Linda's hand. Ginny put a hand under the fork, with its captured pancake, and raised her arm. The pancake fell off. She caught the falling piece and tossed it into her mouth, then sat back with a triumphant smile. Linda smiled back. *My goodness! Has it come to this? How do Mary and Brad deal with it on an everyday basis?*

The meal finished, Linda said, "Mom, there's stuff going on about your money, and I'm trying to defend your interests."

"My money? Where is it?" Ginny asked innocently. "Can I get it back?"

"Your oldest daughter has Power of Attorney, but I'll do what I can. You know what they say about power, Mom—it corrupts!" When she had picked up her mother this time, she had noticed workers laying an expensive wood floor throughout Mary's house.

The trip took twenty minutes, but it seemed faster, and they arrived at Mary's house on time. Ginny held the Christmas gift that Linda had given her tucked protectively under her arm, her purse and gray sweater in her hand. Linda kissed her on the cheek and moved quickly to her car, escaping before Mary's usual disapproving look.

The next day, Ginny said to Linda on the phone, "I don't want you to say anything to get anyone upset."

"I'm not a doormat, Mother."

"Be nice."

"I'm going to stand up for you so that you have your money if you need it. And after that, I'll try to see that it goes according to your will—equally." *Also, there should be plenty of transparency so everyone sees what's going on.* She didn't say that. What she said was, "Yes, Mother."

Her mother's careful instructions—"Be nice"—had already been forgotten with any semblance of social politeness. Battle lines drawn, hostilities were out in the open.

Linda wanted healthy family closeness, with each member having an opportunity to speak and have a say in how to be governed. However, she wasn't sure how to accomplish that. Her behavior was new for them all, and like sheep, they were apt to wander off into the pasture without a shepherd to guide them.

Growing up in the same household, each daughter was unique and strong-willed. Mary was somewhat intolerant and considered herself smarter than the others. She could add a whole column of figures just by looking at it and was also a drama queen, capable of instant tears and heart-wrenching cries, skills that proved useful in family disputes. Linda excelled in languages, was on the debating team, and developed a stubborn streak of argumentativeness. Cathy read everything scientific and had already become a bookworm, her nose lost in a book. Due to their father's *nouveau* affluence, each had their own room—islands often surrounded by stormy seas. Mary painted hers violet—the color of passion—to match a dark purple floral bedspread, Linda chose green and blue to match earth and sky, and Cathy liked everything pink. Although they ate their meals together as a family, afterward the girls usually sought the private confines of their rooms. The house bore a long hallway of closed doors.

Maybe it was the tone of the letter, or its underlying threat, but Linda felt compelled to confront her mother about her upbringing. Umpteen hours in a therapist's office and hundreds of self-help books had prepared her. How would her mother react?

On their next appointed visit, Linda was driving Ginny to the mall, a place they both enjoyed, heading to the walk-in beauty parlor at one of the large department stores. It seemed as good a time as any to say what she had to say. Inside the car, the "whrrrr" of the wheels on the road was audible. Linda held the steering wheel steady, foot lightly on the gas. She didn't know what was on the other side of this confrontation, which had been building for a long time, but she had to get it out as time was running short.

"Mom, I'm going to say some things to you that I've never said before, and I want you to hear me out until I'm done. This is very important to me, so please don't contradict me, or interrupt. After I've said what I need to say, you'll have all the time you want to say what you need to say. Okay?"

Ginny paused and drew in her breath. "Okay."

"I remember Dad being loud, bossy, and moody. His drink seemed more important to him than us. Nobody was allowed to have a different thought or feeling. I felt alone, scared, overwhelmed, and guilty. I tried so hard to please him, but it was never enough."

Ginny bit her lip. She hadn't expected this.

Linda went on. "I felt very resentful, lonely, and hurt for many years. And you, Mother, never let me have my own feelings. If I was sad, you said, 'Don't feel that way.' If I was angry, you said, 'Put a smile on your face,' or 'I hope your face doesn't freeze.' You used me as the sacrificial lamb among my feuding sisters to keep peace. Why didn't you protect me?"

Linda stared at the road ahead. Not having to face her mother made it easier. "My childhood deeply affected me. For one thing, I drank like a fish. And I'm still confused about love and rejection because of the way I was raised; I thought love meant I had to be in pain. It's only now I'm learning to like nice people. You know, it took me a long time to find the courage to say this to you, but I hope we can be honest with each other from here on— no more lies, secrets, or cover-ups."

Thunderous silence. Linda heard her heart pounding. Trembling inside, she braced for a lashing argument.

Ginny remained quiet.

On the dashboard, the clock ticked.

And then softly, hesitantly, her mother spoke. "I don't know what to say."

Time passed. The road stretched. The light turned red, and a herd of cars converged around them. A motorcycle's growl sounded at the driver's door. Linda ignored the leering motorcyclist, but glanced at Ginny who sat with her head turned to the outside.

After a while, Ginny said, "Look what we did for you."

"I appreciate what you did, and I know you tried your best, Mom, but there were some things that were really bad, you know?"

Arriving at the mall, Linda searched for a parking place. Finding one near the door, she helped her mother out of the car, and both were speechless for the moment. They walked side by side into J.C. Penney; it was lunchtime. Linda guided Ginny into a booth along the wall in Ruby Tuesday's. Defiantly, Ginny faced her daughter. "The bad things never happened."

"Just because you don't remember them doesn't mean they didn't happen," Linda countered.

A waitress arrived and took their orders. There was silence between them in the noisy restaurant.

"I thought we had a happy family," Ginny said.

"We had happy moments, Mom, and they were great, but other times things were difficult and hurtful. . . ." She looked at her mother's face. "I know you don't want to hear this."

"You played."

"Yes, I played—mostly with you. For reasons I don't fully understand, there was no warmth from my sisters. Even though Cathy and I shared a room, we constantly competed with each other. With Dad and Mary arguing and screaming at each other most of the time, I was scared. Why didn't you do something about that?"

Ginny struggled with words and then smiled happily, as if she had a solution.

"I know what I want—I want my three girls together!"

What every mother wanted, to fulfill a maternal instinct, struck Linda like a slap on the back of the head. She recalled a recent Thanksgiving dinner at Mary's house. Carrying a heaping plate of Brussels sprouts to the table, Linda had paused.

"How are you doing, Mom?"

"I'm in heaven."

There was no mistaking the ecstatic look on her face. The family sat down to eat armed with brimming wine glasses and a pervading sense of alienation barely disguised among the sisters that ran like a current throughout the meal.

Linda gauged her mother's wistful expression as she sat across from her in Ruby Tuesday's, the chatter of diners and waiters in the background. A patron at the next table bit into his freshly-grilled hamburger, and the aroma made her ravenous. She chose words carefully. "That would be nice, Mom, but we both know it won't happen right now . . . maybe later." A decent family was a gift, a privilege, she knew, available to some. It was unrealistic to expect that from her family at this time. But, if there was a way—what was it?

Having finished lunch, they walked through the busy mall, passing window displays designed to lure them in, boisterous salespeople in kiosks hawking their wares, some intrusively attempting to dab gooey substances on their skin, and shoppers milling about them on either side. A toddler, testing a set of strong lungs, made them cover their ears.

Linda walked a few steps, uncovered her ears and stopped abruptly to face Ginny. "Was family togetherness more important than . . . *me*?"

"Of course not!" Ginny drew Linda into a loving embrace. The simple act had the same effect as untangling a skein of wool.

Enfolded within her mother's arms, with clear and present knowledge that she was loved, Linda's sense of well-being soared. At the same time, she reminded herself that her mother wasn't perfect. She had done the best she could have, under the circumstances. Humbled, she mumbled to herself, *It wasn't Mother's fault, you dope!*

History played back for Ginny. She had held this infant on her hip, until she was ready for the crawling stage and then that first, daring step. She had walked with the youngster to kindergarten and college, until her daughter started to outrun her, lengthening a physical and emotional distance between them, as she traveled through Europe and Central America, and God knew where else and with whom. An incessant craving for adventure and isolation seemed to grip her and so she was always going—away from the family.

Ginny knew that her daughter needed her but had always felt inadequate when it came to the right words, or motions, to make her realize how much she loved her. From the beginning, Mary's insane jealousy towards Linda created problems. Only if she stood on top of them, supervising their every move, were they able to behave nicely toward each other, but if she slacked off, even for a second, they fought. Powerless to change things between them, she hoped that, in time, they would work things out between themselves, as she didn't want to be responsible for another Cain and Abel. Understandably, a special bond between her first daughter and herself had formed during those turbulent war years, yet Linda had been sickly and required extra attention. Ginny admitted to herself that she had done her best to let her daughters know that she had always loved each of them equally, although in different ways. Sometimes they forgot that.

Or . . . *was it something I missed? A sleight of hand? Where had I failed?* Ginny asked herself.

This day in the mall, in what was presumably the finest hour between Ginny and Linda, such enlightenment helped them overcome their sorry, complicated past, with all its slights, miscalculations, misunderstandings, unfulfilled needs, words left unspoken, or inappropriately spoken. There were actions which they had taken or failed to take—like the memory of a devastating hurricane where the survivors are being rescued by boat and helicopter and they were able to reach a clean, wind-blown state of forgiveness in which healing could begin.

They did what any self-respecting, re-connected strangers would have done—they headed to Starbucks to celebrate. Sitting and sipping Chai tea lattés, unanticipated side effects kicked in: Ginny's dementia-induced sadness dissipated, and Linda's urge for a drink weakened.

Chapter Six

Having been raised in an alcoholic household, Linda's emotional maturity remained stunted. There were times, however, when she thought her sisters shared a residual effect, for, although adults, they still childishly interacted with each other.

"Why don't you get your attorney to speak with ours?" Cathy said to Linda on the phone one afternoon.

In the quiet confines of her living room, Linda was reading a book entitled *Toxic Families*. She had the book propped on her knee, her hand holding a yellow marker so she could highlight passages, when the phone chimed.

Baffled by Cathy's choice to side wholeheartedly with the eldest sister, Linda stared out the window as fleeting images from the past danced in her mind. They used to play so well together. *What's the matter with Cathy?* She's supposed to be the bright one, the only one to graduate from medical school.

"You say you want to include me, but you continue to exclude me from family meetings." Linda confronted Cathy. "What's this business about attorneys talking and not us?"

In response, Cathy hung up.

Linda looked down at a paragraph, which dealt with rejection from a sibling and ran the highlighter over the paragraph with enough energy to tear the page apart. She thought, *No, a drink won't help*. Sobriety was the thing she had; without it, she had nothing. *Was it a choice between sobriety and family?*

The next weekend visit was carefully monitored by attorney Brown.

En route to Linda's house, Ginny commented, "I don't want your sisters to hurt you."

"Me neither," Linda replied. Mother's words worked like a salve.

Each time mother and daughter were together, Linda noticed the progress of her mother's dementia. Her language ability had deteriorated. She was restless, with shorter attention spans. There was vacancy in her eyes. She had a strong body odor and she'd lost interest in some activities.

To draw her out, the daughter asked, "Did you enjoy the movie?"

"Yeah, but . . ." said Ginny.

"What about dinner? Did you like it?"

"Yeah, but . . ."

"Dessert was great, wasn't it?"

"Yeah, but . . ."

Linda sighed with exasperation, not knowing how to handle her mother's newfound negativism.

Ginny stood for lengthy minutes in front of a blouse hanging in a closet in Linda's guest room. She had packed and unpacked her suitcase numerous times. When she sat down for a moment, her shoulders sagged, and her head drooped in a look of total dejection and despair. Linda watched her cautiously, her heart breaking. Once a woman of stature, her mother was now reduced to a pitiful human being, who was fading away before her eyes. Linda tried to console herself, as well as her terrorized inner child, and then found herself staring out the window, with a similar vapid expression. Mentally and emotionally exhausted after two days, she tried to remember the many examples when her mother had demonstrated how to be kind and pleasant no matter the situation, or the personality.

Ginny liked action and drama, and there had been plenty of that in her marriage. No sooner had she married into the Cray family than they had their own population explosion. Each of the four couples had children, and there were plenty of cousins for Mary, Linda, and Cathy to play with.

The extended family grew into a close-knit group that promoted the customs of their Italian heritage, without any of them actually speaking Italian, either in the house, or outside. There were the usual religious celebratory rites, such as Baptism, First

Communion, and Confirmation. There were birthday parties and holiday picnics. At most, the family served Italian food, and Ginny learned how to prepare it. When her Welsh parents came to visit, she reverted back to her own custom and served pot roast with carrots and red potatoes. Ginny had told her daughters all about this when they were younger. She had emphasized that money was scarce, after the war. There was a need for the families to share what they had with each other. Plus, the parents had grown up during the Great Depression, and no one forgot what that was like. They had learned to use it up, wear it out, and make it last.

Following the desires of his heart, Roland had left his father's lucrative livestock business to establish his own company that specialized in airplane parts.

As the years flew by, the race to space provided an economic stimulus for many companies, particularly aerospace, and he secured contracts with large companies and the government. His parts landed on space capsules and his status increased.

Chapter Seven

By now, Linda was seeing her mother regularly, and the routine was mutually agreeable. Thinking it would do them both good, Linda drove with her mother in the car to church on Sunday.

As they entered the building, Linda asked, "Mother, do you pray?"

"No."

Mother had been a devout Catholic, so this came as a surprise to her daughter. The family had prayed before meals and during Lent they had knelt around the master bed and said the rosary together.

Ginny was eager to leave halfway through service. After fidgeting without end, she stood up abruptly and walked out without looking behind. Linda moved quickly to catch up to her in the parking lot and hurried to open the car door.

Later, in a large department store, Ginny tripped and fell over a clothes rack sitting in plain view in the middle of the aisle. Linda, standing by her side, reached out to grab her, but her mother had fallen quickly and was already lying on the floor. A salesgirl stood nearby, watching them. Linda helped Ginny get back on her feet and checked for injuries.

Ginny stared at her finger as if seeing it for the first time.

Fearing that it was broken or bleeding, Linda looked, but there was no apparent bruise. "You'll live," she joked, to lighten the situation.

Ginny looked at her and then the finger, as if to make sure.

When it was time to return to Mary's house, Linda put her mother's small suitcase in the car. They approached Mary's home, fifteen miles east of where Linda lived. Feeling light-hearted, Linda reached over across the passenger seat and patted her mother's knee.

"You happy to be going home?"

"I'm going to *that* place." Her tone was sullen.

"That's where you live now, Mom. Aren't you glad to be going there?" The lack of an answer made Linda uneasy.

That night, Linda read a letter from Aunt Dolly:

"Dear Linda,

You sounded very distressed on the phone last night. What you are doing for your mother, you'll never regret. You don't know how much you're reaching her. Be happy with her, now, as she is. Love her, care for her with a smile. Hold her. Talk to her about the fun times, the trips on the boat, when you were little, and most of all, Roland. I know from my mother that you will regret every harsh word, every impatient gesture that you had with her when she's gone. Treasure what you have now, be thankful for it, and be at peace in your mind and heart.

Love always,
Aunt Dolly."

Linda sighed deeply when she had read it. She felt like she was in a cave groping for light.

Another letter followed:

"Dearest Linda,

I was thinking of you and your mother, Ginny. Treat her as a mother, not as a patient. Make her feel as if she is in charge. Let her know how much you need her—ask her advice where possible. When she is with you, you can play Tic-Tac-Toe. Ask her to show you how to bake a cake, bake one, and let her bring the results to Mary. Do things that are familiar to her, reminisce about the happy times in your lives, etc. You will never regret the time you are giving to your mother. The saddest thing in the world is when you must say, 'I should have.'

With love,
Aunt Dolly."

Linda took her aunt's words to heart and tried again.

The weekend following, Linda hurried to pick up her mother, the fifteen-mile drive not bothering her one bit. She made a left turn into her sister's long driveway, made a three-point-turnaround to face the road for a quick exit, and parked. She was thinking, *A little pleasant conversation, get Mother, and split—nice n' easy, breezy. Just what I need.*

Walking gingerly from the dirt driveway, she headed toward the winding walkway that led to her sister's front porch. Thick foliage bordered the paved path. As she passed, she noticed the elephant ear plant had grown in the interval since she'd last been here due to a medical issue. Dark emerald leaves, with raindrops from the morning's downpour, occupied some of the path, and she had to swing her hips to avoid getting wet. She knocked on the large wooden door painted white. As if on cue, the door opened a crack, allowing a hand—with an attached suitcase—to stretch out.

"Directions for Mother's care are on a sheet of paper in the case." The voice belonged to none other than Mary.

Linda's head jerked as if she'd been struck. No *"Hello!"* or *"How are you, sister?"* She wanted to wrap the suitcase around Mary's neck.

A flurry of footsteps and Ginny stepped out from behind the door. Frail and gray, she looked happy and eager to be going. Linda pulled herself together, greeted her mother warmly, and took her arm to lead her to the car.

The suitcase sat on the landing.

Linda, who was unable to lift anything at the time, turned back to the closed door. "Help with the suitcase, please!" She thought she sounded like a drill sergeant.

She escorted her mother down the path to the driveway. Momentarily, she heard the bag's tiny wheels rolling from a safe distance and smiled to herself.

When they arrived at her vehicle, Linda opened the passenger side door and extended an arm to assist her mother into the seat. With a sudden movement, Ginny broke free. She dashed to Mary, still lugging the suitcase, and threw her arms around her neck.

"I love you!" Ginny clung to her elder daughter, as if her life depended on it.

Mary looked over her mother's shoulder to where Linda stood and smirked with satisfaction.

Ignoring her, Linda waited patiently. Similar childhood scenarios floated into mind: particularly, her older sister tormenting her, her reacting like a puppet on a string and Mary play-acting, faking tears. And then . . . the usual outcome. *Mother scolded me for upsetting Mary!* It was all coming back to her. *Would it ever change?*

Finally, Ginny relinquished her hold on Mary and allowed Linda to assist her into the car. After snapping the seat belt around her mother carefully, Linda moved to the rear of the vehicle to pop the trunk. Mary tossed in the suitcase. Linda hopped in, started the engine, and left the property while Ginny waved good-bye through the car window.

The sisters flew away from each other as do moths from a flame.

The fourth weekend marked a difference: Ginny had trouble walking and winced with each step. Sitting down and getting up was a chore. Irritable and belligerent for no apparent reason, she'd sulk one moment and, in the next, take off, with a sprinter's pace. Linda tried to keep up with her mother. Whenever she took a moment to sit down, Ginny didn't like it, as though she wanted her daughter to be up and moving constantly.

They spent the day amusing themselves. The weekend rolled into Monday morning and it was time to return to Mary's house. Within a few miles of their destination, Ginny surprised her daughter with a question.

"What did she say to you?"

"Who?"

"Mary—when you came to the door."

No—it can't be! Mom wants to know my side of the story! Red Sea parting! She offered, "Nothing, Mom."

Ginny's eyes urged more.

A sigh, years of pent up frustration, released. "She didn't say hello or ask how I was. She didn't acknowledge my humanity." She thought, *perhaps my mother might begin to understand some of the underlying conflict between Mary and me.* Ginny gazed incredulously at Linda as if something that had eluded her, some piece of a puzzle, had suddenly become clear.

Waves of gratitude and relief flooded through Linda. She turned on the radio and fidgeted with the tuning dial looking for a happy song.

The dreaded phone call came a few days later.

"Mom's on the way to the hospital." Mary sounded frantic.

"What's going on?" Linda asked, after she started breathing again.

"She tripped on the stoop leading to the front door, and after that, she kept falling all over the place. And then, she fell hard and passed out. Brad and I couldn't wake her up."

"My God! How awful! Did you call 911?"

"Of course! The medics said she'd apparently had mini-strokes and . . . a mini-coma."

"I'm on my way to the hospital. See you there!"

"I'll get there after work."

Things were rapidly changing.

As Linda drove across town, streaking down side streets to beat traffic, she thought, *I'd just gotten used to having Mother live with Mary.* Her sister's house resembled the home her parents had built—a pool, a big yard. The driveway curved from the road to the back of the narrow lot. *Mom's so fragile.* She consoled herself by thinking about the times when her parents had accumulated nice possessions and what that had meant to the family back then.

With a pay increase, Roland embarked on a spending spree. He bought his wife a Thunderbird and a mink coat. Ginny kept the car, but exchanged the fur for a plain, blue, woolen coat. He enrolled his children in private schools.

Mary pursued a business career. She met and married Brad—a cook during the Vietnam War.

Linda prepared for college in Washington, D.C., with a major in political science—a wide-open field with the possibility of numerous career paths. Also attracted to the fast-paced city, Cathy set her sights on a medical program at a nearby university. The sisters visited occasionally when not taking exams and were friendly toward each other.

After college, she thought about furthering her education.

"You're on your own now," her father explained. "I've got Cathy to put through veterinarian school, and after that, she'll need help setting up the clinic."

"But, Dad, I want to study law."

"You can do that." He smiled encouragingly. "Get a job and go to night school."

Her thoughts came back to the present when she pulled into the hospital parking lot.

Chapter Eight

Looking terrified, Ginny sat upright in a light blue gown in a hospital bed.

Linda embraced her. "It's all right, Mother. You're gonna be okay."

A shadow fell across the sheets, and Linda and Ginny turned toward a cleric with close-cropped, red hair and compassionate gray eyes.

"I'm Father Sullivan. I came from St. Anne's." He spoke with a brogue.

Introductions were made.

Father Sullivan took Ginny's hand, blessed her, and leaned toward her. "Are you weak?"

Relieved that someone had finally asked the right question, Ginny nodded, her expressive and lovely, light green eyes speaking volumes.

Father Sullivan and Linda exchanged looks.

Linda asked, "How'd you find her so quickly? I mean, how'd you get here before me?"

"Our computer prints names of new hospital entries from among registered Catholics," the priest explained.

Linda knew her mother hadn't attended church in a while. Neither had she. "I see. I'm glad the church keeps good records."

From the hospital, Ginny went directly into Las Palmas, a nursing home across town. Linda waited in the hallway when they wheeled her mother off the truck and took her to a softly lit room.

Seeing her daughter, Ginny's face lit up. "Take me home—please!"

The plea stopped Linda's heart. Her mother, usually surrounded by family and friends, had always been a woman on the go. Linda used to tease her, saying, "Mother, you've got more friends than the Chinese population." She tried to console her mother. "You had a stroke, Mom."

"What the hell!"

So feisty, Linda thought. It occurred to her that she'd be able to see her mother more frequently in a neutral zone. With great care, she read a letter that Aunt Dolly had written:

"I hope your mother is content. You have the opportunity to visit her often in the nursing home and spend the day. I know that will make you happy to be with her."

She hated going there. The stark reality of the nursing home—its residents at different stages of aging and disease in God's waiting room—was unnerving. It was the great equalizer. Wealth, looks, prestige—none of these mattered anymore, if they ever did. Once powerful men sat in wheelchairs with soup dribbling down their chins. There were traces of former beauty queens. But . . . *Mother is here.* She became a regular, though slightly disgruntled, visitor.

One day, she saw herself in them, and the seeing made her want to help. It made her feel good, and maybe just maybe, someone would do the same when her time came.

Elderly women liked her tending to them in little ways when the staff was not around—pouring milk, fetching a straw, picking up fallen napkins. They introduced her to their kin. Stories about their children's marriages made her think of her own.

Linda was feeding Ginny in the dining room of the nursing home, surrounded by the other residents, most of whom sat comfortably in wheelchairs. The attendants ran between the tables, serving food to them on trays. A pile of bibs lay neatly folded on a nearby counter. The glass windows hadn't been cleaned for a long time, but the sun found its way into the room.

"Is this how you used to feed me, Mom?"

Ginny looked at Linda softly, with a little smile on her lips.

Sally, an attendant passing by, heard the exchange. "She understands you."

It came as a surprise to some that an Alzheimer's patient could still manage cerebral functions.

After the meal, Linda wheeled Ginny to a quiet room at the end of a long hall. She rolled to a stop in front of an overstuffed, floral sofa and sat down. Ginny whimpered as she struggled to speak. Linda leaned toward her to better hear.

"One hundred thousand dollars—for two years!"

Linda calculated rapidly, remembering that the sale of her mother's house had netted a cool quarter million. *So,* she thought, *Mary had used a hundred thousand to add an unnecessary addition, a bedroom, bath, parlor and useless bar to her house, for Mother's residency.* The rest of the money, a hundred and fifty thousand, was yet to be accounted for. She figured a couple thousand a month went toward nursing home expenses.

"You mean the addition to Mary's house? Where you were living before you came here?"

Ginny nodded, sadly. She had planned on finishing out her last days at her daughter's house instead of a nursing home.

Her daughter understood that Ginny's biggest fear was that she'd run out of money—a remnant of the Great Depression—and she'd had it for as long as Linda could remember. But lately, it was getting worse, as if it had merged with fear from the Great Recession. Many shared this anxiety these days, as the gap between rich and poor had widened, and the middle class had downsized. To console her mother, Linda took Ginny into an embrace and spoke over her shoulder, as she stared at the sunlight on a floral pillow.

"Don't worry, Mom, everything will be all right. You'll get what you need. There is a way." She was thinking, *Why are my sisters keeping me in the dark about Mother's finances? I was her financial planner for years.*

As if reading her mind, a staff member showed her a receipt for an insurance payment, as she was leaving. She exchanged a look of appreciation with her. The staff had an idea about their family conflict.

Linda walked down the hall to the exit, speculating, *Had I been involved from the beginning, I'd have steered us down a more conservative route. We might have pitched in and paid for Mother's expenses, as our parents did for our grandparents.* She remembered the letter she'd written to Mary advising her to leave their mother's money in cash and cash equivalents, to keep it readily available in case of need and also to protect the beneficiaries. Mary, the fiduciary, had ignored the letter. Cathy was probably unaware of it.

Chapter Nine

Linda asked herself, *how might I have helped us avoid our present conflict? Was there a way to prevent Mary from seizing control and most of the assets?*

As legal guardian and trustee, with POA, Mary now ruled the family. Attorney Brown's first plan was to have Ginny purchase Mary's house. He said he would have it transferred back to the heirs after her death. Linda, having observed firsthand Mary's clandestine management of the family's finances, plus the irresponsible manner she spent her mother's money, balked at this plan. She doubted the money would ever come out of Mary's house. She figured it would have taken a lawsuit to get it out, and even that was iffy. Worried about their sister's objections, Mary and Cathy abandoned the first plan. Brown then advised Mary and Cathy to purchase rental real estate with Ginny's funds to qualify for Medicaid. His scheme fell within the state's Medicaid criteria.

Not happy with this second plan either, Linda filed a grievance with the state bar, the court of last resort for holding lawyers accountable for their actions.

"Attorney Brown proposes that my eighty-three-year-old mother, with dementia, purchase rental real estate. This is against the Prudent Man Rule meaning it's entirely unsuitable for my mother at her age and in her condition. In addition, he's putting all of Mother's assets in one place, which does not make good investment sense."

Brown defended himself to the bar. He explained that he had to abandon the first plan of homestead due to the wild reaction of Linda. The acquisition of rental property by the mother, his second plan, would allow the mother to qualify for Medicaid or nursing care. He admitted it was a crazy option, but he had no choice. It was a shame that someone of his stature had to put up with someone like Linda.

She responded to his rebuttal by saying that he was supposed to preserve and protect the assets. Instead, he put them in an unsuitable, risky, and illiquid investment which jeopardized their value.

His letter to Linda seared the mailbox before she could get it out.

He wrote: "Due to the inflammatory and libelous nature of your communication regarding myself and your sisters, we will not communicate with you in any manner except in writing. Your sisters' address for the purpose of this trust is my office."

The battle raged on. Linda thought she had steered them away from the second plan. She was alone in this feud with her siblings and their attorney.

And then, the unexpected happened. It started with a phone call from Tom Wentner, a maternal cousin about the same age.

"Are your ears ringing?" he asked Linda.

"No. Why?"

"You wouldn't believe what Mary was saying. You're the black sheep of the family." Tom laughed aloud. "I figured I'd better hear your side of the story."

Linda gave him a thumbnail version.

"That's some story!" He whistled. "I had an idea something like that was going on. I could tell by the way she was talking."

"What's interesting is that it's a common story," Linda added. "The day care and nursing staff say it goes on all the time."

"How sad."

"Yeah. It makes me wonder who protects the elderly."

The topic at the A.A. meeting on December 7 was Pearl Harbor. Linda identified with the topic, feeling like she'd just been torpedoed by the letters from Brown and the bar. As agitated and restless as she was, she sat on a seat near the door. It was doubtful she'd stay the whole hour.

The chairperson began with a report from the intergroup office, the local administration that handled phones, mail, printed meeting schedules, and other assorted tasks. "We had forty-six daily calls, seventy visits for the month: Brazil-6, Canada-1, Argentina-2, Italy-3, France-2, Ireland-3, Spain-1, Norway-5, Australia-2, Germany-3, New Zealand-2, Ivory Coast-5, Thailand-5, United Kingdom-15, Unknown-15."

Linda thought, *I have friends around the world, and I didn't even know it.*

The chairperson paused a moment as if anticipating a comment, or question, but none was forthcoming. "Any other announcements?" The room was quiet. "In keeping with history, let's talk about how we've handled crises in our lives. You can even talk about the crisis of your drinking and how you got here."

"At the end of my drinking," said Liza, "I prayed to God for a sign, and in my case, this meant Jesus Christ. I was visiting a friend out of town and spotted an A.A. symbol, on a church door. I went in, down the stairs to the cellar, took a turn, and saw a large framed painting of Christ on the wall. Just what I needed to see! I smiled to myself and went into the meeting where I shared what had just happened. After the meeting, several women said that my story gave them chills. In over ten years of their attending this meeting, that picture had never been there, until the day I showed up."

Impressed with Liza's story, Linda recalled when she'd hit bottom and had her own spiritual awakening.

The next share was from a woman grieving over the sudden loss of her husband, who'd been killed in a motorcycle accident. "I ordinarily would be drinking over such a tragedy, but I'm not. Instead I'm doing ninety in ninety." Meaning: ninety meetings in ninety days.

A tall, lanky man with a full head of silver hair and thirty years in and out of the program, Dennis raised his hand. "I was in hell for a long time, until I found out that hell has trap doors. I came here because there was nowhere else to turn. I used to wake up and reach for a cigarette, without opening my eyes. I could probably light it, too, with my eyes closed. There was wine by the bed and a box of cookies—all before getting up. I quit smoking three times and went through four divorces . . . but I haven't had a drink in a while."

Joan, seated next to Dennis, was the next person to speak according to this meeting's format. "I had a problem with my leg recently. Something fell out of my car trunk and hit my shin. It cut me all the way to the bone. Then I got an infection and I was really scared. MRSA was setting in." Joan stopped for a moment and examined her leg, as did several others. "It's better now, but for a while I was scared, *really* scared. I remembered what you said about a God box. I got an empty coffee can and filled it with notes about my fears and hopes. I imagined putting my anxieties in that can and left everything up to Him . . . It gave me much relief."

Gene, next in line, spoke, "My journey to find out what's wrong with me led me to realize that my defects stem from my relationship with God. It's not my temper, not my fear, but my lack of faith in God." With each word, his voice rose.

"Gene, lower your voice, please," the chairperson requested.

"Sorry. I get so passionate over this stuff. At my age, I'm really digging deep to get it right, before my time comes." Several members nodded at this. "I'm finding that it's easier to put on slippers than to carpet the whole world."

"The Pearl Harbor in my life," Milton began, "is myself. I was a defect looking for a character." Laughs. "I had to examine my defects and figure out which ones were weaknesses that could be turned into strengths. In so doing, I also discovered that I couldn't make chicken salad out of chicken shit."

"I'm going through something like Pearl Harbor with my sisters, and I'm afraid if I start talking about it, I'll never stop, so I'll just listen today," Linda said. "I'm hearing some good words so far. Thanks, everybody."

"I'll pass," said Kent who immediately changed his mind. "No, I'll talk. I broke my nose serving a game of tennis when I was drunk. My nose started bleeding, but I continued playing. The doctor had to re-break it because I'd let it go too long. Those were the days I thought I was having so much fun. I used to be impressed by deep thinking I found in bars. If someone talked about an emotional crisis, I would've told him to kiss my ass.

"My liver was sore to the touch, and my eyes had turned yellow. I knew I was dying," said Reno softly. "I came to a meeting and stood by the door, listening. At the end of the meeting, they formed a circle of prayer. I realized the open space was for me." He paused. "Afterward, I stood outside smoking. A member bummed a cigarette and I said to him, I think I have a drinking problem. He said to me, 'Thank God. Now everybody knows.' He added, 'Look, we do this one day at a time. Don't drink today. Come back tomorrow.' I thought; *I can do that.* I went home and didn't drink. The power that went home with me kept me sober. The next day, I had twenty-four hours and I've been sober ever since."

Darla spoke about the incident that brought her into the program. "I had been out dining with friends at a local restaurant when I looked down and saw my salad plate filling with blood. Had my friends not called 911, I'd have died, because the blood had penetrated my lungs. The doctors told me that my martinis had burned off the layers of my esophagus." Her pause punctuated the memory.

Passing through town, Ryan had sought the Buena Vida meeting. "I drank and drugged and planned to divorce my wife, until I rolled into a ravine, after a car wreck. Every bone in my body was broken, and the doctors said they were going to amputate my leg, until one young doctor, tired of my screaming, stepped in and saved it." Ryan turned around to take in the audience. "My wife was the only one who visited me in the hospital. As soon as I got out, I crutched my way to the nearest bar. I drilled a hole in my crutches and hid my booze in it—even tried to patent the idea." Laughs. "Later, I had an epiphany and asked God for help. I came into the program and have been sober ever since. I'm very successful in what I do; I own a hundred acres, have two thousand employees, and a *New York Times* best-selling book. I tell you this not to impress you, but to impress upon you what can be done. We learn certain survival skills here. It's up to us to apply them to life, so that we make a life for ourselves combined with moral and ethical principles."

Although the meetings held out hope to all, not everyone got it. Some left after a few visits, never to return. Others came in and stayed a while, sometimes years, and then went out. Such was the case with Dennis who disappeared shortly after this meeting and was later found in his apartment with an empty bottle by his head. A group of friends and relatives buried his ashes at sea, according to his wishes.

But for Ginny's second daughter, the meetings worked just fine. Here, Linda met friends, joined in warm conversation, learned how to think and express herself without wreaking havoc, was accepted, and belonged. She left feeling much better and thought about starting a God can. Even though trouble persisted, she wasn't alone, because a whole new family, from far-away places all over the world, walked with her in this ever-widening, ever-outreaching, spiritual movement known as A.A. In ways she could not understand or appreciate, she was changing, becoming stronger, and forging a new personality. In a happy, little corner of Buena Vida, she was doing all right, which was good preparation for what lay ahead.

Chapter Ten

Ginny and Linda entered the recreation hall while a staff member led the Las Palmas nursing home residents in a lively game of bingo. This was not something that Ginny could do, but she usually liked to be around people, to sit with them and watch. Something was different this day. Linda held her hand and scanned her mother's anxious eyes, noting her mother's restlessness and irritability.

"Mother, there comes a time when you just have to accept. Accept the whole thing. Don't fight it. Just go along with it."

Hearing her, the attendant paused and nodded in agreement. Ginny settled down, seemingly calm for the moment. She smiled at her daughter.

Talk about having to accept, Linda thought to herself. She was having trouble accepting the fact that her mother was no longer available to do fun things. She missed her terribly. Ginny had always been her buddy and her counselor. Her mother had always been there for her.

A nurse handed Linda a baby doll and Linda gave it to her mother. She wheeled her to the television room where several of the other female residents also held dolls. They spoke quietly among themselves, complimenting each other, "Pretty baby."

The scene was tender and reminiscent of old times.

Her mother brought the doll close to her face. "Oh, you silly baby!"

Does she mean me? her daughter wondered.

Linda remembered she had plenty of dolls to play with, including a dollhouse, with a removable roof. It sat on a table in the cellar where she used to spend hours lost in fantasy. Mary also had her share of dolls. By the third daughter, however, Roland was desperate for a boy, and Cathy was his last chance. So, while his other daughters played with dolls and baby carriages, he and Cathy launched toy rockets from the front lawn.

Still capable of an appropriate phrase, though her verbal skills were limited, Ginny was able to get her meaning across. Unconditional love for her daughter shone through her facial expression. A wink, or a blink of an eye, let Linda know she was present and gave her a renewed sense of well-being. She floated, soared and had more energy and enthusiasm for life. Her mother did that for her.

Linda fussed over her, complimenting her on her improved posture. A few days before, she'd been semi-comatose, head tilted back at an odd angle, mouth gaping open and eyes closed. Thinking she'd died, Linda's heart almost stopped. This day, however, Ginny spoke coherently. Her laugh was magical, sweet and gentle.

Chapter Eleven

On another day, after an afternoon rain shower, Linda wheeled Ginny outside for a ride around the block. This was the part of the day she liked the most, because they could be alone with each other and with nature and listen to each other without interruption. The sky was soft dove gray. As they moved along through the puddles, Linda sang, "You are my sunshine, my only sunshine." Ginny tried to hum along and turned back to glance at her daughter. Linda suddenly stopped and braked the wheelchair.

"Your sunglasses are filthy. They're practically opaque. How do you see anything through them?" She wiped them several times with her cotton top and peered through the lenses. "What do you do, spit on them to make them so dirty?"

"Yes!"

After they had gone down the block and turned around, Linda returned to the parking lot outside the nursing home. She reached into her car behind the driver seat, pulled out a thick sheet of canvas, and held it up. She'd painted her mother's image from a photograph.

"Grandma!" Ginny said.

Linda saw the resemblance and laughed.

They continued on their way, one singing and the other humming, as they moved along the sidewalk under shade trees. The path swept under a large Banyan tree where it was littered with dark, purple berries, clogging the wheels of the wheelchair. Linda found a twig to wipe them off while Ginny watched intently.

"Remind me not to do that again."

"What?" Ginny asked.

"Go through the berries. Look at the mess."

Ginny laughed.

When it was evening, Linda wheeled Ginny to her room where her roommate was softly snoring. She dismantled the footrests from the wheelchair then stood before her mother. "I've got to get going, Mom."

Ginny made a dismissing motion with the back of her hand. "Go."

Linda positioned her mother in the hallway, so she could see from both directions.

"Just watch the people, Mom. They're interesting."

With little enthusiasm, her mother nodded.

Linda motioned to the attendant who stood at the desk. "I know you're familiar with the activities. Is there some activity you'd recommend for my mother?"

"Bingo." The attendant looked back at Ginny, as if re-thinking. "But I don't know if she can do that."

"What about television?"

"That would work." Linda proceeded into the television room and positioned her mother between a few residents.

"You'll be okay here, Mom. Look, you've got a girlfriend on this side and a boyfriend on the other."

The attendant laughed out loud. "That's a girl!"

"Oh, sorry!"

Ginny crooked her finger at Linda. Linda put her ear close to her mother's lips.

"D-d-do you think he thinks of me?"

For a second, Linda scanned the room trying to figure out which man, until she realized her mother meant her father. "Undoubtedly, Mom. How could he forget?"

Ginny leaned back with a smile on her face.

As Linda left the room, the attendant immediately catered to her mother who was laughing and seemed too preoccupied to notice her departing daughter.

After the visit, Linda was light-hearted. Ginny seemed content, made happy little sounds, and smiled—a complete role reversal. Ginny was the child, Linda, the parent. Then, it reversed. Linda felt like a little kid. They seemed to swap roles several times during the course of a visit, with neither knowing ahead of time how it would work out.

An old-fashioned housewife in every way, Ginny cooked, cleaned, focused on her husband, saving the choicest morsels of meat for his dinner, and attended PTA meetings for the kids. She volunteered in the school cafeteria and greeted her daughters as she served hot dogs and sauerkraut. The central point of their family, she was forever seeking peace and harmony among her family members who were often at odds. She loved each equally and abundantly and, like glue, kept them together through the years they were under one roof.

As for discipline, a sapling twig lay atop of the refrigerator, handy whenever a squabble broke out. When her girls tried to avoid the rod by twisting and running away, she'd flick the green twig against the backs of their legs.

Stripped of her power, she could no longer demand that her children play together, or even be nice to each other. She knew that Mary and Linda didn't get along and that Cathy was off in her veterinary world, where she'd immersed herself for years. Her daughters scarcely knew each other, only pretending to socialize when they were in her presence. She worried about what would happen to them when she was no longer around. Had she failed to teach them about love and forgiveness? Now with time so short, they were in conflict over a will. It broke her heart to think of her family divided over money. Roland would have had a fit.

In a nursing home that could hardly double as a home like the ones she'd had, hardly able to walk, or talk, she depended completely upon strangers to take care of her. She felt so alone. As much as she abhorred her current residence, at some precious moments, it allowed her to communicate her love to Linda and watch her respond. If she could wrest a few last seconds as a mother to impart softness and gentleness she would remind her that she wanted her to carry on with strength and courage in the days ahead. And to remember, as well, all that she'd tried to teach her. Those moments were etched in her heart forever.

Chapter Twelve

The mess with the sisters continued in August, a hot and sultry month.

Sitting in a wheelchair amidst a crowd glued to the television set, Ginny watched her daughter enter the room. Her face lit up.

"Hello, Mother." Linda reached down and hugged her mother.

"Mmmmm," Ginny moaned.

Anne, a short, staff member of Hispanic and African descent, wide at the hips, ran over, excited and a bit breathless. "You should have seen your mother look you up and down." She held her sides as if to contain the laughter that bubbled spontaneously from her. "Your mother gave me a big kiss this morning. I was dressing her, you know, and I asked her how she was. She crooked her little finger at me, and I bent down to see what she wanted, and she kissed me on the cheek. She's my baby!" Anne beamed, delighted to have had this warm interaction with a resident.

Linda smiled at her mother, who was also smiling, then wheeled her to her room to retrieve a pair of sunglasses. She put on the footrests, because they were going a distance to a manicurist. Even though a podiatrist serviced the nursing home residents, Ginny had ingrown nails which bothered her.

"Mom, this is good for you," Linda said to overcome her mother's objection.

Ginny made a face and jabbered.

"Remember the ingrown nails you had? Besides, the massage is good for your circulation."

The manicurist came forward. "Do your sisters take care of her like you do?" The manicurist draped a towel over Ginny's ankle.

"Nobody does it like me." Linda laughed, and the manicurist smiled at her. "You're lucky to have me, Mom. Who's going to do this for me? I have no husband, or children. I'll have to pay someone."

The manicurist laughed.

Ginny leaned forward and gazed at her daughter compassionately.

"She understands you," the manicurist said.

While Ginny sat in an elevated chair, her feet dangling in warm swirling water, mother and daughter conversed in their own unique way. Ginny babbled, and Linda intuited as much as she could. Sometimes she could tell by the tone of her voice what her mother meant to say. At one point, Linda joked with her about gaining weight.

"Big belly," Ginny replied.

The manicurist and Linda exchanged a glance.

After she applied nail polish, the manicurist led Ginny to the dryer. She held her hands to prevent smudging. Not liking the restraint, Ginny showed displeasure by barking like a dog. The sound made the manicurist lean back, but she kept her hands steady.

Linda tried reasoning with her mother, "Wait just one more minute, please."

When the timer went off, the manicurist released the patron's hands. Ginny made a fist at her, which drew a laugh.

When they returned to the home, Linda paused at the nurses' station.

"I hadn't noticed bloating," a nurse said in response to Linda's inquiry. "Maybe your mother needs to use the bathroom."

Linda turned to her mother sitting in a wheelchair by her side. "I'll see you Monday, and we'll go for a ride in my car. Rest up. It'll be a big day."

Ginny touched her daughter's arm. "Okay, go." With heavy eyelids, she stared into the distance.

"She usually naps in the morning," the nurse said.

"My father did the same thing," she replied, knowing her mother would be asleep, before she left the facility.

Linda turned the corner and walked down the hall to the entrance. Some days the walk took longer. She could see the parking lot and the sun shining on the automobiles. She felt lucky to be walking on her own two feet, free to come and go as she pleased, to have a car and a home. She felt for those who had to stay, including her mother who'd always been active.

Ginny had taken her girls everywhere. They traveled regularly to New York City and became familiar with its famous monuments, restaurants, and shops. She brought them to Ohio and introduced them to her cousins and their children at picnics in the park. Her car became a taxi, providing a ride for every activity. Even though her daughters sniped at each other, she encouraged them to get along despite disagreements.

After an A.A. meeting when everyone but Linda had exited the small room, a blonde woman extended her arm across the door frame, deliberately blocking exit.

"Excuse me." Linda attempted to duck under the arm.

Bunnie lowered her arm.

"*Excuse me.*"

Their eyes locked which slowly brought smiles. Bunnie laughed first.

On impulse, Linda asked, "Will you be my sponsor?"

They made a date to meet the following week.

As they sat sipping *lattés,* under the umbrella of a local Starbucks, Linda talked about a recent boyfriend. "He isn't nice to me."

"No, he isn't."

"But he called and apologized," Linda said. "I like it when he does that."

"I like men who don't do things they have to apologize for." Bunnie leveled her glance at the younger woman.

Linda hesitated, considering such a thing. "I thought I had to accept whatever was handed to me. That's the way it was in my family."

"Not exactly." Bunnie sipped the frothy *latté.* "Tell me about your family." Her posture indicated a readiness to listen.

"My father was a perfectionist, my mother, easy-going. I have two sisters but was never really close with either of them."

"Why was that?" the sponsor asked.

"My sisters and I competed for our parents' favor. Each of us had to be first, best, noticed, and praised. We couldn't tolerate each other's success. My dad used to tell me I was better than my sisters. He'd enumerate their faults and failings to the point that I couldn't stand them." She looked into the street at the traffic passing then turned back to her sponsor. "I finally realized he probably did the same thing with them." She laughed, a brief, staccato sound.

Bunnie nodded her understanding. "Did your father drink?"

"Yes."

"Did he ever hit you?"

Linda wondered how Bunnie knew. "Yes."

"What happened?"

"He'd come home from work and was sitting behind a newspaper in a chaise lounge, with a scotch and soda in hand. My sisters and I sat at his feet, worshipping him, dying for a speck of attention. One evening, he tossed the comic section to the floor. My older sister and I pounced on it and fought until it ripped. That's when he got up and slapped us hard across the face in one swift motion." Linda rubbed her cheek as if remembering. "When we sat down for dinner, the red welts were still glowing."

Bunnie looked appalled. "Was he nice to you at other times?"

"He played games with us and made us laugh. He was emotionally close and then remote. I loved my father. It's just that he wasn't there very much. Now my mother—she was there 24/7."

"I was a princess in my family," Bunnie began. "I got the works—ballet, tap, piano lessons, ballroom dance lessons."

"No kidding. I'm a ballroom dancer myself."

"I know. I've heard you talk." Bunnie smiled knowingly. "My father left us when I was a child. I was close with my mother and aunts who doted on me. I remember playing the piano in a white dress, with skinned knees from tree climbing."

The image made Linda laugh. "A tomboy."

"Yeah." Bunnie relived the moment with a smile.

"Were you married?" Linda asked.

"Twice. My first marriage, I never left the house." She paused and looked away. "I had black eyes and purple bruises."

"He beat you?"

"Every day, until I finally divorced him."

"How long did that take?"

"About three years."

Hard to believe, thought Linda, looking at the stately woman, the epitome of self-respect and integrity.

"My second marriage was much better."

"No more beatings?"

Bunnie laughed. "No, never again."

"Glad to hear it."

Gradually, the two women came to understand each other, and a trusting relationship grew.

Chapter Thirteen

Autumn in southwest Florida was short and sweet, with only a slight change in the heat of the day. Mornings and evenings were cooler.

Ginny was delighted to be going for a ride in Linda's car. Strapped tightly in the passenger seat, Ginny watched as her daughter pulled into MacDonald's drive-thru, barely missing a pick-up. The driver continued to stare straight ahead, oblivious to them, hell bent on a Big Mac.

Gripping the dash with white knuckles, Ginny cried, "Watch out!"

"Thanks, Mom. That's pretty good. You're on the ball, aincha!"

Ginny proudly took credit.

They nibbled on chicken fingers while seated in the car, under the shade of a Banyan tree, in the parking lot. Ginny, holding a piece of meat in shaking hands, carefully negotiated its way to her open mouth. Linda offered her mother a sip from a straw protruding from a chocolate milk carton.

Afterward, as they drove along city streets, Linda pointed out familiar landmarks, such as a popular restaurant and her father's favorite place for a late lunch, on a lazy Saturday afternoon.

"Remember how Dad liked to sit in the bar where it was dark. He always ordered that dish—what was it? Oh, yeah . . . turkey, bacon, and cheese. He was really thirsty after that."

Ginny gazed out the car window, lost in thought. Linda drove through a shopping center and slowed as they approached their favorite department store. An enthusiastic shopper, the elder seemed interested. She'd taught her daughters the fine art of bargain shopping, of discriminating between bling and practical. "You can have that dress, or you can have a skirt, a sweater, *and* a pair of boots." The lesson had served them well.

At Dunkin Donuts, on the outskirts of a strip mall, Linda stopped for a moment. "Be right back." She dashed into the shop and returned with a large cardboard box, which she held open for her mother to inspect.

"Yummy!"

"It's for the staff at Las Palmas. You know; the people who take care of you."

Ginny looked at her daughter warmly.

"Go ahead. Take a chocolate one with sprinkles."

At the intersection to the nursing home, Ginny made excited sounds.

"Yep, this is the turn off." Linda glanced at her mother. "Your new home's a good one, Mom. It smells nice, the food's good, and they treat you right . . . What more can you ask for?"

No reply.

At the circular front entrance, Linda searched for a wheelchair, as the staff had promised.

Mumbling under her breath, she got out. "Hold the donuts. I'll get a chair." Shortly, Linda reappeared with a wheel chair and assisted her mother into it. The large glass front doors swung open to allow them admittance.

Linda wheeled her mother to her room where she dismantled the foot rests, flossed and brushed Ginny's teeth, washed her hands, and combed her hair. Before Ginny lost most of her verbal skills, she had complained repeatedly about hair loss, until it had become an obsession. Mary had purchased a wig, which Ginny wore briefly and then stashed in a dresser drawer. When she forgot to put it away, the cats would play with it. From what Linda could observe, her mother still had a full head of hair.

Ginny played with her dolls for a moment while Linda arranged photos on the bulletin board. Her mother never tired of looking at pictures of herself.

"Blouse, pants, and a sweater on a single hanger," her daughter said as she stood in front of the closet. "I'm trying to make it easy for the staff to dress you, but they never seem to remember." Finishing the task, she leaned over to embrace her mother who grunted uneasily. "Does it hurt?"

Ginny nodded.

"I love you, Mother."

"I love you, too, Inda." The L was gone, for now.

In the dining room, where residents and staff were preparing for a social event, Linda positioned her mother at a table next to a single man. Ginny disapprovingly shook her head, until Linda moved her to another table, with two women. Dressed in beads and baubles, the women chatted amiably and displayed their jewelry. Her mother's beads and watch had mysteriously reappeared after having been missing for a week.

"We have cheese, cookies, and croissant sandwiches for everyone." An attendant wheeled the food cart around. "Come closer, so I don't have to walk so far."

Staff members moved the residents in closer.

"What a nice occasion, Mom." Linda indicated the refreshments. "Good food and fellowship." She sampled a few green grapes. "I'll be heading out. Be back the day after tomorrow."

"Okay." Ginny didn't seem to be bothered by the lapse of time.

Ginny's love nourished Linda, but it worked for Ginny, too. She seemed more capable of adjusting to the new environment, with each visit. And Linda could visit anytime—neither instructions, nor limits on when or where from Mary's attorney. Ginny could call the place her own even if it was an institution. The Las Palmas staff understood her, gave her plenty of attention and kept her busy with activities. Her well-being was their primary concern. Being with others in more or less the same situation wasn't all that bad—really.

Roland and Ginny tirelessly cared for their children even into their adult years. They were excellent cooks and served casual dinners often, sometimes on the lanai overlooking the bay. "We eat like kings and queens," Roland had said. Except for a brief stint to prove he could stop, he drank daily. Early in his seventies, a doctor diagnosed him with liver cancer.

Ginny, Mary and Linda escorted him to Dr. Weinstein. After introductions, Dr. Weinstein sat with one hip on a desk, one leg planted on the floor. He held up an MRI film and gestured with his index finger to light gray areas.

Thirteen lesions, Linda counted. He's a goner, she thought.

"I'm afraid the cancer has spread," Dr. Weinstein soberly informed his patient.

Ginny jumped, made a sound like a squeak. Mary drew in her breath. Linda lowered her head to her chest.

"How bad?" Roland squirmed in the wheelchair.

"Terminal." Dr. Weinstein's voice was shaky.

"Terminal?" Roland repeated as if he'd never heard the word. "You're terminal."

Mary boldly stepped forward. "What about a liver transplant?"

Dr. Weinstein shook his head in the negative.

"Too old." Grimacing, Roland bent over in the wheelchair, focusing on his shoes.

Ginny sobbed openly while her daughters comforted her.

Sadly, the little group wheeled him from the doctor's office to his home where the parents sat on a sofa reminiscing on fifty years together.

The next day hospice came by, tended to the family, and left a booklet on how to cope during the last days of a loved one's life.

The pamphlet in her hands as she sat next to her bedridden father, Linda was on page three, but Roland seemed to be on page eleven of a short book. As if reading her mind, Roland asked her to search under the bed for a cardboard box, which she found beside the dust balls. She placed it next to him.

"Open it."

The contents rolled onto the bed.

"My war memorabilia." The contents were flight instructions, a silk map of China, various medals, and a prayer book, which was darkly stained. He handed her a military pin—Eagle's wings. "I wore this on my shirt collar."

She held it between her fingers, turning it over, the medal picking up the dwindling glint of daylight.

"That's for you."

Their eyes locked.

"Now, put the box back under the bed."

She did as he asked, wishing all the while that he had told her more about his war experience.

His brother, John, came to visit. Linda sat in a chair by the far wall while the brothers conversed.

"Get the box, Linda."

She dove under the bed and pulled it out.

"Give it to him." Both brothers had been flight instructors, but John had never left the States. In this act of relinquishing his war trove, Roland prepared them for the inevitable.

The day after, Linda came to his bedside with a Bible. She'd planned to read Psalm 23 to him, but a current from the ceiling fan flipped the page to Psalm 27, which was longer, and ended with the exhortation to "be strong, take heart, and wait for the Lord."

Roland's eyes were closed, but he squeezed her hand several times, as she struggled to keep her voice steady.

Mary and her family arrived around suppertime to see him. When they were all in the kitchen munching on potato chips, Roland quietly slipped away, four days after Doctor Weinstein had pronounced him terminally ill. Ginny found him, and the shock sent her reeling.

Later, the three sisters gathered in Mary's living room to discuss their father's last request. Mary's husband, Brad, and her son, Matthew, were present.

"He wants his ashes in the Gulf of Mexico," said Cathy, drying her eyes with a handkerchief.

"Remember the picnics we used to have on the beach?" Brad asked. "He'd take us on his boat." Brad wiped his sleeve over his eyes. "Now it's our turn to take him." A loud sniff. Brad, familiar with boats all his life, took control of the situation.

Mary said, "Let's put his ashes in a beer mug."

The group tittered.

Linda objected. "We should use a proper urn."

Ignoring that comment, Mary handed Brad a can of beer. "Mom wants to take them out tomorrow."

"Did anybody write something for a ceremony?" Linda asked.

"Cathy leaned forward. "Like what?"

"I hadn't thought of that."

Linda sighed. *Am I the only one with any spirituality?* "Let's join hands and do it now."

Matthew, from his seat next to his mother, looked at his Aunt Linda, and said, "You lead."

Linda choked back tears. Praying for the right words, she joined hands with her family in a tight circle. "Dad, we are gathered together to honor you and to thank you for raising us with so much love. We love you and we miss you. Rest in peace."

The next day, the family headed out to sea in Roland's boat, which was now Brad's. Brad dropped the urn into a calm, aqua green sea, as seagulls circled the boat.

That was how it went for Roland. It seemed likely that Ginny's fate would be different.

Chapter Fourteen

On a subsequent visit, Linda prepared her mother for a ride in the car—something her mother loved. Once safely buckled in, Ginny heaved a sigh of relief, glad to be leaving.

On the way to a park nestled under the palms by the Gulf of Mexico, Linda bought gas, a sandwich, and chocolate milk. The sky was overcast and it drizzled. People were exiting the beach in a hurry, towing their paraphernalia that made wakes in the powder sand as they passed the car where Linda and Ginny sat. Ducks squawked. Breezes became brisk. The sky darkened. They ate their lunch in the car, with the windows down waiting for the rain.

Ginny became intent on kissing, rather than eating, the sandwich. The drink was another matter since Linda had forgotten to get a straw and Ginny had to drink out of the bottle. They finished their picnic just as fat raindrops pelted the windshield.

The Las Palmas entrance evoked a whimper from Ginny. Linda walked around the car to help her mother out of the seatbelt. Suddenly, Ginny went rigid, her mouth set in a grim line. By tugging a little, Linda found she could slide her mother out of the seat. Ginny began to sob.

"Are you hurt?" Linda asked desperately.

Ginny shook her head, "No," sobbing.

As if someone had been murdered, Linda wheeled her wailing mother into the nursing home, down a long hall to the nurses' station. Everyone stared. The crying stopped as suddenly as it began, and everything went back to normal—whatever that was.

Later, while grooming her mother, Linda accidentally pushed the wheelchair and it jerked forward, banging Ginny's knee on a pipe beneath the sink. Ginny shrieked in pain.

Linda hastily wheeled her mother to the television room. Attendants standing on the sidelines sprang into action when they saw Ginny's misery.

"What happened?" Mike's question sounded more like an accusation.

"I don't know. She started crying when I pulled up to admittance. She's been crying off and on ever since. I don't know what to do."

Mike bent down and put his face close to Ginny. "Are you in pain?"

"No."

"Are you hurt?"

"No."

A nurse stepped forward. "Are you sad? Upset?"

Ginny thought about that a second. "I suppose I am."

"Is it the family division?" That topic was uppermost on Linda's mind.

"Perhaps she didn't want to come back here."

Anne had been watching the whole scene unfold. "Perhaps she was upset that you had to struggle to get her out of the car. She could be grieving the loss of motor skills."

Linda searched their faces. *It could have been anything or everything. Who knew?*

When Ginny calmed down, Linda prepared to leave, with a promise to return in a few days, as she always did. Continuity, she knew, was important. As Linda walked to her car, her shoulders sagged. To see her mother so upset; it just killed her.

Chapter Fifteen

A basket of fresh laundry tucked under her shoulder, Linda rearranged the clothes in a typical disorganized closet, at the nursing home. A knock on the door caught her attention.

Thelma, the Head Nurse, pulled her into the hall. "Your mother has a urinary tract infection. We've started her on antibiotics.

"Good. Is she in pain?"

"She's been very uncomfortable." She pursed her lips. "We're doing all we can to help her."

In the television room, Ginny blended in with a small crowd. She wore the green sweater she liked but was generally listless. When her daughter tried to feed her in the dining room, Ginny kept throwing her head back to stare at the ceiling, after each bite, which made it difficult to feed her. It also prompted several choking attacks.

Anne, Ginny's favorite staff member, came by and clicked her tongue. Linda looked at her imploringly.

"GINNY!" Anne bellowed. "Look at the plate. Put your HEAD DOWN."

For the rest of the meal, Ginny ate with her head in the right position but watched Anne out of the corner of her eye, as if awaiting further orders.

"You're really good at this, Anne," Linda said. "You sure know what to do."

"You're good at what you do, too. You visit your mother several times a week and stay for hours. You take her out and treat her well."

Linda raised an eyebrow, wondering the big deal.

"No, I mean it," Anne insisted. "The other one, your sister, she only comes for five minutes, runs in, gets the laundry, and leaves. What you do is better."

"Why, thank you, Anne." *So that's what's been going on.*

After the meal, Linda groomed her mother and made sure that she had a fresh diaper. They attempted to leave the premises but didn't get far. Ginny started to cry. Linda comforted her as best she could, as did several others. The receptionist came from behind the desk and talked to her. Another resident sitting in a chair in the reception area said something nice to her. An attendant from the rehabilitation room stepped out and smiled at her. A kindly nurse from another ward held Ginny in her arms and soothed her. Linda stood by attentively, listening intently, willing to learn from those who worked in the facility about what she could and couldn't do. There had been a time when she wasn't as open to constructive criticism.

"What do you want to do, dear?" a nurse asked. Ginny spoke at length, but most of it was unintelligible.

The daughter came forward. "I heard her distinctly. She said, 'I want to go home.'" The nurse looked at her as if weighing thoughts. "Yep . . . I heard it clearly."

The nurse smiled as if she had heard this at least a dozen times a day from any of the residents. "Sunshine would be good for her. Why don't you take her out for a spin?"

"That's what I planned to do. See ya."

The weather had cooled somewhat as Linda trudged behind her mother's wheelchair. It had been raining, which in Florida meant a few hours. Sometimes it rained on one side of the street and not the other. Often, the sun shone while the rain fell. A light breeze was refreshing. Ginny's eyes closed, and her head rolled back. Linda maneuvered her breasts as a prop to keep her mother's head straight but found it difficult to navigate the wheel chair and her mother's head simultaneously. They got as far as the big Banyan tree when Ginny cried again. Linda came around to the front of the wheelchair and took her mother's hands in hers.

"No matter what, Mother, you'll be all right. This UTI will pass in a day or two. Cooperate with the doctors, okay?"

Ginny made a questioning expression as if to say, "Is that so, little one?"

They returned to the facility, and Ginny sought oblivion in deep coma-like sleep.

Driving home, Linda's thoughts swirled in her brain, like the water in the tub at the nail salon. Mother really wants to go back to the way she was, before the strokes, before the dementia, before she got so sick that she had to go to a nursing home. She didn't want to return to Mary's house. It wouldn't work, and she knew that; she was too far gone. She was grieving the upcoming loss of her life and she was not alone in that.

That night Linda slept fitfully, and, in the morning, she realized she needed a break from her routine.

"Hey, Harry! What's up?" Linda said to Harry and then waited for his response. "Let's get together. It's been a long time." Blah, blah, blah. Linda thought, *Why do I continue to see this worthless boyfriend? We're always making up and then breaking up.* Her other mind—the bad one—argued back. *Shut up! I need this! Just one more time.*

Harry Rund was most obliging. "Baby! I've missed you, too. Where do you want to meet?"

"Let's go to the Keys. We've never been there, and . . . I'm in the mood."

"What's going on?"

"I've been in the hospital with my mother and that damn UTI, but I think she'll be all right for a few days. The antibiotics have kicked in and she's had a miraculous recovery so let's get out of here." She was talking rapidly, as if on adrenalin, but she couldn't stop herself.

Harry understood. "Sounds good." He made the necessary arrangements, packed the car in a hurry, and met her for a much-needed vacation.

Or . . . so they planned.

The weather was perfect in Key West that fall. Their first night they feasted on delicious fresh fish from the sea. Tired from the long drive and the world's stress and turmoil, they slept in later than usual. Harry was amorous in the morning, and, by the time they finished, the warm, morning light streamed into the hotel room.

After brunch, they toured the island and made plans to snorkel. The following day, they rose early to meet the ship that would take them out to deep water.

The *Santa Cruz* idled patiently as the crowd of snorkelers boarded, with their gear in tow. It was a promising day: clear skies, calm seas and a light, balmy breeze. When they were several miles offshore, the captain anchored the ship and his shipmates rigged a ramp with steps leading into the water. Harry, one of the first ones in the water, took to it like a fish, his lean, muscular arms plying the gentle, lapping waves. Linda, stumbling toward the makeshift steps leading to the sea, pretending she was used to wearing a mask and flippers, was the last one in.

"C'mon in! The water's fine!" Harry beamed from a short distance away.

"In a minute."

Her flipper caught on the side rail, and she grabbed it and took it off. A few other timid swimmers drifted by the steps, and she greeted them warmly, wanting their conversation to last. Impatiently, Harry threw up his hands and swam farther out, until his head was almost dot com size. At last, she immersed herself and paddled around the boat, not having the slightest inclination to drift too far away from it. When she put her mask into the water, she was amazed at the variety of life. Fish of rainbow hues sauntered by, eyeing her curiously, as she observed them. Her fascination was interrupted by a shout.

"Shark!"

The snorkelers propelled themselves toward the ship, as the captain issued orders on a megaphone for everyone to board, especially those who had swum a distance. Harry could have broken a swimming record.

And that was the end of the snorkeling adventure.

Back on shore, resting comfortably in the plush hotel room, Harry and Linda prepared for a busy day of touring the island. Linda picked up her cell, which she had left in the room while they snorkeled and saw that Mary had left four messages—not good.

"Call me when you get this message." Her sister's voice sounded strained. "They're taking Mother to the hospital." The second message was stronger, more desperate. "Where *are* you?" Two more messages mounting in frustration, which Linda ignored as she called Mary. No answer.

She left a voicemail. "Mary, I'm in the Keys. My cell's on now. Call me *please*." Linda scrolled down her contact list, until she found the hospital's number.

"I'm sorry. I can't give you any information. Patient confidentiality."

"I'm her daughter!"

"Sorry."

"Look, just tell me if she's okay . . . please."

The nurse hesitated as if she were checking to see if a supervisor was around. "She's stable. Anything else, you'll have to speak with the doctor. He'll call you."

"The UTI returned with a vengeance," Dr. Amos Sands said. "Your mother became dehydrated and had a high fever. Las Palmas staff called 911 . . ."

As the doctor was filling her in on the latest development, Linda paced the room with the cell glued to her ear as she watched Harry fix himself a protein drink. When the call ended, she fell to her knees by the king size bed, tearfully shaking with fear. Harry came behind her and held her, and she told him what the doctor had said.

"She's stable now. You can probably stay here, until the end of our vacation."

What a guy. "She's my mother . . . start packing."

It was the fastest pack job in the world.

Linda called the front desk to tell them there was a family emergency and they were checking out early. Not waiting for a bellhop, they carried their bags to the front desk and stood waiting for what seemed like an eternity, as the cashier wrestled with aging computers. Linda maintained her cool as she reviewed the billing statement. Luckily, there were no surprises. And then they were on route A1A heading to the hospital and the news that awaited them there.

Chapter Sixteen

Ginny lay in a hospital bed that dwarfed her shrunken body. Mary sat in a chair at the end of the bed, babbling to herself, or anyone who'd listen, not making much sense. Admittedly, it had been a frightening experience. Harry sat down next to her on a vacant chair while Linda stood by her mother's side.

Mary continued to talk out loud, pleased that Harry was paying rapt attention to every word. ". . . and then when the fever was spiking, we thought we'd lost her."

Moved to compassion, Linda crossed the room and embraced her sister, who stiffened in response and didn't return the gesture.

Smoothing her skirt with her hands, Mary stood. "I'm going now." The words were hard, flat, full of hostility. Icy air floated, with her departure.

Harry exchanged a look with Linda that said, "I see what you mean."

Linda turned and moved toward the bed, eyes on her mother suddenly talkative and excitable. Harry made himself comfortable in a chair across the room. Linda looked over at him and smiled.

They stayed a while longer and then walked swiftly toward the elevators. Harry said, "Something you should know . . ."

Breaking stride, Linda turned to listen.

"Your sister was out of town the same time you were. She and her husband were in Ocala looking at retirement properties when the doctor called with news about your mother."

"Now I don't feel so guilty." Linda pushed the elevator button. "Doesn't say much about either one of us, does it?"

He didn't reply.

Exhausted from the long ride and the trauma of her mother's illness, they fell on Linda's bed and napped for several hours in the middle of the day.

They arrived back at the hospital in the late afternoon. Ginny appeared to be better, and they took turns feeding her. Though not much on bedside manners, Harry cut grapes in half and tenderly fed the patient. Enjoying the attention from a young, good-looking man, Ginny livened up, until her heavy eyelids signaled it was time to go.

Harry and Linda occupied themselves for the rest of the day at the beach. The next day, he got up early and left to get back to his home and work.

Linda returned to the hospital room she remembered from the day before, but Ginny was not there. Panic took hold.

"We moved her to another floor," a nurse explained.

The nurses on the sixth floor explained, "Your mother has a stool bacteria and has to be in a private room."

Relieved she was still alive, but still apprehensive, Linda hurried down the hall.

A sign in red letters had been posted on the door: "Quarantined." A plastic bag next to the door held gowns, gloves, and masks.

Fragile and vulnerable, Ginny lay in an expansive room, her pale face arched toward the elevated television in full blast volume. Looking like a moon walker, Linda entered the room. "Hi, Mother. I'm here."

Ginny's eyes darted around the room.

Drugged Linda thought. She noticed her mother's stomach looking like a drum.

Two nurses entered the room and tended to her. One was slim and petite, the other a few extra pounds.

"She seems more relaxed since you arrived," the thin nurse said.

"She looks just like you," said the other.

Linda smiled at them and sat in a chair by the door. "Go ahead and do what you need to do. I'll just sit here and watch."

"The bacteria is highly contagious," chubby replied. "Our disease control physician ordered the quarantine."

After the nurses left, Linda reached for her cell which she kept on regularly now, never leaving it behind, after the snorkeling escapade, although Mary hadn't called since then. She placed a call. "Hey, did you know they moved Mother to another room?"

"What?" Mary listened, pop-eyed.

"Earlier this morning. She's quarantined with a contagious, stool bacteria. I had to put on a plastic gown and mask to see her."

"Oh . . . wonderful."

"Don't worry. You're probably okay. Now about Mom—"

"What about kissing her and touching hands?"

Linda paused, not expecting questions of this sort. "Did you wash your hands after?"

"I don't remember."

"Well . . . you'd know. You'd have diarrhea."

"Oh . . . great."

"No, really." Linda was fairly confident this was not the case, or she would have heard about it by now. "Mom's got to be . . ."

"*When* would I know?"

Losing patience, Linda thought, *This is about Mom, not you, drama queen.* "I don't know when, but don't worry till you get it . . . Say, did you get my message?"

"Not yet. What's up?"

This was the moment Linda had been dreading. She knew she was wading into deep water, but *someone* had to do it. "Have you been able to make . . . the necessary arrangements?"

Mary was silent for a moment, as she wrestled with emotions. Her voice was an octave lower. "A long time ago, I found a paper in Dad's stuff about them wanting to be cremated. Mom told me that, unlike Dad, she didn't want to go in the water."

"What about Beall's? You know how much she loved shopping there."

They both laughed at that, in a moment of connection the way people get silly, carried away, even hysterical, when pressed into dealing with issues of mortality.

When the laughter died down, Linda ventured further. "What's the name of the funeral parlor?"

"Finder's."

"Oh . . . where we went for Dad."

"Yeah. It's prepaid. I bought an urn."

Linda was thinking, *Pre-payment? An urn? My sister has been busy, but, of course, I was left out of the discussion.* "Any ceremony?"

"I didn't get that far."

"I think it's a good idea to pre-plan."

Mary's annoyance broke the surface. "She's only sick!"

"I know, but it's better to be prepared."

A facial tic launched into an uncontrollable frenzy on Mary, distracting her and making her hesitate. "I-I don't know."

"Mom deserves a ceremony, Mary. Something from and for the *three* of us. It's healthy."

"I can't deal with it now."

Linda thought, *Denial will not get us anywhere.* "Why don't you let me find out what's available?"

"Why don't I send you the packet of information they gave me?"

Linda wondered had Mary read it or, more likely, stuffed it in a drawer. "That's okay. I'll stop by and inquire."

Later, at the neatly structured funeral parlor with chairs arranged symmetrically and facing a podium, Linda had a long session with the director's assistant, who gave her a full account of the arrangements her sister had made. Everything looked in order, but she took it a step further and called a church.

She dialed Mary's number. "Hey, it's me, again."

"I'm on the phone." Mary swatted a fly attempting to land on her arm.

Her sister's abruptness didn't put Linda off. "Call me back." A few minutes later, the distinct musical chime of the cell sounded. "Thanks for returning my call. Here's what I found. St. Anthony's has a garden for ashes and they suggest a simple ceremony. You can wait until the moment arrives and have the funeral director make the call. They provide separate urns."

"I figured that. After I bought one, I've been having second thoughts like maybe there should be three."

Linda didn't reply.

Mary asked, "Did you get her glasses?"

"Yes, I'll bring them tomorrow. Are you and Brad going to visit her tonight?"

Mary's voice radiated uncertainty and fear. "What do you think?"

"The nurse said it helped her to have me there. So, yes, go."

"Okay. Bye."

That was the extent of their conversation regarding the life they had shared with their mother. A shame they never learned to love each other the way Ginny had loved them. *Are we going to put aside personal piqués and come together as a family to honor mother's passing?*

Sadness engulfed Linda; it was useless to stop feelings of grief. Her heart pounded. Her mother was leaving the planet, her sister already on Saturn. Her biological family—gone. She stopped at a mall to take a walk, get some fresh air, and lingered by a fountain where a waterfall sparkled in the sunlight.

Chapter Seventeen

The following morning, Linda awoke with clarity. Mary had no intention of having a ceremony; she'd planned to give her an urn with her mother's ashes—nothing else. The funeral parlor had Mary's power of attorney. Mary said that she had already spent several thousand dollars mentioning no details; the big trustee with a secret. Coy and manipulative, Mary had been setting her up for a big disappointment. No reason to expect otherwise.

But Mary didn't have all the power.

Linda decided on a memorial service for her mother. She didn't need Mary's cooperation, or permission. She didn't need her mother's ashes, only her loving spirit. Other spirits, unseen and incomprehensible, their presence known in mind and heart, inspired her.

Arriving at the hospital with renewed vigor, Linda checked her mother's undergarments and tried to feed her. Her mother closed her lips and wouldn't eat. Next, Linda attempted to give her a sip of water. But Ginny refused even this. No amount of coaxing would persuade her otherwise. Linda dialed Dr. Sand's number. The call went to his emergency answering service, but he called her back momentarily. She explained why she called, "Mother won't eat anything or drink water."

The doctor replied, "Your mother's demented."

Such a way with words this doctor has. "Oh?"

"She's out of her element," he said, "but she'll adjust. Right now, I wouldn't be surprised if she spit it at you."

"She didn't do that, but she kept her lips tightly closed. What about the blisters on her buttocks?"

"She had a high fever."

"Four days ago—"

Dr. Sands sighed audibly. "It takes time for them to appear. It's normal. She'll be all right. Don't worry."

Feeling the need for escape, Linda took a little time off to visit her boyfriend. Driving down the highway like a demon, she returned home the following day. She'd found no peace with Harry, but then neither had he found any with her.

From the car, she got through to a nurse. "How's my mother?"

"Much better. We just changed her, and she said, 'Oh, oh, oh,' but we calmed her."

"How are the blisters?"

"The doctor said to keep her on her side, but she keeps shifting her position."

"What about a pillow?"

"Honey, we put pillows there all day, but she moved around them."

"Is she drinking water?"

The nurse took a deep breath. This was the question they all asked, and she hated to tell them the truth. "Who likes to drink water? We adults like coffee and smoothies and other good things to drink."

"So she's getting plenty of fluids?"

This one took the bait. She smiled into the receiver. "Oh, yes, I'm sure."

"Will she be there in the morning?"

"Call ahead to be sure. The doctor gets in early."

"Thanks."

On a later hospital visit, Ginny sat in a chair, her eyes shut, as if willing herself to be elsewhere. Linda gently jostled her, but Ginny dozed on. The nurse came in and both picked Ginny up and moved her to the bed. Ginny's eyes opened to stare at Linda for a second, then, closed in sleep.

The nurse examined the patient. The white blisters were gone, thankfully, and only a slight redness remained. After the nurse left the room, a relieved and weary daughter crawled into the hospital bed and lay beside her mother, placing her head next to hers on the pillow. Ginny squeezed her arm with her left hand once as if to say, "I know you're here, but I can't come right now."

A few days later, Mary called.

"The doctor has called hospice." Her voice was low, heavy.

"I figured as much."

"I just heard about half an hour ago and it's taken me this long to pick up the phone."

"That's okay." Linda felt a strange peace, laced with pity, toward her sister.

"Are you at the hospital?"

"I've got an appointment and then I'm on my way."

"Okay."

At home, Linda retrieved a poster she'd been working on. Colorful pins held numerous family photographs. She sped to the hospital, hoping she wouldn't get a ticket, and called the doctor from the parking lot, as she sprinted to the massive front door.

Dr. Sands hesitated. Linda tensed. "Your mother stopped eating and drinking. We were able to overcome dehydration once with her, but now I have no recourse. She won't take medicine orally; the nursing home is not equipped to deliver the dosage intravenously. . . ." He cleared his throat, "I could order a food plug."

"That sounds contrary to her living will."

"Yes, it is. I wouldn't want to give one to my mother, or wife."

"Mother wouldn't want it."

"Hospice will evaluate her and I'll let you know what's next."

"Thank you." Her arm shook as she called her sister. "Do you have any more information?"

Mary responded, "Only that hospice will be there this afternoon or tomorrow."

"You know, I thought it was strange that she wouldn't drink water for me."

"Really? She did that when I brushed her teeth."

"On Monday," Linda said, "she slept the whole time I was there."

"She was sleeping when I got there, too."

"What time did you arrive?"

"Five. I work—remember?"

God forbid you fail to remind me of my early retirement, due to a near fatal car accident. "I was there at noon. I figured that Mom didn't want to wake up. She's had it."

"That's what Cathy said, too."

"Cathy—who?"

"Cathy, my sister."

Mary had used "my," not "our" sister. Linda tried to keep the sarcasm out of her voice. "Is she coming?"

"No."

The abrupt answer made Linda think, *Mary's replies, dominated by a pathetic hardness, were getting shorter as if she was biding her time for when she won't speak to me. She just can't seem to forgive and forget.* "You sure?"

"Yes."

"She's got more important things to do than be with her mother during her final moments?"

No response from Mary.

"What're you doing now?" Linda asked.

"Working."

"Oh, yes—I remember." Dig. "Can you get out?"

"No, I can't. It's my job . . . my salvation."

"Are you going tonight?"

"I wasn't planning on it."

"Please, go!"

"You think so?"

"Absolutely."

"All right." Mary heaved a sigh of resignation. "I will."

After this dialogue, Linda sat back and marveled at how she was handling her sister with calmness. It didn't sound the way little sister *used to talk* to big sister.

Ginny was sleeping when Linda entered the hospital room singing a happy tune as she slipped on a gown and gloves. Having turned the whole situation over to God, she found renewed love and tolerance and she felt more at peace than she had in a long time. She greeted the nurses cheerfully and they responded positively. "Yoo-hoo!" Linda called to her mother. "Daughter number two is here. Wake up, sleepy head."

She placed a large poster near her mother's bed. Then, she took her mother's limp hand, which registered no response and searched her still, pale face: her skin seemed more translucent, her mouth set in a thin line. Every now and again, Ginny winced, her mouth pursing.

Feeling compelled by a sense of time, Linda spoke as if her mother could hear, using the language of hospice literature and Aunt Dolly. "I know you're ready to go, Mother. It's okay. You've been through a lot. I'd want to go, too. Those who've gone before you and who love you are waiting: Poppa, Margie, Nana, Gran'pa, Sarah, Aunt Rose, your buddy, and most of all . . . Daddy. You remember him, don't you?" She waited a second as if anticipating a response. Nothing, not even a flicker. But she sensed that her mother was listening. "Hey, speaking of Daddy, did I ever tell you about the dream I had shortly after he died?" She adjusted the mask and plowed on. "He was floating upward in a cloudy funnel of rose and yellow light. He was rolling around and laughing, as he ascended. I think that was his way of telling me not to fear dying, so I'm passing the word on to you—don't be afraid."

"I'm not," Ginny said clearly, in a normal voice, her eyes closed as if it was simply too much effort to open them.

"Oh, you heard me? Cool! . . . Oh, yeah, another thing. Someone who knows you will come when it's your time. You will not be alone . . . maybe Aunt Rose." Linda paused, her thoughts projecting into the future. In a whisper, she asked, "Will you come when it's my time?"

"Yes." Weakly.

Linda grabbed ahold of the bed railing, threw her right knee on the mattress, and pulled herself onto the bed. The two lay quietly for a few moments. The plastic gown became hot and cloying. Squirming and fidgeting, Linda pulled at it. "This stupid gown! I want to rip it off."

Ginny laughed out loud.

Happy with the bonding going on between them, Linda said, "Don't worry about me, Mom. I'll be all right. I'll be good . . . you'll see."

"Play."

The word evoked a memory. Back in the kitchen, Mother standing at the sink, a toddler crawling around her feet.

"Yes. I'll play. I always play. I played with you most, I think. I also played with my sisters. And I played alone. I still do. We're playing now, you know." She placed her head on her mother's chest. "You know, I think you should tell Mr. Alzheimer who's boss. You and I communicate pretty well . . ." Her words muffled in emotion.

"Don't cry, Linda." Ginny's face was serene though her eyes remained clamped shut. She spoke softly, "Mary . . ."

"She'll be here after work."

There was a knock was on the door—"Room service." An attendant delivered a lunch tray.

The aroma stimulated Ginny who sat bolt upright, eyes popping open. She drank a whole can of Ensure, devoured a cup of Italian ice, but had nothing to do with the chicken. Linda picked at the meat with a fork.

The phone rang.

"You got her to eat?" Dr. Sands questioned as she explained what they were doing. "Good girl."

"Do you know when hospice will come?"

The doctor replied, "Tonight, or tomorrow morning."

"Will she leave right away?"

"They have to evaluate her first."

"Let me know, okay." She washed her mother's mouth with a wet napkin. Then, she reached for the poster which lay rolled up on the floor, a rubber band holding it together. She held it up and, in a show-and-tell posture, began:

"This one is you as a youth, maybe nine years old. Here you're a teenager. Oh, and here you're engaged to be married. Look how happy you were! This is a photo of you in your white wedding gown. How beautiful!"

Her eyes following every move, Ginny seemed fascinated.

Linda's finger lingered over the next one. "Your three girls." She moved her arm down. "You are on the beach in your house in Buena Vida with Loca, the Tonkanese cat I gave to Mary because of allergies. Here's a photo of you in Mary's house."

"Delighted!" Ginny exclaimed.

Linda paused, struggling with the next, "At Las Palmas."

Her mother leaned forward. "I want to know how I got here!"

"It started with a bad bug. You had a high fever and became so dehydrated they had to bring you to the hospital. Basically, you've had diarrhea for a week. Can you imagine? You've been through a lot, but the good news is that you're better."

Contemplative, her mother looked at her.

"I'm going now, but I'll be back in the morning. It doesn't matter where they take you, Mother. I'll find you." Linda added, "Mary will be here later. Cathy isn't coming. It's just the three of us now."

"Okay, go." Ginny smiled and nodded, satisfied the discussion brought relief from what was uppermost on her mind. Trapped in her mind where the disease held her captive, her mind paced like a caged tiger, trying to put together final messages for her children. She couldn't command the English language like she used to. This daughter read her mind, interpreted, and translated her babble, which was comforting and, in a strange way, helped her to speak better. Must have been those foreign language lessons Roland and she had paid for. The family division, particularly the ongoing war among her daughters, was a terrible thing. Ginny was thinking about some message, some little seed that would help bring them together.

From caregiver to funeral preparer, Linda dragged herself out of the building, feeling emotionally, mentally, and physically drained. She realized how difficult this passage had to be for her mother. Any moment she could go. *It'd be a blessing,* she thought.

Linda had cleared her calendar as much as she could, but some things were necessary—such as manage her own life and take care of her own needs. Every minute she expected a call; everything else paled by comparison—a spiritual time. Death and birth were the two most important moments in a person's life. To have the privilege to walk the last steps with her mother—a cherished honor. She wouldn't miss it for the world. As the minutes ticked, she was getting better at it and remarkably, the need for escape vanished.

Life settled into a routine of visits to see her mother in the daytime and meetings in the evening. As a recovering alcoholic, she discovered that daily meetings, providing thirty to forty therapists, suited her just fine. She had just attended a meeting and was home doing laundry. Her thoughts took her to what her mother had said about getting an education. Well, she was certainly getting an education in the transfer of wealth with her sisters.

Tom, her cousin, called to hear how things were going. They chatted a few moments, and then he asked, "Will Mary be around this weekend? She told me she was going away for a few days."

Another trip? Linda thought. "I don't know—I'll be here."

"Of course, you will." Tom grinned into the phone. "You're expecting me."

"Wonderful! Mother may be waiting on you, too, you know."

"My timing couldn't be better. See you soon."

When they were growing up, Linda and Tom hadn't been close though they were about the same age. She hung around mostly with members from her father's side of the family who lived within close range of each other. Lately, however, since Linda had reached out to him in the absence of her sisters, Tom had made himself available to her, was attentive, and appreciated their newfound friendship. An only child, he'd longed for family closeness.

"Are you going to visit Mary while you're here?" she asked.

Tom thought before replying. "Probably not. Lately, she hasn't been very receptive to me—ever since I started talking with you."

"Really. What about Cathy? You ever hear from her?"

"Not lately. I get the feeling Mary has had something to do with that. It's awkward, but I've made my decision and I'm sticking to it."

"Glad to hear it. You're the first family member to come forward in support. I appreciate it."

Chapter Eighteen

Walking down the hospital corridor, Linda passed the nurses station and smiled at them, including her favorite Head Nurse. Maintenance personnel were busily sweeping the floor just outside the door of her mother's room as she moved around them and entered the room.

"How are you, Mother?"

At the sound of a familiar voice, Ginny came awake. "All right."

"They're taking you to a new home today." Linda touched her mother's hand and glanced toward the open door where the maintenance crew was still at work. "It'll be much quieter there." As if hearing her, they moved closer and the noise level increased. "Stupid vacuums!" Linda got up to close the door as Ginny's laughter filled the room. "Mother, they're coming soon so I won't stay long, because I don't want to tire you out. You have a big day ahead of you."

"Where's the door?"

What door? Her mother's question hung in the air. Hospice literature suggested that sometimes the use of the word door meant death to the departing one, but she wasn't sure that was what her mother meant, so she replied in a way that could have broad meaning.

"When you're ready, you'll see the door."

Best response she could think of in the moment.

Ginny closed her eyes as if preparing for a long journey. A calmness, *a peace that passeth all understanding,* transcended her.

The oxygen tube was gone, but an intravenous needle was attached to her arm. They had only a few moments before hospice was due to arrive.

Mary had called earlier and given her strict instructions about not wearing her out and, had asked Linda to pick up her mother's clothing, at the nursing home. The finality struck Linda.

"Take just a few sweaters," Mary ordered.

"I bought her eight in the last month."

"A few is what they said."

"No pants?"

"She's bedridden." She paused, her speech clipped. "They want to get her settled in any time after three."

At Las Palmas, Ginny's former room was already vacant, with closets and drawers emptied, no radio on the nightstand, and a blank bulletin board; the nurses had wasted no time.

The head nurse came to stand beside her as she surveyed the room. "Housekeeping took her belongings to the linen room."

The linen room, a glorified laundry room complete with boxes and plastic garbage bags piled high amidst detergent bottles, with buckets and mops, depressed her. An attendant pointed to a pile of plastic bags slightly secluded from the others, waiting patiently by the door. He helped her load them into the trunk of her car, piling them on top of each other.

The hospital van, its engine still idling, had already arrived at hospice and was sitting near the doorway, a metallic ramp leaning out of the trunk, as if a wheelchair had just been lowered. Linda hauled a few bags out of her car and entered the facility. She signed in. Two nurses chatting casually greeted her and introduced themselves.

"Let me show you your mother's room." Melanie escorted her down the curving hall. Soft music played in the dim light. The afternoon sun rested on the freshly vacuumed carpet.

Thinking her mother was probably stressed out from the move, she said, "Hello, Mother. How are you?"

"All right," she responded weakly.

Linda surrounded her with teddy bears and a baby doll which she'd found in one bag, probably stuffed in there by one of the attendants.

"Hold her hand while I take her pressure," Melanie said. "She's shaking."

"Please calm down, Mother." Linda patted her hand. "Everything's fine. You're in a good place."

The other nurse, Janice, curiously peered into a plastic bag placed on the floor next to the closet. "What's in the bag?"

"Blouses, pants, and sweaters."

"Some sweaters would be good."

"Okay. Let me sort through the bags and get them out." *What am I going to do with the rest of the clothes?*

"Such pretty sweaters." Melanie watched Linda sort through them.

"They're brand new." Linda stood and arched her back. Her muscles were aching from carrying the bags around. "What if I take her out for a stroll in the wheelchair? Won't she need pants then?"

Routine questions became concerns. "We'll put a blanket on her legs." Melanie nodded to Janice, as if they had done this a thousand times.

The thought of her mother no longer needing pants was disturbing. Linda tried to shake it off by moving toward the sliding glass door. "Nice patio. She'll like this." A small lanai looked onto a garden brimming with native flowers.

Checking Ginny's vitals, Janice didn't look up. "It was designed so the bed could be moved out there."

"That's good. Mother loves to be outdoors."

Linda put the framed photos on the upper shelf. In a small act of defiance, she hung one pair of pants and a blouse in the closet, with a sidelong glance at Melanie who was intently reading a thermometer. She neatly folded several sweaters and placed them in a chest of drawers next to her mother's bed, making the room seem homey, as if a place like this could ever be considered home.

The final steps were becoming more difficult by the moment. Suspense was building. She remembered the times her mother had taken care of her, driving her to all sorts of after school activities, not to mention the times she was sick. Her mother would bring her hot chicken noodle soup and saltines on a silver tray, with embossed nursery rhymes—a family heirloom, having traveled the same route whenever any daughter was bedridden. She never left, not once. "Morning, noon, and night," her mother used to say. Linda sat in the leather chair for a few quiet moments and took in the new surroundings while the hour hand inched forward. "I'm happy to be here with you."

Ginny seemed to hear.

The vigil began as Ginny entered sacred grounds, the last moments of her life. In a coma, breathing heavily, she snored loudly—no food or liquid, for six days. Linda was the only one talking now, but Ginny was still able to communicate by heaving her shoulders or, if it was something of particular interest, arching her eyebrows upward. Though dwindling, her life force persisted.

Resident physician, Dr. Peter Hall, came into the room while Linda sat at her mother's bedside. They were still seeing each other socially, as friends only. He stepped forward to examine the patient.

"Is it important for me to be here—now?" she asked him, watching his ministrations with interest.

"It benefits the dying person and the beloved at the same time," he explained. "You're in the right place. She's aware of your presence and finds solace in it. She recognizes your voice. As for you, the memory will last for the rest of your life."

"I only wish I could be with her as she takes her last breath." Linda glanced toward her mother. "Try not to go in the middle of the night, Mom."

Peter laughed and stepped aside as Linda moved closer and touched her mother's face with lips and hands. She kissed her mother's forehead, leaving a bright coral lipstick mark, and caressed her shoulders, arms, and hands. Ginny seemed relaxed, having been sedated by palliative medicines to help with the pain and restless agitation. Linda wished the doctor would give her some. The days were lengthening like shadows.

"Mother, your time is near. Whenever you're ready, I am, too. I love you. I'll miss you, but it's okay to go." Hospice had coached her on what to say when her father passed. "You're the world's best mother. Look at what you've accomplished. You saw Dad through World War II. You lived through the Korean War, the Cold War when you were raising us, the terrorist attack on the World Trade Center, and our feud over your will. As for that, well, you'll probably do more good for us in heaven. We had so many happy family memories, picnics, parties, dinners."

She turned to the doctor. "How will I know when—"

He knew what she alluded to. "Watch for mottled skin around the extremities, hands and feet. Her breathing might become shallow or ragged."

After he left, Melanie and Janice cleansed Ginny who was slightly responsive. Watching the nurses' activities, she was partly curious, partly terrified, her inner child in a state of shock, Linda spoke soothingly to herself about the natural, normal process of dying. It was the way Bunnie had talked to her the night before, which comforted her. Her innocent eyes were not yet bonded with knowledge, but like a window into her soul. Fear and relief operated simultaneously. The process of losing her mother was strange and new. Friends, Aunt Dolly, and Tom, her cousin, nourished her. Everyone kept telling her she was not alone, but somehow it didn't make it any easier. And yet she found it was beautiful, as God made all things beautiful in time. Her parent's energy was turning less physical and more spiritual, preparing itself for the next realm, whatever it might be, nothing to be feared, no way to be avoided. *To everything there is a season and a time for every purpose under heaven.*

Linda left the facility, her mother on her mind.

Tom and Sally, his wife, called. "We're making good time driving and will be with you shortly."

They met Linda and Harry, the boyfriend, in the foyer of Linda's house. Halfway through the introductions as Tom, Sally, and Harry stood staring at each other, she lost composure. The guests finished the introductions themselves.

They headed to hospice in separate cars. As they signed in, a staff member explained that a priest had just administered Last Rites.

Lying on her side, hands tucked under the pillow near her face like a little child, Ginny's hair was soft to the touch, her skin pale, her hip, under the sheet, skeletal. The oxygen tube was gone. She seemed to be resting quietly, her breathing strong and steady.

Linda caressed her. "Mother, we're here. Tom and Sally just arrived. You remember Harry."

One by one, they made their way to her bedside and spoke softly to her, touching her gently. The radio emitted soothing music. They chatted amongst themselves from the foot of the bed. Linda broke away and stood by Ginny's head.

"Last night, I danced a jitterbug for you, Mother—a feather in my hair!" She left off the black lacy underwear, sequins, velvet-soled, open-toed shoes, thinking she'd said enough.

"She sure did!" Harry stepped forward, happy to gain entrance into the conversation.

"I had curls just like when you used to set my hair."

"Unfortunately, they were gone almost as soon as we got there."

Linda elbowed Harry in the ribs. Tom and Sally laughed. The release of tension felt good.

"Yes, I'm afraid I still have straight hair." She looked askance at Harry. "My date forgot a few dance steps, but I helped him."

"More than a few," Harry admitted.

"We're going to lunch after we leave, Mom." Ginny's breathing was the same, rhythmic and steady. "Don't be afraid, Mom. Remember, someone will come for you when it's time. I don't know who, but you'll recognize them. Might be Dad, Poppa, Gran'ma, Nana, or even Aunt Rose . . ."

"My mother!" Tom cut in. Ginny's sister Sarah had predeceased her by a few years.

"Oh, yes, forgive me—Sarah! Did I forget anyone else?"

"Let me think." Tom scratched his head.

Suddenly, Ginny snorted deeply several times, which startled them and led to exchanged looks. As if on cue, Ginny snorted again, louder than the first time, which made them laugh.

"See. I told you she was listening. She has something to say after all!"

Ginny's breathing resumed its steady pace, as if content that she'd participated in the fun.

"Everyone who was coming to see you has come, Mother. Mary will be back in town tonight. I'll see you tomorrow . . . but it's okay to go." Linda sat down on the edge of the bed, reluctant to leave. "How about we sing a couple renditions of *Happy Trails to You*?" The song had come to mind the previous day and she had been humming it as she walked around the house. She took it as a message that someone, perhaps her father who'd seen every cowboy movie made, apparently thought it'd be a good thing to do. The idea had a sentimental, whimsical humor to it and appealed to her.

". . . Happy trails to you until we meet again . . ." Their voices susurrant, the foursome made a dramatic film-worthy departure.

In the car, Linda placed a call to Mary.

"Thanks for Last Rites. I forgot about that. The priest came at quarter to six last night. Tom had a good idea . . . ."

"You're breaking up. Let me call you when I get off the highway."

Returning from a short vacation, Mary felt relaxed, despite the facial tic, which was suddenly active again. Hours later, she returned Linda's call when Harry and she were shopping.

"Welcome back." Linda smiled into the phone, thinking sweet thoughts, bearing no malice toward her sister. Never had, never would. She thought her sister an odd duck with a truckload of resentment and jealousy.

"What's up?"

"Last Rites were a good idea." No response. "Say, why don't you bring Loca in to see Mom?" Loca, Linda's former cat, had been a wonderful pet for six months, before allergies kicked in. She asked Mary to adopt the cat, thinking, one more animal in that household, wouldn't make much difference. She hoped Mary would take good care of the animal and not hold sibling resentment against her.

Pleased to have such a pretty kitty of high pedigree, Mary took Loca into her home, where the animals thrived under her care. When Ginny took up residence in Mary's home, Loca located a comfortable place on her bed, near the pillows, where she curled into a ball, and they became fast friends.

"I took Mack to visit Mom several times when she was in the nursing home. Loca would be too fidgety." Mack was Mary's dog. All the cats were hers, but Mack was her dog in particular. Her husband, Brad, claimed the other dogs.

"You could keep her in the cage. Loca might comfort Mom." *And me, too,* she thought. She longed to run her hand through Loca's silky white fur.

"Hmmph. Let me think. Maybe in the morning. Bye." Crisp like a potato chip.

"Good bye."

Harry saw the look on her face and reached for her hand, squeezing it fondly. "She causes you such pain. Why do you bother calling her?" He looked at her. "I've overhead several of your conversations and have seen how she stiffened when you embraced her in the hospital."

"I don't know. Just yesterday I told a friend that there was really no further reason for us to communicate. And today . . . I call her."

"It's a bad habit."

"I'm working on it."

"I wouldn't call her at all."

"You know, I receive more kindness and warmth from perfect strangers than I do from her." She held onto his hand tightly. "Basically, I crave the love of my older sister, but she just won't give it to me."

"Maybe she can't."

"I know. All I have to do is accept it the way it is."

"You said she's always been this way. Nothing's changed."

"You're right. She's sick."

Harry looked at her with sad eyes.

"I've learned to pray for her."

Reluctantly, he replied, "That's all you can do."

Later, after Harry had left for work, she thought about how death was like a veil. Her mother and she were walking along life's journey, but the veil lay between them. Her mother was fading behind it, sinking deeper into a coma, approaching mortality. The spirit needs energy to leave the body, she had concluded, probably as much as it had required to unite with the embryonic cell. Soon she would be free.

For the first time in weeks, that night she slept deeply and awoke refreshed. The company of Tom and Sally helped, and they had plans to get together soon. Life was more abundant and exciting after being with loving friends—a stark contrast to the interactions with Mary. As for Cathy, well, only silence.

Time to prepare the memorial, Linda thought. She called various churches she'd frequented over the years, since she'd left the Catholic Church. Raised Catholic, she broke away during college and remained apart throughout marriage. After divorce, she'd drifted among different denominations, never really attaching herself to any of them, never knowing what she sought and seldom finding solace. Occasionally, she'd return to a Catholic church only to sit in the last pew and leave early. She just couldn't get into the heavy duty, rigid, old-fashioned rituals anymore.

She left voicemails at the different denominations she'd visited. Responses varied. "Can you postpone the service for a week or two. We're busy right now." Some returned the call a week later. A priest from St. Anthony's, a local Catholic church, responded within the hour. "Have you selected music?" he asked. A staff member called practically every day with instructions. Impressed with prompt, courteous assistance, Linda felt the arms of the Catholic Church draw her in.

Thinking it might be *the* day, Linda visited her mother at hospice twice. The first visit was early in the morning. Linda approached the bed and leaned down to kiss her mother on the forehead. The distinctive death rattle filled her ears.

Father Henry entered the room and greeted her warmly.

"This is it, isn't it, Father?" she asked.

"Yes, I think so. It won't be long now."

"A few hours, you think?"

"Yes."

"Father, would you say a few prayers for her?"

"Of course."

He blessed Ginny and murmured prayers.

After he left, Linda spent considerable time talking to Ginny. She kept her voice light, stroking Ginny's fine gray hair, which had become even more lustrous. She reached for scissors and cut snips which she placed in an envelope.

Ginny's moan turned into a gasp. Linda stayed a while longer.

In the car, she drove as fast as she legally could around an eleven-mile block. She bought a guest register, flowers, and ordered a prayer card.

In the afternoon, when she returned to hospice, an aroma therapist had just finished with her mother. The room had a pleasant scent. The mottling in her mother's extremities had disappeared. Her breathing was steady, as if someone had turned down the death rattle. Soft music played in the background. For a brief second, Linda was delusional, thinking Ginny might rally.

Then, reality set in.

Nurses, Janice and Melanie, came in to reposition her and halfway through the process, Ginny's eyes fluttered open so that she looked straight at Linda. *Does Mother recognize me?* Linda questioned.

Her mother seemed frightened. Linda moved closer to her and cradled her head as the nurses ministered to her. Her eyes were still open, a shiny, light green hue, as if they bore a hint of sun-drenched palm fronds. A single tear appeared in her right eye and Linda ran to catch it in a tissue, which she saved. The last tear was supposed to be good-by.

Melanie gently closed Ginny's eyelids and she went back to sleep. "I once had a charge half your mother's size who lasted twenty-nine days without food or water."

"Really?" Linda exclaimed in surprise, then thought again. "I don't think that's the case here." Linda glanced toward her mother to see if she'd heard. "I think Mother wants it over with. I know I would."

After both nurses left, Linda remained with Ginny, speaking softly.

"Hey, Mom, Mass will be held at St. Anthony's. Be there, okay?" She looked to see if there was any reaction. "I've arranged to let

Mary have the ashes, because the Catholic Church frowns on dividing them."

In the middle of her monologue, Ginny coughed loudly, which was the response Linda was waiting for. *Mother's still communicating with me!* Linda joked, kidded her, and included her in the day's events. She tried to make it seem like when she was a kid just home from school and Ginny was leaning over the kitchen sink preparing dinner.

Curling herself on an adjacent chair, Linda read from the Bible, which did her more good than her mother.

Chapter Nineteen

Shortly before dawn, lying in the middle of bed, sheets tangled around her legs, Linda awoke with a start. Her eyes fluttered open. She lay quietly, staring at the rotating ceiling fan. *What would it be like to die at this hour, between night and day, when a soul could sneak out quietly.* She pictured her mother's spirit, an ethereal beauty, rising to heaven.

The phone jarred her musings

"Is this Linda Cray?" said an authoritative voice.

"Yes."

"This is Melanie, the nurse at hospice. You asked to be notified. Your mother passed away at 5:15 this morning."

Linda glanced at the alarm clock on the backside of the night stand. 5:20. Her imagination was spot on.

"Can I see the body?" she whispered.

"Of course."

"Be there in thirty minutes."

"Take your time. I haven't called the mortician yet, but I'll need to do so within the hour."

Linda quickly put on her clothes from the day before, which were draped on a nearby chair. She raced down the hallway to the bathroom to brush her teeth, plucked a pair of sandals from a shoe rack in the closet, and darted back to the bedroom to snatch the shoulder strap of her purse from the back of the chair.

On her way to the garage, she cast a longing look at the refrigerator in the kitchen. No time for breakfast. Soon, she was on the highway, going well over the speed limit. A cell phone pressed to her ear, she called Harry.

"Are you up?" she asked him.

"Yeah. I'm drinking coffee in the kitchen. You know, getting ready for work"

"Mom passed. I just got the news and I'm headed to hospice."

"I'm sorry for your loss."

In a strained voice, she managed, "Thank you."

"I'll be there soon, baby. Don't worry."

Another call to Tom and Sally who were still in town visiting friends, but there was no answer. She left a voicemail.

The parking lot at hospice was empty. Bracing herself against a chilling wind from a cold front that had arrived, Linda folded her arms against her chest.

On her side, her eyes wide open with a look of pleasant surprise, as if she had been awakened by a familiar voice, or perhaps a heavenly touch of a long-lost friend or relative, her mother lay quietly, as peace reigned on the pale face cradled by bent arms.

Linda kissed her forehead, still warm to the touch, and stroked the silky gray hair. She knelt. Goose bumps ran up and down her arms, as if she experienced her mother's loving spirit hovering overhead.

Melanie entered the room. "I had just massaged her body with lavender lotion, and she totally relaxed. She had been fidgety until then."

"I'm sure she appreciated that."

Melanie nodded, waited a moment before inquiring: "Will you let me know when you're leaving?"

Linda knew what she was referring to. "Go ahead. Call the funeral director. I'll stick around a while."

Melanie returned to her station. Linda resumed kneeling by her mother's bedside, a familiar place, although things had changed forever.

"Congratulations, Mother. You made the transition. You're in heaven now. Your body is getting cool to the touch, but oh . . . ! look how beautiful you are, even in death." She ran her hands down the sheet that draped her. Nothing but skin and bones, she thought.

The funeral truck was running late.

"It's time to go, Mom. Is it all right?" Linda sensed her mother's approval. She looked up at the ceiling, as if Ginny was watching.

"You may have left your body, but you'll always be with me, Mother. We have loved each other deeply, haven't we . . . ? Good-bye,

Mother, my best friend. I'll see you again." She stood up for only a second, remembering a song she'd heard the choir sing in church, and knelt again. "I thank God every time I remember you."

She kissed her mother for the last time.

"Here's a paper to help you write your obituary." Maureen, a typist at a local newspaper office, squinted from a low chair on the other side of the counter as she let a routine form dangle from bright red, lacquered nails. "We don't write them for you."

"How's this?" Linda leaned over and handed her a rough draft she'd composed over breakfast.

Maureen glanced at it, nodded approval. "Do you have a photo?"

"I forgot." Linda said. "Hold on. I'll be right back."

When she returned, Maureen reached over the counter, took the photo, and scrutinized it. "That'll be $150." She looked at Linda. "Any last minute changes?"

"It's good to go. Oh, by the way, there'll be another tomorrow."

Maureen drew her brows together in question. "How's that?"

"My sister will probably print one through her funeral director."

Maureen stared a second longer, then her face lit up with understanding. "Way to go, gal! More power to you."

Thinking, *Best money I ever spent,* Linda left the office with a swagger. *Something special about a ceremony,* she thought, *something that offered a gleam of hope.* An opportunity lay before them. Funerals brought about reunions. She'd felt an urge to reconnect, an urge stronger than fear of rejection. It was worth a try. Somewhere in time, she knew she'd be called upon to account for her actions and would be judged for what she might have supported, been complicit in or failed to prevent. If ever there was a time to reconcile, the time was now. Guided by a priest, she had left voicemails for both sisters: "I long for a time when we can be sisters again. My door is open. I pray you'll walk through it."

Harry and Linda arrived early for the memorial service for Ginny Cray. The narthex of St. Anthony's, the central hall between heavy wooden doors and the interior of the church, with light streaming in from the stained-glass windows, held a special warm, welcoming atmosphere. They carefully placed a poster—with photos of Ginny at all stages of her life—on an easel to the right of large glass doors leading into the church. Someone had placed a pile of bulletins, with selected songs for the Mass, each bearing Ginny's name on the front page, on a dais. Linda put a guest book and a fancy silver pen she'd purchased for the occasion, on a table close by. Harry easily lifted and stationed two chairs next to the poster so they could sit and wait for friends and perhaps a family member, like Mary or Cathy.

A lady from a florist shop delivered a beautiful array of yellow flowers. Dabbing her eyes with a Kleenex, Linda accepted them with a smile, wondering who'd remembered her favorite color. Another florist brought a large wreath of varied flowers and Linda bent to read the card. "From an anonymous donor."

The first guests to arrive were A.A. friends. Remembering the mystery wreath from an anonymous donor, Linda greeted, embraced, and murmured to each, "Thank you for coming. This means a lot to me."

Harry positioned himself by her side like a bodyguard and joined her in welcoming guests.

A woman close to her mother's age approached. "I knew your mother. We worked together at the hospital auxiliary where we both put in twenty years. My name is Anne."

"Nice to meet you, Anne. I'm glad you came."

"I saw the obituary in the paper and I just *had to come*."

"Thank you so much."

"They tried to penalize your mother for taking time off when your dad was sick. We were all going to quit on account of it. But then, at the last moment, they decided to give her a pin anyway at our annual banquet."

"I remember that banquet. I bought her a suit to wear to it."

Anne smiled fondly. "The green one?"

Linda nodded and bit her lip. She and her mother had been shopping after lunch one afternoon and spotted the suit in Dillard's—a shiny, green and gold brocade, with fancy gold buttons. When her mother tried it on, she was so pleased with how it looked on her and how much she liked the fabric that Linda bought it right away, without even looking at the price. At the cashier, she dismissed her mother's protest, with a flip of her wrist.

Anne touched her arm. "That suit was her. She looked great in it."

"Nice of you to remember." Linda's eyes softened, as if remembering how her mother looked in it.

"By the way, there was a second obit in the paper. I was wondering if you could shed light on that . . . ."

"Oh . . . yeah . . . well, my estranged sisters put that in." She noticed Anne's face clouding. "You know how it is . . . sometimes . . . among family members."

"It's sad that it has to be that way, especially at a time like this . . . Here, let me take your picture." Anne looked Harry up and down as if measuring him for a suit. "You two stand over there, by that stone wall." Harry and Linda posed awkwardly. "Back a little further. I like to get feet in the picture." They took a few steps backward, until their heels scraped stones. Anne looked down. "Nice shoes." This made Harry and Linda laugh and in that second, Anne snapped a photo.

Guests continued to scurry into the church. Friends from the tennis club and dance halls rushed through the heavy wooden doors. Neighbors entered. Arimatheans, a volunteer group who attended funerals as a ministry, arrived *en masse*. Bunnie appeared and embraced Linda at length. Anne commented, "You two look like sisters."

It became apparent that many guests knew each other, and they came together like the pieces of a jigsaw puzzle. The level of conversation inched upward.

The door opened again, and Father Paul entered the crowded room, straining to locate his parishioner. When he spotted her, he hurriedly walked forward, shook her hand, offered his condolences, turned and headed briskly toward the altar, which was a signal for the Arimatheans.

"Do you have a photo of your mother?" an Arimathean asked with urgency in her voice.

Linda motioned with her head. "There's a whole poster full of them."

"No, I mean—one I can put on the altar." Noting Linda's confusion, and without saying another word, the Arimathean reached out and swiped the one by the guest book—a framed photo of mother and daughter in the nursing home. "This will do." She disappeared through the glass doors into the church.

Linda stood staring after her when Harry grasped her arm firmly. "Come on, it's time." As they left the narthex, the guests followed and seated themselves among the pews.

While Harry and Linda made their way down the aisle to the first pew, Linda remembered walking down another aisle, one hand on her father's arm, her mother sitting in the first row so many years ago, on the occasion of her one and only marriage. *Where had the time gone?* No sooner did they sit than the music and the Mass began, causing them to stand. Linda looked around the church to acknowledge the guests one more time and, as she faced the altar, her eyes fell on the photo of her mother and her, which an Arimathean had placed on an altar step. A tremor ran through her. Bunnie and Harry laced their arms around her waist.

The service progressed. Linda looked around, keeping an eye out in case her sisters appeared. Brother Walt, a robust man and A.A. member who wore his hair in a ponytail down his back, belted out the closing song, *On Eagles' Wings*. He smiled at Linda when she glanced at him. *So appropriate,* she thought, *with Mother having passed at dawn.*

When the music stopped, Linda turned to see everyone standing and realized they were waiting for her. She took Harry's hand and they hurried back to the narthex. Although it had been a good turnout, she felt a vague, nagging emptiness and wished her sisters had attended.

Later that day, she turned her attention to Harry, already lying naked on her bed.

Something about grief sweetened their lovemaking that afternoon. Harry held her closely when her emotions overflowed and when she calmed, he made love to her slowly, tenderly, and finished powerfully, as if to reinforce the fact that life was moving on. The physical release relieved them.

Two obituaries about Ginny had appeared in the daily news that week. Mary's was an announcement, Linda's, an open service. It would have been nice to have been able to honor her mother's life as a family, but that didn't happen. Although the three sisters were of the same blood and had shared a common history, there was not even the least flicker of an attempt at forgiveness and reconciliation by Mary and Cathy. There was nothing like the reunion that had occurred between mother and daughter. She prayed for a miracle.

Chapter Twenty

The acid test of remaking life without parents began.

Ginny had taught Linda many things, but now the teacher, the guardian, the policewoman was gone—as were the siblings. Now what? Extended families, like distant seeds blowing in the wind, existed somewhere. In the present, she had the wonderful people who'd attended her mother's funeral, and most of all, herself. Harry was still around, but they were seeing each other less frequently. It was typical for Harry to disappear and be non-communicative for periods of time. What was different this time was that she didn't call or do anything to chase him.

At Christmas time, Linda painted, attended meetings, and grew closer to those who supported her at the funeral. She thought about Ginny constantly, wondering where she might be, what she might look like, what she was doing in the afterlife. Einstein believed that it was possible for multiple dimensions of space and time to co-exist and so, this made sense to her although she didn't understand how. Aunt Dolly, with whom she had many telephone conversations now that her mother was gone, offered, "After my mother passed, I heard her in my heart."

"I know what you mean." The silent voice. Lately, she had gotten into the habit in the privacy of her home, or car, of speaking to her mother out loud: "It's okay for you to talk to me, Mother, in my heart, of course." And there would sometimes be a sensation, which she took to be a response to whatever was going on. Other times, it would just be "I love you." One busy morning at St. Anthony's, Linda was ushering parishioners into overflowing pews trying to make room for one more when she became aware of a poignant internal message: "I'm so proud of you."

Linda and Ginny's talk resulted in reconciliation. Their relationship had turned on a dime after that. Dementia helped them to overcome control issues a little in that regard, because it curtailed Ginny's ability to express herself, and they were no longer butting heads over minor details. All Linda had felt from her mother in that brief span of time was unconditional love. It had never felt so good to be with her mother. Even though their time was limited, even though they had admirably attempted to cram half a century of love into a few remaining days, their connection was stronger, cleaner, and healthier.

Having experienced such love, she focused on selecting and improving relationships which enriched her life.

"I've detached from Harry and our unsatisfying on-again-off-again relationship," she confessed to her sponsor. "Plus I no longer have interest in anyone who has a history of constant abandonment."

"That's just a form of self-imposed punishment," Bunnie commented.

"I'm simply not going to put myself in any intolerable situation, with a man."

Bunnie smiled. "I knew you'd learn to like being treated with love and respect."

"How come it took me so long?"

Bunnie's soft laughter smoothed the question. "You're doing much better. We haven't had many late-night talks about pitfalls. I haven't had to post bail in a while."

Linda laughed and winked.

"You're thinking things through and that's how you avoid bad situations."

"Right. I'm also trying to accept things as they are. Trying, Bunnie, I'm just trying."

Section Two

Chapter Twenty-One

A month after her mother passed, Linda inquired about the estate. Ginny had once shown Linda several bank statements, so she knew there had been three accounts at one time, each with $100,000 in them, held in trust, plus, by now, some interest. *A nice piece of change.*

Attorney Brown, representing Mary and Cathy, who held control of the estate, shockingly replied: the entire sum from all three accounts had been used to purchase a single residence. Linda choked on a piece of pizza she was eating. *Oh no!* They had gone through with the second plan and bought property. Brown explained, "It's rented for two years and can't be touched until then."

Two years! Oh, why did my sisters put $310,000, all the money, into real estate, just before Mother died? She wouldn't have bought green bananas for a sick, elderly client. *What happened to the Prudent Man rule?* Which basically meant don't do anything foolish. She remembered the letter she'd sent to Mary months ago in which she'd written, "Keep the money in cash or cash equivalents, in the bank where it is now, as Mother doesn't have much time left." *Did Mary bother to read it? Did Cathy know about it?* Unfortunately, there was no one to stop Mary from marching into the bank with Power of Attorney papers in hand and cleaning out all three accounts.

In 2006, the economy was booming. For the previous four years, everything had been going up. The stock market had reached a lofty pinnacle. Houses and condominiums were selling like hot cakes. Everyone wanted a home—a dream fostered by the federal government for the past few decades—and a cheap mortgage. Investors were buying multiple homes, retirees, second homes in warmer climates. Debt instruments, such as credit default swaps and collateralized bond obligations, a market of trillions, stood with little backing, the underlying asset and its customary coupon having been divided into so many pieces they resembled bankers IOUs. The risk-reward system had gone entirely out of whack; it was a house of cards awaiting a single puff to bring it down.

Upon learning of the trustees' purchase, she drove immediately to a densely overbuilt section of town, a park development just south of where she lived, to view the single-family residence that represented her inheritance. She found the address and, from her car, stared aghast at a wooden house painted conch-shell pink.

Parking the car, she opened the door, and moved from the street to the driveway to get a better look in the bright mid-afternoon sun. A wooden deck embraced the entrance to the house. Off to the side, a man-made pond had since dried up, leaving the impression it might have looked better at another time, with fresh water lapping at the rounded rocks and fat, lazy goldfish swimming about. A gnarled pine tree stood by, shading the pond. She turned her head to view two rickety wooden steps leading to the front door from the porch. *Wood! A feast for termites! Would the bugs get the money before she did?*

Once over the initial shock, she divided her time between watching the markets and checking on the trust's rental real estate. Caught up in the frenzy like everyone else, she was wheeling and dealing in stocks like the good old days, making a little money here and there. By the summer of 2008, a change had come into the air, stocks were inching downward . . . something was up. She wondered what to do: buy, wait, or . . . sell. Realtor friends gave their input: "I just had a closing and, before the ink dried, my buyer sold it." "People are doing things that are not good for them." "Common sense has gone to hell." "I'm getting out of this job before the lid blows off."

The puff was more like an explosion.

Word leaked out about a credit meltdown. Lehman Brothers filed for bankruptcy and it soon became apparent that the national banking system was in serious trouble. A domino effect tumbled economic beacons—even her old firm—sending shock waves worldwide and ushering in the Great Recession, the worst recession since the Great Depression.

Like many others, Linda glued herself to the news, wanting to know where she stood. Opening the mail gave her weak knees and a rubbery stomach as she saw that her entire investment portfolio had slimmed down considerably.

How was the rental property doing? Unfortunately, the purchase occurred at the height of the market. She made it a point to keep up with the information that came her way by letter from her sisters' attorney, as they were no longer speaking to her. Brown wrote: "The property is currently on the market. Stay away from it and don't upset the renter."

Behind the curtained windows, she knew a single parent who paid her monthly rent on time and raised two children lived quietly, no doubt inconvenienced by a stream of realtors who came by with prospective buyers.

Posing as one potential buyer, she drove by against Brown's directive. A *For Sale* sign in the yard held a plastic box stuffed with printouts of information. She reached in and took a copy. The house was listed at $249,000, much less than what her sisters had paid for it at the height of the real estate bubble. Reality sank in. She shook her head. *My inheritance,* she thought, *a decaying slab of fifty-year-old wood,* or rather, one third of it.

Following their attorney's guidance, her sisters had acted within the law, and made a *really bad* investment. They'd stolen her opportunity to make an informed decision about her intended inheritance, by taking the money out of the bank and putting it elsewhere. Thanks to the economy, most of it had disappeared into the hands of a lucky seller who for all she knew might have been Brown's accomplice.

Sick at heart, worried, and anxious, she wondered how she would keep up. Between the fed's newly imposed low interest rate strategy and mounting health care costs, she felt an economic pinch. One look at her aging car reminded her of the new austerity she was living in. Not as bad as others, but still painful.

Chapter Twenty-Two

Two years later.

Linda had waited the obligatory period for her inheritance, watching a dire economic situation unfold, powerless, thinking about how hard her parents had worked all their lives. Having been their financial planner for decades, she knew what their estate had been worth. They passed their life savings on to daughters who hadn't worked for it, didn't know what it had taken to get it, and weren't able to keep it. The method of transferring assets from one generation to another seemed cruel, unjust, unfair, wrong, and just plain stupid to her. The story of how a cold cash inheritance had turned into a ready-made pile of sawdust seemed unbelievable, but worse was the destruction of a family. Although many families shipwrecked on the shoals of wills, hers had gone down in flames. *How did it get so bad?* The lack of a federal law that would go to the core of family sovereignty—the power to exclude—might be one reason for the mess she was in.

She recalled the family's dynamics. A middle child, Linda was in the center of a sibling rivalry stemming from infancy. The three sisters had always triangulated over something; not once had they worked together toward a common goal, their loyalty to each other lasted only until the next skirmish. In this fight over the will, Mary, the eldest, and Cathy, the youngest, had joined forces against her when she had confronted Mary about the way she'd taken control of the family's estate. To her way of thinking, this was more like a power grab than anything else. It was the first time Linda had stood up to her big sister. The uproar that followed appeared to be all Linda's fault, but who knew for sure? Had she kept her mouth shut and looked the other way, as Cathy had wanted her to do, something else might have done them in. This latest tiff had endured longer than any other argument they'd had and seemed destined to extend to the tombstone.

She pushed back an unruly hair, which was playing with her eye. The pink house was badly in need of repair and probably needed to be leveled, rebuilt, maybe set on fire, a pyric victory over all that was wrong with their family. *Yeah . . . burn the wood pile and start over again.* Glancing at her watch, she realized she'd better get going.

Linda drove away, heading to Buena Vida, the town where she lived, just a few miles north. Her mind was still back in the rental house, and she decided that she was too angry to let Brown and his illustrious law firm get away with what he'd done. She'd write another letter to the Florida Bar, court of last resort.

"My complaint is trust maladministration," she wrote the bar. "Attorney Brown made an unsuitable investment for my mother's trust and lost most of her money. She entrusted him with the fiduciary responsibility, of preserving and protecting her capital for the benefit of all three of her daughters equally.

I don't think my mother was well served by him."

After she mailed the letter, she sat back and thought, *What fiduciaries—my sisters, the trustees, and their legal adviso*r. But the Byzantine law related to Medicaid planning had left the door wide open so that an heir's inheritance could be exposed to such risk.

An attorney friend explained to her over the phone, "Had you acted sooner, you might have petitioned to have the assets immediately transferred into a court-appointed legal guardianship instead of letting them fall prey to a first come, first served maneuver."

Now you tell me, she wanted to say.

Brown claimed he had merely followed the laws pertaining to Medicaid.

Linda had some brilliant legislators to thank for that. Putting an elder's money into a long-term asset carried risk. She had known of some financial advisors who had suffered the consequences of having made unsuitable recommendations, such as loss of employment, or imprisonment. Yet Brown, an elder care specialist, as he alleged, was acting *within* the law.

Linda bravely wrote Brown. "When can I expect my share of my mother's estate?"

He replied in his usual fashion:

"It's a shame about the market crash, but all you have to do is wait a few years for the market to return to its former level. Remember this is all your fault for not going along with my original idea, which was to have your mother buy your sister's house. The transfer of funds and title would have been on a temporary basis. I could have easily gotten it out of there."

Right. Linda read his letter twice, blinked twice, sat back, and thought, Mary feathered her nest with the proceeds from the sale of Mother's house. The house addition was now part of Mary's estate, thanks to the new will Brown had executed. With sweeping powers of trustee, she most likely would have found a way to lay claim to the remaining assets, with no objection from Cathy. To Linda's way of thinking, it looked like her two sisters and their attorney had conspired together in family fraud. As it was getting more serious, she relied on her attorney friend, Jim Cott.

"I'm ready to sue the bastards! How do I get started?"

"Hold on there. What's going on?"

"My sisters lost most of Mom's money. They put all of it in real estate and it's decimated!"

"That's too bad, Linda. Sorry to hear it. Before there's any more talk about suing, you should know you're not alone. Thousands from your generation are arguing over family assets, which have mushroomed from housing and market advances in the last sixty years to seventeen trillion. Court dockets are up 200%. Judges all over the country are ruling on families at war and yours would be no exception." A moment's pause before he probed a little more. "Er . . . what size are we talking?"

"A small mushroom, Jim. My share of the estate is worth about fifty thousand, down from a hundred and change . . . maybe less with this damn recession."

"It'd be worth going to court if it were in the millions."

"Jim, it's the principle of the thing—so what about the size of the estate. A few more zeros can't make that much of a difference."

"I know how you feel, but you have to look at cost effectiveness. It'll cost you thirty grand in court and, if your share is about that, then it's a wash. . . ." He waited for her to say something. "Anyway, here's what you can do: write a letter to Brown and say 'End this never-ending trust.'"

Brown responded by mail within a few weeks. "You're right. It's time to terminate the trust. You have two options. You can choose to continue the trust, or you can take title."

Taking title meant dealing with the real estate agent who had listed the property, and so she put in a call to Vance Hodge whose name was on the ad Brown had sent her.

His voice was brusque, impersonal. "I represent the trustee and can't speak with you."

Even though Linda trusted her attorney, Jim Cott, implicitly, she wasn't shy about seeking other viewpoints. Most attorneys allowed an hour of free consultation. A friend referred her to a real estate attorney named Tripp Crandall whose office was close by. Crandall's specialty seemed to be exactly what she needed at the moment. "Here's his number. Call him and set up an appointment."

Putting on the gloves, as she was getting a more powerful attorney, Linda dressed in a business suit, a remnant of working days, for the next step.

A semi-retired lawyer with a laid-back attitude, Crandall leaned back in an over-stuffed leather swivel chair behind a huge walnut desk that occupied most of his office. He peered at her from beneath bushy salt and pepper brows, which matched a crop of hair on his head, as she explained the situation. Heavily shuttered windows directed the bright afternoon sun to a spot on the floor away from the desk. When she finished, he looked at her.

"You should request that the trust be terminated and take title to one third of the property," he said. "It's in your best interest to do so."

"Could you explain that a little more?" She scooted to the edge of the red velvet chair that felt as if she were sitting on an upholstered elephant.

"The way the will is written, Linda, if something happens and you die, you get nothing."

She smirked. "I bet that's what my sisters are betting on."

"By taking title, no matter what, you, meaning your estate, get one third of the house, or the sales proceeds." He gestured with his hand. "With just a bit of paperwork, you become a tenant-in-common." Crandall smiled, not with his eyes, and added, "It's the partnership from hell."

She had to tear her eyes away from the sunny spot on the carpet, where her emotions wanted to lie down. "Was there any other way it could have been arranged?"

"I just handled an estate for an elderly client who sought Medicaid. She gave everything to charity. That's another option your mother might have considered."

Linda shook her head. "It wouldn't have worked in my family. Everyone wants the money . . . You think you know some people, but you don't."

"That's common."

"Probably it's what we should have done though. Would've been a lot better in the long run. The way it is, the trustee can do anything, including squish my voice as a beneficiary." She ran a hand through her hair. "But now, as a bona fide owner, I get a vote—one in three—but I get a vote." She smiled, liking the sound. Looking at him, she asked, "So, tell me, you're the expert, how will my being a tenant-in-common affect the dynamics of this partnership?"

Crandall picked up a pencil and twirled it between long fingers. "There could be a situation when your vote will be important, say . . . to break a tie or . . . when all three signatures are necessary as in a listing contract." He watched warily to see if she was catching on.

A gleam came into her eye as she thought about that. "The listing realtor gave me a hard time when I called him last week."

"We'll handle that." A fire seemed to ignite him. "Write him a letter saying you'd like an appointment and say 'If you have a conflict with my request, I'm more than willing to notify the Florida Real Estate Commission and terminate the listing.'"

I'm beginning to like this attorney. Linda stood to shake his hand, just as his secretary knocked on the door announcing his next appointment. She left with newly heightened hope. That same day she notified Brown of her request to take title and terminate the trust.

She sent Hodge a copy along with a letter asking for an appointment.

A few days had passed from the time she mailed the letter and heard from Hodge who was suddenly interested in meeting with her. A tall man her age, with a belly to prove he ate well, Hodge escorted her into the library of his firm where a long, narrow table was covered with about twenty pounds of paperwork, analyses, charts, and color photos.

She surveyed the collection. "Looks like you've done your homework."

"As one of the tenants, I thought you'd want to review the listing," he replied.

"I do. Thank you." She pulled a chair out to sit down and glanced at him. "Glad you're talking to me."

Hodge's face reddened. "It's been a difficult transition for me, you know. I'm used to talking with your sister, the trustee. She made it pretty clear that's what she wanted."

Linda smiled. "Little different now, isn't it?" She picked up a colored glossy of the property, which somehow made the wooden shack cozy and attractive. "How about bringing me up to date."

"Right." He launched into a review. "The current market analysis, the average square foot price, and last year's appraisals showed that the property could be listed at $170,000." His expression reeked with sympathy.

She could have choked her sisters. "Then, pray tell, why is it listed at $249,000?"

Proud and confident with his facts and figures, Hodge frowned at a trail of sugar ants trailing across a paper. "Well, er—you know my wife asked me the same question. Heh, heh. Your sisters insisted on the selling price."

"I thought *you* were the realtor." Her words acted on him like a cattle prod.

"You're right! I *am* the realtor! I thought I'd let them list it at that price for a few months and see what happens and then try and talk some sense into them. Sometimes you have to go that way—"

"To get the listing."

She was starting to get to him. "Yeah."

"Good luck with that idea. I think I'll write them a letter."

"Good idea."

When she arrived home, she threw herself on the bed, an arm over her brow, aware of a headache sharpening its claws. She was thinking of the many conversations she'd had with her father over the years she'd managed her parents' life savings.

"What about this stock for five cents, listed on this pink sheet. I found it on your desk while you were on the phone."

"That's a penny stock, Dad—too much risk. Not suitable for you and Mom. Remember your age."

"My buddy has an option fund that pays eighteen percent. I like the sounds of that!"

"Of course you do, but there's risk again. Take a look at this government bond fund, AAA-rated." She had looked at him, thinking, *Dad has little income but he's willing to roll the dice. What if it doesn't work out . . . then what?* A cough cleared her throat. "What about a *guaranteed* annuity or a *federally-insured* Certificate of Deposit?"

Her father had looked back at her blankly.

Over the years, constant worry about her parent's strained financial situation drained her. Sometimes she wished she could have given the account to another broker, just so she could sleep.

It was happening all over again with her sisters, but this time she had no authority over anything. Thousands of dollars were disappearing overnight like flocks of birds taking flight. Her desire to end their partnership and get them out of her life was so strong she would take the loss and move on.

Her letter to her sisters was to the point. "I think you should make the selling price more realistic."

Brown responded for them. "Your sisters want to wait until the market comes back, so they can get more money."

All ships rise with the tide, she thought, but it would take time. She had another brilliant idea. "Why don't you buy me out?"

Mary responded in a tersely typed letter like a one-fingered hello. "Linda, you can buy me and Cathy out. Then you would have complete control of the selling of the house. Cathy and I do not intend to reduce the listing price at this time. Remember that my children and our cousin get a share of the estate."

Reviewing the will, Linda smiled. In her haste to get her hands on the money, Mary had inadvertently cut out her own children and their cousin. *Purely by accident,* she thought and smiled. She moved closer to the keyboard to type.

"Dear Mary,

Thanks, but I'll pass on the offer of buying you out.

Realtor Vance Hodge says we can expect a selling price of $170,000. If we can't come together on a selling price, I'll have no choice but to retain counsel and file a Petition for Partition which means the court will have it appraised and it will be sold." Crandall had helped her with the wording.

"One other thing, Mother's Last Will and Testament revoked any and all wills and codicils previously made by her. The new will stipulates that the balance goes to her three daughters, with no distributions to your children, or our cousin. You may wish to confer with your attorney about that.

Yours truly,
Your sister, Linda"

A few days went by. Attorney Brown responded to Linda on behalf of her sisters.

"My clients still want to wait two years, until the market recovers. You are forcing a sale in one of the worst real estate markets, in thirty years. Basically, if we wait until the market recovers in two years you will make up your money and, in the meantime, the rental is paying all the expenses and turning a small profit. Forcing to sell now and then claiming that this whole matter was a bad investment because we got such a low amount is not something that will be tolerated. Please remember, if there hadn't been for your vehement objections to an otherwise legitimate plan, the other plan we were trying to use would have worked quicker, saved more money and been very easy to undo, without exposure to market risk. The necessity of having to undertake this plan forced us to do so, because you forced us out of the other plan."

His letter sailed into the wastebasket.

Chapter Twenty-Three

Attorney Crandall looked piercingly at her from across his desk. The sun filtered through the blinds and landed on a spot close to his desk. Avoiding his look, Linda glanced at the light on the floor, feeling somewhat numb and hollow. Reluctantly, as if she'd rather be elsewhere, she turned back to him. Crandall, having listened intently to her latest update, leveled wise and experienced eyes.

"Do you know how Petition for Partition works?" he asked.

The velvety armrests on the chair in which she was sitting suddenly held interest. "Not really."

"It allows the court to order a sale. It would happen on the steps of the courthouse. Have you been there?"

A slight bend of her head as she commented, "Can't say that I have."

"Well, I have. It's pitiful. The house might sell for less than $10,000." He watched her face pale. "It might even go for $100." Crandall leaned forward, maintaining eye contact as Linda gripped the velvety pads. "Do you want that?" He had used a softer tone like a concerned parent.

"Of course not . . . A spend down would have been better."

"In this case, yes, but I've seen it go the other way."

After her consult with Crandall, Linda decided that it was useless to pursue a Petition for Partition. Instead, she vainly wrote to the bar again, trying to get them to act. Attorney Brown defended himself vigorously, enlisting her sisters to write letters in his defense.

Linda read Mary's letter first:

"I don't know what kind of low life loser like my sister complains about a great attorney like Nestor Brown, with a fabulous website and more than twenty years' experience. How many attorneys with such good advice does she have? She's a no good troublemaker. I personally have attended Nestor Brown's lectures on elder care fourteen times and if my sister had ONE-TENTH of his talent she'd shut up. I listened to what he had to say and the next day my facial tic was GONE and the doctor said he'd never seen such a rapid recovery. She's frustrated by the economy, jealous, and wants control but frankly is too wussy to handle the challenges of Medicaid, and besides I'm the trustee and don't need her interference, because my attorney has always been cooperative. I'm cutting her off from the family once and for all."

Then Cathy's:

"I'm a busy veterinarian in charge of a clinic and can't get down there to deal with this. Attorney Brown always quoted the law and seemed to know what he was doing."

The letters made no sense to Linda. Attorney Brown's advice had cost most of their mother's assets and a broken family. Who were they kidding? The results spoke for themselves. Her thoughts added up; the course the sisters had chosen was as far as east is to west from the intentions of Mother. Impervious to insults, she knew that they'd thrown her under the bus for an outsider, an attorney, for heaven's sake, and a law with many loopholes.

A few days later, a secretary from the bar, with whom she'd had lengthy conversations, sent her a legal document listing five current complaints against Brown. Well, now, she thought, here's fuel for the fire.

Linda took the latest correspondence from Brown to Crandall who read the first few sentences, shook his head of recently cut, closely-cropped gray hair, and peered over the top of the page toward Linda.

"I can't understand what he writes. Did he flunk freshman English?" Linda nodded in agreement. "Aside from writing in the usual obtuse legal largesse, Attorney Brown doesn't seem to know his adverbs from his adjectives. Dangling participles are all over the page." He finished reading the lengthy rebuttal then raised his eyes to her. "It's your fault." He shook his head. "I don't believe a word of it."

"Neither do I."

Attorney Crandall laid Brown's letter on the desk and picked up her rebuttal. "Five complaints!" Attorney Crandall put the paper down and stared at Linda across the massive desk. "What does that make him—almost a thief?"

She handed him another letter from Brown. Crandall took it in his hand and glanced at her before he read. "He denies what's in the public record."

"In a year, the bar will purge all complaints. It's what the attorneys voted on. Imagine what was in his file before."

Crandall made a sound like a grunt.

When their session was over, Linda mailed her letter to the bar. Her attorney had found nothing in it that would expose her to a lawsuit, but she realized that in other ways she was walking a fine line.

After that, there was a distinct difference in Brown's tone. How long the effect would last was anybody's guess. It had become a regular routine to receive a weekly letter from him. Still up for another round, she drafted a scathing rebuttal and presented it to Attorney Crandall, expecting another green light.

Instead, he sighed. "This has got to end."

"But—"

"You don't understand, the bar seeks blatant thieves, active alcoholics, and drug abusers. They won't do anything with your complaint. It's a lawsuit!"

She shifted her weight on the red velvet seat. "You mean sue, or shut up?'"

"Right."

A close friend had once said, "Stay out of the hospital and the court, unless it's absolutely necessary." With that in mind, she reached out to Jim Cott, her longtime attorney friend.

Cott deftly steered her away from litigation. He advised a letter to Brown. "Say that as a beneficiary of the estate, you hold the trustee and her advisors responsible for the loss of principal and interest. Don't say what you're going to do, just say it."

Her sisters dug in their heels and continued to stonewall, not giving an inch to lower the property price. She updated Cott, expecting him to suggest another strategy.

"Oh, for crying out loud!" He groaned in dismay and frustration. "Walk away and one day you'll get a check in the mail. I hate to say this, but your sister is a . . . 'b.'"

"Excuse me. I didn't catch that."

"B as in bitch."

"Oh, yeah. I know." Hearing it from him was somehow consoling, as if the weight she'd carried for a long time was finally shared.

Cott went on, "If this were an estate worth millions, attorneys would be knocking at your door."

"You mean it's not worth going to court?" Linda's brow darkened with her thoughts.

"I wouldn't."

So that settled it. She'd have to find a way to cope with it and move on. The fight over money had demolished her family. It was as bad as Beirut.

A letter from the bar occupied the mailbox:

"Your most recent letter of complaint has been reviewed; however, we have closed the file on this matter."

Brown's letter lay under it:

"My clients agree to the recommended listing price as long as you don't use this against them in the future and agree not to take any action against them."

A step in the right direction, she thought, *but with the market sliding, even that price was probably optimistic.* She donned sneakers with racing stripes to get to a meeting that night.

Before the A.A. meeting started, Charlie, who seemed to sense her moods, approached.

"Hear from the snakes lately?" he asked.

Linda laughed at the reference. "Same ol' same ol'."

"You gotta stomp those snakes," he advised. "Don't let them get you down."

"I know," she replied dispiritedly.

His glance said he understood what she was going through. "Someday, this will all be over, Linda, and you'll have sunshine of the spirit again."

"I hope so, Charlie."

The meeting began, and they hurried to be seated.

Temporarily blinded because of an eye condition, Hank stood and shared how he had stayed sober for ninety days. His sight had returned, but the Department of Drivers Administration was giving him a hard time about his license.

"I got to A.A. because of a judge in a bathrobe, not a black robe—my girlfriend," Hank said sheepishly. "I come from a small town in Massachusetts. I was a school teacher," said Rick. "My sponsor told me that if I didn't change, my sobriety date would. You can always tell an alcoholic. You just can't tell him much. When I lost my sight and finally went to the doctor, I had to change my sobriety date because of a med. It said on the label to take as needed and I was needy all right, but it was because I liked how they made me feel."

The fading light of dusk permeated the room through a round window in the ceiling. The air conditioner hummed while Hank continued speaking to a hushed audience.

"One of the first things I learned when I joined A.A. was that there was a God and it wasn't me—that much was clear. I had made a monumental mess of my life. A.A. was the last house on the block and I went in willingly. I had nowhere else to go. I needed alcoholics the same as I needed alcohol. In the early days of my sobriety, I practiced steps one, nine, and twelve: I'm an alcoholic, I'm sorry, come follow me. It took me years to learn to do all the steps and to do them in order. I had to learn to be good for nothing—that is, do nice things for others without being paid, but it's worked so far. I'm still sober. Don't judge me by my past because I don't live there anymore." With that, he reclaimed his seat in the front row and crossed his legs at the knee.

With more than thirty years of sobriety, Willy spoke, "I heard in these rooms that anything you lose in life because of alcohol, you'll get back."

"I was really bad," said Riley, "and one day I finally called the cops on myself to lock me up . . . . One thing about self-pity—you know it's sincere." Laughter erupted from the group members.

"What makes my program so perfect is because it's so imperfect," Dick said. "I'm constantly working on my stuff. It's a work in progress. Eventually, it'll go upscale."

Next, Jack spoke. "I once asked what spirituality was because I honestly didn't know. I was a corporate executive in a large pharmaceutical firm, but I didn't know beans about God. One day, I was visiting my son in prison. I told him, 'Son, don't worry about anything. The only important thing is your relationship with God.' As soon as I said it, I realized the progress I had made."

A slim, young woman with rings hanging from her nose spoke up from the back of the room. "I went to the hospital, and the doctors told me I had three days to live. Here I am two and a half years later and this is my first meeting. I'm here because I want to learn how to live. I tried doing it on my own, but it wasn't much fun."

Linda slowly gathered her thoughts and spoke in a calm voice, which was a lot calmer than what she was feeling. "I started drinking at an early age. It probably started with a taste of wine at dinner, with the adults. By sixteen, I was drinking and dating. What a combination! I came home drunk one night and somehow got past my Mom, who was waiting up for me. The next morning, I was still drunk and dizzy. The family insisted on church. I can tell you that the car, the church, and the priest were all spinning. So what did I do? I stopped going to church."

There was a recent addition to the church story. She remembered how it went.

Father Matthew Karpinski, administrator of a local Catholic church, in his late forties with a charming personality, twinkling blue eyes and a warm, inviting smile, entered the main office. Only the heads of a receptionist and secretary who busily answered phones were visible over the counter. The priest greeted Linda and led her into a small reception room. He made himself comfortable in an overstuffed chair while Linda sat across from him on a sofa against the wall. A glass coffee table separated clergy and laity The door remained open.

"What can I do for you?" His tone was pleasant enough.

"I'm back." She was nervous.

Fr. Karpinski's blonde eyebrows crinkled like wrapping paper. "Back from what?"

"From being away from the church for f-f-forty years." Losing the battle with her emotions, tears streaked her cheeks.

The priest smiled. "Welcome back." He could see her struggle, a typical response from one who had abandoned the church and lived to regret it.

"The s-service for my mother was wonderful." She groped in her purse for a handkerchief.

"I'm glad to hear that. Father Howard handles the memorial services and he's really good at it."

She was nodding so dramatically she thought she'd pull a muscle. "I want to join. Sign me up—Oh, and I want to volunteer."

"Congratulations!" he beamed. "Welcome to St. Anthony's! We can always use a new volunteer." He excused himself for a moment and returned with a few forms for her to sign and a list of the various church ministries.

Chapter Twenty~Four

The metallic-hinged door of the mailbox bulged open, as Linda reached in and pulled out the usual junk mail, coupons and white envelopes. Brown's letter was unmistakable, seeming to shout, "I'm here!" Slowly, she walked back toward the garage where she had just parked her car, and inspected the house and yard, which looked exactly like the others on her street in the gated community. She slipped a finger into the back of the envelope to tear it open, her heart beating steadily, her pulse brisker.

"Without waiving any privileges, enclosed please find a copy of the appraisal of your mother's jewelry and the proposed disposition of the same. Cathy would like the charm bracelet, the emerald gold diamond ring and is willing to pay the appraised prices, at the time of the sale of the property. Mary wishes to keep the pearls since they cannot be sold as there is no market for them. Mary suggests that the wedding and engagement rings be sold but could be sold for less than the appraised value.

Let me know your thoughts regarding your mother's jewelry. Unless we hear from you within ten days, this is how the jewelry will be distributed.

All communications from you with our office must be in writing either by facsimile, or mail. Do not use e-mail, or telephone, as it will not be responded to."

Linda smiled because not once had she tried to contact him in any way but mail.

Brown had xeroxed the jewelry pieces in color. A small, gold ring fashioned out of the shape of a frog, with twin emerald eyes and a hole in its side, which her mother joked came from a tiny arrow, reminded her that she'd bought it for her mother as a birthday present. Now was her chance to get it back. An image of her father's wings from WWII caused her heart to swell. *The rings probably held the most value,* she thought. Her mother's engagement and wedding rings and an elaborate emerald and diamond-studded cocktail ring caught her attention, bringing back memories of her parents' former lives.

Everyone would want the rings, she thought.

What if she let her sisters have all her mother's jewelry? Just roll over and let them have everything? Wasn't that what they wanted? Would it solve anything? Just looking at the jewelry did something to her, brought back her father's favorite saying, "Nothing is more important than family."

Sitting at a desk, pulling out a pen and reviewing the inventory one more time, she circled the pierced-frog ring and her Dad's wings, put the copy into an envelope, and addressed it to Brown.

Later that night, she lingered in the guest room of her house. In the closet, she had hung a blouse and sweater that Ginny had once worn. She took the sweater off the hanger and draped the arms over her shoulders, as if her mother were embracing her. On the floor of the closet, Ginny's favorite plaid sneakers lay. Several sizes too big, she stumbled around in them and then took them off and replaced them in the closet. In her bedroom, she draped a Sterling silver necklace that Cathy had given her mother around her neck and noticed that it to be polished. With a little rubbing and special silver solution, the necklace gleamed, and she admired the way it looked on her. From her jewelry box, she took out a small, blue box which held a pair of eagles' wings that the local jeweler had made into a pendant and tried it on for a few minutes. In her office, down the hall again, she knelt on the floor and retrieved a file folder, brushing away the dust as she did so. Inside, there was a letter from her father and birthday cards from her mother. She thought, *This is all I need.* Yet the distribution of her mother's jewelry stirred her deeply.

Within a few days, Brown wrote: "I don't understand which pieces you want. Be more specific."

By now, however, she'd had a change of heart. "Please sell the jewelry and distribute the proceeds equally."

Attorney Brown was not content with her new request. "Pick something you like."

Frustrated and uncertain about what to do, she consulted Attorney Crandall.

"What do you want?" he asked her.

"I don't care."

"He wants you to pick something."

"There's really nothing of value," she said, "except the rings."

"Pick your mother's engagement and wedding ring."

"They'll never let me have that."

Crandall sighed and looked squarely at her. "How can I get you to see that's it's a step at a time. You make a request, then you wait for their response. Like chess."

"I know what they'll say."

"Say it's for sentimental reasons."

Brown response arrived a week later. "Your sisters don't want you to have your mother's engagement and wedding rings. They are the most valuable pieces. You can't have it all! Pick something else."

We will get nowhere with this. It was as if Brown was holding out a carrot only to jerk it away every time she came close. She wrote, "Sell the jewelry."

"Cathy wants a few pieces," Brown wrote. "Mary wants the engagement and wedding rings for sentimental reasons."

With me, it's greed. With Mary, it's sentiment.

Finally, Mary had the jewelry appraised. She wrote, "I'm going to give you the frog ring and some cash."

"Thank you, but I'd like to pass on the jewelry. Please send only a check."

Chapter Twenty-Five

Three years after Ginny passed.

Home sales had perked up slightly, but the median price was down almost twelve percent from a year earlier. The listing agreement on the rental house had expired and Vance Hodge, realtor, was trying to get signatures from the three sisters. He emailed the documents to Linda, forwarding a message he'd received from Mary.

"Linda has stopped everything. Cathy and I can't do anything. Our hands are tied."

My one vote is getting traction! My sisters need my signature. Who'd buy two thirds of a house?

Hodge sent another email. "Did you receive the listing agreement? My wife and I are eager to proceed."

"I'm willing to sign papers but not the release my sisters sent me. They're afraid I'll sue them."

Hodge hated listings when the family was at war. "I'm just a realtor, Linda. I just want to do my job."

"I hear you, Vance." She was thinking, *my sisters created this dilemma. They excluded me from the decision-making, made a poor investment and lost almost all of Mother's money. I'd like to wipe the slate clean, but we still must sell the rental house and settle the estate. Better keep a fire under their feet . . .*

More than a hundred members crowded into the Sunday evening A.A. meeting. For some, it was the end of the week, for others, the beginning—for all, another glorious day in sobriety. They were trudging the happy road of destiny together. The speaker for the night was Grace, a stunning young woman. Her husband sat in the back of the room, smiling at her as she began her lead, in a charming southern accent.

"When I first came in and you all said the Lord's Prayer, it was like nails on a chalkboard. I thought it was a cult and I wanted out. But it's not like that at all. The only thing I had to accept was that there was a power greater than myself. Eventually, I chose to call that power God. Before that light bulb moment, I couldn't control anything in my life and I couldn't stop drinking. But after I surrendered, my life got better."

At the conclusion, the group applauded. Then, one by one, the members stood to compliment her on her lead. The men spoke softly and courteously, their admiration of Grace evident.

A man in his late seventies, known as Dr. Henry because he liked to quote from medical books, thanked Grace and commented. "Every seven years it was houses, spouses, jobs, and zip codes. A shrink explained to me what I was doing. Rather than change myself, I just got remarried and went through the whole cycle all over again. When I finally quit drinking, things began to change. I haven't had the occasion to get a new house, remarry, change jobs, or move in almost twenty years. I'm afraid if I take a drink, I'll get it all back." An outburst of laughs filled the room.

Seated in the first row, Pierre pushed away from the table, making his chair squeak in protest, and stood facing Grace, his back to the audience. "It doesn't matter how many years of sobriety we have. We only have until midnight." Around the room, heads bobbed up and down. "Today, it's just another twenty-four hours . . . Wait a minute. It's June 21—the longest day! That's as bad as it gets." Loud, raucous laughter followed. "If I come to A.A. with a leg missing, there's someone with two legs missing and I feel better . . . That's how it works. You all think you're street smart, but I've got news for you—it's Sesame Street!" There was another round of laughter. "I also got a brother missing . . ." He paused for a second, while he searched the room as if looking for his brother. "I had to detach from him years ago when he wouldn't stop using."

Sitting in the back of the room by the coffee pot, Linda's head jerked. *Detached from his brother?*

As the meeting wound down, the leader asked for the traditional prayer and the members drew into a circle, hands clasped to each other. Later, the cleanup crew moved chairs and tables back to their original position in the rented church hall.

Pierre was pouring himself a cup of coffee. She asked him, "How did you detach from your brother?"

Pierre eyed her closely. "I made A.A. my family. I get my nourishment here."

"It's so hard for me to let go."

"Fill that empty hole here, honey. Get your hugs here!" She didn't know if he meant himself, or others. Her weight shifted, but she took no step forward to embrace him. He noted her hesitation. "Tell you what, let's you and me have coffee and talk."

"I'd like that." She handed him a card.

"You want my number?"

She pointed to the card in his hand. "My number's under the name."

"Right. Then you'll have my number and you can call me back."

She nodded at him. People were milling about and soon they were engulfed in conversations with others.

Pierre called early the next morning to arrange a meeting that same day, late in the afternoon.

They sat across from each other in a crowded restaurant, brightly decorated in yellow and green, a place where you could order anything anytime. A waitress came by with a stack of menus.

"I'm starved." Linda picked up a thick menu, pushing the others away. "I'm having dinner."

"I had a late lunch and am not very hungry. I'm gonna have a milk shake."

The waitress came by, took their orders, and scurried into the kitchen.

"Tell me about yourself, Pierre. Were you born here?"

"Born in France, my dear, and came here when I was twenty."

"What brought you here?"

"I was on the run from trouble."

"Oh." Linda looked down, not wanting to pry, but curious .

"Nothing serious. I organized some protest groups and the government didn't like me very much."

The waitress brought their orders and placed them gently on the table. The milkshake came in two large steel tumblers, which Pierre considered with misgivings.

"Why did I order this?" He spooned thick whipped cream off the top and placed it on a butter plate. "I'm trying to lose weight."

"Don't you like whipped cream?"

"Only in sex."

She chuckled lightly. "Are you flirting with me, Pierre?"

"I love to flirt! I do it all the time." He took a long slurp from the tumbler, not taking his eyes off her.

She smiled at him, wondering how far he took his flirting, and then speared a piece of fish with a fork. "Would you tell me more about how you detached from your brother?"

"Antoine is a multimillionaire. He's worth a hundred million, or so, but he drinks and uses cocaine. This is not the first time he's disappeared."

"Do you and he ever talk?"

"He was supposed to be best man at my wedding, but he never showed up."

"That must have hurt."

"It did, but my other brother filled in. I haven't spoken to Antoine since. I talk to my mother and other siblings. In fact, I got them to go to counseling."

"How did you do that?"

A moment of silence, Pierre's expression was inscrutable, as he read hers. "Linda, I'm famous in my country. I speak at international conferences."

Was he a revolutionary? . . . The people I meet in meetings. She shifted her legs and rearranged the napkin on her lap. "So . . . they came to you?"

"Yes." Pierre continued his story. "I had to sell a bistro that was in the family for one hundred years, in order to get sober myself. I knew that if I didn't sell it, the cycle of addiction would continue."

Leaning back against the booth, Linda took this in, wondering how much was true, and how much pure bullshit. "Sounds like you're financially independent."

"You could say that. I've been successful in my line of work, but my mother owns land that is worth millions. We had a buy offer for twenty-eight million, but Antoine resisted the sale. With the market crash, it's worth maybe ten million today."

"My situation is somewhat similar—same consequences, different numbers."

Pierre sensed an underlying torrent of emotion behind her otherwise bland words. "You gotta let it go, Linda."

"You don't understand. My sisters and myself are tenants-in-common on my mother's property. There are responsibilities. I hear from their attorney almost weekly. After three years, my mother's estate is still not settled. It may never settle. We couldn't even agree on the jewelry. They don't seem to understand that I want our welfare, not evil."

"Leave the money on the table."

"I'm not that financially independent."

"Get involved in A.A. You seem to me to be one of the floaters, not really in the heart of A.A. I meet with members all day. After our meeting, I'm going home to see my wife and then I have two more meetings. Get in the game, gal."

"Actually my sponsor tells me to deal with each incident as it comes up and then let it go. Unfortunately, it stirs up memories. Sometimes, I feel pressure from my deceased mother to reunite the family. Shortly before she passed, she told me her greatest wish was to have her three daughters together. I feel obliged, but don't know how to do it . . ."

"I have the same feelings." Pierre drained the second milkshake and set the tumbler on the table. "Do you have a boyfriend?"

"I'm seeing someone. "

"Good. You seem like someone with a healthy libido. Is he in the program?"

"He sure is." Linda smiled sweetly.

"Invite me to the wedding."

"No, not that."

"Why not? Don't you want to be married? I've been at the altar three times myself."

"Good for you. Me? Once was enough. I like my independence. Besides right now I'm too embattled in the feud, with my sisters."

"Forget your sisters!" Pierre's passion startled her and she put down her fork with its flaky fish hanging from it. "Life is good, Linda. You're not in the parking lot on your knees giving blow jobs to men. That's where alcoholism takes women. You've got a good life. Be thankful for what you have."

"I am, Pierre." She was beginning to understand the rule about pink booties with pink booties and blue booties with blue booties. Women were supposed to talk with women, men with men. She preferred sharing with women anyway.

"Pray for your sisters every day."

"I do, Pierre."

"Keep it up."

Chapter Twenty-Six

In addition to the recession, the country had to cope with summer's soaring heat index. One look at a newspaper map of the country showed mostly red, hot everywhere, and steamy in semitropical Florida. As part of her new life, Linda had been serving as usher at St. Anthony's.

Mass attendance was down, as most of the seasonal residents had migrated north. Too many ushers served too few people on Sunday morning.

Linda approached Fred, head usher of the morning nine o'clock Mass. "Is there another Mass, with fewer ushers?"

"We need ushers this afternoon, at five o'clock."

"I'll be there. Who's head usher?"

"Richie, but he's in the hospital in critical care. Doug and I have been filling in. They only get a couple hundred in attendance. Say . . . would you like to take the lead?"

"I wouldn't mind as long as someone is willing to train me. I don't know a thing about being head usher." She was pleased that he'd asked, proud to accept the position.

"Doug and I will train you, until you get a full crew."

The two men demonstrated how the head usher had to organize and coordinate during a short window of opportunity, the timing, as in a play, had to be perfect.

Fred stood at the open glass doors leading into the church. "Please sit in front." His thick arm shepherded the parishioners.

Doug and Linda followed his lead. It seemed this Mass was for sleepyheads, with most looking like they'd just awakened from a late afternoon nap. A few youths sat stiffly next to their parents. Several single adults tried to sit in shadowy pews in the back.

Linda caught up them. "Would you mind sitting down front?"

"Yes, I would, lady." The parishioner glared. "I like sitting here."

"I'm not moving."

Distressed by their comments, afraid she wasn't doing her job, Linda walked to where Fred was directing traffic.

"They don't like to sit with people." He glanced in their direction with a frown. "All you can do is ask them to sit down front. You can't force them."

When the presiding priest stood at the altar waiting for the gifts of unblessed hosts and wine, Fred remembered he'd forgotten to select a parishioner to deliver them and quickly recruited someone. Collection and Communion went smoothly, but when Father was blessing the congregation, Fred turned excitedly to his assistants.

"Who's doing the bulletins?"

Linda and Doug shrugged their shoulders, exchanging looks.

"I put them on the baptismal font last Sunday." Doug pointed to the font where they could see the bulletins stacked a foot high. "They take them as they exit."

"We'd better grab them and hand them out, or Father Matt will be unhappy."

For a month, the men trained her: recruited more ushers, introduced her as the new head usher, watched her progress, and helped whenever they could, until the operation seemed seamless.

"Good luck next Sunday." They exited the church.

Nervous and excited, Linda was looking forward to her first time, as head usher.

That is, until Fr. Matthew's personal assistant, Martha, called. Martha, with an affinity for numbers and a stiff, businesslike manner that sometimes grated on people, had risen meteorically to the top of the staff when the new priest had arrived.

"I've got good and bad news."

"What's up?" Linda asked.

"You're not head usher anymore. Father promised Amos. You can work for Amos or return to morning Mass."

"B-b-but Father was present when Fred promoted me! He even congratulated me! What happened?"

"I have to go. Call me back if you want."

Martha didn't respond to the call back. Crushed and humiliated, Linda put in a call to Fred.

"I didn't know I had to get his approval for my leads. This has never happened before."

Linda sighed deeply. "First time I was fired before I started."

"Don't you work for Brother Brian during the week?"

"Yes, I'm lector for a weekday mass."

"You better give him a heads up." Fred scratched his head, with a pointed nail.

"What do you mean?"

"What if Father Matthew removes you from *that* job? Brother Brian better be prepared."

Brother Brian and Linda had known each other through A.A. meetings, had worked together in the church and were on good terms. "If I were you, I'd make an appointment with Father Karpinski and iron out your differences."

Linda wasn't so sure she wanted to face the priest alone. "Will you come with me?"

"Fred should go."

Fred picked up the call on the first ring, but before Linda could get the words out of her mouth, he was ready. "It would be better if Brother Brian went. He's clergy and will pull more weight."

The calls went back and forth like ping-pong.

Brother Brian relented. "Okay, I'll go with you. I'm in Atlanta right now and will be back next week."

When Brother Brian returned from his trip, he got in contact with Linda. "I met with Father Matthew and Martha to discuss what happened. Father said he didn't like you asking people to sit down front."

"That's ridiculous! Those were Fred's instructions." She rubbed her temple with her hand. " Well . . . now there are two theories."

"What do you mean?"

"Am I bossy? Or is it that I declined to teach Sunday school?"

"What happened with Sunday school?" Brother Brian stretched out his legs, achy from traveling to relentless liturgical conferences.

"Once I expressed interest, but when I found out how much time and commitment it involved, I backed out and, apparently, Father didn't like that—not at all. He called night and day, trying to persuade me to change my mind and I got the feeling that it was not all right to say no to him. I didn't mean to infuriate him; it was just that I didn't think I could do it. Is he vindictive?"

"Oh, I don't know about that. Maybe you're over-reacting."

She wondered about that. The dismissal had taken her down. She'd been dumped by boyfriends, family members, but never by a priest.

Linda went to St. Anthony's for Mass. Fred, the head usher, was already seating people when she arrived. He spotted her and approached.

"How are you?" He kissed her on the cheek.

She replied, "Fine. You?"

"Good. You want to usher or are you visiting?"

"Visiting today."

Fred understood and nodded.

"Oh, Fred, one thing." Linda looked at him. "I just wanted you to know that I think Father Matthew treated you with disrespect."

Fred reacted strongly to her words. "Thank you. I think he did the same the way he treated you."

She took the last seat in the last pew and knelt. It was difficult to be here and not be ushering. Parishioners passing by greeted her warmly. One usher, Jason, came by, curiosity etched on his face.

"What're you doin' here? I thought you were promoted."

"Demoted. Father fired me." She let it go at that.

Jason looked away.

Maggie, another usher for this Mass, approached Linda. "What happened? You're supposed to be head usher at the 5 p.m. Mass. What are you doing here?"

Linda repeated what she'd said to Jason, but Maggie wanted more details. Father Matthew had rung the processional bell, and the altar boys were marching forward. "Thank you for asking. Maybe we can talk later . . ."

Father Matthew ascended the steps to the altar while Linda averted her eyes, turning pages of the missal. She listened to the priest deliver a homily about love and peace, enjoyed the religious music, which evoked feelings she hadn't felt for a long time. When the time came for the exchange of peace, a woman in the pew in front of her turned and shook hands. Linda nodded to others in distant pews, holding two fingers up in a peace sign. In the past, when she was ushering, she'd shaken a multitude of hands—one of her favorite moments because it made her feel close to everyone, as if she were part of a large family. Suddenly, from the corner of her eye she detected a presence. Fred extended the offering of peace to her, accompanied by the other six ushers.

David pulled her into a warm embrace. "No more nice church lady, eh?"

Rusty choked back laughter. "What volunteer gets fired? That's funny!"

Linda thought, *how kind of them.*

After Communion, Maggie approached Linda. "I'm furious! How can father preach love and peace from the pulpit after what he did to you? And I *know* you're not alone. As far as I'm concerned, a volunteer is a warm body—anyone with a head, two arms, and two legs." She added indignantly, "Who does he think he is that he can fire a volunteer?"

"I was wondering the same thing." The support of friends did much to soothe Linda's ruffled feelings. She asked herself, *Should I stay at St. Anthony's and face this priest or move on later?* There was the issue with her family, too. Stay and make it pay? She remembered the day she and her mother had had a serious talk.

"I always knew that my sisters would someday give me a problem with money, but I didn't know it would be like this. Mary's stolen half of your money, put herself in charge of the estate, and now is going after the rest of it. Cathy doesn't care. I've had it with them. I'm divorcing this family!"

Her mother had cried. "Don't say that! You know how much it hurts me to hear you say it."

Linda had looked at her mother with a sullen expression. "I can't be around them."

"You haven't been around for a while."

"I've been trying to stop drinking. If I stuck around with you and my sisters, I'll start again. The force of habit is too powerful and I'm too weak. I'm not trying to be hostile. I'm just trying to protect myself."

"You isolate yourself from us."

Linda realized she had done to her family what they were presently doing to her.

Chapter Twenty-Seven

A twelve-inch manila envelope from Brown lay poised in the mailbox. It contained a listing agreement and letter of instruction. The attorney had finally stopped pontificating about market trends and blaming her for the losses. Perhaps her complaints to the bar helped. Cathy had already signed the listing agreement and attached a purple sticker on the document.

"If you agree, Mary, send to Linda to sign and fax to realtor. Listing's up so we need new papers. Has Linda signed that release, so she won't sue us?"

Linda squinted at the handwriting, which resembled a medical prescription. Veterinary practice must keep Cathy busy, she thought. The listing price Cathy suggested was wishful thinking. Linda knew what homes were selling for—little had changed. Her sisters, like so many, wanted pre-recession prices, but the fundamentals for recovery weren't there yet. Not much was moving in their mother's estate either. Their mother had passed three years ago, and they still hadn't distributed the jewelry.

Linda drafted a letter to Mary. "Where's the money from the sale of Mother's jewelry? Please advise so we can proceed with other issues."

Brown had informed her months ago that the jewelry had been appraised and divided into three equal pools. She wondered if Mary was holding out, until she had the release, assuring her that she wouldn't be sued for defalcation. Linda was in no hurry to sign anything, until she had her share of the jewelry.

The postman delivered Attorney Brown's second letter in two days. Back to back aggravation. According to Brown, prices were less than what he had previously quoted. Linda wondered if the attorney had delegated the account to a paralegal. There were so many errors lately.

Cathy still wanted the charm bracelet and the emerald and gold diamond ring. He was aware that Linda wanted cash, which was what Mary also wanted. A mysterious cash offer for the bulk of it had appeared, no doubt from the rich veterinarian.

"The question is do you wish to sell the jewelry for this amount, or do you wish to hold out for a better offer?" Brown wrote.

Ignoring him, Linda sent a typed letter to Mary. "I know this is difficult but it seems we'll never agree on who gets what and I think it best to just sell the jewelry at fair market value. When I receive a check for my share, I'll deal with the revised listing agreement and the release."

She placed the letter in the mailbox and on the walk back into the house reflected on what had transpired to get her family to this cold, businesslike relationship. For a second, her thoughts traveled back to a time when they were just starting on their own. They had been somewhat close when their parents were alive, but each had her own path. Mary had a husband and children, Cathy, her books and animals, she, the world of finance. Decades had rolled by, until her mother's will had brought them toward each other again.

After years of conflict over her mother's will and being excluded from any decision-making, Linda, sitting on the listing documents useless without her signature, was pleased she was now directing the trustee and her advisors. The proverbial worm has turned, she thought. *My minority vote is changing the game.* She intended to steer her sisters to a more realistic listing price on the rental property, so they could sell it and get on with their lives.

In the meantime, she spent more time at church.

Seated in the center of the church, Linda knelt and prayed. Fred Martin, the head usher and his wife, Joan, waved to her, as they passed by. Father Matthew was on the altar, but his presence wasn't disturbing. Not this Mass. Nothing would disturb her peace this night.

At the Consecration, the priest paused, read the name on the paper before him, and looked over the congregation. "This Mass is being offered for Ginny Cray. May her soul rest in the peace of Christ and in the promise of the Resurrection."

Deeply engrossed in prayer, Linda thought her mother would appreciate the service, and maybe it would bring peace to the whole family, both living and dead. A thought came to mind, which amused her: The will of my Father in heaven *and* the will of my mother on earth.

Fred and Joan crossed the aisle after Mass to visit with her. Together, they walked through the narthex pausing at the fountain outside church and stood by the heavy, wooden doors which were part of a recent renovation.

"You going to the reception?" Fred wanted to know. "They'll have refreshments."

"It's for newcomers."

"Oh, c'mon, Linda. Join us."

"Nah, I think I'll pass. I'm not in the mood."

"Don't let the priest put you off, dear." Joan was almost convincing. "You belong with us. We want you to come."

"Thank you. Another time."

Her friends started to walk toward the heavy wooden doors. She turned to study the confirmation photos of the bishop and guests along the stone wall. The truth was she just didn't feel like a member of this church anymore, because of the conflict with the priest and had been searching the area for a replacement. She had come here out of good faith, not looking for a fight, but she felt played by him. His behavior provoked her to make a change even though she'd miss the friends she'd made. As she turned to exit, Father Matthew had pushed the heavy door open and was re-entering the church. They passed within inches of each other without a word.

The massive church soared above the two departing figures.

Chapter Twenty-Eight

Kent arrived well-dressed and polished for their date. As Linda greeted him, he handed her a *notice of intent to deliver* message that had been stuck to her front door. She read the name—Nestor Brown, Esq.

"What a surprise! I haven't heard from him for weeks."

"You want to run up to the post office?"

"Yes."

They arrived at the post office and Linda ran in to get Brown's letter. She found a check inside.

"I got money from the sale of mother's rings!" she said with elation.

"That's wonderful. Glad to hear it," he said.

"I'm thrilled that it came. Just delighted!" She laughed aloud. "It only took three years."

"How much did you get?"

"Enough to get a tooth fixed." She thought a moment about what her dentist had said. "I wonder how long it'll take to sell the rental property."

"From what you've told me about your sisters," he said frankly, "I wouldn't be surprised if it took years more." He added, "Hopefully while you're still alive to enjoy it."

She made a guttural sound. "Yeah, hopefully."

After they had dinner, she came home and looked at the lengthy letter expecting another hefty dose of Brown's legalese. She wasn't entirely willing, or ready to hear what the bastard had to say this time. He wrote:

"Without waiving any privileges and nothing in this letter waives any privileges, my clients have grown tired of this constant battering back and forth about this jewelry, especially Mary, who has numerous other matters to deal with and did not enjoy all of the uncompensated trips, gasoline, and time, she was having to spend to deal with this matter. Therefore, she has sold the disputed jewelry and here is your share. It is a shame you could not work things out with your sisters, without spending an inordinate amount of time. Do not send any further letters regarding this jewelry, this is the best price my client could get for the property in question, this ends this dispute."

Letters? Dispute? What the hell was he talking about? Mary had total control, never once asked for help, but it's my fault it took her three years to sell the jewelry. Linda clenched her fists, rolled her eyes. *Get off the cross, Mary, we need the wood!* She read the last line of Brown's treatise: "Also, if you have not already signed the updated listing agreement, please do so and return as soon as possible."

Linda looked at Brown's fancy stationery letterhead then reread his words. She thought, *Was there a shortage of periods and colons? His sentences are always long and confusing, probably to justify hourly charges. Who was paying for that—the estate?* Her fingers itched to write another letter of complaint to the bar, which she knew would be just as futile as the others. She wanted to tell her sister to call off her dog. She'd had enough of this attorney for a lifetime. Yet she knew it was Mary's way of using him to get at her. As for the listing agreement, she called the realtor, Vance Hodge.

"I'm so glad to hear from you," Hodge said. "What's going on?"

"That's a good question, Vance. Tell me—any new development in real estate these days? I know we recently talked about it, but has anything changed? I need some tidbit, please."

He cleared his throat. "Some say the prices have edged down a little more, but there's activity."

"So if we lower the selling price, we might get a buyer to bite."

"I would hope so. Your asking price may be too high. The house is small, with one bath . . . It's wood."

There was always *that* reminder.

"Vance, I'll try again to get them to come down. Thanks for the info."

"You're welcome. Say, why won't Mary return my emails or calls? I've been trying to reach her, but I haven't heard a thing. What's up?"

"I don't know that much because she refuses to speak with me, but she finally sold the estate jewelry and is probably exhausted from the effort. Talk to me, Vance. I'm here."

"I know. Take it easy."

With that, Linda fired off a new letter to Mary. "Thanks for the check from the sale of Mother's jewelry. Glad we got that accomplished! As for the rental house, we may have to lower the selling price."

She put the letter in the mailbox and waited.

Chapter Twenty-Nine

Passing through grief, Linda had felt alone and outgunned, scared and inexperienced, but right. Still, that solved nothing. She had traveled an emotional highway from shock and anger to acceptance and healing. Losing her family, her mother's estate and her inheritance were monumental weights on her mind, but litigation, a grueling lawsuit that would most likely cost her more than she'd gain, was not worth the time or trouble.

By detaching, letting go, being grateful, even content, with what remained, she could start on a new path, with a new direction. She knew her parents had wanted the family to stay together. No matter how often they stumbled, or stalled, they continued with a tenacity and faith that was the hallmark of everything they did and the people they were. We ran aground over the will, she thought, like the fools we are, failing to realize that it was never about power and money. It was a test and we failed. *Will we ever be able to extend kindness and love toward each other?* The thought, more like a prayer, made her yearn for something better and she realized that as her sisters became more hardened and more intractable, she attended more meetings. The words of the group participants blossomed in her mind like fields of tulips.

A.A. members convened for a discussion meeting.

A cardiologist named Omar spoke to the group casually arranged in a circle of chairs at a church hall. "The first sip takes the drinker to a state of mental and physical obsession that only a spiritual remedy can address. In the early 1970s, the American Board of Psychiatrists diagnosed alcoholism as a chronic mental illness. The Diagnostic and Statistical Manual III and IV listed it as a disease. Since then, the condition has progressed in its race against mankind to capture people from all walks of life, including medical professionals, such as myself. I just returned from a retreat with thousands of doctors of the International Doctors of A.A."

Omar had the attention of the group, his voice tone moderate and professional.

"When I first started coming to meetings, my brother-in-law asked me why I didn't just substitute Earl Grey tea." Laughs. "I have to admit the idea appealed to me, but it was a futile attempt to deter my disease. I used to pour Kahlua in my coffee, put on my white gown and stethoscope, and go to work at the hospital. As a doctor, I had more denial. In my group, we call it M-deity. Yet, when I finally admitted I had a problem, I came in with a firm conviction. I knew how to treat the symptoms, like inebriation, tremors, convulsions, bleeding, vomiting, but not the cause. I had to come to A.A. to treat the disease."

Linda's head perked up, as a movement beyond the window distracted her. She looked outside to see pine needles slipping past the clear pane and branches bending in a fierce wind. The sky was a light gray. A storm was brewing.

The storm roared outside, but the meeting continued with only a few glances outside. The rain was pelting the windows loudly. Just then, Kent entered the room and placed his wet umbrella against the door, as he searched for a seat. Linda and he exchanged discreet smiles from across the room.

"There was a man who came to meetings drunk," said Luke. "Nobody wanted to talk to him because he was always angry. He looked like he was going to smack you. Finally, someone realized that he was grieving the loss of his wife and took him to a cemetery. That helped him a lot. Mark."

Mark took the hint. "I think about the insanity of me ever taking that first drink," I've seen all types in these rooms—from Yale to jail. I just know that I can't drink no matter what." He was about to finish, but added more. "I once lived on a farm. It was easy to get guns there. You could open the front door and unload. You were either shooting or in a bar. To this day, I'm not allowed to own a firearm."

A voice piped up from behind him. "Reminds me of Mother's Day at my house."

"Sometimes, I think I'm nuts." Jeff had been in and out of the program, but had six days of sobriety. "I like to think that A.A. goes beyond the drink. After all, it was a symptom of my disease. A.A. has legs; it extends into my whole life. As to my relationship with God, I keep it simple. Today that means that I have to consider how I treat my body. In taking care of myself, I honor and respect God. That's where I'm at today."

Kent looked over to where Linda was sitting and winked. She winked back.

Eric took a turn. "I was certifiably nuts. In fact, I think there are some papers somewhere that say that . . . . Seriously, I was in a lockdown once. The people upstairs wore helmets and I don't think they were football players." Heightened laughter. "I had to act my way into right thinking. Who said that? I'd like to shake his hand. Anyway, here I am twenty-four years later, and I haven't been in a nuthouse since. I owe it all to A.A."

"I didn't think I was insane." This from a redhead named Celene. "I mean, I had a good paying job. Yet why did I leave my desk and guzzle gin in the bathroom? That should have told me something." Laughs. "You know, I just love the laughter in here. It's like the more sordid the stories, the more we laugh. I think it's healing for all of us—only the newcomers are surprised."

The meeting ended promptly at the hour and they filed out of the room in the gentle rain. Pine needles cushioned the tires of their cars, as the members exited the parking lot.

Kent stood by the car as Linda came out of the building. "Hi, baby."

"Hi, handsome!"

They embraced and Kent kissed her on the cheek. "Are you coming over tonight?"

Linda looked up at him, her face radiant. "I'll see you later."

Section Three

Chapter Thirty

The day after Christmas, disappointment and longing had set in, and the A.A. members, who determined not to go back to the life they had come from, forged ahead with tools of recovery.

Terry shared at the meeting. "I called my mother. She told me that she wanted to disown my brothers." Terry's eyes filled with tears. "I didn't know what to say. Hearing those words really made me sad."

Linda shifted in her seat. "The mall was packed with cars. There were people sitting outside Starbucks with star struck looks, because the place was closed. The movie theater was full. Everyone, including myself, was stuffing popcorn into their faces." Laughs. "For the last two weeks, I've been debating what to do about my estranged sisters. The priest told me to call them, but I didn't." Linda let the words sink in. "Instead, I had a nice day with a friend. That's all." She looked down the table where Candy was sitting.

As if on cue, Candy put down her coffee cup. "My grandson called me after so many years. His voice was deep. I missed hearing the change of his voice from that of a boy to a man. You know, I had a lot to learn sitting in these rooms. I have sisters and family here— *you.*" She glanced at them warmly.

"I feel love in church basements," Kate said. "There's a loving God in the rooms. We share weaknesses and that's what brings us together."

"This year I had Christmas in living color." Charlie shook a full head of blonde hair. "Last year, I woke up in a jail cell for a DUI."

"I didn't call my brother," Ana said. "He bullied me and held me hostage when I was a kid. He was disrespectful to the family. No, I didn't call him, but I prayed for him." She looked down the table and exchanged smiles with Linda. "We didn't have a *Leave it to Beaver* family."

From the end of the long table, Susan said, "I lost my house, husband, and car. I've been through four detoxes. I used to sleep with a bottle of Vodka." She sobbed. Terry passed the box of Kleenex. "I finally got a temporary job and I'm starting to make money. Everyone needs money." Her six-year-old daughter sat next to her and cried like her mother. "The judge said, 'I'm sick and tired of whining, sniveling alcoholics trying to get out of the consequences of their drinking. Yet this lady keeps trying so I'm not going to lock her up.' I'm grateful to him for that. I want to quit, but I won't. You all keep telling me to keep coming back and that's what I'm doing."

"I want to re-sister with Linda," Miriam said. She looked at Linda and smiled.

Linda met her smile, with one of her own.

"I've been thinking about how we can assist each other as we go along in life," Miriam continued, "If I can be a better sister with any of you, I can accept my biological sisters who were *never* there for me. I'm learning that it's okay to try, back away and come back when the issue softens or heals."

Helga, the elder of the group, spoke, "I'm seventy-three. My son sent me a nice letter and I appreciate his growth. He's getting over his addiction to drugs and alcohol. I'm unlearning the garbage I was taught and I'm accepting people as they are. There's more to life than being angry. We have women from Massachusetts, Texas, and Nova Scotia here in this room. Where else can you find such a cross section of people? Yet we all speak the same language— the language of the heart. We're all in the same boat. I have found peace within myself because of these rooms. I'm even grateful for the pain because it was a great teacher. I'll see you all next week, if God lets me wake up. The best gift this Christmas was my son's call. He's out of work, but he called me. That was progress."

After the meeting, Linda sought Helga and Eve, with more years in the program and with whom she'd spoken on numerous occasions.

The elder women listened with a penetrating stare as Linda explained the latest incident with her sisters. "I got a check yesterday from the sale of my mother's jewelry," she said to them.

"I would have walked away from the jewelry at the beginning," said Helga. "I would have let them have the money."

Linda grinned. "The money paid for a dental visit."

Eve commented with pursed lips . . . "Cold. That letter to you was cold. Mary's telling you that she doesn't want to reconcile." She cocked her head as if considering. "Is she one of us?"

"That's a good question, but, you know, it's not for me to say."

Eve nodded. "If she is, it could explain a lot. Listen," Eve touched her gently on the arm. "Don't let it get to you. There's not much you can do except pray." She winked at Linda. "Prayer can change anything—even your family."

Helga said, "I was the executor of my father's estate. Neither one of my sisters liked what I had to do, but I followed my father's instructions. It was all spelled out. My older sister thought she should have gotten more and argued with me. I was glad when it was over. It was a learning experience. First, I took care of my dad for the last year of his life. Now I do what's in *my* own best interest. It took years, but my sisters and I are on better terms."

"I really like what you say, Helga."

"You need to cut the tie. I did that with my daughter. After nine years, she came to me. We're together now. I know how hard she tries, and I have more tolerance for her." She looked at Linda and her heart went out to her. "I know how much you struggle."

"How do I cut the tie when I'm involved in business with them?"

"You do what's best for you, Linda. It'll work out in time." Helga had confidence. "It's in God's hands."

Eve added, "My sisters have challenged me my whole life. I've learned to meditate and pray about their troubles. They used to tear me apart with their woes. Now I detach from it all and stay peaceful. I couldn't help but notice how your sisters have challenged you."

"I get so riled up at times," Linda admitted.

"I know."

"I haven't learned to shake it off like water on a duck."

"You're working on it. You're young and active. You still have much to do, but you're learning a lot from your sisters."

"They've been great teachers." Linda said. "Right now I'm probably better off without them."

"You are. And, Linda," Helga encouraged, "try to be at peace with the way things are at the present time, if for nothing else but your sanity."

Chapter Thirty~One

A thick manila envelope from Brown arrived during the holidays. He couldn't have timed it better.

Knowing there'd be no warmth in it, Linda sat down at her desk and wrote to Mary: "In my last letter to you, I asked you to communicate directly with me. The realtor can send me any information regarding our property. Thank you and have a nice holiday."

She enclosed Brown's letter—unopened.

Later, curious about the letter's contents, Linda called the realtor and made an appointment with him.

At a table across from Hodge, in an office that was more like a small conference room, Linda played with a blue pen as she thought about the listing agreement signed by her sisters to sell the rental property. She looked at him, a handsome, strapping guy, with a full head of linen white hair. "Nice tan."

"It's more like a windburn." He ran meaty fingers through his hair. "I rode my motorcycle to Key West, with five guys."

"Long trip." Linda smiled at him. Paunchy, middle-aged men like him liked to ride revved-up motorcycles.

"We camped out and I only got a few minutes sleep."

Linda's eyes twinkled with humor. "My idea of camping out is a Holiday Inn."

Hodge laughed.

"You must be tired," she added. "Thanks for coming in to meet me."

"No problem. I just got off the phone with Mary. She said Attorney Brown mailed you the listing agreement and you sent it back. She sounded very upset." Hodge continued, "She said she was so upset that she couldn't show me the house. She was practically in tears because her attorney is out of town."

"Vance," Linda said in a tone that indicated she was losing patience, "I asked her to communicate with me directly. I'm done with her attorney. Stick-me-with-a-fork-done."

His face registered sadness. "She won't speak with you."

"That's her choice." She met his look with a neutral face.

A familiar plea, she thought. "Vance, you need to understand something . . ."

Hodge braced himself for what was coming.

Linda said, "I grew up with this woman. I've seen her go from calm to hysteria, in seconds, to get her way. When she tries to manipulate you like that, just say, 'I'm sorry you're upset.' Then, be firm and give her the facts."

The wily realtor tried the same logic on her. "I'm sorry you have to be in this situation. I'm the executor of my family and I understand what you're going through." He paused, as if debating which side of the fence he wanted to be on. "Mary said she wanted to get as much as she could for the house."

"Of course she does." Linda leaned her head back on the chair as if taking a moment to reflect. "Vance, from now on, would you please send me any paperwork regarding the rental?"

He looked at her. "May I ask *why* you want to do it this way? I mean Mary said she'd get the paperwork."

"I want to hear from you, the realtor." She wanted to add, *The hell with Brown.*

As if reading her thoughts, Hodge said, "I can't say anything, but—*who does Brown think he is?* He told your sister that it was too soon to sell. I'm the one who's in the field! I know better than him what's going on . . ."

"He's got the worst batting average I've ever seen."

"I'm with you, Linda."

She felt a sense of victory, though a small one at that.

Then, she added, "This tenancy of three embattled sisters needs to end. It's a losing proposition. What's the best price to sell?"

Hodge hesitated then said, "It'll go for $145,000."

"Then, why don't we price it there." She was sick about it. From the beginning, it was such a pitiful loss.

"You know, my wife, who's my partner, was mad at me about this listing agreement. She said, 'Why the *hell* did you let Mary sign at such a high figure?' He frowned as if to show his remorse. "To tell you the truth, I don't know why I did that."

She thought, *Damn real estate agents. Are any of them competent, or have courage to stand up to my sister?*

Hodge took a breath and gathered his courage. With an uncanny ability to leap from one side of the fence to the other, he spoke in a deep, authoritative voice, "I recommend you list it at $160,000."

Linda sighed. "All right. Your price is more realistic. Give me a pen. I'll sign the papers *right now . . .*" She raised her eyes to him. "Can we do that?"

"*Sure we can.*" Hodge quickly made a copy, crossed out the higher figure, and wrote the new number. "That's ten thousand less than the current selling price. Mary won't like the lower figure." He bit his lip. "She'll have my head."

Linda looked at the figure and went with what he'd written. "She already lost most of it. Oh, but we have her illustrious attorney to thank for that."

He watched as she signed her initials next to the new figure. "Why does she need an attorney to price the property anyway?" When she put the pen down, he added, "From what I've observed, she leans on him for everything."

Linda rolled her eyes. "I know."

Another matter pressed on her mind. "Talk to me about sales proceeds. Let's say we sell the property. Who disburses the funds?"

"The title company is responsible. I don't know if they can issue three checks. I once had a husband and wife who held the property jointly try to get them to make out two checks. They wouldn't do it."

She considered his concern and dismissed it. "Probably because they wanted the title company to go beyond what the title said. In this case, it's an outright tenancy in common held by three owners." She thought, *Doesn't he know this stuff?*

Vance looked at her with a serious expression. He knew she had been in finances and imagined she knew what she was talking about. "The buyer usually selects the title company. That's the way it's done in this county. You sure don't want Brown to get his hands on the check. Somebody might abscond with the money."

The conversation upset her and she was suddenly eager to leave. "Well, I've done my part." She stood up.

"Happy New Year!" Vance grinned.

"Same to you. Careful with that motorcycle." She added, "Say, I've never seen the inside of the rental property. Will you show me?"

He seemed surprised. "Of course. How about next week?"

Chapter Thirty~Two

Looking like he'd just dismounted from a horse, Vance Hodge leaned against a fence post in blue jeans and a white T-shirt, as he waited for his client at the rental property. His thick mat of white hair ruffled in the breeze above a cell phone pressed against his ear. He waved at Linda with his free hand as she slowly drove by and watched her park along the side of the street.

Linda exited her car and glanced at the wooden house that had swallowed her mother's entire life savings and which her mother had probably never seen—a wooden shack, with an abandoned garden and waterless pond in the front yard. Hodge held open a wooden gate that led to the front entrance and she followed him into the house. Boxes and crates littered the front room, which served as a living room.

"The tenants have moved in," he announced with a flourish of his arm.

"They didn't waste any time." Her head turned left and right as she took it all in.

Hodge noticed her keen interest. "Here, let me give you a guided tour." He led the way into a narrow kitchen the size of a closet.

Linda stopped to stare at the back yard. There was a lanai, in the traditional Floridian fashion, also made of wood. A wooden fence surrounded the large backyard. She let out an audible sigh. *We get termites and we're done for.*

Hodge walked down an abbreviated hallway barely wide enough for his girth. "Two bedrooms, same size."

A miniature dollhouse, she thought, suddenly feeling like fleeing. She retraced her steps to the living room and swirled around to meet his curious stare. "From three hundred thousand dollars sitting safely in a bank to *this*. My name was on that money!" She him a look of disdain. "From hard cold cash to a shack worth less than half."

"I feel your pain." the realtor lowered his head.

"What's worse," Linda said, "is that it was done without my authorization and against my will. My sisters seized control of my mother's estate and excluded me from any discussion. They and their crooked attorney are responsible for this *mess*."

"I'm really sorry—"

Linda cut him off. " . . . And the law allows this travesty. Totally allows it."

"I know how hard this has been for you and your family."

"That attorney drove a stake into the heart of my family and destroyed us."

He shook his head in sympathy. "I'm executor of my father's estate. Already my siblings are giving me a hard time."

"Executor means fiduciary. You act on behalf of and for the benefit of the beneficiaries. You protect the beneficiaries and the assets."

"My brother thinks I'm lying about the assets."

"Vance, as long as you include everyone, answer their questions, and are open and honest with them, unlike my sisters, you should have no trouble. It's when you start hiding information and shutting off communication and acting secretive that you're in trouble. But don't worry, hardly anyone gets it right. That's why we need independent executors."

Hodge nodded. "I told Mary that I understand how hard it is for your family."

"Hard because she won't speak to me."

He hesitated for only a second. "She thinks you're evil."

"I've been called worse."

Hodge laughed.

She wondered which of her words he was ferrying to her sisters. He had made himself their middleman, since the sisters were not speaking to each other. "So where do I sign?"

The realtor instantly produced the listing agreement. He laid it on a wood frame bar sitting on the front porch. Linda hadn't noticed the bar before and considered it strange to erect a bar on the front porch. She had always done her drinking in the house, or on a back porch. She looked across the street. *Just how friendly were the neighbors?*

Hodge pulled out a ballpoint pen and held it out to her. "Just sign under your sisters' names."

Linda looked at the bottom of the page where it read seller.

"Yes, please initial there." He seemed upset. "Oh, darn, your sisters forgot to sign this line, but don't worry, I'll get their initials."

Linda wrote, but the pen was out of ink. She shook it and tried again. "Your pen's out of gas."

"Here . . ." He dug into his pocket for another pen.

She looked at him with growing impatience, as he fumbled through one pocket, then the other. *What realtor doesn't come with a decent pen?* She knew they were all eager to sell the property. Her sisters had been afraid she'd sue them. The realtor wanted his listing. Now finally they'd agreed on a realistic selling price and perhaps they could move forward . . . if he could only find a pen.

He produced a cheap plastic pen. "Try this one."

Linda made a mark on the side of the document and smiled as the ink flowed. He, looking sheepish, watched as Linda flipped the pages like a pro and signed in all the appropriate places. When she finished, she handed him his pen. They exchanged smiles, then hurried to their respective vehicles.

"Sell this house, Vance!" Linda shouted over her shoulder.

Vance shouted back in a rich baritone. "Don't worry. I will!"

Linda made a U-turn and headed home, shaken by the whole experience and feeling resentful toward her sisters. The flop of the economy wasn't their fault. It was just too bad they didn't leave the money where it was. *Fat chance of unloading the dump anytime soon.* The economy was prostrate, on life support; employment was in the emergency room awaiting a blood transfusion. The real estate market was no longer moribund, but the hot deals came only from scavengers, such as the ones she imagined were prowling the rental property.

A few days later, Linda was shopping for new shoes.

"I can hold them for you for two days." The shoe saleswoman placed a pair of blue sandals in a box and reached for a lid.

"That'll be great. I should know by then which color goes best." Linda glanced at her cell and saw an email from Mary Lou Wolf. *Why would my cousin send me an email with her own name on the subject line?* She opened the message, the tone of it rose to a shriek. "Some of you may have heard that my Mom passed away. Dr. Clyde said she had a massive heart attack and felt no pain. The viewing will be at—"

Not reading the rest of the email, Linda sat down on a bench in the middle of the shoe salon and stared at the screen. Mary Lou was almost her age. Linda unfurled a *Kleenex* with a snap of her wrist and looked up to see the saleswoman smiling at her from behind the cash register. Confused and disoriented, Linda blew her nose and exited the store to sit on a bench in the sun, where she read the rest. Mary Lou's daughter, Marlene, had left a number and Linda dialed it without hesitation.

"Hi, Marlene—" Linda's voice squeaked.

"Hello," the young second cousin replied calmly, as if rehearsed.

"This is . . . Linda."

"Oh, I'm so glad you called. Aunt Jane has been trying to reach you. She called you all day but couldn't get through. What's your number?"

Linda gave it to her.

Marlene continued, "I found Mom lying on the floor between the sofa and the coffee table. She often slept on the sofa when her back hurt. At first, I thought she was sleeping, but when I rolled her over, I started to scream because I knew she was gone. Dad came running."

"I didn't know she had a bad heart." Linda's voice was sounding more like the one she recognized as her own.

"Neither did we."

"Such a shock!"

"Tell me about it!"

"I'm going to see about flights," Linda said. "It's too late today to do anything, but I'll see if I can get a flight for Saturday and be there Sunday for the funeral. I'll do what I can, but the tough part is that drive from the airport." May Lou had lived in a remote part of northern New Jersey. "It's a long way and I'm not a great driver." She thought of what else she needed. "Did she have a favorite flower?"

"Daisies."

"Of course, the hardest flower to find in the winter."

Marlene laughed. "I know. Also, nothing pink. My Mom detested pink."

"Probably because she wore it all the time when she was younger."

"I guess so."

Linda drove straight to a florist.

Sandwiched between a dance hall and a wellness center, poster ads filled the windows of a small floral shop. "May I help you?" The sales woman's name tag read Anne.

"Yes, Anne, how are you today?" Politeness out of the way, she said, "I'd like to order flowers for a funeral. Daisies—in any color but *pink*."

Anne searched through some books strewn on the counter. Meanwhile, Linda scanned the posters on the walls and found a bouquet with white daisies. "How about that one?"

"That's small. You'll want to send something in the hundred dollar range or it won't be noticed."

"That's the one I want to send. It has white daisies, just like she would have liked."

Anne picked up a pen and wrote. "Do you have the address?"

Linda handed Anne her cell and pushed the screen to illuminate the message. "It's all here. Take what you need—phone, address, church, etc."

Anne copied information on a piece of paper while Linda roamed the store. When everything was settled, she paid for the flowers, thanked her, and left. At home, she realized she'd left her cell phone, her only contact with the outside world, on the counter at the florist's. She panicked. What a time to be without a phone!

A quick trip back to the florist yielded—nothing. The door was locked, the lights were off, and Anne was gone. She rubbed the glass window with her shirt and peered through the window, spotting her black cell on the counter cuddled comfortably next to the black computer mouse. She leaned closer, muttering to herself.

A sheriff's deputy sauntered by the store. "See something unusual?"

"Oh, hello, officer. I left my cell phone in the store. It's lying on the counter. See it . . . " She pointed to it.

"It's late Friday afternoon. They've closed for the weekend. You'll have to wait until Monday to retrieve it."

"Isn't there any way to call the owner? I'm going to a funeral out of state and I need to be in contact with my family."

The officer smirked. "Monday." He made a motion with his hand, as if to dismiss her.

Are all cops as compassionate as you? She wanted to say but didn't. Instead, she raced home and got busy on the computer. Flights weren't that expensive, but the problem was arriving at the mountain resort town late at night. Mass and viewing were scheduled for early Sunday. *I want to be there, but I don't know if I can make it.* She doubted that Mary, who lived in Florida, would go, but she wondered about her other sister, who lived closer to New Jersey. *Will Cathy be there? Would there be a confrontation?* It had been years since they'd spoken. *What about the rest of the family? Was anyone else on speaking terms? What kind of a reception would there be? Awkward, awkward.* Linda had a sinking feeling in the pit of her stomach.

She thought of Mary Lou. Though they had been close during childhood, often staying overnight at each other's homes, they hadn't been close for the last forty years. Linda had visited her mother several times before she died, and the cousins had talked lightly about getting together during the summer, but no plan had been made. And now her cousin was gone.

The decision was finally made for her, because no flights were available.

Grief and isolation from those she loved and cared for plagued her during the weekend. A neighbor lent her his phone, so she could retrieve voicemails. She made several trips to Verizon. Thinking about the funeral service and picturing white daisies on the altar,

Linda sought the advice of Father Howard Cookson, after Mass on Monday. He had removed the chasuble and was standing in his alb when she entered the backroom. The Sacristan and Eucharistic Minister were chatting by the sink, as they washed and dried the chalice and ciborium.

"Years of avoiding my family, and now, when I want to communicate with them, I can't. I don't have my cell phone," she lamented.

Seeing the state she was in, Father Cookson asked, "You want to go to the laundry room? It's quiet in there." They walked down the hallway and stepped into the laundry room where the scent of disinfectant was thick. "Let's go to the confessional." Father Cookson closed the laundry room door and led the way.

"It's not a confession, but it could be," Linda said, still confused and disoriented.

They sat down on two chairs facing each other, in the cramped space. Linda told him about the funeral.

"Still trouble with the sisters?" Father Cookson knew about her estranged family.

"My sisters blackballed me to the rest of the family. I expect to meet hostility."

"Why spend the money and go to the effort to be mistreated?" He'd summed up her thoughts exactly. Now she didn't feel so badly about not having gone to the funeral. "Let me tell you about my family. It's similar. My sister married this man I used to call Beelzebub. He used to beat her and throw her against the walls of the house. He threw things at me when I went to visit. My poor sister put up with him. He threw me out when I attempted to visit them. When my sister died, I traveled a long way to say the funeral Mass, but they wouldn't let me. I petitioned with the Monsignor and he told me I could say the Communion prayer. I told him he could take the prayer and wipe himself with it." Father Cookson's face hardened. "I left without even attending the Mass for my sister . . . That's how it went in my family."

"I shouldn't feel guilty about not going?"

He shook his head. "I wouldn't give it a second thought. You did the right thing. When you get close and really look at a person, you see a lot of things that are disagreeable. It's better, sometimes, to stay away and maintain peace."

She thought, *Priests usually speak about love and forgiveness, but this one tells it like it is,* which was why she liked him and sought his counsel.

The lights at the florist shop were on Monday morning and the saleswoman, coincidentally, was just opening the front door. "I tried to call you to tell you I ordered the flowers."

"Thanks. Oh, Anne, I left my cell phone here." Linda glanced at it lying on the counter. She took a few hurried steps, picked it up, and hugged it close to her heart. "I can't even begin to tell you how happy I am to have it back." She activated the screen, which indicated twenty-five unopened voicemails.

"Why didn't you Google me? I would have come to the shop."

Linda's head jerked back. "In all the excitement, I never thought of that."

Anne shook her head. "Well, at least the flowers went out. That's one less worry."

Smiling, Linda was walking toward the door when the phone rang.

"Linda, don't leave just yet," Anne said as she listened to the voice. "It's for you." She raised her eyebrows. "The New Jersey florist." She handed the phone to her customer.

"I'm sorry," the florist said, "but we were not able to get the flowers there on time. Do you want to send them to the house?"

Muffling a curse, Linda shook her head. "You know, I guess it was just not meant to be."

"Would you like to send a plant?" Anne eagerly reached for a book of samples. "Here's some pretty green foliage that will last all year long."

"Not bad." Linda slipped her finger under the page. "Let's see what else you have."

They bent their heads over the book.

Later that morning, she listened to her messages and—lo and behold!—her cousin, Jane, had left a friendly, open voicemail inviting her to call and chat about Mary Lou and what had happened.

Jane was reaching back to her.

A feeling like standing on a ledge overlooking the Blue Ridge

Mountains along the Appalachian Trail passed through Linda. She thought, *Perhaps my cousin and I might reconcile, start anew, and become friends.* Later, they might reunite as an extended family separated by events that had taken them far apart. Hope and longing linked her thoughts.

Later that night, the cousins spoke.

"I had the wrong number," Jane said. "Which is why I didn't call sooner. Marlene gave me this one."

"I'm glad you called. Your mother had problems with my number, too."

"Well, that explains it!" Jane laughed lightly. "I got the number from her."

Linda laughed.

"I was thinking, it would be nice if we could visit. Why don't you come up this summer?" Jane asked.

"I'd like that." Her cousin seemed open to friendship. There were parallels in their lives; Jane had lost both parents and a sister; Linda had lost parents and, in a sense, sisters.

The fourth Thursday of the month, the A.A. members celebrated anniversaries, by distributing plastic medallions, or chips. Casey, leader of the meeting, sat at the head of a makeshift desk, a table turned sideways to the group. A rather large attendance confounded their usual circle of chairs.

As Linda entered the room, she saw that many seats were already taken. A second row had been placed behind the inner circle. She stepped over the shoes of Judge Heike and Eileen and took a seat, thinking she could sneak into the meeting, get her anniversary chip without fanfare, and dash out. Sometimes she liked to do it that way, due to an occasional shy streak, but Casey had other plans.

"Let's have those celebrating anniversaries speak first, okay?" Without waiting for approval, he announced, "Willy is celebrating thirty-two years." Willy was seated next to Casey. "We also have Carla who has one year." A spontaneous round of applause erupted, and Casey had to wait until it subsided.

"Anyone else?"

Proudly, Linda raised her hand. Casey nodded. "All right, Linda! "How many?"

"Thirteen."

"Wonderful! All right, then, we have three. Who'll talk first." He motioned to Carla to start. "Come right on up here next to me."

Carla stood in front of the table where Casey sat. "I didn't think I had a problem with alcohol, until one night when I had a few too many. I was walking through my dining room to the kitchen to refill my glass when my feet went out from under me. I crashed into the wall with my head and shoulders and fell in a heap near the table. I had injured myself, but got up and went out dancing anyway. That's how crazy drunk I was. After that, I came here and admitted I had a problem."

Casey commented, "I remember when Carla showed up for her first meeting with a cast on her arm."

"My arm and I started to heal at the same time."

"Thanks, Carla. Now let's hear from Linda."

"I didn't realize we were doing it this way. I haven't prepared anything." Linda looked around the room. "There's so many here today." She coughed, nervously. "I'm a little rusty so bear with me." She removed her vest to accommodate a hot flash. "I'm getting ready for a long speech," she joked and the members laughed lightly. "All my near fatal accidents came *after* I got sober. I got here sort of like sliding into home plate. I had arrived at a moment when I could no longer deny I had a problem. I said I would drink only when I was upset, or happy. Then, I noticed that I was drinking every day. The day I hit bottom, I was alone in my house, drunk, and sick."

Mark turned clear around in his seat in front of her and stared, the coffee in his cup sloshing. Linda glanced at him, thinking that maybe he'd had a similar bottom.

"My first meeting was seven years prior to that incident, when I'd stumbled into a room I thought was Al-Anon but which turned out to be A.A." She laughed. "We all know there are no coincidences." Light laughter. "I came to my second meeting completely mortified, licked. I was hoping I'd manage my drinking, having no intention of quitting for life.

After that second meeting, I felt better. I felt warmth, safety, kinship. Actually, it was you . . .You got to me by your words and actions—all of you, each of you, in your own way. Yes, it's because of you that I stayed. Or, rather, I felt God's presence through you."

As she was speaking, several more turned toward her and she realized that she was getting a good response. She'd connected with them, or they'd connected with her. Encouraged, she opened up a little more. "Three cousins are currently speaking to me—one on my mother's side, two on my father's. There was a time when no one spoke to me and I was too self-absorbed to notice. One of my cousins, one with whom I'd spent a lot of time in my youth, passed away last week. I was invited to the funeral. In the past, I was actually asked not to attend family functions . . . That pain may have been necessary for my spiritual development even though I didn't think so at the time."

She paused as she saw yet another head strain towards her. Never had she drawn so much attention, she thought. Usually the members yawned when she spoke. "Some of you know that my sisters haven't spoken to me in years, because of a dispute over my mother's will. Yet, I've heard others speak of similar problems that were eventually resolved and so today I have hope for the future. Thank you." Gracefully, she sat down and breathed in deeply.

"Thank you, Linda," said Casey. "One more — Willy," the chairperson beckoned.

Setting a band around his watch to time himself, Willy announced, "I'm going to speak for seven minutes and no more." The members laughed and were eager to hear from their star, with the longest sobriety. Everyone knew how much service Willy gave to A.A. He was always sponsoring someone and going to great lengths to be of service.

"My sister is also a pain in the chockaloosa. She always has been since I can remember. She used to stick a straight pin in my buttocks when she changed my diaper. I can still feel it at times." Laughs. "She's a pain even today. She's not with us yet, but I pray for her." Willy congratulated the other celebrants and talked about the joys of sobriety. "My sponsor told me to avoid my uncle. He said, 'Stay away from him.' That was the best advice he could have given me. It's been thirty-two years since I broke a bone in my hand from banging it on the table to be heard. This program is the best thing I've ever done." He looked at Casey. "Have I gone on too long? I saw you look at your watch."

"No, no," Casey assured him.

"I've got thirty seconds left."

"Take all you want." Casey smiled broadly, going along with the kidding.

"Get ready, then, I'm just gearing up." There were worried expressions. "Naw, I'm just kidding." He said a few more words and then quieted.

"Okay. Now we'll open the meeting to general sharing. We still have a few minutes."

"What I like about A.A. is that we speak the same language. No matter where I go it's the same. We are different, but we understand each other," Nate said. "I am so far away where I live that they don't even recognize me as a Canadian in my own country. But here, it's always the same."

"I had three weeks of anger management with my grandchildren." Mild-mannered Chris B., nicknamed Crispy, as in always fresh, never soggy, spoke. "Their cat, Harley Davidson, was as needy and cloying as they, but I managed to escape his claws and pet him. Thank God for this program. Otherwise, I couldn't have done it. I'm happy to be back and I'm glad to report that my family's still speaking to me."

How fortunate for him, Linda thought. She wondered how she could improve her situation. *Jane, Marlene, and Tom are speaking to me. Who's next?*

Carla caught up to her in the parking lot. "I've been meaning to talk to you."

"Go ahead." Linda laid her purse and an umbrella on the trunk of her car. "I've got a few minutes."

"I heard you talking about your sisters the other day. My brother did the same thing to me."

"Do tell." Linda ran a hand through her short hair and waited.

Carla nodded. "My mother had four million and she named my older brother executor. I went to the house a few weeks after she died and found the house cleared out. My brother had taken all the furniture. He gave my younger brother a million and I got a couple hundred thousand. He kept the rest for himself and his children."

"Is that what your mother intended?"

"No. She wanted us to share it equally, like yours. I've since forgiven my brother and we speak. That was after a number of years. He did something wrong and he wouldn't speak to me; he was insulted that I called him on it."

Linda laughed. "That sounds familiar."

"I asked him why he did it." Carla folded her arms across her chest and let her weight settle on one leg, which pushed her hip slightly to one side. "You know what he said?"

Linda shook her head.

"He said, 'Because I could.'"

"There oughta be a law." Linda blew a puff of air between her lips. "Maybe have an objective guardian execute the will. I don't know what the solution is, but I've been thinking about this for a long time. So many families break up over wills and stay broken for years. It's a disgrace."

Chapter Thirty-Three

Two months later.

Vance Hodge hunched over a round table next to Linda in a conference room the realtors used. His private office was in such a state, he preferred not to use it. Vance pushed a sheaf of documents toward her. As the papers fanned out, she looked at them and then at him.

"Sign each one on the bottom line." Vance indicated where he'd placed a red "X."

Linda inhaled, took another look at the papers, and glared at him. "Not so fast, Vance." The realtor squirmed.

"Didn't I already sign the listing agreement?" She asked.

Vance looked at her over tortoise-rimmed reading glasses. His gray hair seemed thicker and Linda thought, *Maybe motorcycle riding had fluffed it.*

"You may have." He rifled through the pages seeing that the three sisters had signed their initials, until he came to the last page. "Here it is. Yes, you did sign it, but your sisters didn't."

"I thought you were going to get their signatures."

"I forgot." Vance seemed more than a little vexed.

"Talk to me, Vance. What's going on?"

He looked at her. "You know, I'm thinking about how to handle this whole situation. I know you and your sisters are at odds." He paused for what seemed an eternity. "I'm going to play straight with you." He hesitated, uncertain how she'd take what he was going to say. "Mary called me and asked me to manage the property. She got her own tenant, a co-worker, but she wanted a buffer between her friend and herself as the landlady."

"*One* of the landladies." Having made her point, Linda sat back and met his eyes. She reminded him, "She's not the only voice here.

I am, after all, an owner—one of three tenants-in-common." The sisters hadn't spoken to her in years. Their only link at this point was the realtor and it was a weak one at that.

"Right." Vance ran a hand through his hair several times as if trying to smooth it down.

"So now you're also our property manager." *Another fee.*

"Yes." Sweating, he appeared nonplussed. There was another paper which he needed her to sign—a renewal listing agreement, so he could keep his job. He pulled it out from its hiding place and put it on top of the pile of papers. He put the other paper which she had already signed at the bottom. "I asked Mary where she wanted me to deposit the rent and she said she was getting a bank account. She told me to start next month as property manager, but she insists on making deposits herself. I don't know why she won't let me handle that."

"She has to be in charge and doesn't trust you." Linda shifted her weight, stretched her neck, which was getting stiff. "How much rent?"

"Six hundred."

"Geez." Linda bit her lip. "We were getting a thousand a few years ago."

"I know. That's what's happened to the market."

Linda quickly calculated insurance and taxes, her face showing dismay. "We're going to be short."

The realtor's expression showed concern.

"How's it showing?" she asked. "Has *anyone* looked at it?"

This was the part he dreaded. With the current market, the news was hardly shining. "It's been shown a couple of times." He saw Linda's eyes widen and rushed to add, but in a tone that indicated he didn't believe it either, "Maybe more than that."

"What are the comments?"

Vance put his hand to his mouth and coughed. "My wife is the one who has the answer to that."

Linda tapped the pen on the table. "Well—what does she say *they* say? Play it straight, Vance."

He blushed. "Small. That's what they say."

No kidding—and made of wood, not the best Florida house frame. "What's your take as property manager?"

Vance thumbed the sheets of the agreement, which he'd just buried. "Forty percent."

Linda thought sarcastically, *There's a bargain.*

"No, wait. It's thirty . . . thirty percent."

Even more of a bargain! Linda looked down at the pen in her hand poised over the signature line. She turned her head to him. "Look, Vance, I've nothing against your managing the property, but is it necessary? I mean, it's only one property. What about me? I'm available. I could collect the rent and deposit it."

Vance looked sideways at her. "Your sisters would never allow it." Attempting to be more diplomatic, he added. "Besides, then you'd have to put up with the tenant and evict her, if she didn't pay. There's more paperwork with a rental than there is with selling the place." He watched closely for a reaction.

"So you want me to make this easy for everyone. Just shut up and sign the paper, right?"

He bit his lip and looked toward the ceiling.

She bent her head, stared at the line, looked up at him, and wrote her name. "You can stop praying; I signed."

He instantly became more conversational. "I have similar problems with my own family. I'm the eldest. My siblings are angry at me. They don't think I should inherit anything because I bought and sold a property for my mom seven years before she died. They want me to distribute the entire balance."

"Why don't you?"

"I'm afraid they'll sue me. I'm waiting until they settle down. My younger sister is the worst. She's angry. And I don't know why."

"Ask her."

Pain showed in his eyes. "I'm afraid of her. She's crazy." He rubbed the stubble of a beard on his chin. "It's sad. It's not what Mom wanted."

"I've tried to detach from my family mess. But then I get angry all over again whenever I have to face it, like now. It's sad. My mom wanted us to get along." Linda's emotions were rising to the surface.

"I was my parents' financial planner for decades. My mom asked me to help her out, after Dad died, but I was sick with complications from a car accident."

Vance was listening, his dark eyes absorbing every movement she made. "Sorry. I didn't know about that." He lifted his hip and was furiously twisting his hand in his pocket, as if searching for something. Linda noted the strange behavior. "Something biting you down there?"

"Uh—oh, no, no . . . my key was jabbing me . . .heh, heh, heh . . . it's okay now."

She rolled her eyes. "When my mom was most vulnerable, she asked Mary for help and Mary took control like a barracuda after a minnow. Shortly after, a quarter million of Mom's money disappeared into my sister's checking account. That left a neat clean hundred thousand for each of her three daughters, held in trust in a bank in separate accounts, but Mary, using Power of Attorney, pulled the entire sum and gave it to some jerk financial planner who put the money into risky intangibles." She looked to see if he was following.

She waited for a response. When none was forthcoming, she continued, "If there'd been big losses from trading, believe me, I'd have done something." She scrutinized the realtor. "Have you heard of the Securities Investor Protection Corporation."

Hodge nodded affirmatively, with the confidence of an investment banker. "*Sure*, I know about it."

Linda considered his response. "Luckily, it remained intact. Then, on the advice of Brown, and totally excluding me, my two sisters took the rest of the money and bought this house, just weeks before mother passed and the whole freaking economy collapsed."

"That wasn't their fault."

"I know that. Their timing was bad. They should have just left the money where it was. Linda tilted her head back, noticing for the first time a mounted television near the ceiling. She could see his and her images reflected in the dark screen and wondered if she was being secretly recorded. "What's with the television?" She pointed to the set overhead. "You're not recording this, are you?"

Hodge reddened, looking up towards the monitor. "What. . . ? Oh, *that* . . . we use that for real estate viewings." His features pinched as he stammered, "You know, like a virtual tour."

This calmed Linda, but she remained suspicious. "I don't know what happened to Cathy and me because we were close as kids, but with Mary, it's been war since birth."

His head bobbed, as if he were comparing this story with the one he'd heard from Mary. He'd never really talked with Cathy, the busy vet.

"I've thought of suing them, but several attorneys explained that I wouldn't gain anything." She smiled. "The thought of litigation keeps my sisters on their toes." She stopped, realizing Vance didn't need to know this much and might find a way use it against her in a way she couldn't foresee. "There is a way that I could sue their attorney. It's called the intended heir . . . I'm looking into it." She leaned back in the chair, satisfied she'd left the threat of a lawsuit dangling.

"I'm afraid my sister will sue me." Vance held out his hand. "I've kept my mother's money in the bank."

"How much?"

"Several thousand."

"You won't be sued, Vance. Attorneys like big money."

He seemed to relax with her words.

"The worst part," she added, "is the family break up."

"I'm the personal representative of my mother's estate. Personal representatives are usually family members. Something like fifty percent of them are," he said, as if this should explain everything. "Did you know that?"

Imagining others going through a similar nightmare, Linda groaned. "Millions lost each year . . . lots of pain out there."

He nodded. "Well, I've got another appointment." Gripping the edge of the table, he lifted himself. "Gotta run." He wouldn't say, of course, who his next client was. He had his hand on a recorder hidden in his pants pocket.

Linda rose and extended her hand. "Thanks for managing the property." Later, when she had a moment to reflect on their conversation, she wondered if Vance might have baited her. Mary might have put him up to it to judge her reaction, to see how angry she still was, and what she was up to.

"Only shown the place a few times," Vance had said. Linda's mind probed. Their price was at the low end of the market. Where were the buyers or the recovery? Housing had always led America out of recessions, but this financial crisis had caused trillions of home equity value to disappear. Her inheritance—a drop in a sea of the housing market. A thought came to mind, *With all this loss, there had to be opportunity! Yes, yes, why didn't I think of it sooner? There has to be a pony, with all this shit.*

Later, inside the confines of his office, curtains closed, his feet on a pile of papers on his desk, Vance made a call. "Yes, yes, Mary, I got the whole discussion, but I'm not sure we've got anything . . . No, she didn't suspect a thing . . . All right. On my way."

Vance Hodge waited several months and then called Linda with an update on the sales progress of the rental property Linda owned with her sisters. "A similar house down the street is priced at $145,000."

"Isn't ours listed at $160,000?" she asked the realtor. This was the latest price the sisters had agreed upon per his recommendation.

"Yeah."

"Have there been any offers?"

"Not yet."

"Better reduce the price again."

Hodge's voice was gruff. "I need to call Mary first. I mean . . . I only just called you."

"Okay, so call my sisters, the other two tenants-in-common."

"I'll let you know."

"Right." Linda thought little would happen fast. It had taken her sisters a long time to reduce the price. To lower it again was heart-breaking.

But they weren't alone. The economy was slipping and sliding again, with home selling prices notching down another couple percent. American consumers had turned thrifty, afraid of losing money and jobs, and were reluctant to spend.

Chapter Thirty-Four

In another town, not far from Buena Vida, a family had gathered in a spacious kitchen: Mary, her husband, Brad, and Cathy, who was visiting—the Group of Three. It was just about dinnertime. A casserole dish of baked ziti, smothered in cheese, sat on the counter, piping hot. An aroma of fresh baked Italian garlic bread wafted from the oven. The green beans had a few more minutes to go.

Cathy had just poured herself a cup of tea and set it on the table as she pulled out a chair. "Did you send the tax information to our sister?" she asked Mary, who sat at the head of the table.

"No." Mary said bluntly. She stroked the fur of a calico cat that languished comfortably across her lap. Its purr was so loud you could hear it from the other end of the room. The cat lifted its head as if to say, "Don't stop."

Cathy looked from Brad to her sister with a question. "Are you . . . going to?"

"Nope. Don't plan to . . . You can send it, if you want."

"That's going to make her mad," Brad commented from his seat at the side of the table, overlooking the pasta. "How many times has she asked now? Five? Six letters?"

Mary laughed derisively. "I lost count."

Cathy looked worried. "Can we do that? I mean . . . is it against the law, or something? Can we get in trouble?"

"I don't think so," Brad offered, one eye on the casserole. "There's no law that says you have to."

"Maybe we should send it to her . . ." Cathy's voice trailed off when she saw the look on her sister's face.

"Let the IRS get after her. She can rot in hell for all I care." Mary's hand stopped stroking, until the cat turned its head and nipped her. "Ouch!" She chuckled and resumed petting the animal.

Cathy bit her lip, shocked by the extent of Mary's hostility still simmering, after all the years. She'd been angry herself when the rift had first occurred, but Linda hadn't really done anything against her. She'd made a choice to side with her older sister back then. Why had she done that? She didn't want to be cast out of the family. No. She was perfectly happy with the way things had turned out for her. She got to come to Florida, rent free. And she was still on Mary's good side. But still . . . the IRS? That was a different matter. "It's been a long time," she ventured. "She is our sister."

A withering look. Mary replied, "I don't care."

"Can't you . . . just let it go."

"I don't want to discuss it any further," Mary said acidly. "As far as I'm concerned, I'm never going to speak to her again." She threw Cathy a hard, scorching look. "And if you mention her name again, I won't speak to you either."

Sensing body tension, and hearing the tone of the master's voice, the cat bolted and ran out of the room. Her husband raised his eyebrows clearly understanding the boundary, which he knew pertained to him, too.

Cathy sank lower in the chair. She said, chewing on a fingernail, "Oh, okay."

It was time to file taxes.

Dennis Reid, tax accountant, was talking, "Attorney Nestor Brown's in court today and can't be reached." Reid said to Linda, "I need to know the revenue and expenses for the rental real estate property you own with your sisters. And I need the date of death appraisal."

She coughed, then mumbled. "Okay, I'll see what I can do."

"See if you can get the information this week, or else I'll have to file an extension."

"I hear you." Linda sighed and thought about the situation. A few weeks ago, she'd written Mary and asked for tax information. She'd written, "Let me know about the K1, the real estate tax report."

A week later, she met him in his office, a small room at the top of a narrow stairway. The door was locked, but a sign said to knock. She did so and Reid yanked open the door, greeted her, then beat a path back to his chair behind the desk. Piles of tax returns littered the shabby carpet. Linda had to step carefully not to trip on one. The accountant peered at her from behind thick glasses.

She sat down and handed him a manila file. "Here's what I've put together for my taxes so far, but neither Brown, or my sisters, have sent me anything, not even the K1, on the property."

Reid said, "I wouldn't get your hopes up for a K1. These attorneys often don't do them."

"Oh, wonderful."

"You three need to sell."

"I know."

"There's probably a loss." His fingers punched numbers on an ancient calculator.

"Ya think?"

"I'm not too worried. We've got the next two quarters covered. I'm applying the refund to your next two payments."

"You mentioned an extension. How much time will that give us?"

"Six months." Reid grabbed a tax statement from the floor, his usual filing system. "I know you like to be on time and we usually are, but there's so much of it now. I've seen brokerage statements two years late." His voice sounded strained as he spoke with his head upside down. "Well, I've got to file a hundred extensions."

Linda's frustration barometer was rising. "Let me know if you hear anything."

"I will. And you let me know, if you get anything."

"Okay."

Linda composed another letter to Mary. Before turning off the computer, she checked her messages. An email from realtor, Vance Hodge, requested her signature on a document.

"I hate to do this to you, Vance," she said to him on the phone. "But I'm going to withhold my signature, until my sister sends my accountant, or me, the tax information we've requested."

Hodge gasped for air and asked in a squeaky voice. "I understand. Why don't you send me an email and I'll pass it on to her."

"Will do."

As the days and weeks ticked by, Linda's frustration launched into full blown anger, which then bordered on rage. She was having trouble sleeping and the thoughts that were going through her mind were not pleasant. After attending weekday Mass, a habit that usually started the day off right, Linda sought counsel with Father Paul, a trusted spiritual advisor with whom she spoke frequently after weekday Mass about everyday things. "Father, will you hear my confession?"

Paying no attention, a sacristan reached overhead to replace a ciborium in a cupboard.

"Sure." Father Paul pulled the alb over his head and hung it on a hanger, which he stuffed into a small closet in the enclosed room. "There's a secluded room at the end of the hall."

The priest led Linda down the hall and closed the door behind them. "Do you wish to sit or stand?" Two chairs were next to the wall in the windowless room. Light flared from a single, bare, overhead fixture.

"I prefer to stand." Linda took a deep breath. This was not normal confession time, but she felt like she would burst, unless she got the matter off her chest. "Bless me, Father, for I have sinned. It's been—I don't remember how long it's been since my last confession—two weeks, two months . . . two years?"

Father Paul shrugged his shoulders as if this was meaningless to him, and Linda plunged in.

"There's an age old animosity between my older sister and me. She hates me. It's poisoned her. She does things to make me angry and then I hate her back. Then, I'm poisoned. This has been going on since my birth, only it's mushroomed over the years. The problem now is that she's withholding important tax information from my accountant and me . . . I could kill her." Linda's chest heaved with emotion. "I don't act on my thoughts, of course, but they're there all the same."

"That is *monumental*," said the priest, making eye contact. "All I can say is try to endure like Christ endured the crucifixion. Think about the spiritual value of suffering unjust persecution."

Linda's hand balled into a fist, ready for a knock-out punch, but certainly not at the priest who stood looking at her hand.

"Bear your trial well," he said. "Use Jesus as a model; He was betrayed and maligned. He gives full meaning to trials as Christian experiences."

"I'd like to give my sister a trial."

He squeezed his eyes shut tightly and winced. "I encourage you to bear your suffering with joy, knowing it's a means to *and* a guarantee of heaven."

"That's all fine and dandy, Father, but I need to file my taxes or I'll wind up in jail."

"I see . . . "

"The realtor wants me to sign a document and I told him I won't sign until she gives my accountant what he needs. He told me to do what I have to do. My younger sister's in my older sister's camp. I'm not getting any help from my immediate family."

"Maybe that's the way it's supposed to be for now," Father Paul said. "Does she live near you?"

"About fifteen miles from here."

"You have a real mess." The priest looked upward to the ceiling. "A hardship."

"A miracle would help . . . or death. Shall I pray for her death?" Linda's half smile showed that she was joking.

The priest seemed concerned. "Try to detach as best you can. Accept it as it is."

"She'll never change. But I have." Linda paused. "I've got a few years sobriety."

He breathed easier. "I'm glad you told me that."

"I used to drink." Linda raised her left hand to her mouth in a familiar gesture that was not lost on him. "I don't have time for this nonsense. Last week I put in so many volunteer hours it resembled a part time job."

"Keep it up." The priest laughed more normally this time, scratched his head, with a thin finger. "Your sister controls you and your feelings." Linda nodded agreement. "That's why I want you to detach from her effect on you. Be careful. Try not to let her intimidate or provoke you." He looked at her face and saw her tired expression. "Keep trying."

"I'll take care of business and go on my merry way."

"That's the spirit. For your penance say one *Our Father* and one *Hail Mary.*"

Father Paul left the room and Linda walked into the church and knelt. The church was empty except for a few parishioners who remained to pray the rosary. Stained-glass windows threw color, light, and warmth across the wooden floor. She prayed. She was worried and surprised by her sisters' withholding tax information. The way she saw it they'd betrayed their mother by going against her intentions, as stated in the will. Mary had feathered her nest handsomely in other ways—an osprey's nest. And then, there was the matter of what they'd done with the remaining cash. According to the realtor, the rental property was worth less than half what they paid for it. Others had suffered, Linda knew, but that didn't ease the resentment she felt. The matter of withholding tax information added insult to injury. The family is engaged in war exercises, she thought and then it occurred to her in a flash—*I need a better strategy.*

At her request, Hodge and Linda were once again in the conference room of his real estate firm. This time they had both covered the table with papers. Hodge seemed mildly perturbed, having interrupted negotiations with a buyer to keep his appointment with her.

"Did you get my sisters to sign?" Linda asked.

"Not yet." His thick white hair was matted down from sweat.

"They'll sign, don't worry."

Hodge looked askance at her with a dubious expression. He wondered what made her sound confident.

"Did you forward my email to them?" She was referring to her refusal to sign his contract as property manager, until her sisters provided tax information on their rental property. Weeks had passed since she'd requested it and still the information was not forthcoming.

"Never opened it," Hodge said lamely, unapologetically. He knew Mary would've chewed his ass if he had.

"Good thing. My attorney, Crandall—you know him?"

Hodge looked surprised, thought for a second, blew air with his lower lip into his nostrils. "Can't say that I do."

"Well, anyway, Crandall advised me to proceed another way."

Hodge smiled, relieved. "You mean for once my tardiness paid off?"

Linda smiled back and showed him a copy of Attorney Brown's letter. "I circled in red ink the promise he made to provide a tax report for the terminated trust." She pointed to the words she'd written above his promise: *Where is it?* She dragged her finger to the top of the page and read aloud what she'd put there. "It's in our best interests to file the same tax information. Otherwise, inconsistencies reported to the IRS might result in an audit."

Hodge read with an arched eyebrow, shifting his weight nervously.

"Crandall said a real estate tax report, a K1, is probably unnecessary. Your wife said that appraisals and assessments are about equal, and I was hoping you could pull up the public records, so I can get some figures for my accountant."

"Appraisals and assessments are both based on previous sales." Hodge busily tried to access the information on a computer screen hanging on the wall. "Damn. Someone's been playing with this—It won't take my password." He called for help, but no one replied. "I hope you don't think I'm an idiot."

Linda watched his frenetic movements. "I have trouble turning mine on."

After trying his password a dozen times, Hodge found the county's public records. The page held pertinent information, facts and figures. He observed Linda's eyes busily darting from the screen to a writing pad. "Did you get what you needed?"

"I think so. Hopefully, this will satisfy the IRS." Looking concerned, Linda picked up and shuffled some papers she'd placed on the conference table. "Can you help me out with revenues and expenses?" She bit the end of her pencil and waited anxiously.

He leaned forward to better view her notes. "I really can't help you with that, but I know Mary was getting a thousand for rent."

"When did the tenant move out?"

He thought a few seconds. "December. That's when the three of them moved out."

"Three? I thought it was a single veteran." She threw down the pencil. "No one tells me anything."

"A man and wife and their child . . . and dog." Embarrassed, he held his hand to his mouth and coughed a few times.

Linda threw her hands in the air.

"Now I need you to sign these papers here." He pointed aggressively, with his index finger. "And here." After she'd accomplished that, Hodge leaned back in the chair. "You know, I don't get it. Mary asked me to be property manager, but she collects and deposits the rent which is what I should be doing." He looked down at the documents on the table, which Linda had just signed. "I send these to your sisters, but you're the only one who signs."

"You think maybe my sisters have changed their minds?" She pretended to ignore his withering look.

He said sharply, "I'm getting really tired of this sisterly feud—"

"You're not alone. And now I've got to worry about the IRS." Linda looked at him, noting how he seemed to have aged in the short time since she'd known him. She thought little of him as a realtor but considered that he was probably doing the best he could, under the circumstances. "Thank you."

Linda stood up and gathered her paperwork feeling a chill from the risk of an audit.

The deadline for tax filing had come and gone and still Mary and Cathy hadn't provided the necessary rental information.

Hopes that Hitler and Mussolini would cooperate and send the information was diminishing. Weeks had passed since her last letter, one of many, and, cranky from lack of sleep, stressed out from that and the usual minor crises of life, Linda blew up at Kent over some trivial matter and then later had to make an amend to him over the phone. An understanding friend, Kent was able to forgive and forget transgressions without harsh measures. These were significant improvements.

"Your letters aren't working," Crandall said to her one afternoon. "You could sue for financial information, but I wouldn't advise it."

Linda stared out the window of his office at a gathering of ducks, by the pond behind the building. "Any other ideas?"

"Call the one who lives out of town."

"And risk having the phone slammed in my ear?"

"She's the big bucks, right? Just ask her what she's going to do when there's an audit."

Linda sighed out loud. This was getting to be too much. "Have you ever confronted such a thing?"

"Never." The attorney laughed. "It's all you can do. Your accountant can make an amend when the information comes."

"The IRS will eventually get what they want. I'm not looking forward to an audit."

He looked at her with compassion. "I hope it doesn't come to that. No one's innocent when it comes to them."

A little later, she turned on her cell phone and read an email from the realtor: "Cathy has finally signed the lease agreement." Now only Mary was holding back on that document and the vital tax information.

Jim Cott, attorney and friend, returned Linda's call on a bright, Monday morning. Linda grabbed her cell and put aside the electric curlers she was using to set her hair. "It's been a long time since we've spoken, Jim. How are you?"

"We're in the midst of a significant downturn. If you're a builder, a lender, or a borrower, you're in trouble."

"And you? Are you all right?"

"Me? . . . Yeah, I'm fine. Having trouble with real estate rentals, leases, and collections . . ." His voice trailed off.

Linda got the idea that things were not going that well in Jim's world. He was a big player in a local bank that had just gone under.

"I wanted to bring you up to date on what's happening," Linda said. "My sister's withholding tax information, on our rental property."

"The courts are full of cases of people with family squabbles. They're up over two hundred percent from what they were a decade ago. Attorneys are busy collecting fees. It's not cost effective, as I told you before, because in your case the money you'd possibly win would go to pay court costs. The best thing to do is take the screwing and move on. That's what I tell my clients."

"Will I be audited?" A question uppermost in her mind.

"Fat chance. Do you have any idea of the numbers?"

She made a rough estimate on a piece of paper. "Probably pretty much a wash, with expenditures equal to rental income."

"Then it's a non-event. The IRS won't care." He said it like it was routine.

"It's not that I'm worried about. It's when we sell the property and have to claim huge losses."

"How much you figure the losses?"

"Big."

"That's too bad," Jim commiserated. "Sometimes in life we have to get through these situations and bear up as best we can. Things have a way of coming around, Linda. Someday this will come back to haunt her. It's a backache she'll have to endure."

"Thanks."

There was still the matter of getting her tax report filed so she wouldn't spend a night in jail. She called her tax accountant and asked him what to do.

"I can't use your numbers," Dennis Reid said flatly.

"It's all I have."

"You're sure there'll be no K1?"

She was surprised he was asking, as he'd told her previously not to get her hopes up. "My real estate attorney said it wasn't necessary and, knowing Brown like I do, I doubt he'll want anything in print coming from his office, with large losses."

"Attorneys can be like that." Deciding to relent a little and to keep his fingers busy, Reid picked up the letter she'd sent him. "Where'd you get your figures?"

"From the county tax appraiser and previous records. It's the best I can do under the circumstances." She could hear his grinding the numbers on his calculator. "How long do you want to wait? You said the extension would last six months. Do you want to wait until the fifth month, before you file my return?"

"I'll wait one month and then I'll file using your numbers . . . unless something else comes up."

Grace and Linda sat in a booth on the side of a busy restaurant. Leaning toward the younger woman with an expectant look, Grace waited for Linda to say something. Linda was waiting for Grace. The quietness stretched between them.

"How many children do you have?" A safe question, Linda thought as she asked, a good start for middle-aged women, although Grace seemed well into her seventies.

"Four. My youngest, Joe, lives with me."

"He's divorced?" Linda had heard Joe talking about how he missed his children at the meeting.

"Separated. His wife and children live on Long Island." Grace eyed her turkey sandwich and then looked back at Linda. "And you?" The question asked, she lifted the sandwich and took a bite. Chewing slowly, with a full mouth, she watched her friend.

"Divorced."

"I meant your family. Tell me about them."

"I'm the middle of three girls."

Grace nodded, chewed thoughtfully, as if the answer explained a lot. "I have a twin. My older sister who predeceased my mother was a pain. She always nagged my dad and manipulated my mom. She made my dad buy her a sailboat."

Linda nodded her head hard enough to provoke a muscle spasm. "Was your sister named Mary?" Grace laughed. "No really, she sounds just like my older sister."

"Her name was Angelita," Grace said, rolling her eyes. "She was anything but. . . "

Linda's bowl of soup was growing cold, but she was more interested in how Grace had dealt with her family. "Was there jealousy between you and the little angel?"

"No jealousy. I was the caretaker of my twin, because she was emotionally immature, and I resented it. After Angelita and Mom died, things changed between Maria and me. I got sober, for one, and stopped criticizing her. I learned to accept her as she was and let her live her own life the way she wanted. When we get together these days, we laugh and joke and have a wonderful time." Grace seemed satisfied with how her story had turned out and smiled at her friend whose family, she knew, was estranged.

Feeling a rush of jealousy, Linda said, "I had a dream the other night. My mother came to me and told me to focus on what is important. Underneath the grief and aggravation I undergo, because of my older sister's rotten behavior, there is still love. That's the part I don't understand. I should be plotting her death."

Grace slowly shook her head. "When Angelita died, my twin, Maria, said she didn't mourn, or miss her. When I asked why, she said that Angelita was never nice to her."

Linda wondered what she would say when Mary eventually died. Would she spit on her grave, which lately she'd been thinking, or just stand by the tombstone, hands in her pockets, feeling sadness for what could have been.

"Angelita was unhappy," Grace continued. "Her greed and fear drove her to do nasty things. I'm glad I don't have to live like that. I have a good life." Her piercing eyes looked to see if her friend was getting it. Her experience demonstrated how a difficult issue was made more bearable. A few more words should do it. She added,

"I know I'll never be on the street. I trust that God will provide. He always gives me what I need. When Angelita died, it broke the family block. Since then, my twin and I have become more capable of having a better relationship."

Grace's message was clear, and led Linda to consider future possibilities of a relationship with Cathy.

An episode of Jeopardy, the TV quiz show, a brain cruncher, helped Linda forget her problems with the IRS and her sisters. She was sitting on the love seat, with her hand in a bowl of crackers, when Paula, a retired federal judge and friend from a noon meeting, with whom she'd had several conversations, picked this time to call and chat. Usually Paula had a racy story about courtroom experiences and she never glossed over the language she'd heard from the bench. "It'd make a sailor blush," she often said. Linda expected a savory tale and was looking forward to it.

The judge asked how she was doing. "I know you're anxious about not being able to file your tax return. Ever since you mentioned it to me I've been thinking about you."

Linda pushed the television off button. "Just think of how mean they are by deliberately going out of their way to get me in trouble. It makes me shudder to think of how they must feel. If I were Joseph, like in the Bible, they might have sold me into slavery."

Paula laughed. "When I was going through divorce," Paula said, "my husband withheld tax information from me. I wrote to the IRS and asked them to intervene."

Linda grabbed a pencil and scavenged for something to write on. She eyed the newspaper. Perfect. "Tell me . . ." She couldn't write fast enough in the margins. "Exactly how'd you put that?"

"I wrote: I know you need my tax data, but my husband refuses to give it to me. The IRS has the power to subpoena; I don't. Please assist me."

"What did they do?"

"They wrote him a letter and requested the information."

The thought of the IRS writing to her sisters thrilled her. Scribbling the words as fast as she could, Linda asked, "And send copies of the letters I've sent my sisters asking for the information?"

"Yes. And send a copy to their attorney."

"Copy their attorney? Why? He didn't even return my accountant's call."

"On second thought, I might send them one more letter telling them what I'd do if they didn't respond."

Linda thought about that. *How many letters must I send? . . .* "No, I think I'll just go ahead and mail it. Get it done."

"It's your decision."

"I really appreciate your help."

The letter went out the next day—one small, sealed, white envelope, like a raft floating on a river of mail, approaching the rapids.

Chapter Thirty-Five

The postman stuffed a letter in Linda's mailbox shortly after. There was no return address. The handwriting, obviously Cathy's, seemed rushed and sloppy. With trembling fingers, Linda opened the envelope and unfolded a single piece of computer stationery.

A revenue and expense report from the rental property.

The *tax information!*

It contained no note, no message, and nothing endearing—just a copy of the bloody report.

Is my younger sister maybe leaning my way? Linda considered writing a thank you note.

In her office, she examined the enclosure closely and saw they were losing money on the property. To replace the air conditioner system, the veterinarian had loaned money to keep them afloat. She thought about that for a moment and wanted to discuss the report with Cathy.

Cathy's phone rang twice while Linda waited, expecting to leave a voicemail.

"Hello?"

Dear God, she answered! Linda was about to faint. "Cathy?"

Click.

Linda laid down the cell phone on her desk and sat staring at the wall. Hurt rose, then questions. *Had their letters crossed? Had Cathy received the IRS letter before, or after, she sent the information?*

Kent and she sat across from each other at a diner, a greasy spoon, where they played seventies music. A sign on the wall read: "Best place for dinner under $10."

"I had a nightmare last night," Linda said as she buttered a hot bagel.

Kent waited, cocked an eye at her. "Do you want to tell me about it?"

"I was lost. I couldn't find my house or my job. I was frantically running around in circles. Then I woke up, and realized I was in my house and retired. I lay there and thought how lucky I am. I didn't have a hangover. I didn't have to face some authority, because I was on their shit list. There were many of those in my past: Teachers who noted that I didn't get along with others, and managers who were unhappy with my work that filed bad reports. At the time, I remember thinking, Me? Why me? What did I do? It seemed I was always defending my good name. Those days were rough."

Linda bit into the bagel and chewed. She was thinking of how sad Cathy's voice had sounded on the phone. She had little to go on as she had only said hello, but the tone was unmistakable. "Now Cathy, the world renowned veterinarian, with so many awards to her name, has to face being on an IRS list. She gets to answer their questions. It's too bad she didn't send the tax information sooner."

Kent, who knew about the dilemma, with the missing tax information, replied, "She had plenty of opportunity to send you what you needed. I can't say I have much sympathy for her." Then, he bent forward, over his hamburger.

"I was going to warn her, but she already had the news."

Linda became philosophical.

"It's such a mess. I wish I could start my life all over again." She said with a touch of melancholy. "Have the babies my parents expected me to have and were so disappointed when I didn't. Be a better daughter and sister. Do my whole freaking life over."

"No regrets, Linda." Kent admonished. "Everyone has remorse at times, but no regrets." This was the voice of one recovering alcoholic to another.

"I'm grateful for the gifts I was given. I have so many blessings," Linda replied, as if on cue. That was her A.A. training and it lifted her up from a murky swampland of self-pity. She smiled at him across the table. "The only thing I regret is the huge, strawberry sundae I devoured, after dinner last night with you."

"It was a sundae," he reminded her. "Not a drink."

"Right." Linda finished her Texas-size bagel drenched in butter and wiped her fingers on a paper napkin. "You know, as for my family, we've got nowhere to go but up."

He looked at her and his eyes showed sympathy.

"What I want to know is how to convert this liability into an asset, like our literature tells us, and make it a source of comfort for myself and others. *Just how?*"

"Good question," he replied. "Wish I had an answer for you."

She let her glance take in the view from the window. Outside, a few ducks waddled across the manicured lawn and squatted before a pond, establishing residency for the night.

"It's summer. It's eighty-five degrees. Let's get out of here."

Kent reached for his jacket in a compliant gesture.

She added, "Let's take a trip north."

"You want to go to Disney World?" The idea excited him. "I've never been."

"That's a possibility." Linda stared in mild dismay at his mouth where he seemed to have sprouted a green tooth. As he chewed, it moved and revealed itself to be a piece of lettuce. "What about Fort Lauderdale?" she asked.

"We could go dancing at that place they talk about."

It sounded like a good idea. "What would we do in the daytime?"

"Are we beach people?" he asked.

Linda grimaced. "I don't want to lie on a hot beach all day. I like to swim though."

"I'll research the area, see what I can come up with."

The letter to her sister had taken weeks to write, with many drafts, tear ups, and rewrites. She put it off until after a trip to Fort Lauderdale with Kent where they diminished the supply of fresh fish, wore out a pair of sneakers and slept in late, under sheets twisted and tousled from night exercises. She tried again.

"Thank you for the tax information," Linda wrote. "I appreciate your sending it to me. Now I'd like to suggest that we get a new realtor." She knew this would go over like a bomb, but she had a plan, which she'd been plotting for a while. She was ready to put it into action. "Although realtors have shown the property and there have been sales in the neighborhood, our realtor hasn't produced a single offer, in two years. Let's get a fresh start with someone new and lower the asking price for the property so we can get on with our lives."

As she wrote, she wondered how Cathy would respond.

Because Grace had similar experiences with an older sibling and was a minister in a non-denominational church, Linda liked to talk with her and seek her advice. Grace, wearing a floral, cotton top and khaki trousers, looked across a table toward Linda, in a café filled with young families. Children were running excitedly between the tables, as if it were a playground. Early evening sunlight slanted across the furniture casting long shadows across the room. The two women huddled over their meals while a toddler's head popped over the back of their booth, behind Linda, grinning at them with shining big blue eyes. Grace made a funny face at the child who giggled and disappeared.

"Families can be tricky," Grace said, munching on a potato chip. "My cousin didn't want to take care of his mother and I invited him to bring her to my house. My aunt was in my care, for the last seven months of her life."

Linda listened to her friend as she reached into the potato chip bag. "Our meeting tonight is propitious."

"What's going on?" Grace asked.

Linda held up her right hand and pointed a potato chip at herself. "My mistake. I did it."

"What . . .?"

"I was thinking of getting out of Florida because of the heat. I e-mailed my cousin in New Jersey about visiting. A girlfriend who lives in Newark invited me up at the same time and I thought of killing two birds with one stone."

Grace asked, "The cousin in Jersey—is she the sister of your deceased cousin?"

"Yes. After my cousin died suddenly last year, I thought maybe it could be a new beginning for Jane and me. I'm not getting anywhere with my immediate family, so I'm branching out to the extended family. You know—see if that works better. Anyway, I called her a few times, but she told me she only wanted to communicate through emails. She said she was just too busy." Linda rolled her eyes, indicating that she recognized the brush-off.

"You have *history* with this cousin?"

"I didn't think so, but apparently I do. We were going back and forth while I was trying to coordinate plans with my friend. When my cousin wrote that she was going to the Cape for a month, I strongly hinted that I'd like to visit her there. Cape Cod's more fun than Newark, if you know what I mean."

Grace nodded her head with vigor.

"Today she wrote me that she didn't want me to visit her in Cape Cod."

Grace's tone turned sardonic. "What brought that on, d'ya think?"

"I don't know why she was so against my coming up. I've invited her to come to Florida and stay with me several times."

"It could be something different. Once a sponsee of mine was upset because her mother left a whiskey bottle on the table, with two glasses. She thought her mother was tempting her to drink. I told her maybe she had a visitor and was too tired to put it away and wanted her daughter to do it for her . . . Give it time."

"That's what I was thinking. I wish she hadn't mentioned that she was going to the Cape. It brought back memories of the time I had been there with her family when I was barely a teenager. I thought we had a good time eating lobster and going to the beach . . . ." Linda looked at a family of four sitting nearby who seemed to be enjoying the meal. She remembered a similar scene with Jane's family. "Maybe Mary got there first and said something to make her want to avoid closeness with me."

Grace ran her hand across a wrinkled forehead and pushed back a stray lock.

"Before our meeting tonight," Linda continued, "I was singing *All Are Welcome*, with the choir. Not all are welcome on my father's side of the family. We're a family of multiple families. On my mother's side, it's different; my cousin Tom is warm and wonderful and really wants to see me."

"Next time make a plan to see him and get your hugs from him." Grace said. "Stop hurting yourself."

"Okay." Linda smiled. She eyed her sandwich, picked up the bread, looked at the slice of turkey with little appetite, and left it alone.

Grace took a bite of her sandwich and wiped her mouth, with a paper napkin. "You've suffered enough. You've worked too hard in the program to carry this baggage around in your head." As she was chewing, the toddler's head re-appeared over the booth and Grace said, "Hi there!"

Linda turned around and winked at the child, who slipped away again to play with his siblings. She was thinking, *I hope this kid's siblings don't turn into mortal enemies over parental assets.* She picked up her sandwich and nibbled at it. "You're right about baggage, Grace."

"Get this thing about Cape Cod out of your head . . . if you can." Grace looked at Linda with compassion. "I know it's hard, but try. It's an obsession. Think of your cousin and your sisters as children of God." Grace looked out the window across the room. The sun had set; it was growing darker. "I wonder what makes your sisters so sick in their behavior toward you."

"Do you know what it's like to live near a sibling who is hostile?" She elaborated. "She tried to get me in trouble with the IRS." Linda sipped the beverage from a straw.

"Maybe she won't do that again."

"I have to be one step ahead of them and on guard. There's no time for nice sentiments."

"Take care of yourself as best you can. Do what you have to do and then let it go. Try to have as much peace as you can." Grace bent over her sandwich as if in prayer, then picked it up in her hands.

"You know where I feel the most peace? Church. When I get there, I don't want to leave. There's a power and a Spirit that nurtures me like nothing else . . . It's better than a meeting."

Speaking with a mouthful, Grace said, "I'm glad you have that."

"I never had any training in conflict resolution with my family. Nobody ever worked anything out. We didn't talk about anything . . . just buried it under the rug and remained angry with each other."

"Nobody does that well when they're nine years old. We learn this stuff later in life. It'll work itself out." Grace could see that Linda was skeptical. "I know it's hard to be understanding when you're surrounded by pain and suffering. I've been there. Later, I understood that my sister lived a sad life. She was so angry . . . Maybe your sister's jealous of you."

Linda looked away and shrugged, her expression saying she'd heard it before.

"God enables us to forgive and love. Continue to do what's right and be continually renewed." Apropos of nothing, Grace said, "You're going to be awesome."

A moment of silence followed. Linda looked back at Grace and their eyes met.

Linda said, "A decent day for me is exercise, particularly with a little, round ball like a head that I can whack, Mass, and thirty or forty therapists."

Grace laughed. "Can you send a friendship card to your younger sister?"

"I sent her a thank-you note for the tax information last week."

"That's good. Remember that what you give, you actually receive." Grace gulped down the last of her sandwich and wiped her hands on the napkin, which she then crumbled and placed on the empty plate.

The waitress, a timid, Haitian girl, approached and hovered by the table.

Grace looked up at her. "Are we keeping you from going home? You're closing?"

The waitress nodded, her lower lip trembling. "We close at eight."

Linda noticed that most patrons had left, including the playful toddler. She twisted her wrist to see the face of her watch. Eight fifteen. "Oh, sorry. We'll be going then." The waitress nodded in agreement and moved away.

The women prepared to leave. Linda wrapped the rest of her sandwich in a napkin and stuffed it into her purse.

"I always feel happier and better after I meet with you, Grace. You really help me."

"Likewise."

Chapter Thirty-Six

An envelope with Cathy's return address lay beneath a pile of junk mail and uninteresting magazines. The address, typed in bold black letters, made Linda slightly suspicious of the contents. She held it up to the sunlight and looked closer, thinking the thin envelope obviously held a single sheet. Nasty, or nice? Holding her breath, she tore open the envelope—another letter from her sister's wiseass attorney, Brown.

"There's a new development," Linda said to Crandall, her attorney. "I imagine you'll tell me to ignore Brown's letter, but I wanted to be sure."

Crandall had just finished a brown bag lunch in his office and crumbs from a tuna fish sandwich speckled the highly polished desk top. "What's he got to say?"

"The usual accusations and blame. My sister Mary's hostility comes right through that maniac. You remember that she withheld tax information from me?"

"Yeah, I remember." Crandall swept the crumbs off his desk. A crease appeared in his forehead. "Why did he write to you? You don't need anything from him, unless he's writing on behalf of his clients."

"Remember I sent a letter to the IRS asking them to help me out?"

"Yep, you showed me that letter."

"Well, I sent him a copy."

"Oh." Crandall leaned back in his swivel chair, parked his feet on the desk, and smirked, as if relishing Brown's indignation.

"He said to stop trying to get his clients in trouble."

Crandall smirked, recognizing a typical attorney ploy.

"I figure Cathy's letter with the information and the IRS copy crossed in the mail."

Crandall's loud laugh echoed in the cavernous office.

"They tricked me this time," Linda continued. "Cathy's return address was on the envelope and I thought it was from her. They know I won't open anything from him."

"Where was it postmarked?"

"Fort Myers."

"Not one of them was there." His laughter ended with a snort. "But that's no matter."

"Is it illegal to send a letter under false pretenses?"

Crandall thought for a few seconds before responding. "N-n-n-n-o-o."

"So I'm to ignore the whole thing?"

"You got what you needed. What you do need to watch for, however, is your sister using *your* money to pay *her* attorney."

Linda thought, *Mary is probably using the money she swiped from Mom to pay Brown.* "When we sell the property, won't the closing statement be itemized?"

"It has to be. It's the law."

"I might want your assistance at the closing." Linda didn't know whether to take his grunt as agreement. "I'm so mad at Cathy for pulling this stunt."

"She's probably just getting even for your letter," Crandall said. "Doctors don't like the IRS looking at them."

"Her husband's a doctor, too."

"Even worse." Crandall's chuckle sputtered. "Everyone in your family's acting as if they're right and they're trying to prove it."

"What can I do about it?"

"You can let her know you didn't appreciate it. Ask her to refrain from doing it again, or you might report it to the Post Office. That should take care of it." He took his feet off the desk, sat up, as his secretary frantically signaled him from the doorway.

Writing a note to Cathy per the advice of Crandall heightened Linda's sense of empowerment, but, as it slipped from her fingers down the mail shoot, she had regrets. They were sniping at each other when the real problem lay unsolved. Mother's estate still had not been settled. Because of the Great Recession, the estate was mostly gone, as if it had suffered a horrible beating and was near dead. *My sisters never could manage assets,* she thought. *Even as kids, they always blew through their allowance too soon and then asked me for a loan.*

To be healthy and at peace, Linda tried to detach from the whole affair and move on, to live the best life she could, whatever that meant.

Later that evening, realtor Hodge forwarded an email. Cathy had written to him: "Should I use the appraisal price on the property my sisters and I own for tax purposes?"

Hodge replied to Linda, "This is between you and your sisters. I don't want to get involved."

Linda was glad for the opportunity to respond to her younger sister. There'd been so little communication between them since their mother passed, six years ago. She sent Cathy an email. "Would you like to discuss how to treat the property for tax purposes? If we all use the same figures, it should make Mr. IRS happy."

About to seal the envelope, she added, "I tried to protect Mom and you, and all four of us. Do you understand? Maybe it didn't come out that way, but I'd sincerely like us to end this division and be a family. Is that too much to ask?"

After the sticker shock wore off from his last bill, Linda sought a new tax accountant. Riding up a postage stamp-sized elevator, in a recently built professional building, she stood next to a man who appeared to have jumped out of a golf cart. He took one look at her white pants, with lobster figures stitched in red and commented, "You'll be pinched all day." He smiled as she laughed. The door opened, and they went opposite ways down a long corridor.

A receptionist sitting at a desk in the foyer greeted her warmly. "Joe Bidley will be right with you. Please take a seat." She pointed to a row of chairs against the wall. Linda sat and picked up a travel magazine from a coffee table.

Momentarily, a man dressed in a white shirt and striped tie and dark pants appeared. He seemed to have been made with a compass, large round pupils magnified behind round eyeglasses, in a round face. They introduced themselves to each other. With long strides, he escorted her to a conference room. "Sit anywhere you like."

Linda circled the table and settled in a chair with the window at her back, to avoid the sun's bright glare. Handing him her tax return, she asked, "Would you take a look at this and tell me how much you'd charge to do my taxes?"

Bidley sat down across from her, glanced at the date on the report, and said, "You mean for next year?"

She nodded.

He thumbed through the pages and gave her a figure that was less than half what she'd paid her last accountant. *That bastard overcharged me!*

"Do you think there will there be any changes?" he asked.

She watched as he thumbed the pages a second time. "Not that I expect, but there's something I might need your help with." She then gave him a brief synopsis of the difficulty she'd experienced in getting the income and expense numbers for the rental property.

Bidley put down the report and pushed it away from him, as if he'd memorized its contents. "I'm sorry to hear about that."

His compassion impressed Linda. *So far so good,* she thought. The man has a heart.

"It really is a common thing." Bidley leaned toward her over the table, one arm outstretched, palm up. "Let me tell you about an experience I had." He saw she was interested. "I was named administrator of an estate, about the same size as yours. There were four siblings and a mother who died. I couldn't get any of the children to pay for the mother's funeral. I tried and tried. Finally, I hired an attorney to chase them down and bang on their doors. It took months. At last, one of them agreed to pay the funeral expense to bury his own mother." His eyes sought hers and held. "Can you imagine?"

"My sisters didn't attend my mother's memorial service."

Bidley shook his head. "Obviously, you want to get out of this rental property as soon as you can."

"I'm trying."

"I know you are."

The right words, again.

"What about a buyout?" he asked.

"I tried that and my sisters wanted me to buy *them* out—at the price they paid, not what it's worth."

Bidley laughed derisively. "Eventually you'll sell it."

"Depends on the market and . . . my sisters." She sighed and looked at a painting on the wall. "Sometimes I think there's a lesson in it. Like I'm supposed to forgive them, so I can be pardoned for the things I've done." She laughed. "I must have done some pretty bad things, but we don't need to go into that."

"People don't realize that a tax return is the story of their lives—the long and the short of it." He ran his hand over the report with a flourish. "It's all here."

Her eyes widened. There was truth to what he'd said. Nothing she could do about it. "The upside is that I've been following the real estate market closely and am trying to make it a career. It's interesting, but very competitive and requires quite a few fees, as you saw on my itemized deductions."

Sunlight glinted off his glasses as he nodded. "I saw something this year that made me fall out of my chair. A realtor had $150,000 income and $50,000 in expenses."

Linda gulped. "Wow! I'm not going there."

Flipping through the pages, Bidley paused when something caught his interest. "What kind of yield are you currently getting on your portfolio?"

"What's the going rate these days—three percent? I liked it better when rates were higher." She was sure he'd heard *that* from his retired clients.

"Too bad you didn't have some of those high-yielding stocks," Bidley said with a disarming smile, as he lay the report on the table, finished with his perusal.

Linda looked at him, thinking they had arrived at the bedrock of his understanding of markets, and how they worked. Speaking from experience, she said, "Most of them cut their dividends."

"Oh . . . that's right. And then their prices tanked." Bidley pulled the report back to him. "I must admit I don't know much about bonds."

Linda thought, *Or stocks for that matter.*

"Do you have a professional select your bonds?"

"I work closely with the brokerage traders where I keep my account." His expression held interest and something else she couldn't quite read. She added, "I was in the business for many years."

"What was your title?" he asked.

"They called us many names: account executive, financial consultant, stockbroker. If you went to school, certified financial planner." She thought a second and smiled, remembering the office jokes and added, "Stock jockey, stuffed shirt, thieves, liars, whores."

He laughed. "I've done returns for some who had W-2s like telephone numbers." He glanced at her cool porcelain face, then paged back to itemized deductions and re-studied the numbers. "Seems pretty straight forward and simple. You have a lot going on, but nothing complicated." Relaxed and confident, he leaned back against the padded chair. "I'll be glad to prepare your return for next year."

Linda smiled, bent over the table, and put a finger next to the document. "It's down to about an eighth of an inch." She looked up at him. "I remember when it was two inches."

"I bet it was a fun report to work on." He handed the file back to her. "Keep in mind it might get more complicated when you sell the rental property."

"Speaking of that, I have a question to ask you."

"Yes?"

"What do you think about *Facebook?*"

"The one with the botched IPO?"

"Yes. I admire Mark Zuckerberg, the CEO, and what he's done with his innovative social network. I'm thinking I might put the money from the sale of the rental property into it."

"The stock went south and is not doing much," Bidley commented.

"I know, but I think it's bound to bounce."

Bidley blew a low whistle. "It's risky. Think about it."

Grace and Linda spent the better part of the afternoon perched at a table in a local organic supermarket. The older woman addressed a healthy plate of veggies and salad while Linda munched on a greasy, artery-clogging piece of pizza laden with spinach and bleu cheese. After exhausting various topics, Grace coached her friend on the art of letting go.

"When I obsess, I get a pencil and pad and start writing. I ask myself how I feel. A lot of times, it's fear. Why am I afraid? I try to trace it to its origin. I ask myself if I have any other troubling feelings. Then, try to figure out what I want to do. Usually, it's some kind of action and usually I don't want to do it. I talk to God and ask Him to guide me. If nothing happens and I still feel like shit, I write to God and stress how much I need His help. I try to be really specific about the difficulty I have. Then, I stuff the paper in a can decorated with green paper. It's my "God can" can and it goes on the top of the refrigerator. Eventually, I stop obsessing and reclaim my peace and move on."

"Sounds simple." Linda took a bite of pizza. The cheese had a kick to it, but she rather enjoyed the taste.

"Do you pray that your sister Mary has all the good things you'd want for yourself?"

"I usually ask God to take her—quickly." That was the mood Linda was in.

"You've got a lot of work ahead of you, girl. Keep coming back." Grace bent over a spoonful of veggies. "One more thing. Let me tell you what happened to me. I was young. My father, my twin, my older sister, and I were crossing the street when my twin dawdled and got behind us. The next thing I knew a car hit her. My father screamed and dove under the car to pull her out. Luckily, she was alive. Later that night, my parents were in their bedroom and I wanted to be with them, but my mother shut the door on me. I was hurt and I carried that resentment all my life, until my sponsor taught me to see the incident from my mother's eyes. She said my mother must have been distraught. It freed me from my anger, and

I was released from my own self-made prison. I never used to see things the way others saw them. Once I understood that, my life got easier."

Linda paused, pizza held in midair, and looked at Grace who looked back at her the way a sponsor would.

"One day you'll see that it was never about the power, or the money, but other things. This whole episode in your life will teach you what's really important." Grace chomped on the veggies and smiled at the younger woman. She waited a moment then asked, "Say, did you happen to get to the art exhibit?"

Linda set the pizza down and replied, "Sorry. I missed it."

"It was a wonderful exhibit about peace by women artists."

"I was home watching a war movie."

Grace laughed.

"I've been studying the history of Great Britain," Linda added. "It turned out to be about their numerous wars." She licked her fingers then wiped them on a paper napkin. "I was too tired to go out anyway. I played tennis in the morning and Table tennis in the afternoon."

"I don't know how you do it."

"That's nothing. I know a ninety-six-year-old man who does that and then goes out dancing in the evening." She grinned, picturing her friend Jim. "I'm just trying to keep up with him."

A few days later, a letter addressed to Cathy lay on Linda's desk, awaiting an envelope. It was a friendly letter, requesting monthly income and expense of the rental property. Once again, Linda's hand reached boldly toward it and tucked it neatly into an envelope. She could hear Grace's words almost as if she were in the room with her. "Be kind in what you write. Sign your letter with love. Remember you're not doing this for them, but for you. It frees you from their garbage."

The letter, she decided, was a step in the right direction. Feeling so good about it, she wrote a letter to her elderly uncle.

Numerous voice messages and emails from realtor Hodge conveyed a distinct sense of urgency. Both sisters, having signed an extension of his listing agreement, had totally ignored Linda's request for a fresh start with a new realtor. Now Hitler and Mussolini needed her signature.

But in Linda's opinion, Hodge, slower than a snail, had held them up long enough. She was determined to get out from under the thumbs of Mary and Cathy. It had taken time but establishing the estate as a tenancy-in-common had paved the way for a single vote to gain traction, in the seven-year family war. One vote—or lack of it—could shut down the whole operation or at least pause it indefinitely. She made use of that newfound power. She looked for a new realtor in earnest.

Sitting across the desk from Mike Borges, a realtor she'd just been introduced to, Linda listened patiently to his spiel as she settled into a comfy leather chair in a small office he shared. The other desk was vacant, at the moment. She had dropped in without an appointment and had asked to speak with an available realtor. Borges said he had a few minutes.

With eyelashes that could sweep the floor and a friendly smile, Borges had movie star appeal. He leaned back against the chair, adjusted the collar of a golf shirt, and considered her concerns about how her sisters had excluded her and kept her uninformed about the rental real estate. "My standard method of operation is different," he said. "Every time the property is shown, an email will go to all concerned about any comments from the realtor or potential buyers. Whatever is said about the property, or the price, will be equally shared instantly, without editing."

Transparency thrilled her. Linda wanted to jump across the desk and hug him. "I like the sound of that," she exclaimed. "My sisters and their bloodthirsty attorney have kept me in the dark for too long."

"I'd be happy to take charge."

"Not so fast, Mike." Linda held up a hand. "We've got to introduce you to the family."

"I have an introductory letter I usually send out, along with a brochure."

"Perfect, but remember, my sisters may not be open to solicitation. They like to do things their way. Try not to take rejection personally."

Borges raised his head, his deep black eyes searching hers. "I'm treating it like a cold call."

"Good." She remembered cold calling. "It might be difficult selling the property in the middle of a double-edged recession," she said to him.

"I'll do the best I can," Borges replied.

"There's got to be a bottom somewhere." She hesitated, not sure how to explain the rest without running him off. "What I'm going to say next might surprise you, but I feel I have to tell you to give you a better understanding of what you're about to get into." She looked at him, seeing his interest pick up. "You remember World War II?"

A smile spread across his lips and a light glinted in his eyes, as if he was truly appreciating the illustration. Borges wanted to laugh or assure her that it couldn't be that bad. He opened his mouth slightly.

"Hitler had a general do his dirty work—attorney Brown is my sisters' fair-haired Aryan. His name is Nestor Brown. Have you heard of him?" Borges shook his head. No. "They may run your name by him." She waited a second to gauge his reaction, but he merely shrugged, as if made of Teflon. "My advice is to praise him to the skies," Linda added. "I'm just relating what I've learned along the way."

"I know what you're going through," Borges said. "I went through something similar with my family. I didn't speak to my brother for a year and I didn't speak to my father for two. Now we're the best of friends."

Linda thought about that. She said, "Yesterday, the listing expired, and I received five desperate messages from the former realtor."

"Why won't you stick with him?"

"He's slow and incompetent." She added, "Plus, he repeated to me what my sisters said about me and it wasn't very nice or necessary. He also kept forwarding their emails to me. I thought that was unprofessional."

Borges followed her drift and replied, "I'm not a messenger."

"Glad to hear you say it." She looked at him, admiring how he was handling himself. "It's been twenty-four hours since the listing expired and, by now, everyone's aware that my signature is not forthcoming." As if to underscore her words, her cell phone rang. She looked at it with dismay. "It's the realtor!"

"You want me to talk to him and tell him I'm the new guy?" Borges leaned forward, eager to be of assistance.

"You aren't yet, until you get my sisters' consent," Linda reminded him. "I'll let this call go to voice mail." She watched the call disappear. "Mike, it's normal—isn't it?— for other realtors to solicit expired listings."

"Of course! That's how we get business!"

"They won't think I put you up to it?" she asked.

"I don't know what they'll think. In this business, realtors don't need an excuse to prospect new clients."

"Okay. It'll blow their minds to receive your letter so quickly. You'll be ahead of the pack." *If there is a pack,* Linda thought. *How many realtors would want this listing?*

A knock sounded on the door and an agent poked his head into the room. He signaled with his head toward the waiting room. "Your clients are here."

"I gotta run," Borges said.

For the next few weeks, Hodge repeatedly tried to get Linda to sign the listing extension. She ignored him, hoping he'd take the hint and go away. When that didn't work, she sent him a voice mail thanking him and saying she had moved on. Meanwhile, acting as if he'd just noticed that the listing had expired, Borges sent Mary and Cathy an introductory letter, attaching his credentials and several glossy photos of properties he'd sold. He mailed the same package to the three sisters. Nice touch, Linda mused; his photo alone should make my sisters eager to work with him.

"Would love to see you."

Jane's email made Linda's heart stop. In a matter of moments, the stereo blasting, Linda danced around the house, feeling exhilarated, grateful. After a long bumpy road with the paternal side of the family, a streak of sunshine had broken through the clouds.

One cousin was a fine start. She took that good feeling into a meeting.

Twelve members, most clutching steaming coffee cups, huddled around a rectangular table, in a local church building. Leading the meeting was Charlie who chafed under a neck and back brace, from recent surgery. Each person took a turn reading a paragraph from the chapter about steps four and five, in the *Big Book*, which were about self-honesty and admitting to wrongs committed. These steps are crucial for the healing process; skipping them, or skimping on them, could easily lead back to a drink.

"This section reminds me of the labs I used to take in school." Charlie carefully turned his head in the neck brace. "They were always scheduled early in the morning and ran into the lunch hour. We used to pass the liberal arts majors in the halls—like the crypts and the bloods passing each other—the science wonks were always doped up, on drugs, and hung over. To me, steps four and five are our labs." Wincing, he adjusted the straps of the brace.

"I was in labs in school, too," said Eric, a local pharmacist, "We used to mix ethyl alcohol, with cheap orange mix from the vending machine. We'd sip our drinks all day, as we experimented with various compounds. I *loved* lab work."

Charlie stood up, gently stretched, and leaned against the wall.

"You can take the rum out of fruitcake," said Helmut, a visitor from Germany, "but you still have fruitcake. That's what happens when you don't do these steps."

"I was a liberal arts major and I didn't take labs," said Gina, "but I did my fifth step, with a priest. I was so scared. When it came time for him to give me my penance, I was afraid he'd give me a hundred *Hail Marys,* but he was so understanding. He told me he had a lot of respect for A.A. and asked me to say the *Serenity Prayer.*"

"There's so much animosity for us in the real world," said Jean, a former nun. "I dated a few psychologists and I had to drop them because they were so negative about alcoholics. It's too bad they don't come here and see how we struggle." Jean paused and looked down the table.

"I remember my first meeting," said Stanley, "I was listening to a speaker with his head shaved on one side and a tattoo of a spider in a web. I don't want what you have, I thought, but the program grew on me. I used to frequent bars where they bolted the chairs and tables to the floor, so we wouldn't throw them and served paper cups, so we wouldn't cut each other." Wiry, with friendly eyes, it was hard to picture Stanley in a place like that. "I used to take meetings to Folsom prison. The men in C cell were there . . . for life." Stanley looked around the room. "One day, I was at a meeting in another town and a man came up to me and asked, 'Remember me?' He said, 'You brought A.A. to Folsom and it had an effect on me. My life changed after that. The warden noticed. My parole board noticed. I'm the first man pardoned from C cell.' I tell you, I never heard *anything* like that."

His words had a powerful effect on the members, including Linda who spoke.

"I received a letter from my Uncle John. I held it up to the light to see what was in it." Laughs. "I was expecting—Keep out and stay out!" Linda bent her head. "It took me half an hour to open it. It'd been so many years. I was mad at him for some silly reason and cut him out of my life. Recently, I wrote him a letter and said I was thinking of him, wished him well, and was grateful for the good times we had at his house . . . His response wiped out many years of silence."

A member noisily blew her nose. Tears ran down Cassy's reddened face. Lance kept rubbing his beard distractedly. The leader stared off into space as if seeing something from the past.

"He wrote that he played bridge and did crossword puzzles and cryptograms." Linda laughed aloud. "He's ninety-one—the oldest and only surviving member of my father's family. Well, I have to tell you, after that, I googled like mad, until I found his number."

Someone handed her a box of *Kleenex*.

She took one and dabbed her eyes. "He answered the phone— and I told him I wanted to see him. He didn't reply, and I froze . . . ."

A sharp intake of breath from Lance broke the stillness in the room.

Linda continued. "He murmured something about not being up to visitors, because he was alone and had no one to help him with the housework. At first, I thought it was a brush off, but then he explained it would be okay to come for a brief visit." She concluded nervously, "Next week I'm going to see him."

After a few more joking references to drugs and labs, the meeting ended.

A newcomer, just separated from his wife, approached Linda. "Your story is inspiring."

"Thanks. I'll let you know how it turns out."

Chapter Thirty-Seven

Angie, a friend of Linda's with similar family difficulties, attached a transponder to the windshield. "Use the sun pass. It'll make the trip to Jupiter go faster."

"That's mighty nice of you. Appreciate it." Backing out carefully, avoiding kids' tricycles and roller boards, Linda eased out of Angie's parking space in an apartment complex, on the far side of town. Angie and she had attended the same meetings and become close friends. She'd asked her to accompany her on the trip to reunite with her uncle.

They crossed the Florida peninsula on Alligator Alley and headed north, the transponder shrieking at each tollbooth. Upon exiting the turnpike, directions from map quest proved too difficult for even such savvy navigators to follow. The surroundings turned distinctly rural.

"I think this is the wrong way," Linda said. "We're supposed to be going east, towards the Atlantic ocean."

"Too many cows," Angie concurred. "Make a U-turn at the next light."

Finally, the two women arrived at the end of a cul-de-sac and Uncle John's house. Linda got out of the car and surveyed the surroundings. She told herself to be brave, threw her shoulders back, and approached the portico.

The front door slid open to reveal an aging man with a square face and penetrating dark blue eyes, a replica of her father, as she had last seen him. One eye, she noticed, was encircled by bright red skin. Uncle John, her father's older brother, was the last surviving member of his family. Linda sucked in her breath, knowing how much her uncle detested emotional weakness, and how prone she was to emotional display. She introduced Angie to her uncle.

"Pleased to meet you." Uncle John stepped to the side and gestured for them to enter his house.

Angie passed within. Awkwardly and nervously, Linda followed, tripping over the hurricane shutter brace at the foot of the door. Angie held out her arm. Linda quickly recovered her balance. Not noticing, her uncle led the way with a gimpy, but sprightly step, into a spacious family room overlooking a lake.

"Have a seat." Uncle John gestured toward a love seat set against the wall while he himself sat down on a sofa facing a wide screen television.

The girls made themselves comfortable.

"Have you had lunch?" Linda inquired, glancing at her wristwatch.

"Not yet."

"Let's visit here for a few moments and then go eat."

"Fine with me." Uncle John pointed to his eye. "I woke up with this."

"Did you forget to duck?" Linda joked, relieved that he had brought it up, because she was about to ask him about it.

Uncle John laughed. "You shoulda seen the other guy." His quip put the girls at ease. "I've seen this before. When you get older the blood bleeds into the skin." He indicated other red spots on his body. "There's nothing I can do about it. It usually lasts a few weeks and then fades."

Although the skin looked troubled, the eye was clear. Linda was concerned, but not alarmed. "It's really good to see you, Uncle John."

"Likewise."

"How long has it been?"

"1867—right after the Civil war."

Their laughter broke the ice.

"Longer than I thought." In a flash, Linda remembered the last time she had seen him. "You were there when my dad passed." Twelve years, but she had ceased speaking to him long before that and they both knew it.

"You've never been in this house."

Linda could see the hurt in his expression and instantly regretted her actions. "It was my fault, Uncle John. I was nuts." She drew imaginary circles in the space around her head with her finger. "I go to A.A. now and I've changed. That was something I used to do when I was drinking—cut people out of my life when I got mad at them." *There, it's out, I've made my amends to him.*

Uncle John seemed concerned. "Have you always had this problem?"

"Probably."

Angie and Linda exchanged glances, as if they were from a secret society, which, in a way, they were.

"This is a beautiful place you have here," Angie said, changing the subject as she took in the room's furnishings. "It reminds me of my aunt's place."

"Angie's an artist and a teacher." Linda relaxed and threw her arm across the back of the love seat. "She has her own studio."

Uncle John asked Angie a few questions about her choice of career. Linda let them talk a few minutes and then reentered the conversation.

"It was in the school system in our county that I met your granddaughter. Have you heard about that?" Uncle John shook his head and Linda explained. "I was a substitute at an elementary school and an attractive, young student teacher entered the classroom. I was her supervisor for the day. She walked up to me and said we both had the same last name."

"Oh, right!" Uncle John beamed. "I did hear about that. She got a job right out of college. She's teaching fifth grade at Shadowlawn."

"Shadowlawn!" Angie exclaimed. "That's where I teach! Are you related to Selma Cray?"

Both Uncle John and Linda expressed surprise.

"My granddaughter!" Uncle John said excitedly. "What a small world!"

"My second cousin!" Linda sat shaking her head in disbelief. "Three hours in the car together and now I discover that Angie works, with a member of our family."

"That's so *amazing.*" Angie tilted her head toward Uncle John. "I teach her students art and we share a common room."

"Let's go celebrate over lunch." Uncle John eased himself off the sofa and steadied himself while the girls gathered their purses and prepared to leave.

As they approached the restaurant, Uncle John walked briskly and said to them over his shoulder. "There's no beer in this place. Oh . . . right, you—quit."

"Right." Linda smiled, figuring he was just getting used to her new status, as a nondrinker.

Once seated in the brightly lit restaurant that served breakfast and lunch, Uncle John spoke lovingly of his deceased wife, Tess, of sixty-three years. He turned to Angie. "Are you married?"

"Going on forty years. We broke apart once, but couldn't stay away from each other."

"Good," Uncle John approved.

The waitress came by and took their orders. It seemed like only minutes had passed when she returned with their meals. The three of them bent over the plates.

After chewing and swallowing toast and eggs, Linda asked her uncle, "How are your sons doing?"

"Brian's busy with his family and job." Uncle John polished off a piece of bacon. "Dan's doing fine. He has an avid interest in WWII."

"What a coincidence," said Linda.

"He reads about it all the time."

"So do I." Linda stirred the ice in her water glass. "I'm fascinated by Churchill. He kept everyone going during that time." She stopped stirring, sat up straighter. "I like the speech that goes: 'We shall fight on the beaches, we shall fight on the landing grounds—"

"'—We shall fight in the hills,'" Uncle John joined in the quote. Uncle and niece finished together. "'—We shall never surrender!'" He smiled at his niece. "The British people did a *fantastic* job."

The waitress sauntered by, catching the last part of his comment. "Why, thank you!" She glided to the next table with a broad smile.

"She thought I meant her—" Uncle John chuckled. "—I'm not retracting the statement."

Both girls, having heard the exchange, smiled at him. When the check came, Uncle John tucked it under his plate, as if to hide it from the girls.

Linda reached out with her hand. "Will you let me get *that*?"

Uncle John didn't reply, but only stared at her with a blank expression.

"I know *that* look," said Angie. "It means: Don't even *ask*."

Uncle John relaxed and laughed, obviously pleased with Angie's observation.

The drive through the winding streets that led back to his house seemed less complicated the second time around. Once inside again, he gave them a detailed tour of his photo gallery, including several photos of his brother and him fishing off the Venezuelan coast. "Your father hated to get up early, but I told him that's when the fish bite. I remember one time we went out in the boat at six in the morning and got our first bite at nine. Your dad said that proved we could have slept in for another three hours. He had a great sense of humor, your dad." Uncle John's eyes filled up.

Linda cleared her throat.

They came upon a few photos of the two brothers in their WWII uniforms.

"There's a newspaper article about me on the other side of the window." He pointed to a weathered frame she hadn't noticed until then.

She took a few steps and leaned over to read it. The article said that he was commissioned a lieutenant in the U.S. Air force.

As a cadet, Lt. Cray was selected to enter the All American Bombing Olympics and scored the highest marks of the team which ranked sixth highest of all teams competing. He was graduated as a distinguished bombardier and was appointed an instructor.

So that's how it went. She turned to him with admiration and he met her glance with humility.

"Your dad was also a teacher, but he was sent on a mission to bomb Japan." Uncle John braced himself by putting both hands on the desk. "He had eleven missions. A shell struck his plane, the B-29, and he made a forced landing at Okinawa." Uncle John paused and looked at the two young women. "It's funny what you do in a situation like that. Your dad said he grabbed his head, as if to make sure it was still on."

Linda made a sound meant as a laugh. She was looking at the world through her father's eyes, from the cockpit of a B-29, as it flew over the Pacific.

"Your dad was—what?—nineteen-years-old and responsible for the lives of eleven men." Uncle John shook his head sadly. "After that, he swore that he'd never fly again." His face lit up unexpectedly. "The next day was VJ Day."

"August 12, 1945." Linda had memorized the date—Victory over Japan.

"You don't know how it was back then," Uncle John explained. "You didn't have much choice."

"I met a man who landed on Normandy beach on D-Day," said Angie. "He fell out of his small boat, and his comrades fished him out of the sea."

"When they landed in those boats and saw their friends getting killed, they didn't want to get off." Uncle John gestured making a pistol out of his hand and pointing it to his head. "If they didn't, they'd be shot."

"Frank got lucky," Angie continued. "His comrades took him to a nearby village and the French countrymen dried his clothes and gave him a pair of wooden shoes. He said he saw 137 days of combat. He walked by a concentration camp, was curious, but couldn't bear to look inside. When the Army asked him if he wanted to reenlist, he told them that he had a brother in Italy and another one in Hawaii, all fighting. He just wanted to go home."

"Did your father talk to you about his experiences in the war, Linda?" Uncle John asked.

"No."

Uncle John had a look on his face that indicated he didn't understand why. There was silence while they browsed among the photos in the room. Uncle John showed them a photo of the founders of Walmart. A crew of a dozen men stood around a rustic wooden table.

"See that guy there, to the right." He pointed with his index finger. "He was my friend. One of the original group that founded Walmart. Nice guy. I told him I bought shares, paid about eighty a share. He told me he owned 80,000 shares and his cost was pennies."

Linda smiled. "I'm always interested when someone makes a fortune in stocks. That was my trade."

Uncle John watched as Linda and Angie peered at the photo. The man he indicated was small, with wire frame glasses, a rather nondescript-looking fellow. The next photo showed the same man, years later, with a broad grin, stretching a lanky frame contentedly in a chaise lounge.

"Once we went to a boat show and he pointed to a twenty-five million dollar yacht. Even though he could easily buy it, he didn't. That's the way he was. So humble." As an afterthought, and with a lowered tone, he added, ". . . He died last year."

My uncle's lonesome. Many of those he loved and admired had gone before him. He misses them and probably thinks about them as he sits around the house doing jigsaw puzzles. A dozen of his prized puzzles had been laminated and hung on the adjacent wall.

"Have you got any photos of Selma?" Angie finally asked.

"This way." Uncle John led them down a hallway where there was a large family portrait. Angie stepped closer and bent for a better look.

"Yep. That's her all right. Tall, beautiful. . . with long, dark hair." Young Selma looked back at them from the photo as if appreciating the compliments.

Angie and Linda left shortly after that.

"There was a lot of healing between you two," Angie said as she gazed out the window watching fields go by in a blur, as the tires chewed up the space between Jupiter and Buena Vida. "It gives me hope that the broken ties in my own family can be restored."

"I imagine my uncle is already calling Selma," Linda said as she chomped on a juicy pear. "Word about our visit will be old news by the end of the week. I can just hear my older sister—Uncle John had a visit with my sister? Not Linda!"

In the days that followed her visit to Uncle John, Linda mailed letters to her uncle's sons, Dan and Brian, busily corresponded with her cousin Ron, and booked a flight to visit her cousin, Jane. With every communication, she expressed a heartfelt desire to reconnect with extended family members and their families. Hands reached back. Plans were made with joy and jubilation. Linda had allies. The number of those willing to speak with her was growing, up from zero, which was where it was when she'd entered A.A. She longed to reconcile with her immediate family members, but knew they were not quite ready. Despite their chilliness, she found she could stand up to them, of coping with whatever treachery they might throw at her.

As long as the law allowed first come, first served, gross disparities in the distribution of power and wealth would persist. Adult siphoning of parental assets would continue. She imagined an independent court-appointed custodian to prevent some from taking advantage of the system. The thought made her smile.

The afternoon mail delivered a jolt.

Cathy wrote: "I insist that you stop having realtors contact Mary and me. All correspondence from you is to go through our attorney, Nestor Brown. And we would appreciate it if you would stop holding up the sales process on the rental house and sign the listing agreement with Vance Hodge. Do it now!"

Linda smiled and put down the letter. *Busted.* She closed her eyes, thinking about the demand. *Whip. Whip. I can almost feel the sting. But my sisters no longer have total control. They need my signature to collect the inheritance.*

Hodge had erred in more than one way: like failure to answer questions regarding the house showings and not bringing an offer in two years. What was there to like?

She spoke with her attorney, Crandall. "Cathy gave me the boot with cleats."

Crandall smiled. "Don't do anything. Nothing at all." He watched her reaction closely.

Linda remained cool and calm. "Won't that imply consent? Like it's all right, or—something?"

Crandall wavered a moment before answering. "Don't worry about that." His eyes locked on hers. "One thing is positive. Cathy wrote the letter. That's a change."

It might have been a change, but Linda figured that Mary had a say as to what was written. The letter was shocking and mean.

It bothered her and she wanted to talk to her priest counselor about it. Father Howard had been a priest for fifty years and, at times, could be irreverent though he usually knew what he was talking about.

Celebrant for daily Mass, Father Howard saw Linda approaching and asked, "Any news?"

"Just this." She handed him Cathy's letter.

The priest read the letter and looked at her. "I'm glad she's your sister and not mine. Whew! That was a nasty letter. What kind of work does she do for a living?"

"She's a veterinarian."

He thought for a second before answering. "Be thankful you're not a poor, sick, little animal in her shop."

Linda nodded, her lips pursing. Lately, she was leaning more toward church counsel than her own attorney. It had reached that point.

Just then, Rob, a maintenance man, swerved past them, carrying a bouquet. "You going to be ready by eleven, Father?"

The priest nodded.

"A funeral?" Linda asked. Most funerals were held after daily Mass.

"This one's a cremation." Rob had a twinkle in his eye as if there was a private joke between the priest and him.

Father replied without missing a beat, "That's the last time his ash will be in church."

Rob let out a thick, appreciative laugh and then, peering around the church, quickly stifled his mouth with his hand. Father Howard seemed pleased with Rob's response.

They must joke around like this regularly thought Linda. When Rob moved down the aisle, she resumed their discussion.

"After meeting with my attorney, I wrote a brief note to my sister. I insisted on a new realtor and a lower price to get the house sold as fast as possible."

Father Howard nodded in approval.

"Say Father, you know about A.A. and the *Big Book?*"

"Yeah, yeah," the priest replied as if he knew enough about it, more than he wanted to know.

"Well, it says that I'm supposed to write someone I dislike and tell them that I regret the ill feeling between us. What do you think?"

"You already did that. Your sisters still poop on you."

She had to agree with him—a sad truth.

"You're not alone. My brother hadn't spoken to me in years and suddenly he gets a divorce, loses his job, is lonely, and he's calling me every week. He came down to stay with me and after a few days he announces he wants to leave. He says, 'You don't feed me.' I told him there was plenty of food. He says, 'No, it's not the food I like. I'm going.' So he took off. You see, Linda, you're not the only one with a nut case in the family."

"I've got two."

Father Howard nodded and saw that some people had entered the church for the funeral. He started to leave, but then turned to her and said, "They'll have to answer to God for that." He stuck out his chin. "Hang in there." The priest took a few strides, stopped, and turned again. "They're not the only ones who have to answer to God."

"What do you mean?"

"I can't say much. You'll hear about it soon enough. Just come to church on Sunday." With that, he left her.

Chapter Thirty-Eight

Driving into the church parking lot, Linda saw people from the previous service lingering in clusters, talking animatedly. She passed them and entered the church, pinning an usher identification tag to the lapel of her jacket. A few parishioners approached and asked what was going on. She explained that she'd just arrived and knew nothing.

Linda looked around, sensing a ripple of tension among the congregants who had whispered among themselves.

Just then, the side door burst open and banged against the wall. Father Matthew led an entourage comprising Martha, liturgical director and his personal assistant, and Dwayne Sumner, choir director. With purposeful strides, they marched to the first pew, directly in front of the pulpit on the altar, and squeezed in so that they sat shoulder to shoulder. The rest of the group scattered throughout the pews behind the priest. Father Matthew, dressed in a dark suit sans traditional priestly collar, folded his arms across his chest, and stared straight ahead. His cohorts did the same.

The pastor was popular, a golden orator who'd made the parishioners laugh. Largely due to his efforts and charisma, a sum the size of a legislative campaign had been raised for the church's expansion, which went up in short order. Unfortunately, about a fourth of the funds was unaccounted for and that had raised more than a few eyebrows in the diocese.

"What're they here for?" Curious and concerned, Linda asked Mason, the new head usher, since Fred Martin had taken ill.

"Patience, o' ye of little faith," Mason replied with a wicked smile, as if he knew what was coming.

The ousted priest's entourage didn't bode well. Especially since the Bishop's entourage, consisting of the Monsignor, his chief of staff, and other princes of the church, were just outside the front door, gathering steam.

At the sound of a bell, Bishop Hank Lang, flanked by the Monsignor, entered and proceeded to the altar. Fathers Pedro and Howard, from St. Anthony's, followed close behind. Spying the rebellious priest in the front pew, the bishop bristled visibly. Father Matthew glared back defiantly.

The service progressed with the bishop keeping close to the usual liturgical ritual.

Bishop Lang faced the congregation with a face that appeared calm and confident. "I'm happy to be here, but I'm also sad and hurt. I have come to let you know that your administrator, Father Matthew, is on temporary leave of absence." He moved his head from left to right to take in everyone. "A deacon will temporarily fill the position."

Linda looked at the priest, seated with his arms folded across his chest. She thought, *It doesn't look like he's on leave.*

The Bishop attempted to continue when a group of angry parishioners stormed out in a staged protest. One woman ran to the altar. She stood in front of him and shouted her displeasure, shaking a closed fist held high. The Bishop looked down at her with a mixture of shock and dismay. Another man ran up the central aisle and put his foot on the first step of the altar as if ready to launch himself against the Bishop. Incited by the heat of the excitement, hecklers joined in.

The Bishop raised his voice, in order to be heard over the din. "This is a Mass, not a forum for debate. We are here because of Jesus Christ and we are to behave accordingly."

Gradually, the dissenters settled down and resumed their seats. However, when it came time for the handshake, the mob descended upon Father Matthew in further demonstration of their loyalty and affection, which created more disruption.

At the end of the service, the ousted priest exited by way of Linda's section in a promenade, as if he were still presiding, greeting parishioners and embracing them. As he came abreast of Linda, he looked at her with a twinkle in his bewitching blue eyes and commented, "We came to peace, didn't we?"

Linda smiled and shook his hand, remembering the conflict they'd had and the trouble it had caused both of them. "Sure, Father. We came to peace. Good luck to you."

Father responded by grabbing her brusquely and pulling her into a close embrace. Then, he was gone. Stunned, Linda straightened her blouse and rolled her shoulders backward to relax.

It was not finished.

Returning to the dais, the Bishop announced, "I will explain some things to those who are still present. Some things that I can't put in print, but I will tell you that Father Matthew had a child . . ." He let the weight of that sink in. ". . . and there are also economic reasons which I am sure you can understand. Bear in mind that this investigation started, because the parishioners of this church came to me with complaints and reports that things were not the way they were supposed to be. *Remember that.* I'll be available to answer questions." With that, he left the altar and walked down the central aisle toward the front door.

Linda realized she was not alone in writing a letter of complaint.

The altar vacated, a man grabbed the microphone and bellowed, "This is the people's church. We want Father Matthew back!"

Someone wrested the mike from him and, within moments, they were scuffling on the floor. Parishioners nearby stood like statues.

The Bishop became engaged in responding to parishioners' questions and exclamations at the front entrance: "I didn't know there was a child," said one. "—What?" "I knew it had to do with sex," said another. "Was the girl underage?" "I want you to know this is the first time in thirty years that I came back to church!" Tears streamed down a woman's face. A man countered, "You picked a *hell* of a day to come back!" "Keep coming back, girl! Don't let this sway you." A man pointed to the figure of Christ crucified which hung over the altar. "Come for Him." "That shows you the caliber man our former administrator was! This was Mass! Not a baseball game!" A sobbing couple approached. "We're here visiting from Germany. We've never seen anything like this!" "So what if there was a child!" a woman screamed in his face. "I have a child! Having a child does not make him bad!"

"I have to follow the rules of the church," the Bishop explained, as the woman turned on her heel and stormed off.

A heckler elbowed his way forward through the pressing mob, snuck up behind the bishop, and punched him squarely in the back. "I loved that priest!" he shouted in a perfect example of what can happen when parishioners get carried away.

The Bishop grimaced silently in pain.

"Let the bishop go," the Monsignor, who had seen the assault, spoke in a commanding voice. "He has another service."

As the crowd dispersed, the Bishop hastily exited.

Over the course of the next few days, more calls, emails, and conversations centered on the situation at St. Anthony's. The incident drew attention. The story hit the front page of several local newspapers, with full color photos of the acclaimed and expanded church. A headline ran *Sex and Money Cause Priest's Removal.* By noon, all the papers in Buena Vida had sold out. Twelve million had been raised to fund two renovations, but several million was missing. A full-scale investigation was underway. Once proud and confident at the pulpit, Father Matthew didn't look quite the same on the front page. He looked more like a hoodlum. The story ended by saying that most parishioners wanted this priest back *regardless* of the circumstances. Sentiment for the ruined priest, reflected in Letters to the Editor that could have filled a book, ran the gamut from those totally against him to those who adored him.

Father Matthew refused to give up, without a fight; he and his cohorts, including members of the fund raising committee, were busily sending letters to the parishioners portraying the bishop as a domineering tyrant. The parish was divided. Meanwhile, everyone awaited the outcome of the investigation.

Inside the beautiful stained-glass building, Linda stood among a group of parishioners who debated the issue.

"That Bishop has done this before. He thinks he's God," said a man who towered over her. "I'm not giving him a cent!"

Linda didn't think his weekly one dollar contribution would be a great loss. "The Bishop is not under investigation," she gently reminded him. He abruptly turned his head away from her. "Father Matthew is under investigation."

"*Hmpph.*"

A couple arrived late for service. Linda greeted them, handed them song booklets, and led them down the side aisle, searching for an empty space for two.

"Miss, what do you think is going to happen?" The woman whispered to her.

"I don't know." *Why does everyone think I have the answers?* She held out her arm, guiding them. "There's room in this pew."

At the end of service, there was quite a stir over a letter from the Bishop enclosed in the bulletin. Wanting to keep up with the saga, Linda grabbed a bulletin and pulled out the letter. The bishop wrote that it was his responsibility to safeguard the unity of the church. He had called the errant priest to accountability and initiated a financial review.

He concluded with an entreaty for prayers for all parties. Linda read the letter more than once. The Bishop was trying to be professional and fair, but he faced a wall of hostility. She knew about that.

Another Brown letter arrived the following day—a thick envelope with taped edges. Linda decided to call her friend, the retired judge.

"I can tell you're upset." Paula said on the phone. "I hear it in your voice."

"Attorney Brown never has anything nice to say to me. After six years, I'm tired of his letters."

"I'm surprised he lets himself get so personally involved that he would stoop to such tactics."

"Last month he sent me a letter with my younger sister's return address. You recall she was the one who finally sent me the tax information."

"I remember," said Paula. "Have you complained about him?"

"I wrote to the Florida bar twice to no avail. There were other complaints, but at the end of the year, they expunge the record."

"I remember going to a seminar about that years ago when I was a federal judge. I voted against it."

"Well, . . . they passed it."

Paula sighed, then coughed relentlessly. Years of smoking filterless cigarettes had taken their toll. "I haven't gotten to the second part of the serenity prayer: *Courage to change the things we can.* You want to open the letter with me on the phone?" Paula's curiosity was getting to her.

"Nah, I pass."

"Are you sure? It might be evidence." Paula insisted.

No response.

The judge backed off, "Call me if you change your mind."

They said good by and Linda thought: *Eventually, when my sisters consent to sell at the market instead of a pipe dream and the house sells, there will be three checks, according to the warranty deed, . . . hopefully, . . . and one of those checks will be mine. One third. Mine.* A much-reduced sum than what Mom intended, but it'll be something. Since the downturn, the US economy was weak, the recovery anemic, A malaise seemed to have come over the land. Not a single offer on the rental property. She was on a strict budget, until it sold.

It was time to meet Grace for dinner.

Grace looked at Linda across the table in their usual place—a soup and sandwich shop, with an eye-popping bakery. Grace had ordered a full meal and a cherry pastry and was going at it with gusto. Linda nibbled on a sesame seed bagel, not sure if she was hungry enough to eat.

"What's going on with you?" Grace asked.

"Not much," Linda lied. "How about you?"

"I'm staying at the home of the pet owners. I'm watching their reptiles and walking their big dogs. I didn't want the job. I prefer kitties."

"You've been successful in your business." Linda was thinking about how Grace had supplemented her income through pet-sitting.

"Yes, and I love it." Grace sat back with a smug expression. "Now tell me *what's going on?*" When the younger woman didn't reply, Grace persisted. "I can tell by your expression that *something's* going on. *What is it?*"

There was so much to say Linda didn't know where to start. After thinking a moment, she said, "How do you deal with a sponsee who's drinking and desperate?"

"I tell them to call back when they're sober."

That was the preferred method, Linda knew. "She was drinking sadness and working herself up. She told me she was crying so much she was bleeding."

"When there's blood, call 911."

Linda nodded. *Good direction.* "Thanks. I wasn't sure, but I told her to call back when she wasn't crying."

"That was the right thing to say." Grace looked at Linda. "What's going on with your sisters?"

Linda wished that she had tabled that subject. "It's dead in the water for now. My sisters won't speak to me except through their attorney and I won't speak to him. Did I tell you that I returned his latest letter?"

"Really." Grace glared, showing disapproval. "What if it was a buy out offer?"

"We've already tried that." Although exhausted by the mere discussion of the topic, Linda didn't want to leave it at that. "There's no other offer, just more harassment. You have to understand, Grace, I've been through this before. For six years, I've received correspondence from their attorney. Every week, it seems, I hear from that bastard. There's a stack of letters from him in my file." *Mount Everest.*

Grace raised her eyebrows. "He's made money." A wicked smile played at the corners of her lips, as if she was enjoying the conflict.

"No kidding." Linda knew who was paying—the estate. A pause ensued with neither of them saying anything. "I've indicated how I'd like us to move forward—new realtor, lower price. I said I'd sign a new listing . . . They know that."

"What if it was a listing?"

"From him? He's an attorney—not a realtor," Linda stated. "The only other thing is the tax information, which my new accountant can chase down. I've detached from the rest of it. I hardly think of them anymore. They want to run the day-to-day management of the rental and that's okay with me, just so long as they don't bitch about it." She shrugged her shoulders. "I've been watching war movies recently. You know, Churchill had bunkers. Well, I've got a bunker! A.A. meetings!"

Grace looked at her like she'd lost her mind.

"Before Hitler started bombing London," Linda went on, "the British took great pains to preserve their telecommunication lines. They encased their cables in tunnels beneath the city. While the Luftwaffe blistered the skies, Churchill talked with the heads of seventy nations. Well, you know, I've got a cell phone. I may not talk with prime ministers, but I have the numbers of hundreds of recovering drunks. I make calls . . ."

"Go heavy on words like 'Thank you' and 'I appreciate it.' Phone calls are good," Grace advised, "but I'm more concerned about your state of mind, because resentments can easily lead back to a drink. Last time we talked you were defensive when I asked you where your property was located. You asked me why I wanted to know as if you were hiding something."

Linda recalled the conversation. "Sorry. I didn't mean to put you off."

"I can't wait until you sell that place and get out of it." Grace murmured as if in prayer.

"The house is there for a reason . . . but I haven't the foggiest notion what it is."

"You don't have to know. Let God."

Grace lifted the cherry pastry that lay on a paper napkin, next to her clean plate, and held it close to her mouth. "I haven't seen you at the eight o'clock meeting."

"I haven't been able to get up early."

"Why don't you come to the noon meeting?"

Linda looked at the ceiling and considered how that would fit into her schedule. "I might."

Grace was encouraging, "The noon group's good."

"Maybe you'll see me there." *A possibility, not a promise.* Linda looked down at the bagel, which had hardened meanwhile and realized she wasn't interested in eating. She threw a napkin over the last of it and pushed the plate aside. She reached for her purse.

Grace stood, seeming satisfied with herself.

Linda glanced at her watch. They'd been sitting for an hour. Where had the time gone? She felt release from something she didn't know she was holding onto and thought that Grace's strong sponsorship was helpful in ways she hadn't expected. That she could feel relief so quickly, right after their talk, was encouraging.

"I've got to give Moose his snack and walk him," Grace declared. Moose was a dog that Grace took care of and he was as big as a— well, his name said it all.

Later that evening, Linda sprawled on the sofa, feeling like a warrior laid out on a stretcher. What could she do to bring the Cray family through the shoals of estate settlement to safe, tranquil shores?

Chapter Thirty-Nine

Attorney Brown paced his office, fretting and fuming. In his hands was the letter he'd sent to Linda, which had come back to him: *Refused, return to sender. Who the hell did she think she was?* When he calmed down, he had his secretary set up a conference call with his clients, the sisters.

"She's done it again," he said on speakerphone. "We're going to have to try something more clever."

"Like what—?" Mary asked testily.

"Give me a few days . . . I'll think of something."

"Okay," said Cathy. "We'll wait to hear from you, but don't take too long."

For the next few days, Linda had a strange foreboding, compounded by the end of the week being Friday, the thirteenth. A hundred degrees read the heat index. Linda dragged herself home, took a cool shower, and remained indoors the rest of the day.

Late afternoon, the postal truck lumbered by. A metallic click of the postal box lid awoke Linda from a nap. She roused herself and went outside to check the mail. Inside, a folded-over, air mail express package that must have cost at least five dollars pushed against the walls. Linda struggled to get it out. From: The Colony Group. Sounded like a real estate firm. Probably regarding the rental property. She thought, *A simple letter of introduction would have sufficed.* She decided not to open the package, but go directly there and introduce herself. Take a friend. Someone with a GPS.

A little later, she showed up at Hal's driveway and waved to him, as he came out the door. A friend from the tennis courts, Hal sprinted across his lawn, his long legs used to crossing short distances in good order.

"Have you got it?" Linda asked from the driver's seat with the window down.

"GPS right here." He held the passenger door open and asked, "You want to come in for a minute?"

She ignored the invitation to view his bachelor quarters. "Hop in and set it up."

Hal jumped into the passenger seat and placed the GPS device on the dash. As Linda read the address to him, he commented, "That's only a few miles from here." He typed in the address, paused, and re-typed it. "Sometimes you have to play with these things," he explained.

She nodded. "Are you ready?"

"Sure. Let's go!"

Linda put the car in drive and soon a recording of a woman's voice spoke. "Calculating."

Hal smiled. "The GPS is great. I use it all the time."

"Shh!—I missed what she said."

Hal quieted and turned up the volume.

"Turn right," the voice blared. Then, "Destination reached."

Linda turned into a complex of medical buildings. "Where's number 840? Do you see it?"

"It has to be here. Maybe it's around the back."

Linda drove around the building, reading physicians' doorplates. No real estate firm. Nothing remotely resembling The Colony Group. *Why would a real estate firm be here?* It came to her like a flash. "You know what we've got, Hal? . . . A red herring. It's bogus. If I open the package, I expose myself to more of Brown's bologna and I'm not willing to play that game again." She turned the car and headed back to the highway.

"What do you mean? I don't get it."

"Let's go get something to eat." Linda smiled at him. "I'll explain over dinner."

They arrived at a quaint restaurant and Hal sat across from her at a side table overlooking the water. While enjoying grilled tilapia, she explained the story of her family and what was going on.

Hal had a story of his own. "I was the youngest of eight. My parents couldn't afford to raise us so they parceled us out to orphanages. Later on, they made good money in the furniture business. I was only a baby when I was adopted. My siblings, all seven of them, lived in the same area and stayed close. They totally forgot about me, until it came time to settle the estate. In order to do this, they had to account for me and they told the judge that I'd died." He took a moment to butter a second roll, which he popped into his mouth. "After the money was dispersed to the seven of them, they contacted me."

"How nice of them," she commented sarcastically. "I bet they felt guilty about depriving you of your share."

"Not really. I told them not to worry, because I didn't want the money." He glanced out the window, to watch a fisherman in a rowboat toss his line into the water. "I went to visit them and they were really surprised. After that, they went on with their lives and I with mine. I'm not really close to any of them. Last couple of years—I lost two of them."

Linda wondered what he'd lost—surely not their love and affection. Perhaps on the other side, there would be repentance and remorse—amidst the gnashing of teeth. Still, hearing his sad story made her realize once again she was not alone. She had to hand it to Hal; he'd lightened what would have been an unlucky day and made her feel better.

"Let's stop for a sundae. You want to?" Hal asked.

"Love to!" Ice cream, especially after this latest episode, would be comforting. Linda flipped down the visor and applied a fresh coat of lipstick.

Hal expounded on his hunting prowess and sharpshooter skills as they sat spooning ice cream. "I won many contests in my younger years. I still have eighteen guns in my house."

"You ever use them?" Linda wasn't sure she liked what she was hearing. He was sounding violent.

"Nah. Not too much anymore. I used to go out to target practice. It helped me deal with my anger." Hal licked the spoon nonchalantly as if this was a conversation he'd had everyday.

Linda's hand stopped in mid-air, the spoon dripping vanilla bean ice cream on the dark table top. "Anger?" She looked at her date who'd been a real peach moments ago. "What are you angry about?"

"Remember I told you I was adopted?"

". . . yes."

"That was only part of it. My mother was an alcoholic who abandoned me."

His words sent a chill down her spine.

"I *hate* alcoholics." Hal looked at her as if seeing through her. "I could *kill* them all." Linda shuddered, gulping down a bite and preparing to run for cover. Good thing she hadn't told him anything.

Hal focused on the last of his dessert and then smiled at her, as if he hadn't just dropped a live grenade on the table. She played it cool on the drive back to his house.

"Happy birthday!"

The pleasant sound of Bunnie's voice made Linda smile. She was her number one sponsor. "Thank you for remembering and for calling," This was the personal touch she'd longed for.

"How was your party?" Bunnie asked.

"Great. I have many loyal friends."

"You've made a family!" Bunnie said with enthusiasm.

Linda smiled and nodded. "For a while there, I felt like a sail stretched taut against the sky. I asked, Is this all there is? I had received one card in the mail and only my cousin Tom had called. That was it. On this birthday, I received several email cards and a card from my Uncle John, which was the highlight. Then at the party, my friends showered me with kisses, hugs and attention. I've never felt so nourished and content in my life."

"That's wonderful news. I'm happy for you."

"How's your vacation going?"

In Cape Cod for the summer, Bunnie was staying, with her older brother. "This is the best vacation of my life. Bobby puts fresh flowers in my room every day. The kids are great."

The longest time they'd been separated, Linda missed her friend. "I'm so glad to hear that. You have a great family. How's the weather?"

"It varies," replied Bunnie, and then, as an aside, added, "It's been unusually warm." Not surprising, Linda thought. All over the world people were talking about the same thing. Russia was so hot that wildfires had broken out in a drought and destroyed the wheat crop. Lake Michigan was the warmest on record—compliments of global warming.

"And the food?" Linda asked.

"Wonderful. I've had lobster, crab, cod, of course," Bunnie remarked. "What about you?"

"Fine," Linda said sensibly, not wanting to burden her friend.

Slightly suspicious, Bunnie asked, "Your health?"

"Good. I'm doing much better. I've been communicating with my extended family. My cousin, Jane, says she's looking forward to my visit." Linda continued, "When I first reached out to Jane, she was reluctant to befriend me. Now she can't wait to see me. How cool is that?"

"Linda, you ooze gratitude and the promises. It does me good to hear your story. And there might be more family visits later."

"That's what I'm hoping. When I get back from my visit with Jane, I'd like to see my uncle again. I've written his sons, but they haven't responded . . ."

"Maybe they'll show up when you're there," Bunnie suggested.

"That'd be nice."

"A.A. spreads healing. No one can predict it, but it happens. Once an alcoholic has spent some time in recovery, there's a greater chance that the rest of the family will come to wholeness. I've seen it happen more than once." Bunnie hesitated a moment. "Anything else?"

Linda wanted to tell her about the removal of St. Anthony's administrative staff, like a surgery that was still bleeding, the mysterious air mail package in the latest skirmish with Brown and her sisters. Instead, she said, "We'll catch up when you return."

Bunnie sighed as if relieved. "I really need this vacation."

Linda remembered that Bunnie sponsored several other women who probably required as much time and attention as she. "You deserve it!"

"Thank you. You can tell me about your trip to visit your cousin when I get back."

"That's a plan."

Memories from years of working with this particular sponsor came to mind. Bunnie had always taken her calls and always gone the extra yard. Through thick and thin, Bunnie had been a loyal friend and brilliant guide, giving her a shoulder to cry on for every broken dream and rejoicing with her through every victory. Linda vowed to be there for Bunnie, as she'd been for her.

Her cousins lived in a remote part of New Jersey. She would fly into Newark airport and drive there. For accommodations, they'd steered her to a local hotel. She was coming up to make amends, to reconnect and start anew.

Linda stuffed clothes into a suitcase, hoping she'd arrive in time for dinner.

The flight went smoothly. Upon arrival at Newark airport, Linda called her cousin, who answered the phone on the first ring. The impact of what she was doing hit her and she was suddenly at a loss for words. Fortunately, Jane did most of the talking and encouraged her to get on the road. They were waiting anxiously for her arrival.

It took a mini-course of instruction in the Hertz rental parking lot with an attendant, which resulted in a dead battery and an upgrade, but the GPS proved to be a godsend. Only once did the feminine voice bark: "Calculating." The voice guided her through a lengthy detour, until she was back on track. Traffic bogged down in typical rush-hour-Friday-night-crawl, until she reached the outskirts of urban areas where the landscape turned into rolling, green mountains.

Jane met her in the hotel lobby where they stood a few minutes staring at each other. A more rounded version of her former string bean frame, about the same height, with dark brown hair caressing her chin, Jane's dovelike eyes welcomed. Her second cousin, Marlene, the spitting image of her deceased mother, down to the voice and laugh, made Linda pinch herself to make sure she hadn't stepped into a worm hole and warped back to the distant past.

Dinner was relaxed and easy. They were hungry. The conversation centered on the food they were eating.

A refreshing coolness greeted Linda as she stepped out of the hotel the following morning, for an early stroll. Her cousins were expected later that morning. Exhilarated, she raced downhill, feeling like a filly wanting to gallop through the soft grass and jump fences. She called Marlene. "What are you doing this fine morning?"

"Working on a paper for a class I'm taking."

"Can you pick me up a half hour earlier?"

"What's up?"

"I thought we could walk around the town square. It's so beautiful outside."

It didn't take Marlene long to decide. "See you at 9:30."

Jane led Marlene and Linda through the square, pointing out landmarks. Empty storefronts along Main Street showed the effects of the recession, as in Buena Vida. Later, they drove to Jane's house, not far from downtown. Inside her home, Jane showed Linda the blueprints for a new kitchen.

"With the money I've inherited, I'm doing some things around the house," Jane explained. "Last spring, we put in a new driveway. I don't know what I'm going to do with the rest of it."

"You're lucky you have a pile of money to work with." Linda bit her lip after she said this in an effort not to show anger, or bitterness. "My inheritance is an anthill." She looked at Jane, who seemed to know of the situation, but chose not to say anything. Jane was good at staying neutral, as she walked a tight line between cousins.

Jane stepped to the sink and washed a dish from lunch. "I've lived in this same house thirty years and, believe me, I was getting pretty sick of my kitchen. I've never had a dishwasher in all this time. I have a washer and dryer, which is good. I haven't had to go to the river."

Jane's husband came in from cutting the lawn, covered from head to foot in grass clippings. For some reason, the county required residents to own at least an acre of land. Considerably older than his wife, Joe stood with his hands on his waist. "Welcome to our home!" He made no move to shake her hand, or embrace her. "I've got to finish mowing the lawn. See you at dinner."

"Don't work too hard," Linda replied. Riding on a lawn mower had to be more fun than work, thought Linda. She glanced at a chair along the wall and noted a stack of albums, which Jane had assembled. "How about showing me your wedding photos?"

Not needing a second invitation, Jane motioned to Linda and the two sat at the dining room table. Marlene and Ann, Jane's daughter, followed. Jane placed a thick album on the table and opened it. Page after page Linda smiled at the photos of Jane's prim and proper wedding. Jane looked beautiful in her white flowing dress, with its long train. They switched to baby albums and the younger set immediately became very interested.

"That's a photo of me at my birthday party!" Ann exclaimed.

"Yes," replied Jane. "You were three when I took that one."

Marlene said, "I'm sitting next to you. Look at the size of that cake."

When they finished reviewing thirty years of a successful marriage, Jane turned to Linda. "What about your wedding?"

Linda gulped. "It was quite a scene."

Jane looked at her as if encouraging her to fill them in on the story.

"Oh, I had a traditional church wedding and wore a similar white dress," Linda stated calmly, knowing the ending would surprise them. "The reception was at my parents' house." She recounted the rest of the story, and concluded with the fate of the guests landing in the pool."

Jane commented, "Maybe it was an omen."

Linda nodded. She imagined her cousins were shocked, but to her it had seemed almost normal—quite understandable, in fact. She realized they were becoming comfortable in each other's company. ". . . What happened to *us*?"

Jane looked at her with a question.

"We were close during the first two decades of our lives, our families shared so much." Linda stopped, feeling emotions welling up inside, not knowing if she could go on.

Jane followed her line of thought. "Then for the last four decades—nothing!"

"You married, had three children, one stillborn, went through all the religious rituals of baptism and confirmation, saw your children graduate from college, and stayed married to the same man for three decades—where was I?" Her voice rasped. "What happened?"

Jane shook her head sadly, considering the loss of what could have been—of lost opportunities for friendship and closeness.

"After graduation, everyone scattered," Linda said. "I didn't hear from anyone."

"Our cousins were like brothers and sisters . . . " Jane added.

The fact that Jane had also missed Linda's life was beside the point. Mindful of her cousin's recent loss of mother and sister, Linda stepped forward and affectionately put an arm around her. "Let's not let that happen again, okay?"

Jane looked at her with moist eyes. Linda could feel a connection between them strengthening and it gave her the courage to speak up and encourage a solid continuing relationship.

"Anytime you need me," Linda said to her cousin with a view of hope for the future, "you let me know and I'll be there."

"Same for you," Jane replied.

Section Four

Chapter Forty

The art of making amends, crucial to maintaining harmony in personal relationships and the world , fascinated Linda. It boiled down to different situations calling for different approaches. She thought about her family. They were at a point where even minor hassles seemed overwhelming. *It's gonna take time,* she thought.

The phone rang and Linda answered it.

"How are you?" Bunnie, her main sponsor, the woman she most admired, asked.

"Been reading about amends," Linda confessed.

"Who are you making amends to?" Bunnie's tone was cautionary, as if a move like that would be best talked out first with her.

"Nobody yet, it's a generic reading."

"Oh, good." Bunnie paused a moment and then added. "I was in the emergency room last night."

Knowing Bunnie, fifteen years older, was having some medical issues, Linda asked, "What happened?"

"My foot went numb," the sponsor said. "It had been slightly numb before and I ignored it, but then it went completely numb. It hurt, too."

"What did the doctor say?"

"I have to see a neurologist. It's coming from the lumbar region." Bunnie asked, "What's the latest with you?"

"Not much."

"Just as long as you don't drink. You're a sober, adult woman. You can do anything you want."

"Gee, Bunnie. When you put it that way, it makes me feel free."

"That's the way I feel."

"More than that. I feel a new sense of well being."

Bunnie nodded, as she listened to the younger woman.

"It's hard to explain, but I've noticed that more people want to spend time with me."

Bunnie expanded her line of thinking. "There's a peacefulness about you that they like. It's catching."

"Whatever, I think it's A.A."

Unable to argue with that, her sponsor nodded again in agreement.

Linda was on a roll and wanted to talk. "I hear a still, small voice within me that's like my conscience. Sometimes it sounds like an alter ego, or inner child, sometimes I wonder if God is talking to me, or a relative, like my Dad, or Mom. I can recognize a special tone, the way they used to talk to me, but the important thing is that I hear it. I didn't used to. What it says is usually apropos to whatever is going on in my life and it guides me . . . you know what I mean?"

After her burst of a talking jag, she suddenly stopped. She could hear sniffling on the other end of the line.

"That's good," Bunnie said and then blew her nose loudly. "Why don't you write in your journal about that?"

All the words Linda had a few moments ago had left. Now she struggled for words.

"I've noticed a change in you," Bunnie continued. "There's an openness and friendliness in you. You have challenging ideas, not shallow thinking. You're taking action, not engaging in wishful thinking. You have an honest desire to share, not be selfish."

Linda had seen these qualities in her sponsor, but never dreamed anyone would ever say they belonged to her. She spent a few moments gazing out at a pond behind her house where ducks paddled into view, squawking amongst themselves, as if bickering. They floated into the wider part of the pond, leaving a V-shaped wake behind them. She thought about the upcoming holiday. "Christmas is coming. What are you and Chet doing?" Chet was Bunnie's partner.

"We don't know exactly yet, but we're going to keep it positive and light-hearted—no drama!" Bunnie said. "It works for me!" She chuckled in a motherly way. "I wouldn't want to go to your sister's house for the holiday," she said. "From what you've said in the past, it was uncomfortable for you."

This jogged Linda's memory. "I never felt welcome at Mary's house. She waited until the last moment to invite me. When I was there, I couldn't wait to leave. If it weren't for my mother, I wouldn't have gone."

"I hear it in the meetings. Every year many complain about family dinners and not wanting to go, because of the drinking and drama. Yet they go and it's the same every year. We get sober and we find we're free to go where it feels good. We don't have to live like that anymore." After a moment, Bunnie asked. "Have you made any plans?"

"My cousin Tom invited me up to Savannah to be with his family."

"That was nice of him."

"He's good to me and I will go to see him."

"What about the estate chaos?" Bunnie finally asked, "Anything positive on that score?"

Linda explained, "I'm going to meet with my new accountant to plan a strategy to get the tax information this coming year. I don't want to repeat what I had to go through."

"That's good you have outside help."

"Got to—with my family."

"Remember you have a larger family in A.A." She thought a moment. "Why don"t you reach out to your extended family, after you see your new tax man."

Joe Bidley, tax accountant, invited Linda to have a seat at a long conference table where the chairs bumped against the wall. He listened to Linda and felt compelled to talk about the experience with estate settlement hassle. "A client of mine accounted for every penny when he was left in charge of his mother's estate. At first, he said his siblings distrusted him, but as he continued to account for every penny, they gradually lost that and became nicer. It took almost a year before he settled his mother's estate. His siblings and he have been friends since."

"A year is better than eight years," Linda said, thinking, *I wish he'd been in charge of our estate.* She wouldn't wish what she was going through on her worst enemy.

"I thought I'd send Cathy a postcard so she'd be sure to see the message and say something like please have your attorney give my accountant what he needs by such and such a date, or I'll write to the IRS again."

The accountant shook his head. "Don't expect much cooperation from the IRS."

"It worked last year. Unfortunately, that's what it took to get my family to act. Last year I had to file late because of them."

Bidley thought a moment. "Put in there that you need the information by January 31st for tax planning. Then you can say that you'll hold them accountable for any penalties, or fees, that might be incurred, if they don't get it to you on time."

They went back and forth, until they got the wording just right.

"I'll send it right after the New Year." Linda made a note in her planner.

Linda rose and shook the accountant's hand. "One more question. Can the IRS withhold a refund, if they don't have the real estate information?"

"Not likely. It comes from a different department. I'm not saying it's impossible, just that I've never heard, or seen, anything like that. People file and amend all the time."

"Oh, good." Linda prepared to leave.

"By the way, after you signed a POA for my office, my secretary sent a letter to attorney Brown and we received the numbers for last quarter."

The news gave Linda instant relief and she let out a sigh and sat back in the chair. "That sounds like my problem is solved." She took a moment to savor the news. "Saves me a postcard." She smiled, then thought to ask, "How do the numbers look?"

"There's a loss of $700 which Cathy loaned to the tenancy."

We're still losing money. Linda wondered how much Cathy was out of pocket and how she felt about having to keep the tenancy afloat. One benefit of being kept in the dark, she thought, was that they didn't ask her to pitch in, which they couldn't do legally anyway, since they got themselves into a financial mess. She faced her accountant and asked, "Why don't you go ahead and get the rest of the numbers?"

"Okay. I'll plan on doing that."

By no means was the war over, Linda thought, but at least the bombs weren't dropping as frequently. She thought about how quiet her sisters had become of late. The removal of discord from her life was a blessing, but she wasn't fool enough to think their animosity had faded. No, it was more like she was numb.

In the news she read that the economy was still weak. The Great Recession has swept across the US like a tsunami, taking its toll in millions of lost jobs and homes, and trillions in wealth that simply disappeared. Congress forced the Fed to disclose more than three trillion in loans made during the peak of the financial crisis to foreign and US-based investment banks.

Linda thought, *And my sisters paid cash for that dilapidated rental house.*

Chapter Forty~One

While the mission was to reconcile and reconnect with any family members who would allow it, the immediate game plan was to meet a long lost cousin at Uncle John's house—reunion time. Although they had been close as teenagers, he being two years older, Dan and Linda had not spoken since college. For a brief time, their careers coincided as public school teachers in the same school, but, while Linda had ventured into finances, Dan had made a second career in building homes from scratch, his father's for one. This visit, she had come alone purposefully to reconnect with him and start anew.

She rang the doorbell. A few seconds later, the door swung open.

Dan stood, grinning, and greeted her. "What have you been up to for the last *forty* years?" he asked and then laughed aloud.

She stared at him with shining eyes. Except for being bald with an odd yellowing of his scalp, he had changed little. Short, thin, with laughing eyes, a quick wit. He held his arms open and she walked into them.

The embrace was strong and warm.

They chatted briefly. He turned and motioned for her to follow him. "Come in. Dad's waiting for you."

She followed him into a large room where his father sat comfortably watching television, from a floral sofa. They exchanged greetings.

"How was the trip?" Uncle John asked, extending his hand and letting her draw him into an embrace.

"Uneventful," she replied. "I didn't get lost this time."

There were smiles all around. "Are you planning on staying at the inn like before?"

"I was going to, but Dan invited me to stay at his place." She glanced at her cousin who nodded.

"She can sleep in the guest room," Dan explained cheerfully. "It's ready. I changed the sheets this morning."

Uncle John nodded. He would not have her stay at his place. It wouldn't be proper. "I made reservations at Favio's. Since it's almost six, we'd best be going."

A short distance from his house, the restaurant had the atmosphere of a pub, with an emphasis on steaks, fries, loud music and a thick crowd of beer drinkers clustered around the bar. They elbowed their way into the dining room and located an empty booth against a wall. A waitress approached, as they seated themselves.

"I'll have a glass of red wine and my son will have an appletini—his favorite."

The waitress nodded and didn't write it down. "Happy hour's two for one."

Dan flashed a smile. "Right. Extra thin slices of green apples, please."

"That's his appetizer," Uncle John joked.

"Water for me," Linda said, "No ice please."

"Happy hour ends at six?" Dan asked.

"Yes," replied the waitress. "You've got a few more minutes."

"Bring me doubles, then." He laughed, as if this was amusing.

Linda's eyebrows rose above widened eyes. *Since when does my cousin drink like this?* They usually had a little wine at parties, but nothing like this. A faint alarm went off in her head.

Uncle John made a whistling sound of admiration. The waitress nodded, without registering surprise and disappeared into the kitchen. Linda reached over to a stack of menus leaning against the wall and passed them around.

"I already know what I'm having," said Uncle John. "Short ribs. Best in town."

"He always gets the same thing," said Dan. He nodded toward the waitress. "I'll have the same."

Linda searched the menu for something lighter than beef and found an entreé for salmon. She turned to Dan, "We have some catching up to do, my dear."

"I know we do." The thought pleased him. Plus, we have all night, if necessary. I want to hear about everything you've been up to."

"Me, too." It was hard to believe they had let so much time pass without communication.

But that was in the past. She wanted to stay in the present and make the best of things as they were.

The waitress reappeared and set down Uncle John's wine glass plus six appletinis in front of Dan who inspected them approvingly. Linda choked at the sight. The waitress took their meal orders and whisked into the kitchen.

Linda watched him carefully as he took an eager, thirsty sip of the first 'tini.' The action reminded her of how she used to down a gin and tonic and she worried about him. He gently placed the drink on the table and looked at her. Well, she thought. Now is as good a time as any to let him know. She raised her arm slowly, pointed to herself, and, facing Dan, mouthed, "A.A."

Dan wasn't fazed. Without a moment's hesitation, he pointed to himself and remarked, "Al Anon." They broke into wide smiles and considered each other anew, as if they'd just met. Seeing the six apple-flavored martinis lined up, waiting, and sweating, she wanted to ask, "Are you sure?" Instead, she turned to her uncle and inquired as to his health.

"I'm fine." Uncle John's eyes moved to his son, with a certain sadness and concern. "Dan's the one with the problem."

Dan was silent, as he sipped from number two.

"What is it?" Linda asked.

"I've got a brain tumor." He touched the top of his head as if greeting it. "We just found out."

Her eyes begged for more information.

"My girlfriend was with me the night it happened. She woke me up because I was convulsing. She took me to the hospital and they ran some tests. It's a small tumor. I've been getting chemo treatments, but I'm going to Duke University to find out more about it in a week and see what else can be done."

"They're the best," commented Uncle John. "If anything can be done, they're the ones to do it."

"I admire your courage, Dan."

Dan shrugged, as if he had resigned himself to it. "These days there's so much more they can do."

"Modern medicine can work miracles," she said. They had just reconciled, after so long a separation. Mercy!

In the rooms, things were about the same in Buena Vida, with the exception that Linda was more actively participating. She was sharing at each meeting, sometimes just a few words, or a few minutes, arriving earlier and leaving later, sometimes standing in the parking lot talking, and attending and participating at business meetings—good signs that recovery was in progress.

"Let's hear from the lady in the shoe department." Arthur was leading the noon meeting. He preferred to lead standing up, so he could see the fifty-one members who showed up. The most they'd ever had at this particular meeting. Everyone craned their necks to see who he was referring to. Way in the back, along the window-laden wall, Charlie, with flaming red hair sat comfortably. "That's the section where people sneak in and slip out," Arthur explained.

"This is the first place I learned to act responsibly," Charlie replied. "I had to be taught all over again. If you're new, don't try it without help. Get a sponsor."

The sharing snaked its way to the center of the room, where Gary was sitting.

"When I came in, I applied myself to A.A. with a fervor. I went to evening meetings and stayed out with newcomers, until midnight. My wife complained. I tried to justify myself to my sponsor." Gary shook his head, as if the experience had caused him pain. "He told me that I was acting the same way as when I had been drinking, by not letting anyone know where I was, or what I was doing. I started calling my wife. I told her that I was with A.A.ers and that I'd be home around midnight. She still didn't like it, but it was an improvement. You see, I had to learn to take responsibility for my actions and their consequences, try to achieve the greatest peace and partnership with those around me. I flat out had to act differently."

Suzanne twisted her head. Green earrings in the shape of an olive with a pimento, like you might find in a drink, dangled from her ears. Funny jewelry for a meeting, but then again, if you knew her, probably appropriate. "Alcoholism can't exist where behavior matches values," she commented.

"Let me tell you what happened to me." Darlene spoke up from a seat by the door. "I tried to commit suicide one night when I was drunk and I woke up in a psych ward, on the fifth floor of the Buena Vida hospital. That place was locked down good and tight, as I was. I unpacked my suitcase and put on a Tee shirt that read 'Don't worry. Be happy.' It amused the staff to see me walking around with that on. I told the other patients in rehab that I was working the twelve steps and they asked to know what dance I was working on. The more I tried to explain, the more questions they had and we weren't getting anywhere. So I finally just told them that I practiced at the Presbyterian Church and then they wanted to come." Laughs. "I haven't been back to the psych ward ever since and I'm still doing the twelve steps!" Louder laughs.

"Now to celebrate lengths of sobriety," said Arthur, as he opened the tray that held medallions.

Pablo always had something interesting to say, but this time, he dug deeper into his memory box and talked about the time he'd attempted suicide. "I was a click away," he said. "I held a loaded gun to my head and was just about to pull the trigger when I looked up and saw a photo of my sons." He became emotional. The room was still. "I thought about what they would be like without a father and I couldn't go through with it. I threw the gun in the back of my truck and drove downtown where I saw this cop parked. I pulled up alongside him and told him that I had a loaded gun with me and that I didn't know if I was going to shoot myself, or somebody else. He told me to follow him." Pablo was steadier now that he had gotten the hard part out. "They held me in jail for a few days and then I entered a rehab. Years later, I was at a meeting when a guy walked in with half a face. He had shot himself in the face." Pablo's emotions got the better of him. He paused and looked out at the sea of faces watching him. "That could have been me."

"I'm coming up on nineteen years and I can't believe it," said George. "I'm going to my parents' fortieth wedding anniversary. Before, they couldn't wait for me to leave; now they want me to stay. My mother used to hide her purse because, after I was there, she was missing twenty dollars. Now she finds an extra twenty and I'm a good son."

Greg spoke about his attempts to get a year's sobriety. "I kept trying to work the steps, but then I'd start drinking again. I used to call my sponsor and ask him which meeting he was going to and then, I'd go to a different one." Laughs. "I'm glad the eleventh step is where it's at. For this militant atheist with zero character flaws, I couldn't do it at first. I thought I was having a spiritual experience one day, but my sponsor told me it was a nervous breakdown. He told me to move a muscle and change a thought. Finally, I managed to get a year and I've been coming ever since. For me, the first step was the door step."

Linda came to stand before the group. Ryan handed her a chip in an ornate box the size of a matchbook and embraced her.

She began, "I've always considered myself a poster child for a bad example in A.A. Yet here I am getting a medallion." She looked at the members and smiled. "When I came in, I didn't do anything I was supposed to. Why did that surprise me? I came here looking for a way to manage my drinking . . . and get a date." Laughs. "But I guess it worked out. By the end of the first year, I was still as crazy as a bed bug and I wound up in a near fatal car accident. For months afterward, I couldn't understand why I had been spared. People remarked that it wasn't my time, or that I was here for a reason. That was baffling. I was a money manager, pushing money around all day, buying and selling, and I couldn't see a deeper meaning in doing that. I kept wondering what special thing I was saved for. Today, as I stand before you, I finally have an answer. If ever there was a moment worth living for, it's this."

The last speaker, a slight woman who'd maintained her good looks into her nineties, reached for the microphone and held it in thin hands. Bev's voice was raspy, probably from numerous speaking engagements; everyone wanted to hear her story, which contrasted with the quiet, charming, stable presence she'd demonstrated over the years.

She began, "I hope my voice holds out. I intend to give you what you've come to hear." With a twist of her head, a full head of luxurious dark gray hair, and an uplifted chin, she faced her audience of a hundred. "My drinking surely and slowly got out of control. My husband had enough of it and left. So there I was, drunk, broke, and with four, little children to raise by myself. So I did what any self-respecting drunk would do—I got a real estate license!" Laughs. "I was very fortunate in that I had a very successful career and my kids didn't want for much."

She held them spellbound, in the palm of her hands, as she gave them a glimpse of her life.

"The roaring twenties! The crash of twenty-nine! The Great Depression! Prohibition and repeal! WWII! The sixties—Oh, my God, the sixties! . . . If you can remember it, you weren't there."

The room erupted into uproarious laughter.

"I bumped into a man who'd been my drinking buddy in a record store and he told me that he no longer drank. He wanted to take me someplace special. That place was my first A.A. meeting! Of course, I went to my first meeting drunk, but what else did you expect? Eventually, I sobered up and stayed sober and have stayed sober to this day." She became more confident with each word, and poised for the finale. "My life turned around. It's the best life I could've had. I have no regrets. The people I've met in these rooms are some of the best people one could ever hope to meet and they've inspired me in so many ways. The women I've sponsored are admirable and trustworthy. I've been blessed by coming here forty years. Thank you so much!"

Before her last words had been spoken, several members stood at attention, hands ready to applaud. The rest of the room stood as she finished and then the entire room burst into a frenzy of applause. The chairperson waited quietly before passing out the medallions, until the applause died down.

An elderly gentleman rose and spoke. "I'm Bob and I'm *not* an alcoholic."

The first thought that went through Linda's head was, *Sure, we all say that initially.* Earnestness about the man's speech began to weigh on her thinking.

"I represent the people who love you——your husband, wife, significant other, father, mother, sister, brother. We love you and what you're doing here and we support you in your efforts." Bob, speaking as if he was used to addressing large groups of people, carried an air of confidence and authority like a CEO, or president, of a large corporation.

No one interrupted. In fact, no one breathed. They seemed to hang on his words.

"I urge you to continue to help yourselves and us." He pointed to the list of the twelve steps written on a white parchment about five feet long and hanging from a nail behind the roster. "Let me tell you what this organization has done for me." He stopped and beheld a young man seated next to him, a blonde lad with a bright green shirt and a wild darting look that spoke of someone new to the program. "My son came down here from Boston University to help me celebrate my seventieth birthday. He's here for three days and told me that he wanted to get to a meeting. He was willing to leave the festivities and come here. I said I wanted to go, too. For my son to take time out from the party and come here says a lot to me. I applaud him and you and wish this fellowship long life."

There was another long-sustained applause.

When the meeting was over, Linda stood in front of Bob and his son. She smiled at him. "Spread the word."

The executive returned a warm smile. "I'd like to tell everyone about the good of A.A."

During dinner, one evening with Mercedes, a close Jewish friend, and accountant, Linda re-capped the story of how her sister had usurped power and manipulated their mother's money, which had led to her rebellion and their subsequent ongoing family division.

Mercedes listened carefully, and then replied, "I have two cousins who haven't spoken to each other for twenty-five years." She watched Linda's stunned reaction, then, added, "They live in the same apartment building." Nodding as her friend's reaction grew, she took a sip of water and sat back. "I also know of a gal who ripped off her parents while they were still living. Using POA—I'm sorry—Power of Attorney, she siphoned their assets and left them broke. The whole family is not speaking to her as a result."

"Did anyone take legal action?"

"No."

"It figures," Linda said with a twist of her lips.

"What do you mean?"

"It's hard for family members to take action against each other. Like me. I couldn't sue. Besides, too many attorneys advised me not to." She gazed across the roomful of diners, and then turned back to Mercedes, wanting to put some objectivity into the discussion. "I read in the *Wall Street Journal* how banks are no longer honoring POA's, to avoid liability. Misuse of the POA is the first step in a swindle."

"I heard something like that." Mercedes reached for a dinner roll and worked a pat of butter into it with her knife. "They never used to challenge that kind of document before, but, I guess, stealing from your parents is on the rise."

Linda nodded. "One of the big insurance companies, Met Life—I think, put the loss around three billion a year which includes credit card fraud, forgery, and outright theft. Can you imagine? I mean, it's got to be one of the worst kinds of crime—stealing from the ones who loved and raised you."

Mercedes frowned as she shook her head. "You get old and feeble, and your kids rob you. There should be a law."

"I wish legal support was around when *I* needed it. It could've saved me much heartache." Sadly, Linda thought, *Too late. The assets are almost gone.*

"Sometimes the big estates get hit hard."

"I read about a famous singer whose estate, worth millions, was supposed to go to needy children, scholarships and the like. Not a penny to date has gone to his intended recipients. Everybody's suing everyone else."

Mercedes said, "That could take years."

"Some say it may never be settled." Linda stabbed a meatball on the outskirts of a mound of spaghetti and popped it into her mouth. She chewed thoughtfully, then added, "Disputing heirs, multiple executors, lawsuits, and plenty of litigation—even an overturned state intervention."

"So much for public confidence in the probate process," Mercedes sighed. "I should have been an attorney."

Digging for another meatball, Linda nodded as if she had been thinking the same. "My mother's estate wasn't that big, and we didn't go to court, but, nevertheless, her intentions went by the wayside."

Her friend pondered the words, thinking about her own family and the possibility of feuding with her siblings.

"I'm thinking about a state guardianship, with a court-appointed committee to distribute my assets according to an ironclad will to a national scholarship fund. Bequest it to *anyone* but family." She seemed enthusiastic about this idea. It led her to take it further. "Let someone try to sue the government!"

With a snide laugh, Mercedes asked, "You think that'd change things?"

Linda thought about that before replying. "Might, might not. It's worth a try. *Anything* would be an improvement."

"So tell me . . . what's the latest with your family estate? What's going on?" Mercedes asked.

"Same. We're still divided. I've been busy reaching out to extended family members who want to see me. I just reconnected with Dan, my cousin, who lives on the East coast."

"When do you see him again?"

"Soon. Who knows how much time he has." Pause. Sadness. "He has brain cancer."

"I'm sorry." Mercedes was beginning to appreciate her friend's travails.

"Hey, help me out with something, okay?"

"Sure. What is it?"

"You remember my trip a few months ago to visit and reconcile with Jane?" Linda asked.

"Your cousin who lives in New Jersey?"

"Yes. There was an incident with her that has me in a tailspin."

"And—?" The accountant leaned forward, eager to hear.

"She came to town to visit Mary. She was within five miles of my house and never even called. Talk about hurt feelings. I positively ached."

"Why'd she do that?"

Linda shrugged. "She said she didn't want to rock the boat."

"*Whose* boat?"

"Probably my sister's. But—get this—she invited me to visit her up there."

"*Hmpph.* Why don't you write her a note and say that you don't have travel plans at the moment? Invite her to visit you—*anytime.*" Mercedes advised, "Keep the door of friendship open."

"Right."

Chapter Forty-Two

The days passed peacefully, and spring sidestepped into summer. Mornings were still tolerable, but by midday, the temperature rose into the nineties. Dan and Linda grew closer after their reunion. They developed the habit of speaking to each other on the phone regularly and planned another visit. Linda invited Kent to accompany her.

Dan met Linda and Kent on the driveway with open arms. After a brief visit in Dan's living room, they got in the car and picked up Dan's girlfriend, Marty, and Uncle John then headed to a restaurant nearby. Despite the crowded parking lot, they found a spot near the front door. Inside, the waiter delivered a monster appetizer that would have fed an elephant. After dinner, they dropped Uncle John off at his house, and the two couples spent a leisurely evening walking around a hotspot called City Plaza, clowning around and acting like teenagers in love.

Kent went to bed early while Dan and Linda stayed up late talking.

"What do the doctors say about your brain tumor?" Linda asked as they huddled over the kitchen counter.

"I'm flying back to Duke University for more testing. It's been two months since I started the oral chemo. They expect to know if it's working or not."

Linda watched his face, seeing fear lurking behind his eyes. "Would you call me with the results?"

"I will."

Linda nodded, wondering how long she'd wait before calling him. "How much time do you have in Al-Anon?"

"Ten years." Dan watched her carefully. "You know, I was thinking the other day about when you first told me you were in A.A. There was this weird reaction. I thought, If she thinks she's an alcoholic, what does she think of me?"

Linda smiled. She'd heard it so many various times in meetings. She remembered how long it had taken her to admit it. She'd hidden in other rooms for years, before admitting the real problem was alcohol. Well, she thought, if he is one of us, he'll get there on his own. It never worked to force someone into admission.

Dan looked at her steadily, not saying a word.

"Tell me," she said, "what's going on with your brother? I don't hear you talk about him."

"We haven't spoken for years."

"Tell me about that," she urged.

Dan explained at length how it had started at the university when Brian had first met his wife Carey. "She was chasing my brother. I think she saw me as a competitor for Brian's attention. To this day, she's still jealous, and she eggs my brother to take sides against me whenever the occasion presents itself. My brother hasn't spoken to me in over ten years."

"Ten years!" She recouped quickly. "How awful."

"I had to be out of town for a week after Mom died and, when I returned, Dad handed me a check," Dan said. "He explained to me that Carey had admired one of Mom's bracelets. He said it was his to do with as he wanted and he gave it to her. I was incensed because not a word had been spoken to me. My father insisted that it was innocent. I asked him if it was so innocent, then *why the check*? Now I'm afraid to think about what will happen after Dad dies."

"Watch out for the power grab." Linda related what had happened in her family. "My part in it was that I had a warning years before when my mother's sister passed. I saw how greedy and selfish Mary acted and I failed to warn my mother to take appropriate action. Had I acted responsibly from the beginning, my family division might not have happened. I'm not saying that we would have been buddies because it was never like that between us, but it might not have turned into what it is now."

"That's what I'm afraid of. What do I do?"

"Talk to your attorney. Now, while there's still time."

"There aren't many assets left," Dan was sliding away from the target. "I know my dad has some money, in a life insurance plan."

Uncle John had always been on the wealthy side of the track, as Linda recalled. As the firstborn, he was well taken care of.

"Do you have a copy of his will?"

"Yes." It was the way he said it, that made Linda believe he had hardly looked at it.

Suddenly, Dan stood up from the stool and embraced her. They stood that way for some time, locked in each other's arms. Linda shook with emotion.

"If you start crying, then I'm gonna cry, too."

Linda laughed and calmed. "I'm glad you're back. Don't leave me!" Linda admonished in a teasing way.

"No, never. I'm going to stick to you like glue."

On Sunday, Linda and Kent met with Brian, his wife, Carey, and Uncle John at a local restaurant while Dan prepared for his trip to Duke University Medical Center. It had been years since she'd seen and spoken to Brian and Carey. A decade of silence seemed to be the norm in her family.

Carey's attitude toward Dan was evident in the way she kept referring to him. "You know the *way he is*." She glanced conspiratorially toward Linda who didn't share her sentiments.

When an opening came, Linda seized upon it. "I want to thank you and Brian for visiting Dan in the hospital, after his initial seizure from the brain tumor. That was nice of you." She wanted to add, "About time." She didn't say that.

The scene at the restaurant was fairly pleasant, with everyone on friendly terms.

The next morning, Dan's house registered a sense of quiet and emptiness. Dan had left before dawn to catch a plane. Linda was composing a thank-you note to him, which she planned to leave on the kitchen counter, as they departed. Kent had his arm over her shoulders as they sat on the sofa watching the morning news. She heard a sound and picked up her cell phone.

An email from Dan.

"This is composed on the plane," he wrote. "I just want you to know for sure that I feel delighted and blessed to have you back in my life. I am grateful and look forward to remaining in touch. Marty and I are planning to visit you sometime this summer. Love you, Dan."

Kent glanced over her shoulder and read the email. "You can answer him tomorrow."

"His words are so eloquent," she replied. "My thank-you note looks like something a six-year-old would have written." She got up from the sofa, sat on the kitchen stool, and tore up the note. She was about to start anew when she noticed the time of his email—6:15 a.m. She suddenly thought about what he faced. How he must feel. A bad diagnosis was a possibility. Hastily, she emailed him: "You are a gift to me. I know that God walks with you to that appointment. No matter what, you will be all right."

Bunnie had said the same words to her when she was sick. *This is what it means to pass forward.* The power of the program helped her push the send button. That done, she wrote a simple note of gratitude which she left on his dining room table—a white note, with the name Dan, scribbled across the top lying on his black-lacquered table. He'll see it right away when he gets in, she thought.

The next day Dan called. "The doctors said the tumor has stopped growing and they expect shrinkage."

"That's great, Dan," she said. "Did you see the note I left you?"

"What—where is it?"

"On the table. The black one. By the refrigerator."

"I thought I left that note for myself, as I was packing my overnight bag." He took a few shuffling steps to pick it up and read it. "Got it. Thanks."

"Say, Dan. I sent a card to Mary's husband when I heard he had cancer."

"And? "

"Mary's attorney sent me a nasty letter."

"Not nice," Dan said sadly.

"Well, I guess I just get on with the rest of my life, right?"

"Yes."

"It was worth a try." She'd gambled and lost—for now. "I was hoping my brother-in-law, who used to be so sweet to me, would accept an olive branch and try to bring our family together."

"Not this time."

"They want to keep it the way it is." Just looking at the letter Brown had sent made her bristle.

"It's their choice. Not much you can do about it."

"Acceptance."

Dan offered words of encouragement. "What you can do is nurture the family relationships that are working."

"Those are with the extended family."

"The ones who want to see you."

Chapter Forty-Three

On a later visit, Linda, seated at a round table in Uncle John's kitchen, was watching from a window as an egret stretched its legs in a lake choked with purple lily pads—a tranquil scene. She was talking to him, "I've reunited with your two sons. As for my other cousins, I drove up to see Robin, in the mountains in New Hampshire. Ron finally gave me his phone number, after a dozen emails, and we've been talking. I'm getting to know his wife better."

"It's healing for them and for you, too," Uncle John said softly and sipped from a glass of red wine.

"I helped your sons get together." She'd wanted to tell him this for some time.

"How'd you do that?" he asked.

"When Dan told me that he and Brian hadn't spoken in ten years, I encouraged him to call him. I said I loved each of them and wanted the three of us to have coffee. I sort of pushed Dan a little."

Uncle John smiled and took another sip. "I didn't know that."

"It worked." She elaborated, "They had lunch the following week, and now they're meeting regularly." She shifted her gaze back to the lake where the egret was now stalking his next meal—a fish or a tasty frog? She was thinking, *Would anyone in the family do that for her and her sisters?* She turned back to her uncle when she realized he was speaking to her.

"That's because they had good parents."

His comment thickened and registered. "That's it, Uncle John!" she exclaimed. "My sisters don't get it, do they? The way they treat me is a direct reflection on our parents. They think they're hurting me, but they're hurting themselves."

Uncle John nodded. His expression turned serious as if something was troubling him.

"Something on your mind?" she asked.

"There's something I need to say . . . I was driving the new car Dad had given me, as a reward for my efforts in the business, and saw your Dad in the garage, taking out my bicycle, just as I was pulling away. He hadn't wasted any time getting his hands on my bike. I stopped the car, rolled down the window, and yelled at him. I told him to put my bike back . . . I regret having said that." He rubbed his eyes.

She quietly waited for him to finish.

"Another thing, I never told your father how proud of him I was when he was in the service."

She watched him drain the glass of wine and felt compelled to say something soothing. "I'm sure he knew, Uncle John."

His brow furrowed, as he set the empty glass on a side table. He seemed lost in thoughts. Turning, he said, "When the Japs shot at his plane, your dad cried out, 'They're trying to kill me.' After that, he refused to fly again, but he got lucky because the war ended just then." Uncle John laughed lightly.

She wanted to hear more and leaned forward; her hands braced on her knees. He took the cue.

"Let me tell you a little about our family you may not be familiar with," he said. "We didn't always talk about this around the dinner table when you kids were growing up."

"I'm all ears." She smiled encouragingly. Dying to know more was closer to the truth.

"My Dad, your Grandpa John, survived by stealing bread from restaurant tables, swiping newspapers from news stands and hawking them to passersby. He'd made a deal with illicit employers—the Mafia, I think—to climb telegraph poles to retrieve racing results before they reached the city."

"Sounds like a street urchin."

"That was your grandpa." He smirked and watched as she raised her eyebrows and sat back as if to distance herself. "Jobs were scarce, but he searched the obits and found an opening in the Chicago stockyards. He applied and got the job. Apparently, he was good at it, because he soon rose to manager. Your dad hated the slaughter houses. Me?" He smiled with a measure of pride. "I loved the family business and was deep in it."

"Tell me what that was like, Uncle John."

"We were a livestock commission merchant company registered with the Department of Agriculture and subject to their rules and regulations. We rented office space from the stockyard in a building where other commission merchants and butchers were located."

"And your customers were?" she asked.

"Livestock dealers who bought animals from farmers and shipped them to the stockyard in our care, to be sold to slaughter houses. Each dealer had a separate pen for his cattle. Our commission was $0.75 per animal before WWII and a $1.25 after. The market opened early when my father, or I, would take a buyer and a butcher in a pen and price the cattle. The buyer would bid, and an auction would take place until both sides agreed. The cattle were then weighed, and the sale price per pound was marked on the ticket."

"How did you get paid?"

"The dealer took the ticket to the office where it was calculated how much money he netted, after expenses like our commission, and stockyard expenses were deducted. A check was issued to him for that amount. Next, we billed the buyer. We received two commissions." He held up two fingers.

"Nice work. My father didn't want to get in on *that*?"

"Your Dad went with Grandpa and me to view the operation and nearly collapsed. He couldn't take the smells, sights, and sounds of the distressed animals. Besides, ever since Charles Lindbergh came to town to produce airplane engines, he was infatuated with airplanes. That's all he talked about. He made hundreds of miniature planes to play with. Even his teachers noticed his mechanical skill."

She whistled low under her breath. "Charles Lindbergh. Airplanes."

Her uncle smiled, as if he knew about her secret passion for planes. "Your dad liked to go out with the boys to the local hot spots where they lived and breathed aviation. He'd sneak home at dawn and would be taking off his pants when your grandpa came into our bedroom to wake us up at five a.m." His smile grew wider as he continued. "I'll never forget it. Dad would holler, 'Time for work. We've got a big load of cattle coming in.' I'd look at your dad, pants down around his ankles, and he'd look at me, and Grandpa would say, 'Why, son, you're already getting dressed! Good to see you're finally getting some ambition!' I thought I'd die laughing."

Comical, she thought. Years later, married with children, her dad manufactured airplane and space capsule parts under government contract. Yeah. My dad did all right—*on his own.*

Another year passed. Rental income had lightened on the property the sisters owned, but a small profit materialized at the end of the year, which meant that the tenancy didn't have to borrow from the rich veterinarian. Linda reviewed the financial data Brown's secretary had sent and laid the paper on her desk to review after she went to a meeting.

At the meeting, the table was set with books and a financial ledger for keeping track of contributions. Eleanor stood at the head of the table and saw Linda come in the side door. She asked, "Would you like to chair the meeting today? Our regular chairperson hasn't showed up." Other than court-orders, attendance was voluntary.

"Sure, no problem," Linda replied and made her way to the chair. She looked at the ledger, noting the number of attendees at the last meeting—forty.

Other members filled the seats around the table. Eleanor sat down next to her husband.

"It's time," Eleanor reminded her. "We'd best get started." The group was mindful of the rented time they had from the church.

The meeting went smoothly, and at the end, Linda said, "Thank you for sharing. I learned so much from you. This week has been filled with sorrow and joy for me. A family reunion's taking place, and I was not invited." As she said this, she noticed a few heads bending in her direction. "My sister, who lives near here, is in charge of the reunion and she won't have anything to do with me.

Two of my female cousins are staying with her. Anyway, yesterday, my sisters and cousins drove to the other coast to visit our uncle and his sons. While that was going on, I was in church serving as Lector. So there I was on the altar, feeling disgruntled, sad, and yes, sorry for myself. I tried not to think about them, but it was like trying not to think about pink elephants." She paused and looked at them, noticing that they seemed to hang on every word. "Then today, I remembered that my uncle's sons hadn't spoken to each other for a decade and yet they were together, with my sisters and cousins. I became happy, because I had a small part in that reunion. So, even though I felt like something bad had happened. Actually, something good was happening."

The meeting over, there was the usual hustle and bustle as volunteers tidied the room. The treasurer held out his hand for the collection money.

"I see you're still working on the family stuff." Familiar with her story, Frank had occasionally mentored her. From New York, he had slept on park benches before joining A.A.

"Not getting far with it."

"Linda, just let the joy shine. Eventually, they'll come to you."

She looked at him, wanting to believe what he was saying. "They don't call or write."

"My kids wouldn't speak to me for thirty years."

Thirty years! She eyed him with some misgiving. "Are you speaking now?"

"Sometimes. I had to give it up for a while because there was no response from them." Frank tossed his empty coffee cup into a nearby trash can. "I still call them once or twice a year, just to let them know I'm thinking of them. You do the same thing. Keep calling. It leaves something in the air."

She found this amusing and laughed.

He said, "You could jot a note to your female cousins who were here and say something like, 'Gee, too bad we missed an opportunity to get together.'" He watched to see how she'd take the suggestion.

She looked away, focusing on the coffee pot where members had congregated, and mumbled something he couldn't hear.

Frank nodded, knowing how she felt. "They're using you as a target. You have joy, and they're miserable. It's their way of trying to beat you down. Good and evil coexist, Linda. Just keep letting the joy shine through. Eventually, they'll want it, too." He looked at her as if he could see something budding, through the dense foliage of her demeanor. "Be humble. God works in His own time."

"I called my cousin, Ron, in Virginia and tried to talk him into coming down. Next thing I know he says he might arrange to visit Uncle John when I'm there. They haven't seen each other in years."

"See? He wants a piece of the action. It came from within. Eventually, everything will work out. You don't have to worry, Linda. God's in the kitchen. He's mixing it up right now because you want it."

"Frank, I didn't know I wanted it until I came to A.A. For years, family was the last thing I thought I wanted. I ran away from them. I avoided them. I never visited them. I only went when my mother insisted. It was in the rooms, listening to everyone share, that I realized what I was missing and I've been after it ever since—here, there . . . everywhere."

"You can make A.A. and church family. There's plenty for me. Plenty for you."

Moved and encouraged, Linda made her way to her car. As she buckled the seatbelt, she reached for her cell phone to call Dan.

Dan answered on the first ring. "What's up?" They had spoken only yesterday.

"I wanted to congratulate you."

"On what?"

"Wasn't yesterday the first time in many years that you, your dad, and your brother were together at the same time?"

Dan hesitated for a second, thinking about the question and holding it up against ten long years. He put it together. "You're right! It was!"

"Fantastic!"

"Oh, I think it had something to do with the fact that Brian's kids have grown up and moved away, or . . . it could be the cancer."

"Dan! It's the love he has for you!"

Listening to her, Dan suddenly became silent. When next he spoke, his voice rasped, "I'm going into a store. I have to go."

She took the hint. "Love you. Take care."

"Love you, too."

The challenge: the female cousins—a tight-knit clique in the Cray family, whose walls had ascended and thickened—then, the sisters.

Through the estate hassle, Linda had realized just how much hostility Mary carried for her. She thought back to nasty childhood incidents and caustic remarks. Hatred for another was like drinking poison, hoping the other person would die. She pitied her sister. By now, she thought, Mary must be *really sick.* As for herself, she had forgiven both sisters. Most of the inheritance was gone, but it was never about the money. The three were numbskulls not to realize that. She wasn't bitter or resentful—disappointed maybe. Now she had a peaceful spirit and wanted to spread it around. She took Frank's advice and wrote a note to Robin and Jane, cousins who had recently visited Mary. She threw in an extra line about how she had encouraged Dan and Brian to settle their differences and added that they were now buddies.

Robin responded. "That's nice that you helped our cousins, but don't expect me to help out with your sisters. They don't want to reconcile with you, and I don't want to get involved in any way. My trip to Florida is supposed to be a relaxing time. Besides, I have no car when I'm down there so I can't visit you . . . *blah, blah, blah.*"

Linda threw up her hands in defeat.

Then the phone rang.

"I feel so awful that I didn't get to see you when I was in town," Jane said. "I'm not going to let that happen again. Would it be all right if I came to visit with you for a few days after I visit your sisters?"

Linda felt a happy rush of adrenalin and remembered Frank's words. "Let's plan on it!"

Chapter Forty-Four

Up on the top shelf of a closet packed with coats and jackets, Linda gripped the edge of a brown video box labeled: *How It All Began*. It was a VHS video her mother had made for each of her daughters. Since it was a VHS, not a DVD, it had sat on the top shelf gathering dust. Part of it lay untouched because she wasn't sure she wanted to view it.

Clarence, a good friend, tall with thinning, soft, blonde hair, had video equipment in a third story room of his house on the river where he often entertained guests. "Yeah, I can play a VHS," he replied to her request. "Bring it tonight. We'll watch it after we get a bite."

The kindness and care he showed to others had attracted Linda to him. He volunteered his time generously around town by cleaning the beaches, singing with a group at nursing homes and showing films at another. Every holiday, he threw a party at his home and invited many of his friends, couples, and singles, to bring a dish and come over. Although forever single, and not a frequent dater, he was popular with the ladies and seemed to have an interest in Linda.

She said to him, "Thank you! I can't tell you how much this means to me!"

The video, a series of still, somewhat unfocused clips, had been cut from old tapes. The color was not that good. It ran two hours, and Linda barely moved. The video contained scenes of her mother and Mary as a baby, family reunions, parties, important occasions, dogs, cats, houses they'd lived in, holidays, snow days, camping, Girl Scouts, a celebration of her paternal grandparents fiftieth wedding anniversary, vacations to Puerto Rico, Canada, and Florida with her immediate family, vacations that the uncles and aunts took by themselves to Bermuda, meals including roast beef and a pig with an apple in its mouth, and the last house the family had lived in together, where they built a landscaped garden and terrace rivaling Babylon.

After it was over, Clarence turned to look at Linda. "Sometimes a movie like that can make you sad."

"I'm overwhelmed," Linda said. "It was hard to look at because of the blurry film." She awaited an aftereffect. "I think I just want to go home now and relax." Clarence understood. "Come, walk me to my car."

He joined her at the stair landing, and they made their way down the stairs, through the cluttered kitchen, and out the door to another staircase. An architect, Clarence had designed and built the house when his knee problems were nonexistent.

"Take it easy on the steps," she cautioned as he maneuvered his bulk down.

"Oh, I'm fine. It's you I'm worried about. You all right?"

"Fine. Just dandy," she said too quickly. "Don't worry about me."

Nervously, he watched her back out of his driveway and onto the street. "Look out! You almost hit my mailbox."

"Oh, sorry," she replied sheepishly. Slowly, she finished backing out.

The following night Linda sat quietly reading a book by Thomas Merton. Merton had a knack for writing that soothed her and helped draw out emotions lurking behind thoughts. Memories like clouds clustered and drifted over the horizon of her mind.

Her first reaction to the VHS, now that she'd stepped away from it and gained perspective, was that her mother had gone to great lengths to capture scenes from their childhood and to arrange them in chronological order—an invaluable gift.

As she'd viewed each scene, she observed little affection between her sisters and her. No cuddling, no holding hands, no watching out for each other. What vividly struck her at one point was a hangdog look on her younger sister's face, present in almost every shot, until she reached her later teenage years and acquired self-confidence, just before she went away to college. That look was on her face, at about the same age, moments before her drinking career went into orbit. She thought about all the parties her mother had helped her host at home—girls she camped with, classmates and neighborhood friends, Girl Scouts. Where were the friends from childhood? The lack of connections in her life reminded her of the trademarks of alcoholism—isolation, self-centeredness, and arrogance.

She shared these thoughts with Clarence as they sat on a sofa in his house.

"We were all like that," he said. "I don't think any of us did any better than you. I didn't keep any childhood friends either."

"I was in a world of my own."

"Well, I was an only child, but still, I was immersed in jobs. I traveled a lot. I didn't really make friends easily."

"I made friends but didn't keep them. I regret that. Today I'm trying to do things differently."

"Does that include me?" Clarence asked.

She took his hand in hers. "You know it does."

He looked at her with softness in his eyes. "Was there anything else about the movie you want to talk about?"

"Just that I want to have close connections with family and friends and am willing to do whatever it takes to get there. I hope it's not too late."

"Sometimes the little things make a difference," he said.

"I sent a birthday card to a cousin I haven't communicated with in forty years."

"Nice. How'd that work out?"

"He wrote back that it was filled with so many nice sentiments that he got suspicious and asked his wife if he was dying and nobody had told him yet."

Clarence's chuckle filled the room. "Listening to you has given me courage. I've got one of those ancient family films. You want to watch it with me?"

"Sure. Bring on your past. We'll view it together."

Chapter Forty~Five

The pink sugar shack, the rental property, hadn't sold. It was still on the market.

The extended family was circling, however. Jane sent Linda an email announcing that she'd be in the area in March and wished to visit for a few days. "Would you meet me and take me to your house?"

Overjoyed, Linda responded, "Where would you like to be picked up?"

After a few days, Jane replied, "They can drop me off at Dillard's." A major department store.

Linda thought. Why couldn't her family drop Jane off at her house, like normal people, instead of making Jane lug a suitcase around a mall.

She sought Father Thomas after morning Mass the following day and briefed him.

Remembering her history, the priest offered insight into the problem. "They're playing games. Expect the unexpected. Don't put yourself in the wolf's mouth."

"What about picking Jane up at the end of Mary's driveway?"

"The wolf's mouth! *Don't go there!*" He shook his head violently. "Just say, 'Wonderful! Let me know where to meet you.' Otherwise, they'll think they have you guessing and confused."

"Already there, Father," she said sadly.

He folded his arms across the green chasuble. "They want to kick you down the street some more."

"The meeting place is her choice. She's the one hauling a suitcase."

"Good. Leave it there." He smiled and looked over her head to where the next parishioner waited to speak to him.

For those who'd continued to inquire about Father Matthew, there was a letter, carefully considered in prayer, from Bishop

Hank Lang inserted into the church bulletins on a Sunday late in October. The ushers had orders not to distribute the bulletins, until after Mass.

Having peeked to see what all the fuss was about, as she left church, Linda read the one-page letter later that evening when she could give it more attention. The bishop began by stating how he'd been notified of serious allegations by St. Anthony's parishioners, and had the responsibility to discover the truth and to act accordingly on that information. Throughout the process, he'd been concerned about the good of the church, the spiritual well-being of the priest, the parish faithful, and the diocese.

Once the canonical process began, Linda read with growing interest; a church court had been convened. The tribunal consisted of a three-judge panel of priests, and experienced canonical experts from outside the diocese. Father Matthew had chosen a canonical advocate, or lawyer, to represent him. Now he could describe what had transpired at the canonical trial, which he'd informed them from the outset that he'd do.

By collegial decision, the judges discerned a pattern which demonstrated that Father Matthew had violated his fiduciary responsibilities to the parish, his priestly promise to celibacy, and his promise of obedience to his ordinary. The judges rendered a decision that he no longer was able to function anywhere as a priest.

A weighty decision, and a conclusion, which reflected the serious nature of the acts committed. No tribunal would render such a grave decision lightly, wrote the bishop, or without careful consideration of the evidence and due process.

The priest offered no appeal, claiming to have removed himself from active ministry, something he couldn't do on his own. Removal from the clerical state required a canonical process under church law.

Bishop Lang stated that he continued to pray for the priest's spiritual well-being, for healing for the people of St. Anthony following the scandal, and for the wounded church. He entrusted those involved to the power of prayer.

The letter encouraged them to move forward in their lives. We're all trying to do that, thought Linda.

Morning had broken, the blackbird had spoken, dew blanketed the grass, and a fresh sweetness filled the air from a wet garden when Linda turned on her computer to read the first correspondence of the day. The conflict with her sisters had been quiet for so long that it was tempting to think it was over. Linda knew that it'd only be a matter of time before Cathy, who'd been feeding the failing rental property, would grow tired of supporting it. Rent just couldn't keep up with expenses. So it was no surprise, really, when another sales contract appeared, this time through *her* tax accountant. Her sisters' attorney, Nestor Brown, who'd been sending Joe Bidley quarterly rental information on the property her sisters and she owned, took it upon himself to forward a contract as well. Why her sisters continued to worship the man who'd lost most of their inheritance remained a mystery.

She downloaded the attachment and was thrilled to see a new real estate agency was handling the sale, with a realtor named Richie Vettia. So long, Vance Hodge! Cathy had written, "Sign and return promptly." Please, or pretty please? Linda intended to use her minority vote to sell the property. She looked at Cathy's note again. Had the reign of Mary the Dominator ended? Was she sick? Stomach ache?

Bidley made an unusual offer. "I'll be happy to act as an intermediary for your continuing family conflict."

She wrote back, "Thanks, Joe, but that's not really your role as my tax accountant. I think you should return the document to Brown and maybe remind him that he's a lawyer, not a realtor." Linda figured her sisters were desperate to sell. As an after thought, she sent Bidley another email. "A realtor usually sends that document to a client after discussion, but I don't know the realtor, no one's contacted me, and there's been no discussion."

Bidley replied, "I'll send it back to Brown . . . with your email attached."

"Okay."

A few days later, Richie Vettia, the new realtor selected by her sisters, contacted Linda and scheduled an appointment. His office, located across the street from the beach, was heavily decorated for the holidays, with a large, five-foot Santa Claus standing by the front door. A plump receptionist wearing a tight red sweater ushered her into his office.

"Nice to meet you," she and the realtor said at the same time as they reached to shake hands. Richie was young, early forties, with thick, wavy black hair and eyes equally dark. He wore casual dress pants flaunting a trim waistline and a light blue, Polo shirt. Handsome, Linda was thinking, as she took a seat across his glass-topped desk and looked at the comparative analysis he'd placed before her.

"Take a look at these figures, and I think you'll see why we want to sell the house for $160,000. These are properties that my office has handled," he said proudly.

The prices seemed high. "I notice the square footage is considerably more than our property and they're more recently built."

His head snapped back, as if he'd been slapped. "Not at all," he defended but leaned forward to review his figures.

Linda reached for papers a friend had prepared for her. "Here's a similar analysis, with comparable square footage."

The realtor glanced unhappily at the list, prepared by a rival firm.

She continued, "As you'll notice, those listed for less have sold. The rest are still on the market."

Richie's face soured. "That's what I was thinking. I tried to tell your sisters, but they insisted on this price. The older one— Mary?— wanted the higher price. The younger one was at least willing to look at the comps."

Linda imagined their meeting. "I didn't come here to argue with you, or to be a difficult client, but to tell you what *I'd like* to do."

He leaned forward, his black eyes alert and glistening.

"I'd be willing to sign a sales contract with a lower selling price." She exchanged a look with him. "We'd be lucky to sell it for less."

"Oh, I think we can compete," Richie said smoothly. "What if we listed it for $150,000? Would you be agreeable to that?"

"The whole street's a ghetto—pickups motorcycles, garbage cans! You go one block over, and the view is much nicer!"

"A block doesn't make much difference, really."

"It's made of wood!" She raised her hands and spread her fingers to emphasize. "Who buys a wood house in Florida these days?"

No reply. Richie chewed his lower lip.

She went on. "And the inside! Have you *seen* the inside?"

"No." Sheepishly. Richie's enthusiasm wilted like the floral arrangement on a shelf behind him.

"Wait till you see the inside," she continued. "The damn thing is blocked up and dark. The rent doesn't cover the expenses. It's been a losing proposition, since the beginning. My sisters were fools to put mother's money into this shack."

Damp spots had appeared under his armpits and were spreading to the front of his shirt. "If I can get all three of you to agree, it could be a starting point." A bead of sweat slid down one thick hair. "It could help you get off square one."

I like his attitude, his asking rather than telling, and his willingness to find a middle ground. She picked up his report and noticed that most properties had sold for less than the asking price. "All right, I'll agree to that, but only with the stipulation that if it doesn't sell within a short time, say a few months, then we lower the price."

"We're making progress!"

His confidence seemed a little premature, but she liked the sound of it. "Thanks for your help."

"I'll be in touch."

Her hand was on the doorknob when she turned back to him. "Look, Richie, try not to get your hopes up. You don't know what you're getting into."

The warning failed to dissuade him. "I like to think positive."

"That's good . . . just don't hold your breath."

Several weeks had passed when Vettia sent a voicemail. "Linda, please call when you get this message."

She did.

"We've got a potential buyer for your rental. Expect a signed sales contract at our asking price by Monday." He held the phone to his ear with a coy smile.

"No kidding! After eight years, this is the first offer we've had. I'm thrilled!" Her face beamed with delight. Then, a whole series of bad memories rushed into her head making her pause and consider. She asked, "What about the clause I requested? Did you remember to put it in the contract?"

"*What* clause?"

"The one where if it says that if it doesn't sell within a few months—then the price goes down. I don't mean to be a pain. This is just in case."

Vettia ran a hand through his hair. "I put something in the contract to that effect."

"Such as—"

"That based on feedback from the other realtors the price would be readjusted after a reasonable time on the market." *This woman's driving me nuts*, he thought.

"Not bad." Linda knew that she could always refuse to sign a contract renewal, if her sisters stalled in lowering the price. Enough wasted time. *Why won't he just admit it?*—

"Admit—what?" the realtor asked.

She realized she must have spoken her thoughts aloud. "Oh, nothing, nothing. I'm just happy with the way you're handling things." She heard an exaggerated sigh of relief through the phone. "You're the most professional realtor I've met since this whole business began."

"I don't mind getting in the middle if it'll help."

"It won't. Trust me. We've been down this road before."

"I understand."

"Let's hope it works this time. Congratulations on getting them to agree to a lower price. That's awesome."

Big smile. "Just doing my job."

"One of your tougher jobs, right?"

He laughed, thinking, *If she only knew.*

Chapter Forty-Six

Ron Lagonegro, the eldest male cousin, had inherited a rich sense of humor from his mother who liked to laugh at her own jokes. An attractive man, he enjoyed wine but didn't let himself go to extremes. Always ready with a joke, Ron was fun and easy to be with. You couldn't help but like him.

In her efforts to reunite with the extended family, Linda found him uncharacteristically aloof. She'd started with an email, to which he responded succinctly. It took longer to get his phone number. Hallmark cards send on holidays and his birthday produced slim results.

"I'd like to see you sometime," she suggested during a phone conversation.

"Linda, a trip to Florida is not in my plans. I'm busy visiting children and grandchildren."

"It's been more than forty years since we've seen each other."

No reply.

After the holidays, she tried again, "Hey, Ron! How are you doing? What are you up to?"

"I'm on a staycation," the cousin joked. "I'm home for a while. I just lit a fire in the fireplace even though it's a balmy twenty-nine degrees in our part of Virginia."

She laughed. They chatted at length about the weather and news.

"In a few days, I'm going over to Uncle John's to meet your brother. It would be a bonanza if you were there."

"Oh, is that the weekend he's going down?" Ron asked.

"That's the one. I'm excited about seeing Allen after forty years. We were close when we were kids . . .You know," she added as an aside. "Uncle John asks for you."

A pause.

"I've thought about it," Ron said, "but there's no particular reason for me to come down. If I could play a game of bridge with Uncle John, I might reconsider. It's a long way to go just to visit."

Linda gently persisted. "He's an old man . . . It would mean so much to him. He picks out a great restaurant, and we laugh and reminisce about old times . . . I'd love to see you again." No response. "Does this mean that I'm going to have to travel to Virginia to see you?"

He laughed aloud. "Afraid so."

She remembered how he had avoided her when they were younger. *I must have been a royal pain.* "I'll let you go. Nice chatting with you."

"You, too. Have a good trip. Say hello to my brother for me."

His forwarded email surprised her the next morning. She noticed that he had sent it to other family members.

"Yesterday, Linda called and told me that Allen was going to visit Uncle John and she was going to meet them for dinner. I decided it was time I joined in the fun. I called Uncle John to make sure that we could play duplicate bridge together. I'll be arriving at his house early Friday morning. We'll play bridge at his club, and then I'm staying with him that evening. Allen arrives Saturday morning. We'll spend the day together and then I have to leave after dinner. I'm looking forward to seeing everyone. It's been a *very* long time!"

Gradually she felt herself lightening, getting giddy. There was some progress, after planting seeds like an agribusiness. She called her uncle to hear how he was taking the news.

"I'm very excited," he said.

"How long has it been?"

"Forty, or fifty, years."

"This is going to be an incredible reunion. It's been that long since I've seen Allen, too."

"I see Allen every year when he comes to visit." He added, "I'm going to have to get extra sleep the following week."

She thought, *at ninety-four, extra sleep was the right answer any time.*

"You know what, I'd like to come over on Friday, too. You wouldn't mind, would you?" she asked.

"Not at all. Come on over. Let Dan know."

"Will do."

Dan replied in an email. "I'm sleeping off the effects of my latest chemo drip and am lying low, but I'll get your bed ready."

Grinning to herself, she started the journey and, in her excitement, missed a turn on the highway, which delayed her arrival by an hour.

Dan stood in the driveway anxiously awaiting their reunion. She fell into his embrace, both of them happy, feeling like kids again.

"Can you believe we're pulling this off?" She asked with a radiant smile.

"It's wonderful!" Slimmer now, Dan's lengthy chemo treatments showed effects. His teeth were a brighter shade of yellow and he had not a hair on his head. He looked at her. "Have you lost weight?"

She looked back at him. "Not really. You?"

"About the same."

Right.

Inside his house, telltale signs of foreclosure were evident. There were fewer knickknacks adorning the shelves in the living room. Bigger pieces of furniture, like the sofa and the dining room table, remained. One bed huddled in a corner of the guest room, where there had once been two. He'd laid extra blankets on the bed. She rolled her suitcase into the closet, and they sat down to talk for a few minutes on the sofa, before meeting Ron and Uncle John for dinner.

"You have voice messages." Linda pointed to the blinking red light on his home phone.

"It's just the bank," Dan said. "They call two, or three, times a day and I just let them leave messages."

"What's with that?"

"They want me to provide documentation," he said nonchalantly. "They lost theirs."

"Duh."

They both laughed.

Dan made himself comfortable on the sofa and stretched out thin legs. "The last time my attorney went to court at their request, the judge asked for documents. Their rep couldn't provide them, so he dismissed the case. The poor rep, a young woman, was totally flustered. My attorney said she looked like she was about to cry."

"It's happening all over the country. The banks have been sloppy in their record-keeping in the foreclosure mess. Many stay in their homes and don't pay the mortgage."

He pointed to himself. "It's been three years for me."

"Lucky you."

"I'll stay here until Dad's health gets to the point when he'll need me full time, at his place. Then, I'll live with him and go back and forth. Eventually, it'll resolve itself."

Dan worries about his dad, and I worry about both of them. She looked at his shrunken frame. He seemed so small lying on the sofa. "Tomorrow, for sure, I'll need a meeting."

Dan nodded. "I've got that institutional meeting in the morning, and then we can go to the noon A.A. meeting."

A double header, thought Linda. *How appropriate.*

They arrived at Uncle John's where Ron was emptying the contents of the mailbox as a favor to his uncle. Linda jumped out of the car and ran to greet him. Ron warmly returned her embrace. The reunion was off to a strong start. Linda stood aside and watched her two cousins have their own reunion. Then, they went inside.

After greetings and taking seats in the living room, Uncle John measured a small space with two fingers in the air and repeated the gesture several times. "This is how close we came to first place in bridge this afternoon."

Ron laughed. "You see how competitive he is?"

"Don't forget the bed!" Uncle John reminded him.

"Oh, yeah! C'mon, Dan, let's get to it. Your dad wants to put half his bed in the guest room." He headed toward the master bedroom, and they followed. "After all this time, I get to share a room with my brother."

"Allen's coming in tonight."

"Oh, wonderful!" exclaimed Linda. "Will he join us for dinner?"

"No, he won't arrive until late, because of the storm. Around eleven, I think." Two major storms were set to converge over the northeastern shore.

The four family members dined at a restaurant close by. The men ordered drinks while Linda clinked ice cubes in a glass of water.

"Congratulations on your anniversary!" Ron said, referring to a previous conversation.

Linda pulled out a bronze medallion from her wallet and passed it around the table. Her uncle held it in his open palm and rubbed his thumb on the lettering. "Sixteen years!"

"That's how long I've gone without a drink," she admitted.

Dan looked down at his apple martini, with a mixture of chagrin and relief.

"I want you to know," Ron said, "that it's because of you that I'm here!"

Linda grinned. "I just gave you a nudge, that's all."

"I have a medallion in Al-Anon," Dan said as he leaned across the table intently looking at Ron.

Ron puzzled. "What's that?"

Dan replied proudly, "It's a support organization for people who have relationships with alcoholics." The point was not lost on Linda and him, who exchanged glances, but the others seemed oblivious. His father sipped red wine and admired the waitress.

Dan explained, "Both my adopted sons were alcoholics. We call them qualifiers."

Linda cringed and threw him an incredulous look. *Just your adopted children.* Still, it was good that both programs were out in the open, for the first time as if a blast of cool, clean air had entered the room and swept away deep, dark, hidden secrets they'd tried desperately to conceal. Linda recalled watching her father drink while her mother insisted in hushed tones, "Your father's a heavy drinker, not an alcoholic. Alcoholics live under bridges in cities like New York. They wear big coats and hide half-empty liquor bottles under them. You see, dear, it's out there, *not here.* We don't have anything like that in *our* family."

Her uncle and cousins were watching, and she realized she must have been staring into space.

"This reunion is a miracle," she said. "Ron wasn't going to come." She turned toward him. "Yet here you are." She dramatically opened her arms, palms up.

"That's what did it—the challenge!" Ron laughed with an open mouth, throwing his head back, the way his mother used to do.

The rest of them enjoyed a laugh, too.

"It made me wonder what you've got going on in Virginia—some bootlegging maybe?"

Ron grinned at her.

"When did we last see each other?" she inquired.

"Your wedding, which was great! I arrived in semiformal attire and returned home in a bathrobe." Another big laugh affected the others like a contagion.

"Was that it? My goodness—that was forty years ago!"

"Same for me!" Dan exclaimed. "That's the last time I saw you both, before Linda started on a mission to reconnect."

"I went to Jane's house; then your sister's in New Hampshire—"

"I was first!" Dan claimed.

"Your dad was first," Linda corrected, "then you and your brother."

The four were crossing a lengthy bridge of time and memories. Uncle John and Ron decided that they'd last seen each other at Mary's house, about twenty years ago.

"Where was I?" Linda knew the answer to that question, and she bent her head as a quietness spread. "On another subject," she said, "Tell us about Germany, Ron. When you went to Nana's hometown, what was it like?"

Uncle John showed increased interest and set down his glass.

Ron addressed the group. "I was on a business trip, traveling by myself, in Duesseldorf, nothing unusual, when the thought occurred to me that I was close to the town where Nana had grown up. After our meetings, I took a bus to the train station, arrived in Wuppertal later that afternoon, and found a phone book. There was only one Nottenbaum in the whole book so—forgive me for what I'm about to say—I ripped out the page and stuffed it in my pocket."

"You're bad, but I would've done the same thing." Dan said as he drained a third martini.

Ron smiled at him. "I found his name on an apartment building: Heinz Nottenbaum. I buzzed the intercom. No answer. So I buzzed every button on the list and, eventually, somebody let me in. I rode the elevator up to his floor and knocked on his door. A woman I assumed to be his wife answered and I pointed to my nose and said *Nottenbaum*." He touched his nose to demonstrate. "She called Heinz and he came running and standing in front of me was a guy who looked just like me. I pointed to my nose again and said his last name over and over and he suddenly seemed to understand what I was getting at because he let me in."

Uncle John chuckled and then his attention drifted away. Dan and Linda sat enrapt.

"We sat on his sofa for hours with his wife, who spoke a little English and helped us piece it together. He finally admitted he had an uncle who'd gone to America. I said, Uncle Herman, and he laughed hysterically. I called my mother in the States, and she gave me hell for calling her at three in the morning, but I explained how urgent it was and she confirmed that Herman was our great-grandfather. Heinz and I were exuberant, yelling and embracing in recognition that we were indeed related. He broke open a bottle of wine and we drank it all. He showed me pictures from his album and . . . there was one of him . . ." Ron paused, let his glance move from one to the other, then continued in a lower tone, "in a Nazi uniform."

The family exchanged sullen looks across the table.

A Nazi in the family! The awareness lingered.

"They didn't have much choice in those days," offered Dan to soften the blow and their heads bobbed slowly in agreement.

"He came to the States after that, didn't he?" Linda asked.

"Yeah, for two weeks we played charades until I thought I'd go crazy! His wife Karen was translating all the time."

"That's great how you found him and dared to just walk up to his door as you did."

"Today you might not get away with that," Dan said.

"I'd read that the town was industrial. Did you learn what role it played in the war and what happened to it," Linda commented.

"They made ball bearings, I think, and the town was destroyed—bombed relentlessly."

"Meanwhile on the other side of the world," Dan added, "Uncle Roland was bombing the hell out of the Japanese."

Uncle John seemed to have emerged from a stupor. "He told me later, when he was back in the States, that the Japs meant to kill him." He shook his head sadly. "I don't know what he was thinking when he was over there."

"He was flying the most advanced airplane ever built," Dan said confidently, with good reason. Having been a pilot himself, he'd spent many hours with his uncle, and owned a library of books on aviation. Posters of airplanes hung on every wall of his house.

The men looked at her. Looking back at them, she felt renewed pride. *Dad would be pleased to see us together.*

The plan for Saturday was to meet for lunch at a restaurant on a river where the five of them could sit outside. In the morning, Ron and Uncle John went to the beach, and Dan and Linda attended an institutional meeting of Al-Anon. This was service work he'd been doing for years.

Chosen designated driver, Linda valet-parked at the restaurant. Cars pulled up, and people streamed into the restaurant, for it was proving a popular spot for late lunch on a weekend. Dan stood waiting in line with a gadget in his hand that would light up and buzz when their table was ready. Linda bumped into someone blocking her way. The stranger turned—Allen!

With a leap, she landed in his arms and wouldn't let go. He embraced her strongly, as if he, too, didn't want to let go. Emotions swept through Linda, and she gasped for air while the others watched, particularly Ron, gauging her reaction and slightly surprised.

The waiter situated them at a table overlooking the river where youths paddled by on surfboards, the latest water sport. Lunch unfolded with jokes and remembrances until Ron made a comment that riveted Linda's attention.

"Cathy was crazy to travel to Rome, with an expensive Rolex watch and jewelry like that. I mean, what did she expect?" Conversation halted abruptly as they let him continue. "Her husband tried to help, but—"

His voice trailed off while Linda's thoughts took off like wild horses. *Was Cathy harmed?* Even after the trouble they'd had, she still harbored kind thoughts for her little sister. "Is she all right?" she asked.

"Oh, yeah. The thief ran off," Ron explained. "She lost the watch, but she wasn't hurt—luckily."

Uncle John, who was having trouble hearing over background noise, tuned out and let his attention wander. He leaned against the side rail, staring at the river where the paddlers slipped quietly by. He whispered to Linda, "It's good to be with family!"

She nodded and smiled at him and then the most unimaginable scene unfolded.

Uncle John addressed the family, "We had a lengthy discussion last night about your sisters and you, Linda. We want you to know we have a better understanding about what caused the rift between you three and we support you completely."

Linda looked at each one of them as if to confirm what her uncle was saying.

Ron said, "I'm on your side."

"Count me in," said Dan with a grin, having been a source of information for the others.

"And me," Allen said. "I kind of figured out what it was about."

The moment was a joyous one for Linda. She felt overwhelmed and pleased. The dragon had been slain. From here, she could go on and live the life she was supposed to lead, knowing that some members of her family knew another side of the story. It made all the difference in the world. There had been no formal courtroom drama, no legal ruling, but this reunion was just as good and satisfying.

After lunch, Ron took off in his rental car to catch a flight back to Virginia and Uncle John took a nap, which left the remaining cousins to themselves.

Returning to their uncle's house, Allen sat down at a table in the kitchen and motioned for the others to join him in front of a laptop. He flipped open the lid. "I brought along a CD of our family history. Would you like to see it?"

Dan and Linda eagerly sat down on either side of him. Allen had been meticulous in his organization of photos. The story unfolded as Allen clicked. Great-grandparents were pictured arriving in America with young children, who grew up to be parents and grandparents. At one point, the cousins, baby boomers, appeared at family picnics. A newspaper article about the apparent suicide of their great-grandmother appeared, and the cousins exchanged looks.

Allen explained, "Our great-grandfather, Herman, immigrated to America in 1889. A Socialist, he was forced to leave, before the authorities arrested him. With limited funds, he left his wife and three daughters in Germany. A friend of the family arranged it so that his wife and three daughters could travel to America with him, but he took advantage of Herman's wife on the ship. He bragged about it in a bar and Herman became so incensed he bit off the man's finger." He stopped and looked at them with an expression that said, *I know. First time I read it I about gagged.* He continued, "He must have had a really bad temper, maybe a drinking problem. His spouse, our great- grandmother, later threw herself into the Passaic River. News sources gave various accounts of her delicate condition and dementia."

Dan and Linda read a few of the news articles about their great grandmother's tragic end without comment. It took a few moments for the history of their family in the early nineteen hundreds to register. Stunned, Dan sat back, thinking, *What a family.* Linda's expression was frozen. She was thinking, *Never heard of a bar scene like that.*

"I went ahead and made copies for you." Allen handed each a neatly wrapped disc. He waited, seizing the moment, and turned to Linda. "I'd like to ask you something personal . . . How did you get this far with your sisters, without cracking up?"

"Good question. God and A.A. are my salvation. Without them, I don't know what I'd do. Keep in mind that Mom's estate is still not settled."

"It's been a while since she passed."

"I know."

Dan was fidgeting in the chair, leaning from side to side, acting as if he was impatient to say something. "Mary gets away with it because Cathy doesn't object."

"I'm surprised at Cathy," said Allen. "Not so surprised about Mary."

"She made Linda out to be the black sheep," Dan added. "Then, she excluded her from any estate planning and cut her off from the family."

"I really feel for you," said Allen sadly.

She acknowledged his support with a warm smile. "Not exactly what Mom intended when she said share and share alike."

Dan and Allen exchanged looks, which settled on her.

She looked out the window to the lake where ripples fanned out from landing ducks. "It's okay. I have forgiven them." After watching their reactions, she added, "I try to adjust myself to conditions as they are."

"You survive," said Allen. He added, "Did you know that Mary's husband is sick?"

"I heard," she replied. "I sent him a get well card."

"That was nice."

She looked at him. "Her attorney sent me a letter."

"Her attorney did *that*?" Allen shook his head in disbelief.

"That's only the tip of the iceberg!" Dan laughed, remembering what she'd told him.

"My sisters and their attorney are a challenge."

"I'm glad I didn't have to go through anything like that," Allen replied. "I'm sorry you had to."

Conversation drifted to family memories, and she excused herself to use the restroom. When she returned, Dan asked, "Anyone for the beach? We talked about having a little ceremony for Mary Lou." Mary Lou was their deceased cousin.

"Let's go," said Allen enthusiastically.

A brisk wind whipped their hair, as they stood on the white sand. Sunshine poured down on them. The surf roared over Dan's words. "We miss you, Mary Lou, and we remember the fun times we had together as children. We pray that you are okay where you are."

Allen said laughingly, "I got a tingle at the back of my head." Massaging it with his hand, he added in baritone, "Hey, Mary Lou, we know you're listening, and we want you to know we love you. We'll see you again."

How much sooner for Dan? Linda wondered. He was fighting the lions of cancer like a gladiator. The doctors had recently told him that his brain tumor had shrunk, and they were clinging to that good news.

"Yes, that's beautiful, we'll see you again in a *long* time!" Linda squeezed their hands tightly.

Allen departed later that evening. Uncle John decided to have a night to himself.

Driving alone with Dan, Linda was in a thoughtful mood, and she knew Dan would understand. "You know, for years, I've asked myself how my sisters and I might reunite. What would that look like?" She asked aloud, and Dan looked sideways at her as she drove. He had felt too weak to drive and besides, she was the designated driver for the weekend. "This weekend taught me something. No rehash of the past, or the mistakes we made or our resentments and hostilities, but a simple *I love you* and a move forward." She gripped the wheel tightly, with both hands.

Dan reached over and patted her wrist. He waited until she'd made a right-hand turn. "You know, I'm thinking about my brother. Our relationship's better, but it has a long way to go. I want an explanation and an apology for some things."

"What?"

"My problem with my brother is his wife," he declared.

"I know, but what are *you* going to do about it?"

"I'd like to talk to her about what she does to keep our family apart."

Linda grimaced. "Why not just have lunch with your brother?"

"Are you telling me what to do?" Dan replied defensively.

"Just a suggestion."

Dan stared out the window as if he needed some time to consider it.

"We had an awesome reunion this weekend," Linda said as she stopped at a light. "Can we do it again next year? Who else can we get to join us?" She thought about their eldest cousin. "Robin?"

"I don't know about that," he mumbled.

News about the reunion in Jupiter had traveled. One of the toughest family members, besides being tight with Mary and Cathy, Robin Leport was a strict disciplinarian and straight shooter. Like her brothers, she'd been pursuing an interest in genealogy with results resembling a college term paper, complete with index and bibliography. The latest topic making the rounds had to do with their relationship to Heinz. Picking up the phone, Linda made a call.

"If Allen said he was our fourth cousin, then he was probably right," Robin stated emphatically.

Linda drew in a slow breath, striving for patience and tolerance of a cousin she didn't particularly like and who didn't like her either. "I'd like to know more about the other side."

"What do you mean?"

"I've read about Nana's history, but not a lot about Grandpa's. I'd like to know more."

"I've got quite a file on his side already. I'll send it to you."

"That would be terrific." Linda wiped her brow and prepared herself. "Next year we're going to try for another reunion. Do you think you can make it?"

"Maybe."

The click of disconnection resounded in Linda's ear. So much for that brave attempt, she thought. This cousin is as hardhearted as my sisters. Robin would pass through Buena Vida soon, but Linda knew she wouldn't call or stop to visit. *Why do I bother?* she asked herself.

Shortly after their conversation, a letter surfaced in a PDF from Robin.

"Well, this is THE day. The news finally came this morning over the radio just as I was rolling off the runway, back from my mission, the last one of the war."

Whoa. Linda leaned toward the monitor reading a letter her dad had written to her grandfather during the war.

"*I meant to write three days ago, but the news kept getting worse. I was so morose and dejected I couldn't write. But today I'm the happiest man in the world! You must have received my last letter telling about the missions I was on.*

"*My mission against Kobe was at night. The flak was rough, and they caught us in searchlights, but we got through. The next mission, claimed to be the roughest of the war, was a daylight raid on an aircraft plant north of Tokyo. We'd previously flown raids against it and lost a total of sixty ships (planes) on that one target. When we flew over it, they shot the hell out of us. For five minutes straight heavy flak pinpointed us. The Japs shot out my number three and four engines just after "bombs away" and smashed a window inches from my face. The plane suffered numerous holes in the fuselage. I was never so scared in my life! I couldn't keep up with the formation, and the fighters were waiting to pick me off like buzzards. I called the leader of the formation and told him I couldn't make it, so he slowed up the whole formation to my speed and escorted me off the coast of Japan. Then, at a safe distance, he designated a ship to escort me to Iwo Jima while the rest of the ships went home. I landed, but I couldn't keep from shaking all night.*"

She leaned back and closed her eyes. What a close call. After a moment, she turned her attention back to his letter. She scrolled to the last paragraph.

"*You asked me if I didn't want to try something else besides cattle business. Hey, are you trying to get rid of me? Dad, actually I'm glad you asked me because there is something else I might want to do—something that involves airplanes. We can talk about it when I get back. Roland.*"

Linda considered how her Dad loved aviation which didn't pay much back in those days. The discrepancy between her grandfather's good fortune, which had passed on to his older brother, and her father's financial insecurity, she realized, had been left unstated while she was growing up. Her father had always loved and admired his brother. They seemed to get along just fine—so different from her and her sisters.

The letter went into a folder on her computer. She typed a brief thank you note to Robin.

Chapter Forty-Seven

The first offer fell through. Another potential buyer appeared. The new realtor yielded quick results. Richie Vettia wrote, "A buyer has made a lower offer. What do you want to do?"

She assumed he'd already asked her sisters. "Take the money and run!" The escape from this partnership was worth anything.

After a lapse of time, Vettia wrote. "The buyer can't get insurance, because of the roof and has lowered the offer. Please advise how to proceed."

Linda shot back, "Take whatever we can get." She dialed his number, and the realtor came right on the line. "What's going on? Who's holding up the deal?"

"Nobody right now. All three of you agreed to the offer."

"Really? Now how was I supposed to know that?"

"Things were moving right along, until this problem with the insurance."

"Well, the cat's out of the bag now. We'll never get rid of it, unless we fix the roof." Vettia agreed. "Does Cathy know that if she doesn't approve the lower offer, she's footing the bill for a roof? I mean, I know it might interfere with the purchase of her next Rolex, but . . . is she willing to do that?"

"I don't know. She asked for an estimate of a new roof."

"How much does a roof cost these days?"

"It's a small house. I would say nine grand."

The inheritance was shrinking by the second. She sighed. "Let me know what my sisters want to do."

"I'll do that."

Nothing to do but wait.

Dan's brain tumor had grown again and a second tumor had been discovered in another area of his brain. The doctor recommended a few weeks in rehabilitation to help him adjust. Dan refused.

Linda communicated with relatives. Robin wrote: "It's sad you're losing a good friend." Allen replied: "Thanks for the update." Ron said: "Keep me posted. I want to know what's happening." Jane, who'd come to visit, expressed heartfelt thoughts, "I hope he goes peacefully and that it doesn't get too difficult for him."

She asked Clarence to join her on the long trip to visit her relatives in Jupiter.

At an Irish pub in a strip mall along the highway near Dan's house, members of the Cray family and Clarence huddled together somberly. Seated in the corner was Uncle John, with Linda and Clarence on his right. Across from him sat his son and daughter-in-law.

"It's good to see you again," Linda addressed Brian and his wife, Carey. "It's been a while since we visited."

"Good to see you, too," replied Carey politely. "I wish it were under different circumstances." She was referring to Dan who was absent from their lunch at the pub.

Home alone, lying in a hospital bed in the middle of his living room, attended by a nurse, Dan was enduring the last stages of brain cancer. Linda and Clarence had stopped first at his house for a brief visit. Dan had recognized her and seemed happy. The plan was to meet the rest of the family for lunch and then return.

His usual upbeat self, Uncle John, wouldn't let sadness get him down. Brian, on the other hand, was sullen and quiet but greeted Clarence with practiced ease.

The waitress came by and took their orders. The pub was dark, even darker in the corner they'd chosen, with an overhead TV providing the only light. Clarence immediately took an interest in the baseball game and commented on it, which drew Brian into a lively conversation.

Linda turned to her uncle. "It looks like Dan's getting excellent medical care."

"He has round-the-clock nurses now, and they're doing a good job," the patriarch replied.

"I'm glad to hear that. I was really worried about him being alone in the house."

"It's all been taken care of."

The food arrived, and they devoted themselves to their plates. Linda took a bite of the asparagus served in a ramekin, then picked at the fish in a sandwich, suddenly feeling nauseous. The others had hearty appetites.

Noticing her actions, Carey asked, "You don't like asparagus?"

"I like it without a tub of butter."

Carey made a clicking sound in her mouth. "Sometimes they do that, but usually it's good."

Linda waited for a break in the sports conversation that her cousin and friend were still pursuing. "So . . . where do we go from here?" She was addressing no one in particular.

Brian looked at her with a question. "Oh, you mean—my brother. He'll stay at home until the money runs out and then he'll go to a nursing home or the hospital."

Thankfully, Uncle John changed the subject. "Your father read in the war manual that he was only supposed to go up a certain number of times, I think it was eleven, but he had already gone up twenty-six times. Each time he flew, he was aware that other crews hadn't returned." He paused until their expressions indicated they understood. "He figured he was next . . . So, he went to his commanding officer and told him he had flown more than the required number of flights and he was done. The officer warned him that if he didn't fly the plane, he would be court-marshaled. Your Dad said he didn't care; he wasn't going up again. A week later, another pilot dropped the bomb on Nagasaki, the war was over, and he didn't have to go up again. Can you imagine that? One minute he was a war criminal and the next, a war hero."

This story reminded her of *Catch 22.* "He was lucky." A half smile shaped her mouth, as she swirled the ice in her glass, wishing her cousin Dan could be with them.

"Very lucky," Uncle John repeated. "His crew members really appreciated him."

"They reunited with him in his later years," Linda said. "Most of them had some form of cancer when they met. As you know, my Dad died of cancer."

"I'm not surprised," said Brian as if he knew. "All that stuff flying around."

Conversations from other patrons filled the room. The waitress reappeared in the dining room and wound her way to their table. She asked, "Is everything all right?" She frowned at Linda's meal, which looked untouched.

Linda met her stare. "I'm working on it." She smiled. "Slow eater."

Satisfied with the response, the waitress moved to another table, and the patriarch continued where he'd left off.

"One of the crew members kept a journal," Uncle John said, "and it was in that box of war medals that Uncle Roland gave my son." He meant Dan.

Carey leaned so far over that her hair was almost in Brian's cream of tomato soup. "Where *is* that box?"

"I've looked for it," said Brian. "but I can't find it anywhere."

"Maybe Dan gave it to his stepdaughter when she was visiting last week." Carey put her long hands on the table and pushed her chair against the wall.

Dad's war medals in the hands of a complete stranger. Linda swallowed hard. "I'd like a copy of that journal, if it's possible," she said instead, swallowing her pride. *Let it go, let it go. Maybe some little boy has a hero.*

"Me, too," said Brian. "I'll see that you get one."

First, they had to find the box, Linda thought as she put down her fork. She'd given up trying to eat.

Afterward, they returned to Dan's house. The nurse announced their arrival and moved a chair for Uncle John to sit next to his son, close to his head. Struggling to keep his eyes open, Dan absentmindedly surfed channels on the television. Carey walked into the large open room with the hospital bed in the middle of it and went straight to the back of the house, without so much as a glance toward her brother-in-law. Brian acknowledged his brother and immediately looked for the box of war medals. Clarence took a neutral position by a sleek, black, dining room table, next to the back of the house, and chatted with Carey. Linda perched on a bar stool at the kitchen counter, her back to the kitchen, so that she could view the scene between father and son.

"Hey, there," father greeted son. "We're here to see you."

Dan turned his head and a look of love passed between them. Holding the remote control in his hands, he inadvertently raised the volume.

"You know, son, there's a button on that thing that has *never* been used."

Dan's eyes questioned, and his mouth turned in a slight smile through a haze of pain medication.

"*Mute!*"

Grinning, Dan hit the button. The room was suddenly quiet, except for Brian's scuffling feet as he traipsed from room to room.

"Who's that?" the patient asked.

"Your brother," replied Brian, "looking for the box of war medals. Do you know where it is?"

Searching his memory, which was getting to be more of a chore with each passing day, Dan said, "In the garage . . . as you're looking at my car . . . to your right."

Brian hurried toward the garage barely missing a nurse bent over the dryer in the laundry room.

Linda slid off the stool at the kitchen counter and approached the hospital bed. "Hey, cuz, how are you?"

"Any better and I'd be with the angels." Dan motioned in the air with his hands.

She didn't think he meant to put it that way. Gently, she rubbed the top of his head and took hold of a lock of hair under her uncle's watchful eyes.

The patriarch explained, "He's got hair again since they took him off the chemo."

"Look—no gray!" Linda tugged at it playfully, and he didn't seem to mind. "You have more hair than I do and yours is dark brown. How'd you do that?"

With a shrug of thin shoulders, Dan smirked.

His father leaned forward. "We just had lunch at Duffy's."

"Good lunch?"

"Delicious! The manager asked for you," said Uncle John. "He wanted to know where Mr. Apple Martini went—What should I tell him?"

A trace of yearning. "Did you bring?—" Her cousin groped for words.

"Bring—what?"

As if he'd finally remembered, Dan's head jerked up and down. "Apple martini!"

His father laughed. Linda rolled her eyes.

Suddenly apprehensive at the background noise, where Carey and Clarence sat idly chatting, Dan whispered earnestly, "Who's *that*?"

Linda turned to see Carey passing between Clarence and a chaise lounge in the back of the house. "My friend Clarence and your sister-in-law," she whispered.

His face lit up in surprise. "Oh! First time."

"No, it's not!" Carey shot back, surprising everybody.

Brian returned to his brother's bedside. "I can't find the box in the garage. Any chance you gave it to your stepdaughter?"

Nothing registered in the patient's mind. Cancer, gaining strength and mass, crowding out memory, had mutated and was defeating the medicine that had previously worked.

The nurse leaned in and placed a bowl of ice cream on the tray in front of him.

"I brought you *creme brûlé* ice cream," his father said, "knowing how much you like it." He turned to Linda. "We used to share some after dinner. He'd split it down the middle and then we'd argue about who got the bigger half."

Having seen them in action on a prior occasion, she smiled. Dan, still capable of feeding himself, was digging into the ice cream with a spoon. Dinner once, or twice, a week with his son was one of the joys of her uncle's life, at ninety-four.

Finishing the bowl, Dan announced, "It's time for my nap." His head rolled on the pillow.

Linda embraced her cousin warmly, murmuring words of affection she thought only he could hear.

Her uncle, who stood nearby, stepped forward as she turned, drying her eyes on a sleeve. "I know it's hard to see him like this."

She sniffed back a tear. How much longer was anybody's guess. The nurse said some patients lasted months; others went more quickly. Her cousin still had fight in him and resisted, or denied, the tumor. The struggle drained his energy. Linda embraced her uncle and then called Clarence, who was already standing by the door, as if eager to depart. She passed Brian in the narrow foyer leading to the front door and pulled him into the narrow kitchen. "I know your brother gets on your case occasionally, but he loves you."

He bristled like he'd been stuck with a pin. "All my life my brother's been mean to me."

She met his eyes as if seeing him for the first time. His words reminded her of what she'd been through, and she realized they had something in common. She never knew about Dan and Brian's relationship, had never known Dan this way. "You're not alone," she said to him.

Brian said, "I heard about your trial. Just so you know, I'm proud of you." He turned on his heel and continued his search for the missing box of war medals.

Linda felt a great tide of relief. Support from the extended family was healing.

A few weeks later, she and Dan spoke on the phone. He appeared lucid, remembering things they had done together, asked a few pertinent questions about her life, and expressed love and affection for her—a brief, but satisfying conversation. What more could be asked of him? Was it just a few months ago they'd stood on the beach?

Chapter Forty~Eight

Uncle John called to say that his son, Dan, had passed and Linda made a hasty trip to visit him.

"We knew when he had only twenty-four hours left," Uncle John explained as he leaned forward on the leather sofa in his house. "His systems were shutting down. Hospice sent in a special nurse for the last day, and we were there with him. He went in his sleep, no pain. He was comfortable."

It was the best that could be expected, after a protracted battle with cancer.

"Last time I spoke with him," she replied, "I told him to seek our relatives in heaven."

"They were waiting for him."

She inquired about his health, which was good, and then asked, "Have you had other company recently?"

"It's been quiet. Say, how's your sister? I haven't heard from her in over a year."

Surprised he was asking, she replied. "I don't know. She chooses not to speak to me, you know."

"I wondered," he murmured, "if there's sickness . . . "

"Her husband."

"Oh."

Linda added, "She thinks she's punishing me with her silence." A robust laugh intended to demonstrate that she had adjusted to the situation.

"Right!" Uncle John also laughed, showing he approved of her attitude. "You're happy."

"I'm happy in the new life I've made for myself," she explained, adding, "I get to see you in a few weeks!"

"When Allen comes down! I'm looking forward to it."

"Me, too. Will your son be there?" Brian, his younger son, was always so busy with work and travel.

"If he's around," Uncle John said, "he'll come." He said this in a way to indicate that he would have a say in this.

"Oh, good. I haven't seen him in a while although he sent me an email recently. I'm having lunch with Ron and his wife next Friday in Sarasota."

"Good. Let me know how that goes."

"I'll tell you about it in person shortly. Oh, and Jane's coming to visit in March." Linda couldn't help but feel pride in the progress she was making with relatives who wanted to see her. She was at last able to tick off more than one entry on the list.

"She's a wonderful woman."

"Sure is. We always have fun."

As an aside, Uncle John added, "Your sister, Cathy, liked that story about you and Jane in Nana's house."

"Oh?" Linda didn't know what Cathy thought these days, unless someone leaked word as her uncle just had. She was surprised that the visit to grandmother's old neighborhood had been passed around and gained popularity.

"She asked about you." The patriarch smiled into the phone. "Just thought you might like to know."

"I appreciate that." A deep sigh. She wanted to say, "Then why the hell doesn't she call me?" But instead, she said, "I would like to see her and—"

"— Where Mary is, you can't come." He finished the thought for her.

Linda thought, *If I make a move toward my sisters, their attorney comes after me with a pitchfork.* After a second, she came back with, "I can't tell you how much I appreciate that you understand the situation. It's so comforting to know that I'm not the only one who knows."

"You're not the only one, but there's not much you or anybody can do about it. Mary's made up her mind for good, I'm afraid."

"How do you know that?" she asked.

"Several years ago when Mary and Brad were visiting, I asked her about her relationship with you, and she reacted strongly."

"I expected that," she replied. "Somehow, I thought Cathy would do something, like what Jane did."

"Tell me again what she did," he requested.

"Oh, at first she went along with Mary and didn't want to rock the boat. Then, when she got to understand the situation better, she basically said, This is bull, and she made a plan to see me. She announced it to everyone, and no one stood in her way. Cathy could do the same thing, you know, find a way to reach me."

"Maybe when Mary passes," Uncle John said, "Cathy will reach out to you. Right now I think she's too afraid of Mary." He thought about what he had just said. "I have learned," he began in a stronger, more assertive voice, "that sometimes you have to speak up and take a stand against bullying in any form, even if it's in the family. Otherwise, you become part of it. We saw that in the war."

"Would Cathy do that?" Linda asked meekly. "I don't know." Her voice trailed off.

"The good thing is that you've been seeing your cousins and getting along with them," Uncle John was encouraging.

"I started by reconciling with you and then things just sort of spiraled," she said, smiling, and thought, *Like the Allies have taken Italy, Germany still a holdout.*

Another year had passed, and it was time to celebrate sober anniversaries.

"Who's got an anniversary in January?" Booker, the chairperson for the evening, asked fifty assembled group members. A few hands waved in the air, proud faces behind them. The chairperson nodded. "Stuart and Linda will be our speakers."

Surprise registered on Linda's face, but then she remembered that, luckily, she'd brought notes for the afternoon meeting where she was supposed to speak, but which she'd missed.

"Stuart will go first."

Stuart had a short message for his length of sobriety. "After my first meeting, a woman came up to me and told me she had just been diagnosed with cancer, and her doctor told her she didn't have long to live. I told her just to keep praying. I said I didn't have that great a faith, but that's what I was doing." He waited a moment and then resumed. "A year later she and I both grabbed the same loaf of bread in a supermarket, and we recognized each other. She told me the doctor told her she was going to live and she was still sober. That was my small burning bush."

The chairperson leveled his gaze at Linda. "You're up."

Taking her plastic water bottle in hand, she walked slowly to the front of the room and turned, clearing her throat, feeling slightly nervous.

"I'm happy to be here tonight," Linda started with enthusiasm. "I didn't expect to speak, but I came prepared. I've got notes." She held up a stack of index cards and saw smiles. "I've been thinking about what to say because I knew I'd be speaking at the end of this month. So whenever I had a thought, I wrote it down."

She shuffled the index cards and settled on one the color of lime.

"What it was like, what happened, and what it's like now," she began. "Back then, it was rough seas, white caps, hundred foot waves, terrifying swells. Today it's a placid lake with gently lapping waters along the shore." She was referring to her state of mind.

By the looks on their faces, she could tell they liked the images and understood what she was talking about.

"You've heard the expression: A.A. got me to God, and God got me to A.A. Well, in my case, my family got me to A.A., and I'm grateful for that. My family gave me a valuable education. Everyone drank too much, and there were many parties. One uncle had a habit of passing out and rolling under the curtains. He thought he was hidden, but we could see him." Laughs. "To my knowledge, I'm the only one who's made it to A.A. so far."

She looked at the door as a latecomer entered and quietly took a seat.

"I had my first drink in my teens. I was very close to my Dad who had an enormous capacity for drinking. When he died, my sister wanted to put his ashes in a beer stein." Louder laughs. "The first real sign of my drinking problem happened in college when

I passed out after eating fish and chips and drinking a pitcher of beer. The nuns didn't buy my story about an allergy to fish and grounded me. It was a royal pain to have to sign in every hour all weekend. I blamed them."

Her throat had gone dry, and she reached for the water bottle and took a sip.

"The first A.A. meeting I attended was for my former husband who definitely had a drinking problem. Seven years later, I got to my second meeting for the right reason."

Warming to the subject, aware of hundreds of eyes focused on her, she felt calm and natural.

"About four years ago, I realized *I* was the problem. At that time, I had absolutely no contact with any family member. I listened to you in these rooms and observed what you did to make amends and restore lost family relationships. Gradually, following your example, I began to reach out to my relatives and have enjoyed successful reunions. My immediate family is another matter. That door is closed at the present."

Here she stopped to draw a deep breath.

"Let me tell you about my cousin Ron. At first, he ignored my emails, but finally, after about six months, he responded. Then, when Dan had cancer, I made an effort to get the whole family together asI've seen you do. They wanted to know what I was up to. Ron said he had no intention of participating, yet he was the first to arrive. He told me the sun, moon, and stars had lined up to make that happen for him. It was God."

Heads nodded.

"Today several family members talk to me, some don't, but . . . we'll see. Last Friday my cousin Ron, his wife, and I met for lunch and we have plans for next year. Amazing, isn't it?"

Gong. Church bells sounded the hour.

"Is it over?" she asked Booker.

He looked at his watch. "You still have a half hour."

"I'm not speaking *that* long!" Gentle ripples of laughter.

"Take as much time as you want." He encouraged. "With only two speakers, we have plenty of time."

"There is stability and steadiness in my life today. I'm well-connected with the fellowship and have an ever-widening circle of warm, loving friends. When I came into the program, my life was a mess, but now it's quite . . ." She looked at them and smiled, finishing the sentence, " . . . acceptable. Thank you."

Rousing applause.

Booker's arm blocked her attempt to sit down. "Pick a topic. Use one of your cards. No—not that one, the white one."

Linda put aside the yellow card, picked up the white card and read, "A fellowship of warm, loving friends."

"That's it! That's the one. Okay, anyone want to comment?"

People who ordinarily didn't speak, spoke, including one shy guy in the second row, with a backward baseball cap and a slight stutter. Most commented about what she'd said; she appreciated the supportive response.

A lovely, young woman with blonde hair to her waist and laughing blue eyes couldn't stop hugging her. She handed her a medallion, seventeen in Roman numerals, after some discussion about how many "I's" came after the "V." Another woman came close and talked to her as they walked outside to their cars. Linda smiled, pleased and content. Best anniversary yet.

Chapter Forty-Nine

Not long after the anniversary meeting, Vettia informed her the rental house had sold.

After nine long years, each sister received a third of the sales proceeds at the closing.

Linda wondered what to do with her shrunken inheritance. Buy a new car? Donate to charity? Try to recoup? The DOW was up 6,000 points since the financial crisis had begun. A fledging, new technology company looked promising. Facebook's initial public offer had floundered due to a computing glitch. The company's leader had a brilliant idea, and she knew he wouldn't give up. *Buy low,* she thought.

When April rolled around, it was important to do taxes. With the real estate closing and the settlement of the estate, this was bound to be interesting.

"Thanks for sending me a draft of my tax return," Linda said to her accountant. "I looked it over, and I think I spotted an error."

"What is it?" Bidley asked.

"Those numbers I gave you, well, . . . it appears that you divided by three."

"I did."

"You were probably thinking of my sisters and me. Three beneficiaries."

"I was."

"The numbers I gave you are the numbers to use. You didn't have to divide." She was thinking, *The amount is small enough. Don't make it worse, turkey.*

Bidley quietly reviewed his copy of her return as if doubting he could have been so stupid. "Are you sure?"

"Yeah. It says right here. The property was purchased for $310,000, sold for $105,000. My share was a third. If you don't have a copy of the settlement sheet, you can look it up on the county tax register."

"I remember it now. So all I have to do is multiply by three, that'll make the figures . . . " he rapidly calculated, "You'll have . . . hmmm . . . a good-sized loss. That's the difference between what you would have inherited and what you received. I'll fix it tomorrow morning and resend it. Anything else?"

"No. The rest looked okay."

The next morning the file came across the internet and Linda opened it. Seeing the real estate results—a fiasco—on a tax return had an unexpected wallop. The loss created a negative adjusted gross income, something she hadn't seen in her entire working career.

She wrote Bidley. "That's the first time I ever saw numbers like those."

"You won't owe any taxes this year." He added, "Probably not for several years."

"Will I get audited?" She was almost afraid to ask.

"Probably not. What are they going to say? The numbers speak for themselves."

"I guess it takes a little getting used to." She was still in shock.

"I've seen worse."

She raised her brows. "I know I'm not alone. Others lost assets in the Great Recession, but maybe not the same way."

"For sure."

"The good thing is that I went back to my career and tried to make my education and experience work for me. The firms I worked with taught me many worthwhile things about how to invest and make money. I challenged myself to recoup what I would have received. I mean, my inheritance had gone from a nice-sized boulder to a pebble. I knew I should practice my usual mantra of balance and diversification, but I was itching to make up for the loss." She paused, knowing he would have disapproved had he been her financial advisor. "I took a chance and put the entire lump sum into a new hi-tech stock. I figured what the hell." She could imagine his frown.

"Which one?"

"Facebook. Remember the botched initial public offering?"

"Who could forget? So you went ahead and put the inheritance into it? The whole amount?"

Linda nodded with a smile. "I waited until it hit bottom and had a little bounce. For once, my timing was perfect."

"The stock's moving in the right direction," the accountant said. "Maybe you'll recoup what you lost."

"It would be great to recover what my mother would have bequeathed me had my sisters not gotten their grimy hands on it. If I make it up, I'll lose my resentment."

"You won't have to pay taxes until you sell."

"I don't plan to sell it. I'm going to let the profit ride."

"I bet your sisters can't say the same."

Linda laughed. "You're probably right."

"It might make you feel better to know that banks no longer accept Power of Attorney papers from siblings, after the death of a parent."

She sighed mightily. "I can't tell you how glad I am to hear that. Something needed to be done."

In the days that followed the filing of her tax return, Linda reflected on the loved ones she had lost and what they had meant to her. Preeminent among them was Bunnie, who had kept her going, listened for hours to her problems and been a dear sponsor and friend. After a valiant battle against cancer, Bunnie had slipped into a coma. No one, not the doctor, nurse, family, friend, or partner could do more. Although there was no replacing any of them, they had taught her how to live. She had built new families in the church as well as A.A. and had become active in service. Those renewed relationships with family members grew stronger. She and Jane had become quite close.

Linda was driving to the airport to meet Jane for her annual visit to Florida. Spring's balmy breeze rustled palm fronds, and the trees swayed gently, as she approached the cell phone parking lot bordered with colorful florals. She turned off the car, sat back, and reached for the newspaper lying on the passenger seat. The news about her favorite tech stock, *Facebook*, pleased her. The stock had hit new highs in three digits and made her inheritance more than whole.

Her cell phone beeped, and she saw a text from Jane saying that she was at gate five. Linda laid the paper down and started the car.

At the arrival gate, she saw her cousin standing and talking to a taller, slender woman with straight posture and an expensive-looking light-weight coat. She thought, *Who's that?*

Happily, Jane waved over the shoulder of the mysterious woman who slowly turned and smiled—Cathy!

The End

CPSIA information can be obtained
at www.ICGtesting.com
Printed in the USA
BVHW080254060220
571497BV00001B/73